Graffiti Red Murder

Murder

A Monica Spade Novel

ALEXI VENICE

Published by: eBookIt.com
Edited by: Megan McKeever Editorial
Cover Art: Alexi Venice and Bo Bennett

Books by Alexi Venice

The Monica Spade Series
Conscious Bias
Standby Counsel
Graffiti Red Murder

The San Francisco Mystery Series
Bourbon Chase, Book 1
Amanda's Dragonfly, Book 2
Stabscotch, Book 3
Tinted Chapstick, Book 4
Sativa Strain, Book 5
#SandyBottom, Book 6

The Pepper McCallan Series
Ebola Vaccine Wars
Svea's Sins
Victus – Margaret River Winery (Part I)
Margaret River Winery (Part II)

Dedicated to the trans community

Table of Contents

1

March 2020
Placencia, Belize

Monica Spade and Shelby St. Claire strolled along the Caribbean shoreline while Monica played fetch with a local dog. He circled, dropped the water-logged tennis ball at her feet, and yipped at her to throw it for the umpteenth time. She picked up the soggy fuzz, the dog dancing in the foamy tide before her, and hurled it into waist-deep water. He swam out to the sinking ball and nabbed it before it joined the crustaceans.

She clapped. "Good boy! Bring it here!"

On their second day in paradise, Monica had purchased a small bag of dog food for the stray she had dubbed Beach Boy. He devoured the food on their condo patio while she chased away cocktail hour with a few beers. He was a mixture of happy-go-lucky and caginess, allowing Monica to scratch his brown and white ears but darting away if she tried to pat his body.

"I should get a dog when we return to Wisconsin," she said.

"You aren't home enough to take care of a dog," Shelby said.

Monica sighed as she hooked a wayward strand of black hair around her ear. "I suppose not. I'll tell you this, though, if I were a stray, I'd definitely want to live on the beach instead of the cold streets of Apple Grove."

She threw the ball again and Beach Boy flew across the shallows, plucked the ball from the foam, and returned it to Monica's hand, wagging his tail and whining.

Shelby looked down her pert nose at him. "As a stray, do you really get a choice? Isn't it a matter of where you're born?"

"I'd stow away in your luggage so I could come here." Monica threw the ball again, water droplets forming a perfect arc in the air behind it.

"You'll probably catch fleas from him." Shelby quickly released Monica's hand.

Monica suppressed a grin. "He's wearing a flea collar."

"That just means they'll jump off him and onto us."

Ignoring Shelby, Monica scratched Beach Boy's ears when he returned. "I haven't felt any fleas. Have you?"

"My skin has been itching all week. Look at these red welts." Shelby stopped and displayed her arms, rolling them over in the golden glow of the late sun.

Monica pretended to inspect Shelby's toned arms while admiring her tan. "You have beautiful, flawless skin."

"That's why I don't play with feral dogs." She scratched at imaginary spots then resumed walking. Shelby was attractive in a sassy, self-confident way. Muscular legs, ripped abs, square jaw, and hazel eyes that could go from compassionate to stormy in an instant.

"You play with me, and I can be a wild beast in bed," Monica said.

Shelby snorted.

Monica had spied a few red bumps, but they were probably from mosquitos or gnats. She didn't say that though, because once Shelby latched onto a belief, her bite was as unshakeable as Beach Boy's. "Would you prefer that I not play catch with him on our walk?"

Shelby looped her hand through Monica's arm and leaned in close. "Yes. This is the last beach walk of our vacation, and I want it to be romantic."

Monica was relieved to hear the flea nonsense had been a pretext for garnering her undivided attention. When she didn't throw the ball for Beach Boy, he trotted along beside her, content with their companionship.

"I can't believe we leave tomorrow." Shelby's tone drifted toward melancholy.

"Hm. I'm sort of excited about returning to my firm and the practice of law."

"I'm impressed they haven't called you this week."

"I told them I needed uninterrupted private time to process my knife fight with the beguiling butcher."

"Thank goodness you're a better fighter than she was." Shelby hugged Monica's arm.

"I think I got lucky." After a few more steps, Monica said, "Can we not talk about that murder trial? I've worked hard to forget that nightmare, so I can start fresh when we return."

"Not half as hard as I have." Shelby raised her right arm, displaying the raised skin around her wrist from the zip tie that a Ukrainian thug had used on her. Her left wrist was equally scarred, but not half as bad as her psyche.

Monica gently stroked her thumb over Shelby's wrist. "I'm so sorry. Your nightmare was worse than mine."

"I had no idea that being a lawyer's fiancée in a small town could be so dangerous."

"I'm sorry I failed to protect you—"

"Come on. You didn't see that coming. Who would've ever guessed?"

"Still. You're my fiancée and I feel responsible." Monica raised Shelby's left hand so they could admire the blue sapphire set in a braided gold band on her ring finger. "One of a kind. I hope you like it."

"Love it. I can't wait to buy you one."

Wings flapped in Monica's chest but she didn't say anything. In a desperate move to lock down Shelby's heart three months ago, Monica had publicly asked Shelby to marry her. Surrounded by their close circle of friends, Monica had taken a knee in the ice sculpture garden at the Apple Grove fishing tournament. Shelby had said yes, and Monica had placed the outrageously expensive, custom-made ring on her finger. A ring Monica was still making monthly payments toward.

At the time, Monica had been terrified that Shelby's ex-lover, the gorgeous Coco Rivelli, was still interested in Shelby. Coco fueled an ongoing source of insecurity for Monica because Shelby had admitted that Coco had broken her heart but hadn't yet confided the details, feeding Monica's fear that Shelby still carried a torch for Coco. A limber yogi with a devastating *je ne sais quoi*, Coco was a clever business owner too. Her yoga studio was packed seven days a week. How could Monica compete with beauty, brains and success?

Suddenly, a movement in the water caught Monica's eye, sending her hand to her brow to cut the glare. "Did you see that?"

They waded in toward a dark figure to discover a turtle swimming through the sea grasses, his curved flippers gracefully swishing back and forth.

"He's beautiful!" Shelby exclaimed.

"I can't believe he's this close to shore." Monica admired the gigantic green and brown shell of the ancient animal.

As their shadows fell over him, he angled into deeper water, so they retreated to firm sand where the water licked their ankles.

"What time is our dinner reservation?" Monica had yielded control of the social calendar to the woman who cared more about it.

"Seven. I want to hang out in town afterward and hit up Tutti Frutti for dessert."

"I'm addicted to their gelato," Monica said in a hungry voice. "Nothing like it back home."

"My body will thank me for leaving it behind." Shelby anchored in place, so Monica pivoted around her like a tetherball. "Turn around and head back?"

As she completed her turn and came face-to-face with Shelby, Monica cupped her jaw and eased Shelby's sunglasses on top of her curls. She stared deeply into Shelby's hazel eyes, accented by gold flecks shimmering in the slanted light. "Thanks for the best week of vacation ever."

Shelby tilted her head back to admire Monica's soft green eyes and the tiny freckles sprinkled across her nose. "Same."

"I could definitely come back here next year. How about you?" Monica asked.

"If you bring me," Shelby said flirtatiously.

Monica leaned down and gingerly grazed Shelby's lips with her own, tasting a mixture of sweet and salty.

Shelby pressed her bikini-clad body against Monica, wove her fingers into Monica's thick black hair, and coaxed her into a loving embrace. The lingering heat of the day enveloped them as they swam in and out of a lazy kiss, content in their unhurried pleasure, sated from a week of sex but still burning with passion.

After a time, Shelby arched back and playfully tugged on Monica's lower lip with her teeth. "I suppose we should go back and shower before dinner."

Monica cradled the back of Shelby's head, savoring the intimacy. "I love you."

Shelby squinted, tiny creases playing at the corners of her eyes and a smirk pulling up the right side of her full lips. "I'm just in it for the jewelry. Don't get too attached."

Monica stiffened. "Jewelry, huh? And I thought you were in it for the spankings."

"Don't you dare."

"I accept the challenge." Monica firmly slapped Shelby's left butt cheek, producing a shocked squeal.

Beach Boy barked.

"You're going to pay for that." Shelby rubbed her cheek and lunged at Monica.

Monica easily dodged the attempt and started running backward, taunting her. "You loved it, and you know it."

Shelby's coquettish smile told Monica everything she needed to know.

When they returned to the condo, Monica helped herself to a Lighthouse beer and went out to the patio. "You want to shower first? I'm going to feed Beach Boy and catch up on the news."

"Perfect." Shelby disappeared into the bathroom.

While waiting for Shelby to shower, dress, and apply her proprietary mix of makeup and hair product, Monica leisurely consumed two beers and a small bowl of peanuts, Beach Boy resting at her feet. She wasn't looking forward to saying goodbye to him.

The gentle surf lulled her as she absent-mindedly thumbed through her newsfeed. When they had first arrived, she had ignored her phone to distance herself from the brutal murder trial she had just completed. Despite being a lawyer who specialized in healthcare law, Monica had been baptized by fire in criminal court while serving the needs of the government to represent a woman who had stabbed her boyfriend multiple times. Monica's efforts had resulted in a legal bill the size of a small nation's debt. She hoped the government would pay her soon, as she needed the money to keep her new law firm, Spade, Daniels & Taylor, afloat.

She and Shelby had put their lives back together in Placencia, repairing the psychological damage from the brutality that had spilled out of the courtroom an into their personal lives. Monica had weathered the attacks on herself as superficial combat wounds, but Shelby had been affected in a deeper, more profound way. She was a high school art teacher, not part of the justice system, so she had been blindsided by the assault and still wore the sheen of trauma. Monica felt guilty about Shelby's pain and was committed to restoring her sense of equilibrium.

Shelby hollered to give Monica the all-clear for the bathroom, where Monica took a five-minute shower then dressed in a loose shirt and black capris. There was no point in trying to dry her long, thick hair in the tropical humidity, so she ran a brush through it and called it good. Preferring an *au naturel* appearance on vacation anyway, she had left her makeup in Wisconsin.

Shelby, on the other hand, took pleasure in applying a tasteful amount of coppery eye shadow to accentuate her hazel eyes. Her thick brows picked up the same tones of the golden corkscrews framing her face. Dangly earrings shimmered through long tendrils of hair, and coral lipstick drew Monica to the chevron in the center of Shelby's upper lip.

"You look gorgeous tonight," Monica said, as they grabbed their cell phones on the way out the door.

Shelby turned and brushed Monica's lips with her own, leaving a coral smudge behind.

Monica drove them in a rented golf cart down the main drag of Placencia, a charming little tourist town. They parked under the *Rumfish y Vino* sign, a trendy, second-story restaurant they were excited to try. Once they were seated on the balcony overlooking the street below, Shelby ordered a mojito, and Monica, a Belikin beer.

The scent of tropical flowers filled the air, and the distant sound of the surf blended with the background music. A smattering of people on foot and bicycle chatted on the street below—tourists dressed for dinner and locals bustling to and from work.

Sparkling strands of holiday lights decorated the railing and overhang, adding to the romantic ambiance in the sultry twilight. The soft glow cast Shelby in a more glamorous version of herself, if that was even possible.

When their drinks arrived, Monica raised her glass. "To returning next year."

"I'd love that," Shelby said.

Despite the repeated pillaging of her credit card over the past week, Monica was thrilled at the prospect of returning with her beautiful fiancée—hopefully, her wife—next year at this time. Feeling brave, she said, "If the law firm has a good year, let's rent a house on the beach."

"In that case, here's to your law firm having a record year." Shelby clinked Monica's glass with her own.

2

The next day, Monica and Shelby dozed during the flight to Atlanta, where they were met in Passport Control with armed guards wearing surgical masks. The masks, a new development, were almost more alarming than the assault rifles, conveying the impression that they were entering a biohazardous war zone. Monica was never comforted by anyone carrying assault rifles, and even less so when she couldn't read their facial expressions. The guards' eyes swept suspiciously over the passengers, as if they were armed with a deadly contagion.

Surprised at the new protocols, Monica and Shelby watched as an agent wiped down the surface of the kiosk with a sanitizing wipe after each passenger, then signaled for Monica and Shelby to approach. Through her mask, the agent mumbled instructions about setting their passports on the glass and looking into the camera for a photo. After the machine spat out a sheet of paper confirming each woman's identity and logging their entry into the United States, the agent raised her hand, stopping them from proceeding to the next station.

"I need to take your temperature and ask you a few questions."

Monica froze while the agent ran a thermometer over her forehead and read the electronic display.

"Normal," the agent mumbled. "Have you traveled to China recently?"

"No."

"Do you feel short of breath, or do you have a cough?"

"No."

"Thank you. Welcome back to the United States."

Never feeling less welcome or on shakier ground, Monica stepped past the agent and lingered while Shelby was similarly quizzed. Monica recalled reading some headlines about a new coronavirus but hadn't realized that it had sparked this level of precaution and scrutiny.

The women proceeded through the stamping of their passports and soon found themselves in a food court waiting for their flight to Minneapolis. As they glanced around, they noticed that about half the travelers wore masks, some made of bandanas and others of yellow surgical material.

"Should we be wearing masks?" Shelby asked.

"I'm not sure. Where would we buy them?" Monica spun around in place, looking at the smattering of tourist shops —from Gucci bags to one-dollar trinkets—but didn't see any masks or scarves for sale.

They found a Mexican restaurant close to their gate and sat at a table for two with their burrito bowls. Weary from travel and stunned by the fear in people's eyes, they didn't chat much over dinner. Monica had a foreboding sense, her mind struggling to catch up with the evolving news about a highly communicable, deadly virus from China.

Later, as they sat in the gate area, Monica took a deep dive into the news feed to learn more. If the newly identified coronavirus weren't bad enough, there was even more grisly news. She gasped, covering her mouth with her hand.

"What?" Shelby asked without turning her head.

"Have you seen the news about suspicious murders of trans women in Minneapolis and Chicago?"

Shelby raised her face to Monica, her eyes glossy from travel and the pages of nonsense in *Cosmo*. "What now?"

"This is really bone chilling." Monica kept her voice low. "Last month, a trans woman in Minneapolis was shot at pointblank range in her apartment. The killer stripped off her clothes and spray-painted a penis and scrotum on her entire torso."

Shelby's hand flew to her mouth. "That's the sickest hate crime I've ever heard."

"Even worse, the same thing happened a few months earlier to a Chicago trans woman, except she was killed by a slit to her throat. Again, a penis and scrotum were spray-painted in red on her torso." Monica looked up from her phone to Shelby's astonished eyes.

"What is this world coming to?" Shelby asked.

"Hate crimes and a new coronavirus. Welcome back to reality." Monica clicked off her phone and jammed it in her pocket. "Vacation is officially over."

"Is it safe for us to hold hands in public?" Shelby asked, all liveliness in her tone gone.

Monica picked up her hand. "Yes. And soon, we'll be married. No one can take that right away from us."

"Let's not fool ourselves, Mon. There are obviously psychos out there who think it's okay to murder and defile a person just because she had gender-affirming surgery." Shelby's voice grew louder and higher. "Where does it end? Are they going to start shooting all the gays now?"

Monica gestured for Shelby to keep a lid on her emotions. "Let's not jump to extremes, and since we're about to board a plane, let's not talk about shooting, okay? People are on edge enough with temperature checks, masks, and questions about fevers and coughs."

Shelby glanced around to confirm that no one was paying attention to them. She briefly ran her fingers along Monica's cheek. "You're right. I'm just so shocked. I hope they catch the killer. Or killers. Do you think it's one or several?"

"Good question. One person who's mobile or maybe a copycat crime. The article indicated that the police in Minneapolis and Chicago are working together to investigate."

"At least they're taking the murders seriously," Shelby said. "That hasn't always been the case for the trans community."

"I know. The article implied they're prioritizing it."

Their flight to Minneapolis was uneventful, and after a two-hour drive to Apple Grove, they pulled into Monica's driveway as dusk was disintegrating into a chilly nightfall.

"A lot of snow melted while we were gone," Monica said, as her headlights swept over the smaller snowbanks next to the driveway.

"The great thaw begins," Shelby said, her voice heavy. "I'm so glad we returned on a Saturday, so we have all day tomorrow to do laundry, grocery shop and rest."

"Me too. I'm exhausted. I need a vacation from our vacation."

3

The next morning, Monica jotted down a grocery list while watching the news on TV. She was horrified by the images of New York City—hospitals overflowing with patients who needed ventilators. Hundreds of patients were dying despite physicians' best efforts to treat them with everything from blood transfusions to steroids. Nothing seemed to aid the lungs in their fight against the coronavirus. The governor implored manufacturers and the federal government to send more ventilators to the hospitals. He also begged healthcare workers to come to New York to help relieve the nurses and first responders who were falling sick.

While sipping her black coffee, a shiver of fear snaked through Monica's body. *When will this hit Apple Grove?*

The ring of her phone startled her, pulling her attention from the TV to Jim Daniels's name and bearded photo on her screen. "Good morning, Jim."

"Welcome back. How was your trip?"

"Awesome, but we're freaked out about this coronavirus."

He blew out a sigh, and she pictured him sitting at his kitchen table, oatmeal clinging to his silver beard. "I know. It's spreading like wildfire and everyone is scared. My colleagues in Madison tell me that the governor is getting ready to sign a shelter-in-place order."

"What's that?"

"An executive order that all citizens have to remain in their homes. Some businesses will be exempted if they're essential to society, like hospitals and clinics, but I doubt our law firm will be able to stay open."

"Seriously?"

"I'm not joking. We need to talk about closing the doors and working from home. Nathan and I plan to meet at the office in an hour. Can you join us?"

She gulped, her eyes traveling over her bare kitchen. They needed groceries, and fast. She decided she could buy them on her way home from the office. "Of course. See you then."

"Sorry to hit you with this your first day back, but we have a business to run."

"No worries. I had the benefit of a vacation."

"That makes one of us. See you soon."

Monica set down her phone and tossed the remainder of her coffee down the sink. Her stomach was suddenly too upset to tolerate the black acid. As she turned from the sink, she felt like a gawker at an automobile accident, her eyes roaming back to the TV, its grisly images and CNN ticker spewing macabre news. After staring blankly at the images of covered bodies being wheeled to white truck containers at hospital loading docks, she turned off the TV and went to the bedroom to get dressed.

Shelby was awake and thumbing through social media on her phone. "Mind if I post this pic of us on the beach?" She held out her phone for Monica to see a romantic photo of them standing at the water's edge.

The vacation pic was so incongruous with reality that Monica questioned the wisdom of posting evidence of their trip as tragedy unfolded. "Um. I'm not sure, hon. Have you seen the news?"

Shelby rolled her eyes. "What now?"

"This virus is killing people at an alarming rate. Italy is shut down. New York City has over 500 people dying per day. The hospitals are overrun. The nursing home residents in Washington State are dying, and the Wisconsin governor is considering ordering us to shelter at home. I don't think we should advertise that we just traveled."

"Ordering us to shelter at home? Can he do that?"

"In an emergency, yes. The experts are calling this a pandemic, so he wants to stop the spread."

Shelby harrumphed. "My friends who were on spring break are posting pics."

"Most of your Insta friends are high school kids. They don't know any better." Monica changed out of her sweats and t-shirt into jeans and a black collared shirt. "You're the teacher, so you're held to a different standard."

"I'm talking about my teacher friends, not my students." A moue punctuated her furrowed brows.

"Do whatever you like," Monica said a little too quickly. "I have to go into work for a few hours. I can pick up groceries on my way home, okay?"

"What? Work? It's Sunday."

"Yes. Jim said the governor is going to close our law firm, so we have to make a plan to telework. That's what I've been trying to tell you. Our lives are going to change abruptly."

Shelby's eyes snapped up from her phone. "Do you think school will be canceled?"

"There's a good possibility."

Shelby whipped off the covers, jumped out of bed, and rummaged through Monica's drawers, shrugging on several layers over her ginger-tanned body. "Then I'm going to the grocery store right away. We need to stock up on everything."

Monica blinked in surprise at the abrupt change in attitude.

"If what you say is true," Shelby said, "the shelves will be empty by the end of the day. We need toilet paper."

"I'm pretty sure it isn't that kind of virus. It attacks the lungs."

"How do you know?"

"I've been watching CNN. If they sell ventilators at the grocery store, buy one of those."

Shelby looked at her, puzzled. "Aren't those just in hospitals?"

"Yes. Sarcasm, Sheldon."

"Maybe you can order one from Amazon. I'm buying toilet paper."

Monica briefly closed her eyelids so Shelby wouldn't see her rolling her eyes. "Fine. I'm sure we'll use it eventually. I started a list of food items and left it on the counter." Monica pecked Shelby on the cheek. "Thanks for going without me."

They walked together to the kitchen where Shelby poured herself a cup of coffee and opened the fridge door. "Oh no. We're out of milk."

"Yep. Black coffee or Starbucks. Take your pick."

"Ugh." Shelby rested her elbows on the counter. "What a way to end our vacation."

Monica gently rubbed Shelby's lower back. "I know. Who would've guessed? At least we had a vacation. I suspect Nathan and Matt will have to cancel their trip to the Florida Keys."

"Seriously?"

Have you been listening at all? "The virus is spreading at an alarming rate. Governors are racing to close down their states, so yeah. What sense would it make to go to Florida and shelter in place there? Or worse, risk getting the virus by traveling to and from?"

"Do you think we were exposed to it on the way home?"

Monica thought about how to answer that without upsetting Shelby. "There's a good chance."

"Ew." Shelby shivered. "Breathing the same air as all the other people on the plane!"

Monica shrugged. "Honestly, what's done is done. That's the past. Let's focus on what we can do to stay safe in the future."

Shelby tilted her head and looked at Monica, suddenly eager to learn more. "Like?"

"The experts are saying the virus can be transferred on droplets through the air when someone sneezes, coughs, or even talks loudly."

"So, basically, an average day in a high school classroom. I'm doomed."

"You aren't doomed. Let's just buy groceries, make it through today, and see what tomorrow brings. Wear a bandana over your nose and mouth when you go to the store."

"I'll look for one." Shelby opened the fridge again and stared at the empty shelves. She moved a few jars and found a blueberry yogurt in the back. Rolling it over in her hand, she squinted at the tiny print. "I can't see a thing without my glasses. What does the expiration date say?

Monica leaned in. "Expired a few days ago, but it's yogurt. It should still be good."

"Waste not, want not." Shelby tore off the cover, and, as she ate, she opened Monica's cupboards to take inventory. "We should buy a boatload of oatmeal, flour, pasta and all the essentials."

"Sure." Monica was relieved that Shelby was getting a handle on reality.

"I'm going to start making food that we can freeze, like soup."

"You're very smart." Monica kissed Shelby on the forehead. "And I'm a lucky woman to have you in my life. As soon as I return from the office, I'll be your *sous*-chef."

"Deal." Shelby eyed Monica from head to toe. "Shouldn't you be going?"

"Yes, but I wanted to make sure we had a plan. All good?" Monica removed her Visa card from her phone case and set it on her grocery list.

Shelby's gaze followed the gesture. "Thanks." She ate a bite and thought a private thought, then asked, "I assume it's okay if I hang out here while we weather this storm?"

"I'd be honored."

"I'll swing by my house and pick up some more clothes for school."

Monica decided not to point out the lack of logic if schools were closing. "I'll make room in the extra bedroom closet."

"I already took over that closet." Shelby's hastily uttered words were followed by an angelic expression. "If that's okay, I mean."

Monica hadn't realized, but her surprise instantaneously warmed. "More than okay. There's a dresser in there, too, that should be empty—"

"Already moved into it," Shelby said with a flick of her spoon and a coy wink.

Victory goosebumps ran over Monica's skin. "If you need more space, I can go through my clothes in my bedroom dresser. I'm sure I can donate some that I don't wear very often."

Shelby tossed her empty yogurt container in the recycling. "You're so sweet to offer but I couldn't..."

"I want to. Seriously."

"In that case, thank you." Shelby brushed a kiss on Monica's cheek as she passed by.

Monica watched her saunter down the hall toward the bathroom.

I think she just kicked me out of a closet and two dressers. Aren't I the luckiest woman in the world?

4

As Monica unlocked the front door to her law firm, an incongruent mixture of pride and fear flooded her veins. Spade, Daniels & Taylor had been open for less than a year, and now Jim was forecasting they would have to close due to the pandemic. *How are we going to pay everyone?*

She pushed through the doors and admired the light gray wall color and modern furniture in the reception area that Kathy, the chief cook and decorator, had selected and ordered. Had it all been for naught?

Monica heard Jim singing softly—*still haven't found what I'm looking for*—so she moved quickly down the hall toward the kitchen, detouring briefly to drop her coat and laptop in her office.

When she entered the kitchen, Jim was still humming the U2 song while pouring water into the coffee maker. He glanced up at her. "Hey, stranger."

"Oh good. You're making coffee. I drank only a half cup at home because we were out of milk. Not a fan of black. After that vacation, though, I'm too broke to swing through Starbucks. I hope we have milk here." She walked over to the fridge and opened it to plenty of food, including milk.

He rested his hip against the counter and peered at her over his half-glasses. "I could've told you Belize is expensive. Nice tan, by the way."

She smiled through her scattered emotions. "Thanks. Maxed out my Amex card on this one, so I really need to get back to work. I can't believe we managed to squeeze in a vacation before this pandemic exploded."

"Me, either. I was tempted to warn you off from going 10 days ago, but who knew it was going to proliferate so rapidly and decimate New York City?"

"The new Wuhan, right? I'm still in a state of shock."

"Me too." He moved to the cutting block of knives, selected a paring knife, and slit the tape on a box of donuts resting on the counter. "Figured you'd be hungry after travel and need something to counter the bad news." He pushed the open box toward her.

Monica's shapely black eyebrows arched. "What do we have here?"

"An assortment from Dunkin'." He waved his bear-sized paw over the box. "You go first."

"Don't mind if I do." She grabbed a napkin and helped herself to a glazed jelly donut. Not waiting for the coffee to brew, she chomped into it. As the strawberry jelly melted in her mouth, her body and mind immediately relaxed. She closed her eyes and savored the sugar bliss for a second. "This is just what I needed. Thanks Jim."

He hummed knowingly. "Pretty harsh reality out there. Unfortunately, I think it's going to get worse before it gets better." He pushed his half-glasses onto his forehead and removed a mug from a peg under the cupboard. As the coffee maker sputtered mid-cycle, he grabbed the carafe handle and jimmied it out, pouring himself black concentrate. A small puddle spit on the warmer before he jammed the carafe back in.

"What's going to get worse before it gets better?" asked Nathan, their third law partner, as he glided into the kitchen, radiating his perennially good mood.

"This pandemic. The overcrowded hospitals. Quarantines. Businesses closing. The economy. You name it," Jim said.

"Going apocalyptic on us?" Nathan asked, flinging his longish, brown bangs out of his face. "What's changed since we discussed this last week while Monica was gallivanting across Belize?"

"Don't you watch the news?" Jim asked.

Nathan similarly interrupted the struggling coffee maker, also making a mess of pouring himself a mug. "I do, but I'm trying to keep a positive attitude. Matt and I are going on vacation next week, and I don't want anything to fuck it up. That includes this impromptu partners' meeting and whatever you have in store behind that untrimmed beard." He leveled a look at Jim then turned to Monica. "Welcome back, cupcake. Your tan really sets off your emerald eyes."

She pointed to mug and said around a bite, "Thanks. Pour me some too, please."

He did, and she topped off the coffee with some milk. "Did you just call me cupcake?"

"If the shoe fits…" He gestured to his chin. "You have donut dust all over your lips and chin."

"Then perhaps 'sugar' would have been more appropriate, don't you think?"

"That sounds too…" Nathan turned to Jim. "What's the word I'm looking for?"

"Sexual," Jim said, his own donut leaving a blanket of sugar on his beard.

"If you called me 'sugar tits,' that would be sexual, but sugar is more respectful than cupcake," Monica said.

Nathan squinted at her in disbelief over the rim of his mug. "You're busting my balls over cupcakes, sugar and donuts?"

A gravelly chuckle flowed through Jim's donut-filled mouth. "Okay, kids, no fighting before breakfast."

Monica adored Jim. He had advocated for her at their former law firm, Daniels, Smart & Whitworth, when one of the partners, Charles Smart, and his entitled son Richard, had criticized her for standing up for her physician clients in a racially charged murder trial. Their attack turned personal when they discovered she was a lesbian, culminating in Charles threatening to fire her.

After sacrificing her social life—staying in the closet for three years at the firm from hell— Monica couldn't tolerate their unlawful behavior any longer. Jim had stood by her side, trying to protect her from Charles and Richard, but when that proved futile, he represented her in a claim against the Smarts, negotiated a settlement, and suggested they start a new firm together, suggesting her name first on the marquee. Nathan had been in the process of leaving the firm too, so Jim and Monica had snapped him up as their third partner.

Monica had grown especially close to Nathan, who had saved her bacon during the Stela-the-Slayer trial by subbing for her when she had unexpectedly fallen sick.

"Are donuts the first item on the agenda?" Nathan asked with amusement, his eyes ping-ponging between Jim and Monica. When neither answered, he said, "Fine. I'll have one too. We might as well get jacked up on sugar and caffeine for our first Sunday partners' meeting." He selected a sprinkled donut and politely took an exploratory bite, his long fingers keeping the donut away from his designer sweater, his version of Sunday-meeting-casual. His expensive blue jeans were cuffed at the ankles, highlighting his tobacco, wing-tipped ankle boots. Boots that Monica considered proper courtroom attire rather than an impromptu weekend business meeting.

"Are you and Matt really going to the Keys?" Monica asked.

"Why not? It's just Florida."

"I expect Trump to close the airports," Jim said through a bite.

Nathan snorted in disbelief. "He said last night that he considers the 'Kung Flu' to be like any other flu, and that it will all just blow over soon."

"He's a lying, racist windbag," Jim said. "The nation's top physicians are saying COVID-19 is more deadly than the flu and spreads just as easily—"

"Easier," Monica added.

"Maybe I should inquire about a refund for our trip," Nathan said between bites.

"I'd highly recommend it," Jim said, allowing a pause while they all chewed. "Now, turning to our firm, I expect Governor Eberhardt to issue a stay-at-home order next week."

"Where did you hear this?" Nathan asked.

"I've got friends in Madison who are writing it, and they emailed me a draft."

"Look who's connected," Nathan said.

"Anyway, only essential businesses are going to be allowed to remain open, and we aren't one of them. So, we need to make a plan for teleworking. That's why we're here."

Nathan ran his fingers through his thick hair, leaving a trail of donut sprinkles. "How am I supposed to litigate my cases? I have witnesses to prepare and depositions to take. Litigators do all of that in person."

Jim shrugged. "You'll have to postpone them or do them by Zoom."

"By Zoom? No one takes depos by Zoom."

"Get used to it," Jim said. "I think it will be the new world order very soon."

"I don't even have a Zoom account. No one I know does that." Nathan sputtered expletives in disbelief.

"I've already asked Janet to subscribe to Zoom's secure account for all three of us, so we can confidentially meet with clients," Jim said.

"I have three trials scheduled in the next six months," Nathan said, slurping some coffee. "Zoom isn't a substitute for the courtroom."

"I saw Judge O'Brien at Rotary last week," Jim said, "and he told me that he's postponing civil trials so he can prioritize the criminal docket. He's going to close his courtroom to spectators and put the jury in the gallery in masks."

"He's a crazy old misanthrope," Nathan said. "My clients need to get these cases over with to settle their financial affairs. They can't stay in legal limbo for God knows how long."

Jim patted the air with his donut. "I'm just relaying what I heard, and O'Brien is neither old nor crazy. A bit eccentric, maybe. The courts have to honor the Constitutional right to a speedy criminal trial, but civil cases carry no such guarantee. He told me the judges are going to shut down almost all proceedings. I would expect courts to reopen in several months under new guidelines."

"If we're ordered to shelter at home this week," Monica said, "then you won't be going to Florida, Nathan. I'd call about that refund if I were you."

Nathan turned on Monica. "Easy for you to say. You still have sand in your hair and tequila in your brain."

"I drank Belikan beer while I was there, not tequila, and guilty as charged."

"Let's focus, children," Jim said. "Set aside the resentment, Nathan. This is an unprecedented situation. A pandemic. I, for one, don't want to get COVID. I can't imagine you and Matt want to risk getting it either by going on spring break."

Nathan rubbed his eyes and groaned, looking more like a 12-year old than a man in his early 30s. "Not fair."

Jim blinked patiently. "Who said anything about a virus being fair? Now, back to the firm. Janet is coming in later today to inventory all of our computer equipment, including printers, so she can send everyone home with the proper equipment. Kathy, Cheryl and Sandie will telework from home as well."

"What about the phone lines?" Monica asked.

"Janet knows how to forward calls to our cell phones. The phone tree will work the same, but your cell phone will now be your work phone."

"There are a million details to this," Nathan moaned, reaching for a second donut but stopping himself midair, instead closing the lid on the box. He longingly ran his thumb and forefinger along the fold.

"That's why we're here," Jim said. "We need to retool our mindset to work at home in an electronic environment. We won't get much use out of our paper files because printing and mailing is a major hassle from home."

"Come again?" Nathan asked.

"You'll be ordered to shelter at home. Think isolation. The CDC says COVID can live on surfaces as well as travel through the air on droplets. Healthcare workers in New York are putting their clothes in the washing machine with Clorox as soon as they get home. In other words, don't touch stuff that others have touched."

"I guess I'll have to email all my pleadings and motions," Nathan said. "What about masks? Should I be buying those?"

"Yes," Jim said, "but good luck. I ordered some on Amazon, and it says they won't be delivered for three weeks. Dominique told me she can sew some if she finds a pattern."

"Not only a district attorney, but also a seamstress?" Monica asked, impressed.

"She can do everything," Jim said with pride.

"How many days should we close the office?" Monica asked.

"Hopefully, just a few weeks," Jim said.

Nathan's expression relaxed. "I suppose I can suck it up for a few weeks."

Jim winked at Monica. "Might be two weeks. Might be six weeks. We'll see what the state and federal governments do."

"Nothing like living on the edge with a fledgling business," Monica said sarcastically.

"What a shitstorm," Nathan muttered. "I suppose I should start packing my equipment and files for home."

"Take a photo of the serial numbers on the equipment and text them to Janet so she can make a list," Jim said.

"This is getting pretty real," Monica said.

"Remember that the partnership owns the equipment," Jim continued, "so we need everything to come back to this office." He looked at Nathan. "You took out a loan to pay into the partnership, so we can't afford expensive equipment walking out the door and never returning."

Nathan gulped, his sharp brown eyes taking on a more serious hue. "We can't afford an interruption in business either. I just hope I can make the payments on my loan. We're going to hemorrhage cash paying for this place while we work at home. How depressing."

"I know," Jim said, rubbing his thick hand through his beard. "The three of us need to stay in close touch, so we can remain nimble as the situation evolves."

"I'm down with that," Monica said. "I can ask Kathy to set up recurring 8 a.m. phone calls on our calendars."

"Make it a Zoom call, so we get used to the technology," Jim suggested.

"What if I don't want to look at your hairy face every morning at eight?" Nathan said.

"I'd be happy to turn around and show you my hairy ass," Jim said.

Nathan rolled his eyes. "Thanks for that mental image. Seriously, we don't need a daily phone or Zoom call. Let's just text each other."

Jim cocked an eyebrow and shrugged, avoiding disagreement. Monica could tell he would have preferred a more formal way to touch base each day, but he probably didn't want to force communication on Nathan. The more mature play was to let Nathan come to the same conclusion in his own time.

"Let's wrap up this meeting before you two start making fart jokes," Monica said. "We can see how the first week goes, then we can formalize regular Zoom meetings if we need to."

"Sounds great," Jim said.

She returned to her office and sat down in her white leather desk chair, admiring her glass desk and well-appointed office. The trappings of early success. She ran her finger along the top of her desk, picking up a thin layer of dust that had accumulated during her week away. *I'm going to miss this place. Immediate access to Jim for his sage advice. Bouncing strategic ideas off Nathan. Kathy's food. Kathy's wisecracks. Kathy's help. How am I going to work full-time from home when I'm not surrounded by this supportive cast of characters?*

Fortunately, she didn't have time to ponder these pandemic worries because her desk phone rang with a call from Al Bowman, the president of Community Memorial Hospital and her main client.

"Monica Spade," she answered.

"When did you get back from Belize?" Al asked.

She appreciated his thoughtfulness. "Yesterday."

"Lucky you got back into the country. I heard the president is closing the borders to more countries."

"In addition to China?"

"I heard he's considering all of Europe. Have you seen what's happening in Italy, and now in New York?" he asked.

"Yes. Terrifying."

"Well, it's on its way here."

"Do you have any cases at the hospital?" she asked.

"Not yet, but the Governor's Executive Order and the Department of Health and Human Services are going to shut down our outpatient practice and elective surgeries."

"What?"

"I have an advance copy from the Hospital Association, and that's what it says—no more surgeries and no more outpatient clinic visits."

"For how long?"

"Two-week minimum, then reassess."

"Oh no, Al. That will hit the bottom line pretty hard, won't it?"

"Decimate our bottom line is more like it," he said.

"How can I help?" Monica asked, her own financial future suddenly looking vulnerable. She was waiting to be paid by the government for the Stela trial, and only the state bureaucrats knew how long that would take. She needed to do some work for the hospital to keep the cash flow going, but if the hospital spigot dried up, she'd go belly up.

Al was talking over her thoughts. "I have a project for you that's wholly unrelated to COVID, but much more troubling on a personal level for one of my surgeons."

"What's that?"

"The police want to interview Dr. Kershaw about murder."

"What? Who?" She removed a blank legal pad and began taking notes.

"Two of Dr. Kershaw's patients were murdered."

"While they were in the hospital?"

"Fortunately, no."

"Is he a suspect?"

"I don't think so, and the surgeon is a she, by the way. Dr. Nicole Kershaw."

"How sexist of me. Please continue."

"Dr. Kershaw is a plastic surgeon who specializes in gender-affirming surgeries."

"You mean, like sex reassignment? Breast implants and genitalia?"

Al cleared his throat. "Yes. Anyway, two trans women were murdered, and Dr. Kershaw did the gender-affirming surgeries for both of them."

The news brief that Monica had seen in the airport only yesterday flashed through her mind. She closed her eyes for a minute to absorb the devastating information on top of the shocking pandemic news. "Didn't those murders take place in Minneapolis and Chicago?"

"You know about them already?"

"Read about them in the news but there weren't too many details."

"The most important detail is that Dr. Kershaw performed both surgeries, and she's afraid the killer will come after her."

"Oh no. Why is that?"

"She's transgendered herself, so she considers herself a prime target for a hate crime. Her former name was Nicholas Kershaw."

Monica scribbled a few notes. "When do the police want to interview her?"

"They called her today, but she said she wouldn't be available until tomorrow. She needs you to prep her as well as attend the interview."

"Smart doctor. I'd be happy to," Monica said. "Do you have her contact info?"

Al gave it to her. "You'll have to prep her at her home because we've already canceled elective plastic surgeries, and we're trying to send as many employees home as possible to decrease the risk of transmission of COVID at the hospital and clinic."

"I can do that," Monica said. "I'll call her right away."

"Sorry to ruin your Sunday."

"No worries. I'm at the office anyway."

"Are you going to keep your law office open?"

"Not under the current draft of the Governor's Order. We're transitioning to teleworking."

"Fortunately for you, it's easier to run a law office teleworking than it is a clinic and hospital. You guys can lie from anywhere, but we have to see patients in person."

She heard the teasing tone in his voice and laughed. "Yes. We're changing the firm's name to "The Teleworking Pettifoggers.""

He erupted in laughter.

"Have you considered offering virtual visits to patients?" she asked.

"The Information Security department is setting up those accounts and connections as we speak."

"Good for you. I assume you can bill for those?"

He sighed. "Not as much as an in-person visit."

"Again, I'm so sorry. I have a feeling we're all going to take it in the shorts during this pandemic."

"After we're done shitting them," he said.

She was surprised by his uncustomary vulgarity.

After they rang off, she felt less secure about her law firm's future than she ever had. She dug around in her bag until she found a bottle of Pepcid. She popped one in her mouth and chewed the chalky disk, hoping for relief. If COVID didn't kill her, an ulcer might.

5

While rounding up some office supplies she might need at home, Monica stared at her desk phone. She didn't have a landline at home, so it wouldn't be useful there. Something so critical yesterday was now as antiquated as the telegraph. Their office space was slated to become the Smithsonian of what a legal practice used to look and feel like—before the pandemic. She pictured her glass desk gathering more dust, but forced herself to set aside the imagery, instead turning her thoughts to Al's request to prep Dr. Kershaw for a police interview about two murdered patients.

She googled Dr. Kershaw and was surprised to see an entire page devoted to the doctor's groundbreaking work in sex reassignment surgeries—both female-to-male and male-to-female. Although the doctor had been practicing only four and a half years, she had built quite a reputation in the niche specialty. The medical articles and media clips indicated there were only a handful of plastic surgeons in the United States who specialized in sex reassignment surgeries. *Elite club,* Monica thought as she dialed the number Al had given her.

After a few rings, a contralto voice answered, "This is Nicole Kershaw."

"This is Attorney Monica Spade. Al Bowman asked me to call you."

A sigh of relief.

"I understand the police want to interview you?" Monica asked.

"Yes. Can we talk in person?"

"Of course. What's your preference? My office or your home?"

"If you wouldn't mind coming to my house, I live at the north end of Lake Wissota, off County Highway S."

Monica pictured the winding road and huge, manmade lake. Whenever she drove around the lakes area, her internal compass flipped and she lost her bearings. "Can you give me your exact address so I can plug it into Google Maps?"

Dr. Kershaw rattled off a fire number for her street address and described the fastest route, as Monica quickly entered the address in Google Maps and followed along on her iPhone screen. The doctor lived off the beaten path, leading Monica to wonder how she made the serpentine trek to the hospital for emergencies on winter roads covered in ice and snow.

After they ended the call, Monica disconnected her computer and printer and carried them out to her small, white pickup truck. A beater-with-a-heater, it had sentimental value because she had purchased it from her grandfather, now deceased. The tiny truck had taken a hit to the driver's side last year when a thug had run her off the road during a murder trial, but a body shop had done a reasonably good job of repairing it. She still suspected that Charles Smart had hired the thug who the police had never found.

She loaded her office equipment into the passenger seat and went back inside to retrieve a few odds and ends. As she piled them in a small box, a feeling of loss pumped through her, not unlike what she had experienced when moving out of her previous law firm, DSW, or as it was referred to among lawyers in town, Dumb, Slimy & White. *This is different,* she told herself. *Those guys were douche canoes, and I couldn't wait to leave. Spade, Daniels & Taylor is my firm, and I'm not giving it up. Think positive thoughts. We'll be back in a few weeks.*

She carried her overstuffed box, a plant sticking out of the corner, out to her truck and set it on the passenger-side floor. The plant reached for the window to capture the bright sunshine previewing spring. The mountains of dirty snow piled high in the law firm parking lot were no match for the intensity of the sun this day, as the temps were predicted to climb into the low 50s. She swung in behind the wheel and started the engine.

While she drove the potholed streets toward Highway 53 north, she called Shelby.

"Hey," Shelby said in a faux-sexy voice. "Miss you already."

"Me too. Listen, something unexpected came up at work. I have to go meet with a doctor to prepare her for a police interview. I'll be home in a few hours. Sorry about the delay."

"No worries. I'm almost finished grocery shopping. After I drop these at home, I think I'll hit up a CrossFit class to work off some of those mojito toxins from Belize. My liver is the size of a football."

While Monica liked the sound of Shelby referring to her house as "home," alarm bells rang in the back of her mind. "Are you sure? Going to the gym is like returning to the airport. People crammed together and breathing hard—"

Shelby snorted sarcastically. "Zip it, Mon. I'll lose my mind if I don't work out. Seriously. I'm sure the coronavirus hasn't spread to Apple Grove yet."

Monica was too stunned to speak, her mind somersaulting between relationship harmony and science.

"I interpret your silence as disapproval?" Shelby asked.

How to disagree without making it personal. "From what my hospital client told me, the coronavirus is everywhere. The governor's order is expected to close gyms like the CrossFit Box."

"Then I'd better get my workout in today, right?"

"That's one way of looking at it." Monica bit the inside of her cheek.

"Gotta go," Shelby said. "At the checkout counter."

"Thanks for buying groceries," Monica said, doubtful that Shelby was really at the checkout counter.

"Actually, you're buying them," Shelby said.

Monica couldn't tell whether Shelby was being factual or snarky. She pictured the mounting debt on her credit cards, and Al Bowman's dire financial prediction. She swallowed a surge of anxiety and tried to sound confident. "At least I can contribute financially, if not in person."

"That's right. Gotta go." Shelby hung up.

Monica looked at her phone to confirm she had been dropped. She suspected that Shelby was irritated that she had to grocery shop alone, but Monica was at a disadvantage by not seeing Shelby's expression. Her eyebrows could go from questioning like the squiggly tilde in piña colada to furrowed thunder-brows in the span of 60 seconds. And that was only her eyebrows. The color of her eyes could change as fast as a mood ring. One minute purple, the next, blood red. *Maybe a workout would do her good.*

Fifteen minutes later, Monica found herself winding around the lake country, quickly becoming disoriented. She missed a critical turn off County Highway S and had to double back on a paved road with several lake houses to her right along the vast shoreline of the 6000-acre lake. To her left, the farm fields were brimming with shallow ponds from the ice age known as winter.

She finally came upon a rugged wooden sign at an obscure driveway, upon it written in faded blue paint, "Aqua Vulva." That was the name Dr. Kershaw had provided over the phone, no doubt a play on Aqua Velva aftershave, a reflection of yesteryear. Bordering on unprofessional and a bit schmaltzy, the sign certainly was an attention grabber. Monica wondered if the doctor was as playful as her driveway sign.

She turned onto a long gravel driveway framed by a budding tree canopy, the surrounding woods thick with underbrush on both sides.

Not wanting to surprise anyone, Monica politely tooted her horn to announce her arrival. The single toot set in motion a cacophony of barking, clucking and quacking. She opened her truck door to meet her hosts—a colorful flock of designer chickens rushing around the corner of a detached garage, pecking at the ground, puffing out their chests, and straining their necks in curiosity. A yellow Labrador retriever eased himself out from under a bush, stretched and yawned, then gave a solitary warning bark that lacked any menace.

The dog approached cautiously as Monica walked across the driveway and moved slowly toward the front walkway. Much larger than Beach Boy, the lab sniffed her hand and circled her, smelling her shoes and pant legs.

"How are you today, buddy?" she asked.

He shimmied his body, his tail whacking the side of her leg.

"Do you have a tennis ball that I can throw for you?"

He tilted his head in the negative, still eyeing her up. When he decided she didn't pose a threat, he abruptly turned his rump to her and led her down a cobblestone path bordered by overgrown shrubs and shaggy, untrimmed trees. The flock of chickens scurried behind her, keeping their distance but following like hapless hens. A cock-a-doodle-doo from somewhere behind the garage punctuated the ambient noise of the colorful menagerie.

They emerged from the thick brush to a wide deck protruding at an odd angle from the house. A well-trodden dirty path ended at a faded wooden door, which looked more like a back entry than a front. A propane grill stood a few steps to her right, a charred brush and pair of dirty tongs hanging from it.

Even taking into consideration that March was the ugliest month in Wisconsin—brown piles of discarded snow instead of flowerpots—the entrance looked like a college frat house rather than a surgeon's house.

She automatically reached for a doorbell but couldn't locate one. Now she was glad that she had tooted her horn. As she raised her hand to rap on the door, she heard the bolt lock click. The door swung open to a man in a green sweatshirt and dirty jeans, his swarthy face unwelcoming.

"Hello. I'm Monica Spade, the lawyer retained by the hospital. Is Dr. Kershaw here?"

The disheveled man unabashedly scanned her from chin to boots and back up, like an owl considering a field mouse for lunch. "I'm Geoffrey. Come in."

"Nice to meet you." Even though his predatory look left a sour taste in her mouth, she defaulted to politeness, something she strived for in her professional life. That, and prevaricating, but she hadn't done that yet on this file. The day was still young.

He extended his hand so she grasped it. *Should we be shaking hands during a pandemic?* As long as they were touching, she decided to give him a firm squeeze, lest he think she was a pushover.

As soon as they released, she slid her hand into the pocket of her sherpa-lined denim jacket, fishing for a bottle of hand sanitizer. Empty. She immediately wished she had worn her black wool coat with its fully stocked pockets for traveling to the courthouse and client meetings. Lotion. Kleenex pack. Hand sanitizer. Lipstick. She looked more professional in it too. At least she had thrown on a black shirt before going to the office, breaking up the Canadian tuxedo look—denim jacket on top and jeans on the bottom.

"If you wouldn't mind leaving your boots at the door," Geoffrey mumbled with a hint of Southern drawl.

Monica was accustomed to the protocol for the sloppy winter months, so she quickly unzipped her black Angela Scott ankle boots, now covered with salt stains, and toed them off. She reminded herself to polish them when she returned home as she had paid a fortune for them as a gift to herself for surviving the Saudi Arabian student murder trial.

Not bothering with hospitable small talk, Geoffrey guided her down a dark hall. She noted a bathroom on their right, and a book-filled study with an upright piano on their left. They emerged into an open-concept kitchen with a view through an archway to the living room. A bank of windows faced the quasi-frozen lake, a gleaming layer of water covering the thick ice.

The place had the architectural bones of a majestic 1970s lake house that hadn't been updated. The eclectic mix of furniture looked frayed, and the scattered books, newspapers, pillows and throw blankets indicated a lived-in space.

A blonde woman of medium height turned from the kitchen counter and smiled. "I'm Nicole Kershaw."

Monica entered the space. "Pleasure to meet you, Dr. Kershaw. I'm Monica Spade."

"Please, call me Nicole." Monica took the second hand offered to her in as many minutes, all the while questioning whether she should be shaking hands with anyone.

"I just put some coffee on," Nicole said. "Why don't we sit at the kitchen table?"

"Sounds great." Monica wondered if she should excuse herself to the bathroom to wash her hands.

As if reading Monica's mind, Nicole said, "We bought a ton of hand sanitizer in preparation for the pandemic. Here, help yourself." She pointed to a giant squirt bottle on the table and pumped a blob of foam into her own palm, briskly rubbing her hands together like a surgeon.

Monica followed her lead.

Geoffrey didn't participate in the cleansing, adding to Monica's growing curiosity about him.

Nicole and Monica sat opposite each other at the oak clawfoot table, while Geoffrey rested his butt against the kitchen sink, the dirt and stink of chicken coop chores clinging to his jeans.

"I see you met Geoffrey?" Nicole asked, gesturing in his general direction.

"Indeed," Monica said. Like Nicole, he was of medium height, slightly shorter than Monica's 5 feet, 10 inches. His face was covered by thick, black stubble that accentuated his deep-set eyes. He possessed a gritty appearance with an undercurrent of sleaze, but maybe Monica was judging him too harshly, since he obviously hadn't showered in a few days.

"Geoffrey, would you mind giving Monica and me some privacy?" Nicole asked in a whiskey voice that was pleasant to the ear without having the accompanying rasp of a cigarette smoker.

Geoffrey nodded without speaking, a practice that looked well-honed. He turned and poured himself a cup of coffee, then shuffled out to the living room where a Milwaukee Brewers spring training game was playing on a mammoth flat screen TV. If Geoffrey was committed to not eavesdropping, Monica thought another room might have been more suitable. She could still see the top of his head at one end of the sofa, and his feet hanging over the arm at the other.

Monica's gaze slid back to Nicole. "Thank you. I prefer to meet with clients in private because we need confidentiality. For me to do my job effectively, I need to know all the facts, even if you think something might not be relevant or important. Tell me everything, okay?" She leaned down and removed a yellow legal pad and pen from her brown suede attaché case, which boasted a few battle scars from being stomped on and thrown under a chair during her last murder trial.

Nicole's intelligent, light gray eyes studied Monica, performing some sort of private calculation. "I appreciate your expertise, Monica, and have no problem telling you everything."

"Very well then. When were you contacted by the police and what was the officer's name?"

"Friday evening on my way home from work, an Apple Grove detective called me and left a voicemail. Do you want to hear it?"

"Sure."

The doctor cued up her phone and hit play.

Monica immediately recognized Detective Matt Breuer's baritone voice. He was a good friend and her law partner, Nathan Taylor's, boyfriend. Matt's message was short and to the point, asking Nicole to return his call without telling her why he was calling.

"I know Matt," Monica said.

"Is he a good cop or a bad cop?" Nicole asked.

6

Monica contemplated Matt's character before replying in a tone intended to convey neutrality, "I've worked with Matt before. He's fair."

The coffee maker beeped. "Would you like a cup?" Nicole asked.

"Sure."

"Cream or sugar?"

"Both."

While Nicole prepared the mugs, Monica asked, "Did you return Matt's call?"

"Yes. We agreed to meet tomorrow. He's bringing another detective. From Minneapolis, I think."

"Here? At your house?"

"Yes. Will you come too?" Nicole asked.

"That's why Al Bowman hired me—to protect the hospital's and your interests."

Nicole cocked her head in question as she set the mugs on the table.

"I represent the hospital first. Since you're an employee, I can represent you too, as long as your interests are aligned. If at any time your interest becomes adversarial to the hospital, then I have to withdraw as your counsel."

"You mean, like, if I murdered my own patients?" Nicole said with glib sarcasm.

Blindsided, Monica didn't know whether to smile or run for cover. "Um, yes. Should I ask if you did?"

"Of course not." Nicole rolled her eyes at her throwaway comment, as if Monica lacked any sense of humor.

Despite the weird vibe, Monica pressed on. "Now that we have that settled, I'll come to the police interview tomorrow on your behalf."

"I'd like that." Nicole tossed a long chunk of hair over her half-bare shoulder, exposed by the jewel neckline of a taupe sweater sitting askew.

Monica studied the woman across from her as she asked, "What did Matt tell you about the two patients who were murdered?"

"He just gave me their names so I could look up their medical records."

"Did you?"

"In a heartbeat. I have access to the electronic medical record from home, so I printed out a few of my notes." She tapped her long fingers on a small stack next to her, her laptop within reach, open, and the screen glowing blue.

"What are their names?" Monica asked, her pen poised over her legal pad.

"Michelle Adler from Minneapolis and Veronica Remington from Chicago."

"Let's start with Michelle Adler. Tell me what you remember about her. I want to know your casual observations rather than your clinical impressions."

Nicole pressed her eyes shut and briefly scrunched her face. "Unfortunately, those types of details are hard to recollect two years after performing her surgery. I've seen so many patients since then." She opened her eyes and stared into the middle space between them, tugging on her memory. "If I recall correctly, Ms. Adler seemed pretty well-adjusted and happy, aside from gender dysphoria, that is. I think she worked at a big corporation in Minneapolis—an insurance company or retail giant, something like that. Her corporate health insurance covered the surgery. That sticks out in my mind. Not all do, you know, and this is an expensive surgery—at least $60,000, and that's just for the bottom half. Anyway, Michelle had really done her homework about the surgery—watched several videos depicting it and had been in counseling for a few years. She was aware of the WPATH guidelines and had followed them to a T before seeing me."

Monica stopped writing and held up her hand. "Okay, what are the WPATH guidelines?"

Nicole smiled, revealing straight white teeth, the result of orthodontia work early in life. "Sorry. WPATH stands for World Professional Association for Transgender Health. The organization has published standards of care. Any healthcare provider who works in this field is familiar with WPATH guidelines."

"What do the guidelines suggest?"

"They're quite extensive, but for gender-affirming surgery, which Michelle was interested in, they go into detail about the preparation leading up to the surgery."

"What type of preparation?"

"You have to understand that this isn't just a surgery to fix a shoulder or remove an inflamed appendix. It's an emotional and physical transformation that involves a team of professionals, from counseling to hormone therapy to surgery."

"What are the pre-surgical requirements?"

"WPATH lists several, so I might miss a few, but in short, here they are." She ticked them off on each finger as she spoke. "The patient, whether male or female, must have well-documented and persistent gender dysphoria. The patient must have the mental capacity to make an informed decision about sex assignment surgery. The patient must have a full year of hormone therapy for the patient's gender goals—in Michelle's case, from male to female. A full year of living in the identity of the gender goal, again for Michelle, living as a female. Last but not least, two referral letters from the patient's providers. One from a primary care physician with whom the patient has had at least a one-year relationship—usually the endocrinologist who has prescribed the hormones. The second letter is usually from the patient's mental health counselor."

"Wow, that's a lot of prep work." Monica scribbled down the requirements.

"That's just the minimum. Customarily, my patients have been seeing a counselor for a number of years, and gender-affirming surgery is the final step in a long process. I know it was for me." Nicole ran her hand through her long, disheveled hair, dark at the roots and blonde at the tips.

Monica's pen hovered. *Is now the right time to ask Nicole about her own transgender story, or should I save that for later?*

"Anyway," Nicole said, foreclosing that line of inquiry, "Michelle came to me as a fully informed patient who knew what she wanted."

"And what was that?"

"Sex reassignment surgery—bottom first, top later— with a tracheal shave."

"Just to translate for me, are we talking about pelvic surgery, then breast implants, and what's the shave part?"

Nicole's business-like expression softened into that of a teacher. "The bottom surgery is called a vaginoplasty. Basically, we remove the penis, called a penectomy, remove the scrotum, called an orchiectomy, then create a clitoris, labia minora and majora, and a neovagina from the scrotal skin."

Monica squinted, trying to envision a neovagina created from scrotal skin. "Is there enough skin? Wouldn't the neovagina be hairy?"

"We have enough skin to create a neovagina that's about 5 to 6 inches in depth. And, no, it isn't hairy because we treat the skin with a laser before we transplant it to create the canal."

Monica gulped. She had a thousand more questions about the clitoral anatomy, but those could wait. "And the tracheal shave? What's that?"

"We reduce the size of the Adam's apple, a distinctly male characteristic, to complete the transformation." Nicole leaned her head back and arched her neck, pointing to a tiny scar at the top of her neck where the skin met the back of her jaw. "We try to hide the scar in the shadow of the chin."

"Yours is small and very well hidden. Why is that important?"

"If the scar is visible on the neck, the trans woman can be clocked."

Monica thought back to her first criminal case that involved a privileged white man punching a Saudi foreign exchange student outside a bar. "And by 'clocked,' you mean punched or beaten, right?"

Nicole's blonde hair swung from side to side. "I can see how you might think that, considering we live in Apple Grove, but no. By 'clocked,' I mean discovered, found out, or outed, as a trans woman. It's a common term in my world."

"Oh. Learn something new every day," Monica said, writing.

"Straight people wouldn't understand."

"Maybe not," Monica said, looking up from her notepad. "The straight people I work with are pretty empathetic. You know I'm gay, right?"

"No. Al didn't tell me that. Then again, why would he?" Nicole looked at Monica with a fresh set of eyes. "Excellent. I think you'll appreciate the nuances of this situation more than a straight person would."

"I'll try my best," Monica said. "Now, continuing with Michelle, how did the surgery go?"

"Everything went terrifically. Pleasing aesthetic result and her neovaginal canal was deep enough for penetrative sex with her partner."

"Did you ever meet her partner?"

"Probably, but if I did, I don't remember."

"Do you know if they were still partners at the time of her death?"

"No clue. We didn't stay in touch. Like any surgery, the patient follows with me for a few months, then, after healing, goes about her life. Occasionally, I receive a Christmas card or wedding announcement, something happy like that. Not a call from the police that my patient has been viciously murdered, the victim of a hate crime." Shocked and hurt, Nicole raised her chapped hands to her face and rubbed her forehead.

"I'm sorry. This entire situation has to be so upsetting for you."

Tears spilled over Nicole's long lashes, turning her mascara to muddy rivulets. "I just feel like I failed her somehow."

"Why?"

"Was she clocked from her tracheal shave, even though I thought I did a great job?"

"Maybe the detectives will share more information tomorrow."

Nicole pushed back from the table and paced to the other end of the kitchen like an antsy athlete. She pivoted in her rainbow-colored Crocs to face Monica. "I mean, is someone targeting my patients? Trying to get at me through them? Am I next?"

Monica shifted in her chair, careful to avoid the dog that had settled at her feet. "Who would be trying to hurt you by killing your patients? And why?"

Nicole snorted derisively and rolled her shoulders. "I've made my fair share of enemies since I entered this specialty, compounded by being the only transgendered surgeon who performs sex reassignment surgery."

"Help me understand."

"Where do I start?" She glided back to the table, folding herself like a scythe into her chair. She crossed her legs and kicked a foot out in metronomic irritation, in the opposite direction of the dog. "My life history. I was bullied all through high school. Horribly bullied because I was a scrawny, effeminate boy who got straight A's. My name was Nicholas then."

Monica nodded, picturing the young Nicholas.

"I grew three inches taller after high school, so college wasn't so bad. I did well academically. Made some friends. Had a few relationships. After medical school, I underwent gender-affirming surgery during my residency in plastic surgery. I was 31 years old and working alongside Dr. Broussard in Canada. I was so flattered that he agreed to perform it, as he was the preeminent surgeon for many years, instructing a lot of us in the field how to do vaginoplasties."

"Uh-huh." Monica wrote his name on her pad.

"He's still a leader in the field and has been a great mentor to me."

"So, why would someone want to harm you or your patients?"

Anger replaced her pensive look. "I'm active in the trans community as an advocate and counselor, so I'm quite visible. I march in parades, volunteer to lobby at the state and federal level, speak at conferences, and the list goes on. When you're on the public stage, you're a target. People are crazy, and the crazies fear the unknown. They fill in the blanks with fiction, like conspiracy theories, or some other outlet for their hate, and hate leads to violence." She stopped and sipped her coffee. "Case in point—QAnon or Neo-Nazis."

Monica raised her eyebrows. "Good examples. It does feel as if the world is back-sliding and getting less safe."

"Hate against the trans community has been the topic of many late-night conversations for Geoffrey and me." Nicole glanced toward the living room where Geoffrey still lay, the game not loud enough to cover his snoring. "When I began my plastic surgery practice in Apple Grove, I purposefully included the subspecialty of sex reassignment surgery and advertised nationally. You've probably seen my website."

Monica nodded.

"Well, so have the paranoid, crazy haters. At the beginning, protesters actually lined the parking lot outside my clinic, just like they would an abortion clinic. I'm the poster child of trans women, and that can be either really good or really bad."

Monica nodded, her silence encouraging more.

"The haters probably think I'm recruiting young men into my clinic to become women." She threw her hands up. "I don't know. Anyway, I get hate mail regularly. Death threats call me a freak. A monster. A mutilator. Queen of the faggots. You name it. Condemning me, my practice and my patients."

"That's twisted and horrible."

Nicole waved off the sentiment. "I've learned to live with it. I don't even open the mail anymore. Geoffrey does. Then he burns it out back." She again glanced appreciatively at the living room.

"That's why we live out here, off the beaten path. And I have a conceal and carry permit. I'm armed to the gills—a gun under the seat in my car, one in my bag wherever I go, and one in every corner of this house."

Monica resisted the temptation to look more closely at the nooks and crannies. "You might want to stop burning the mail because it could serve as evidence if someone targets you. Has anyone tried to harm you physically?"

Nicole pursed her lips, her eyes turning darker. "On multiple occasions. Crazed drunk Neanderthals confronted me in the hospital parking lot one night. Fortunately, hospital security was making their rounds and two guards intervened."

Monica covered her mouth in surprise.

"That's nothing. Geoffrey and I have been physically threatened when we're out as a couple. Not necessarily in Apple Grove, but when we travel. I'm trained in self-defense and Geoffrey learned the hard way—on the streets in Miami. He knows how to protect us."

"What's Geoffrey's last name?" Monica asked in a gentle voice that she hoped didn't sound too interrogation-like.

Nicole arched her plucked right brow.

"As your lawyer, I need to know everything," Monica said.

"Fine. Geoffrey Gold."

Monica made a note. "Where did you meet?"

"At a plastic surgery convention in Miami where I was giving a presentation. At the time, over a year ago now, he was working for a pharmaceutical company that hosted a fishing expedition for a small group of physicians."

"Which pharmaceutical company?"

"Injectafyl, a company that makes breast implants."

So, Geoffrey is a boob guy. Monica's gaze inevitably drifted to Nicole's chest. Perky breasts cantilevered the sweater in a firm, distinct outline, characteristic of implants, but they weren't porn-star-size. She quickly raised her gaze to meet Nicole's. "Does Geoffrey still work for Injectafyl?"

"No. He quit that job before he moved to Wisconsin. He hasn't found anything in the region yet, so he mostly takes care of our flock, maintains the house, puts the dock and boat in the water, cooks, buys groceries, you know?"

Monica didn't know, but she thought Geoffrey had a pretty nice gig, taking care of the joint while Nicole was at the hospital. Nicole obviously loved him, though, so Monica hoped it was requited. "Do you remember the date of the plastic surgery conference?"

"You're really testing my memory now."

"That's my specialty."

Nicole stared at the ceiling for a second. "Let me see... I'm pretty sure it was late 2018."

Monica wrote that down. "Circling back to the issue at hand, is there anything else about your former patient, Michelle Adler, that you think I should know?"

"No," Nicole said in a defeated tone. "She's been on my mind ever since Detective Breuer gave me her name. I just keep thinking over and over, 'Why her?'"

"Do you think proximity has anything to do with it? She was killed in Minneapolis, which is only a 90-minute drive from here."

"I thought about that," Nicole said and paused for a second. "Veronica Remington was murdered in Chicago, which is only a five-hour drive from here. My patients come from all over the country, so I did wonder if there's something special about these two cities and their relationship to my practice here in Apple Grove."

"Again, maybe the detectives will be able to shed light on a geographical connection tomorrow. Before I lose my train of thought, is there anything specific you remember about Veronica Remington that I should know?"

"God, I wish I could remember something specific. A clue or something, but I can't. I had to look at the medical record just to refresh my recollection about her surgery."

"That isn't unusual. When I meet with physicians on medical malpractice claims, they usually don't have a specific recollection of the patient if the care was provided more than a year ago. As this case progresses, if you remember more, feel free to call or email me."

Nicole looked relieved as she nodded.

"Do you have any questions about how to handle yourself tomorrow?"

Nicole glanced down at her stack of medical records. "Can I share confidential information from the medical record with them?"

"Yes. In a homicide investigation, you absolutely can share the details about the patient and the care, but only about the deceased patient, not other patients."

"Good to know. Is there anything I shouldn't say?"

Monica regarded the doctor closely and thought about her earlier sarcasm. "I wouldn't be glib about the murders and tossing a comment out that you aren't the killer. They aren't going to appreciate sarcasm in a setting like this."

"I get it. What I said earlier was in poor taste."

"Maybe so. In addition, I always caution my clients to use common sense when speaking to law enforcement. No confessing minor infractions of the law that might get you in trouble, or worse, detract from your credibility."

"Infractions?" Nicole looked like a deer in the headlights.

"By way of example, and not implying that you would do any of these things, but maybe you occasionally smoke dope. Don't mention that. Or, if you drink cocktails when you drive your boat around the lake. Or, if you gave a patient a narcotic without a prescription. I don't know. I'm just naming random possibilities."

A deep, throaty chuckle bubbled up from Nicole. "None of those apply to me. Don't get me wrong, I've had my share of fun, but I'm a law-abiding citizen. I can't afford to lose my DEA or medical license over something stupid like smoking weed." She nervously glanced over at the slumbering Geoffrey, adding as an afterthought, "We're both law-abiding citizens."

"Then we don't have anything to worry about, do we?"

Nicole forced a smile that, if meant to be reassuring, had the opposite effect. "Well, I did get arrested a few times in college for marching in protests."

Monica raised her eyebrows.

"For gay rights. I might have been arrested for disorderly conduct after lipping off to a few officers. Those were later expunged for good behavior—or something like that. I forget what my lawyer told me."

"Okay. No need to mention them, right?"

"Trust me, I won't."

"If you have a question tomorrow while we're talking to the detectives," Monica said, "just ask to speak to me in private before you say anything, okay?"

"Good advice," Nicole said.

"Based on what you've told me, I'm not concerned about the police speaking to you. Are you?"

"No. I'm just torn up over my patients and this entire situation."

"Me too." Monica lay her hand on top of Nicole's and patted it a few times. "I should get going."

"Thank you for driving out here to talk. I'll walk you to the door."

As they passed the library, the upright piano snagged Monica's attention. Like the rest of the furniture, it, too, looked old but well-used. "Do you play?"

A genuine smile smoothed Nicole's worry lines. "When I get the time. It relaxes me. Looks like I'll be playing a lot more now with the coronavirus shutting down my surgical practice."

"Might be a silver lining," Monica said.

"Unfortunately, playing piano doesn't pay the bills."

7

When Monica exited into the dappled sunlight on Nicole's faded wooden deck, she noticed that the midday warmth had ebbed, reminding her that March still had some fight.

The chickens and ducks had retreated to their coops behind the garage, and the dog had stayed inside the house, so Monica didn't have any companions on the return to her truck through the unkempt forest.

As she glanced around the property, her eyes caught on a motion detector camera strapped to a tree about 12 feet to her right. A critter cam. She looked directly into it for the series of photos it inevitably was snapping. She wanted Nicole and Geoffrey to know she had spotted it, sending them a message that the cam was too obvious and should be moved a few feet back.

Monica's parents had critter cams at their lakefront property, which was located two hours north of Apple Grove. Her parents delighted in removing the memory cards and looking at the photos of the deer, bear, wild turkeys, raccoons, skunks, beavers and domesticated cats traveling through their woods. Monica was no stranger to the camera's capabilities.

At present, Roger and Colleen were wintering in Arizona through April and had asked Monica to check on their place up north. She and Shelby had spent a cozy weekend in February enjoying walks on the frozen lake, reading by the fire, drinking hot chocolate, and watching movies. Colleen had complained to Monica that Shelby had been to their lake property, but only after they had departed for Arizona. They were dying to meet the woman who had stolen Monica's heart.

Whenever Colleen called or texted, she pummeled Monica with questions about Shelby, especially since the engagement. Even though she came out to her parents early in life, Monica had never brought a girlfriend home. She was nervous about bringing Shelby home because their relationship was still so fresh. Would her parents be judgy? Worse, would they say something embarrassing?

Dragging herself back to reality, Monica suspected that Nicole's critter cam had less to do with capturing nature and more with capturing people. She wondered if it was the type that sent the photo or video to the owner's cell phone.

She got into her truck and backed up next to the garage, careful not to run over any poultry, then drove slowly along the winding driveway while peering into the woods. She spotted two more cameras strapped to trees on her way out. She pictured the streetwise Geoffrey becoming accustomed to the culture of the Wisconsin Northwoods. His clandestine camera placement needed some work.

As she pulled onto the two-lane highway, Monica was reminded that she needed information, and her number one information gatherer was Kathy, the wispy-haired law firm receptionist who wore leopard print half-glasses and routinely baked goodies like cinnamon rolls. When Kathy wasn't reading Vince Flynn novels at the reception desk, she enjoyed a spicy assignment. Monica called her on speakerphone.

"Welcome back from Belize," Kathy said. "Was it a hot, romantic and beautiful vacation?"

"Very," Monica said, her face flushing at the memory of Shelby frolicking in the water in her skimpy bikini. "We're actually grateful to be back, safe and sound."

"No kidding. Janet called me a while ago and said the governor is expected to close everything in the state, including the law firm, so I came into work to pack up my stuff."

"Good move. Jim said the order will be issued tomorrow, so we all need to get set up quickly at home."

"It won't take me long to pack my equipment, but I can't help but feel sad," Kathy said.

"Me too. I feel like we're closing the firm after we just opened and worse, we never got an opportunity to say goodbye to each other. It's weird."

"I agree."

"Do you have a strong internet connection and a space to work at home?" Monica asked.

"Oh yes. I have an antique desk in my sewing room that has great ergonomics. No worries."

Monica was tempted to remind Kathy to pack her her RumChata, a Wisconsin cream liqueur she stashed in a desk drawer, so she could operate at the same level of buzz while teleworking, but she decided against offending the woman whose help she needed. "Hopefully, we'll be back at the firm, business as usual, soon."

"I don't mind teleworking. I can't afford to get this virus. Winter colds always knock me on my ass, so I'm sure I'd be on a ventilator in the ICU if I got this."

"Me too. The news coverage of the overflowing hospitals looks really scary."

"They say it's just a matter of time before it arrives in Apple Grove."

"I guess staying at home and isolating is our only hope for right now."

"We're good at that. As we speak, Don is grocery shopping and stocking the freezer."

"He's a good man." Monica pictured Shelby doing the same.

"Is there something I can help you with?" Kathy asked.

"As a matter of fact, yes," Monica said. "I'm wondering if you could look up a guy who used to live in Miami. His name is Geoffrey Gold."

"What's he got to do with anything?"

"I'm working on a new file."

"On a Sunday?"

"Al Bowman called me earlier today and asked me to prepare a plastic surgeon for a police interview. Time is of the essence." Monica explained the two murders and their linkage to the only transgendered surgeon in America, and her boyfriend, Geoffrey Gold. She downloaded Nicole's belief that someone might be trying to harm her by killing her patients.

"That's fucked up," Kathy said. "How do we know there are only two patients who've been murdered?"

If Monica had been walking, she would have stopped in her tracks. Her vacation-addled brain hadn't yet considered that possibility. "You're absolutely right, Kathy. When we meet tomorrow, I'll ask Matt to check on that."

"Matt? As in Matt Breuer, Nathan's boyfriend?"

"Yes. He's the local detective working the case. He and the Minneapolis detective are coming together tomorrow to interview Nicole."

"What about a Chicago detective?"

"Not coming with them. At least, that's what Nicole said."

"I'm surprised they're even investigating a trans woman's murder." Kathy tut-tutted. "Not exactly a high priority in the past."

"Devastatingly sad, but true," Monica said.

"Once I get plugged in at home, I'll do some digging into Geoffrey Gold's background in Florida. I take it I can use any method at my disposal?"

That question piqued Monica's curiosity. "Do I even want to know what you mean by 'at your disposal?'"

"You don't know my full background, do you?"

"No. I only met you at Daniels, Smart & Whitworth, and that environment wasn't exactly conducive to chit chat or socializing."

"Well, the idiots at DSW were the reason I started drinking at work. I actually had an exciting life before working for those bastards."

"Do tell."

"Oh, my dear, I could entertain you with wild stories over a beer sometime. Here's the abridged version. Before I started at DSW, I had a series of, shall we say, strategic positions. I worked for the federal government in Washington, D.C. right out of college. I can't discuss in what capacity, but it was with the Bureau of Alcohol, Tobacco and Firearms, and I saw a lot of action. That was back in the early 90s, when no one wore a body cam."

"Sounds dangerous."

"It was. After a few years of that, Don got a job with Miller Brewing Company distribution, so we moved to Wisconsin. I worked for the Wisconsin Division of Criminal Investigation for several years—"

"Wow."

"Then I had a few kids, took some time off, and returned to the working world as a do-everything-for-everyone at DSW."

"Fascinating. Do you keep up with your old contacts in the government agencies?"

"You bet your tush I do."

"Handy set of resources to have at your fingertips."

"You can say that again."

"You're full of surprises, Kathy."

"Not even my best quality."

"I'm sure." Monica chuckled. "Thanks for helping me. I'll make sure to keep your work life more interesting than it was at DSW."

"Not a high bar."

They ended their call.

Monica next considered calling Al Bowman to update him, but she didn't think he'd be interested in her conversation with Nicole. Maybe she'd have something of substance to share with him after the meeting with the detectives.

She used the remainder of the drive to mull over Nicole's personal history and subspecialty practice, and the media attention both had garnered. *Could the fear and hatred of gender-affirming surgeries be so strong to foment a killing spree? Is there any connection to Nicole, or is her involvement pure coincidence? Are there others?*

Twenty minutes after leaving Nicole's, Monica turned down her own tree-lined street, a working-class neighborhood on the north side of Apple Grove. She didn't live on the tony streets of doctors and bankers, but she respected her neighborhood, where people worked hard, watched out for one another, and allowed their kids free rein to play in the front yards and roam. Everyone knew each other on a first-name basis, and she was delighted that she belonged to a true-blue community.

She parked on her narrow, concrete driveway next to the house, since knobby tire tracks from Shelby's Jeep ran directly to Monica's single-stall garage. The descending angle of the sun created streaks of pink cotton candy across the sky, as Monica unloaded her office equipment and set the boxes inside the kitchen door. Savory aromas from the kitchen greeted her. *Aha. Back to our routine. I work. Shelby cooks dinner.* Her heart smiled, and she might have drooled a little.

"Hi, Mon. I'm in the kitchen," Shelby yelled over the hum of the stove vent.

"I'm unloading a few things." Monica peeked around the corner to see Shelby in pink Lycra boy shorts and a loose, white tank top. Her coppery, defined legs stretched from floor-to-ceiling. She looked like a sweet piece of candy that Monica could lick from head to toe. *Is she even wearing a bra?*

"Like your outfit, sexy," Monica said while gently setting her computer monitor on the dining table.

"Have to flaunt my tan before it fades." Shelby swiveled her hips.

"I hope you didn't wear those shorts to CrossFit class. Pandemonium would break out—people dropping barbells on their toes and tossing kettlebells into the air—distracted by your gorgeous legs and ass."

Shelby tossed her curls over her shoulder, showing a tanned expanse of neck. "Don't be silly. I wore something skimpier."

Monica kicked off her boots and threw her jacket over a chair. She moved to the stove, where Shelby was stirring a pot of barley soup with bay leaves floating on top.

Snuggling up to Shelby's back, Monica gently tickled her below the tight hems of her shorts, finding the crescents of her butt cheeks.

"Mm," Shelby said, a shudder running through her.

Monica raised the back of Shelby's hair and kissed her neck, first with closed lips, then with tongue sweeps down her spine.

"What's this?" Shelby trembled, arching her booty into Monica and leaning her head back against Monica's shoulder.

Monica planted slow kisses on Shelby's tanned neck, drinking in the salty taste, reminiscent of sun and sea.

Shelby simultaneously gasped and sighed as she reached for the dial and turned off the stove. "I haven't showered," she breathed. "Wanted to start dinner."

"You taste sexy and smell even better." Monica cupped Shelby's breasts, her warm palms caressing the undersides, her fingers skating over Shelby's rising nipples.

"You're turning me on." Shelby squirmed, rubbing her ass back and forth, craning her neck, so she could turn and kiss Monica on the lips.

Monica would have none of that—yet. Instead, she tilted Shelby's head and plunged the tip of her tongue into Shelby's ear, exhaling through swirls.

"Oooooh," Shelby purred, her hands covering Monica's now, encouraging her to be rougher.

All the blood in Monica's body made a U-turn, speeding south, engine roaring. She lingered over Shelby's ear lobe, nibbling. "Been dreaming about you all day."

Shelby reached up to the vent hood over the stove, her fingers fumbling for the off switch. She spun in Monica's arms to face her, wanton lust burning in her hazel eyes. "I want you so bad right now."

"Then you shall have me." Monica reached under the loose tank top—no bra—and massaged Shelby's small breasts while kissing her into next week.

When Monica pulled back to move lower, Shelby swooned, her body swaying so hard that Monica had to hold her by the ribcage so she wouldn't topple over.

"You make me dizzy," Shelby murmured, her voice husky.

Monica smiled into Shelby's hazel eyes, the gold flecks on fire. "Wait till I go lower."

Shelby purred like a cat.

Monica moved her hands to the bright pink boy shorts, hooked her thumbs in the waistband and slowly, oh so slowly, lowered them over toned thighs, creamy knees, shapely calves, and smooth ankles, kissing and nibbling her way down.

Shelby's hands rested on Monica's shoulders for balance as she stepped out of her shorts. "We've never made love in the kitchen."

"It's about time we remedy that." Monica breathed against Shelby's curls. "Tilt your hips toward me."

Shelby arched against the stove like a yogi bending backward on the mat, lifting her landing strip to Monica's mouth.

Monica dove in, tongue first, not wasting any time on breathy kisses, teases or caresses.

"Whoa," Shelby moaned. "Fuck!"

Monica latched onto Shelby's center then surprised her with bold tongue strokes, moving in a figure-eight pattern.

Shelby gripped the warm stovetop with her palms, saying in a tight voice, "My hair…in soup. Move."

Monica loved that she licked Shelby into incoherency but backed off long enough for Shelby to sidestep the pot of soup.

Her own lips glistening with Shelby's crème fraîche, Monica wiped them with the back of her hand and glanced up to see Shelby's eyes dive ten shades darker. "You're deliciously wet."

Shelby placed one hand on the counter and the other against the side of Monica's head in a loving, coaxing gesture. "More."

On her knees, bowing before her goddess, Monica would sell her soul at a discount to have Shelby look at her that way for the rest of her life. She rested her hands on Shelby's hips, holding her in place with commanding palms. "Give yourself to me, you CrossFit goddess."

Shelby arched nimbly into Monica's mouth, a *fuck-me-now* smile playing at the edges of her lips.

Monica buried her face, French kissing Shelby's folds, moving her face from side to side, intentionally covering everything but the bullseye.

"Pleeease," Shelby hissed, her hips chasing Monica's tongue.

Monica knew what Shelby wanted but ran her tongue around Shelby's gem in deliberate strokes, steady and strong.

"God," Shelby moaned, spearing Monica's hair and cupping the back of her head. "You're torturing me…"

Monica brought her middle finger around and deftly curled it into Shelby's vagina, instantly locating the sensitive ridges that drove Shelby nuts. She tickled with the tip of her finger as her tongue struck the chime.

"Fuck yeah," Shelby groaned.

Monica's own body throbbed with passion as she tasted the essence of Shelby, feeling Shelby's core shivering and spasming around her finger and over her tongue.

"Oh, yes. Oh...thaaat," Shelby mumbled, barely forming words, her voice trembling with pleasure and anticipation.

Monica lapped like a kitten drinking milk.

"Fuck...fuck me," Shelby murmured, as garbled sounds toppled out of her mouth between pants and gasps.

Monica was shouldering all of Shelby's quivering body now, as she inserted two fingers and found a rhythmic combination between her tongue swipes and finger slides.

Shelby's hips thrusted to and fro, until her entire core froze for a hot second—during which Monica could feel the heartbeat of Shelby's impending climax—then Shelby exploded like a finale of fireworks.

Monica clenched Shelby's ass, holding her in place, so she could savor her. The goddess in her mouth, shattering at her touch.

A high-pitched squeal emanated from Shelby, making Monica smile. As a finishing touch, Monica swiped her tongue around and across her throbbing hotspot again.

"Nooooo...too much," Shelby hissed, her fingers wedging between Monica's mouth and her spent bundle of nerves. "Too soon."

Monica backed off and instead kissed the inside of Shelby's thighs, up and down one, then the other.

Tremors subsiding, Shelby mewled in response.

When Monica licked her way back to the golden core and swept her tongue in a feathery swoop around and around, Shelby's body tensed and she bucked into Monica's mouth again.

Monica backed away long enough to say, "I want you to come again for me."

"I can't—"

"You can." Monica kissed her again. "Relax and trust. Give yourself to me."

Shelby sank into Monica's mouth, her hands digging into Monica's shoulders. "Just a little...Oh, yes...like that."

This was Monica's favorite part—the second time around. She felt like she had Shelby's soul in the palm of her hand.

Monica backed off a hair, looked up at Shelby, and said, "Tell me you want it."

"Fuck, Mon."

"Tell me." Monica sent out a tongue dart.

Shelby laughed through a pant. "I want to come again."

Monica played hide and seek until Shelby's fingers dug into Monica's scalp, pleading for more.

Monica slowly lay back on the kitchen floor and guided Shelby down with her, her tanned thighs astride Monica's head.

As Shelby lowered herself, her hands sought and found Monica's, their fingers intertwining.

Monica leaned up and thrust her tongue into Shelby's vagina, eliciting a growl from Shelby, who lowered herself onto Monica's face.

Later, as a primal scream escaped Shelby, Monica's own core swelled in anticipation of an orgasm. Monica felt deep waves crash through Shelby's body, as she quivered then tumbled over Monica's shoulders in a heap.

Monica's own orgasm rumbled deep within her, giving her a mini version of what Shelby usually gave her.

Shelby released Monica's hands and wrapped her arms around Monica's head, scooting down to conform her planes over Monica's curves.

"That. Was. The. Best." Shelby exhaled a contented sigh.

"Yeah?"

"Did I feel you come too?"

"A minigasm. First time I've experienced that while giving you one."

"Score!" Shelby fist-pumped the air.

Once they caught their breath, Shelby stretched out over Monica like a slinky cat.

They lay in the waning light, as the sun hovered above the tree-lined horizon.

"Let's take a shower, so I can give you a proper orgasm," Shelby said in a sated voice.

Monica uncurled from Shelby and rocked up to her feet, holding out her hand.

8

The next morning, the women were jolted awake by the pre-dawn ring of Shelby's phone. Banging her hand on the bedside table, Shelby found the obnoxious device, then held the bright screen to her ear. "Hello?"

Surfacing to consciousness during the commotion, Monica struggled to find her bearings, trying to remember if they were in Belize or Apple Grove. *Apple Grove,* she decided. *My house or Shelby's?* Her eyes traveled over the familiar furniture in her room, cast in an orange glow from the streetlamp on the corner. *My house.* She breathed quietly, straining to hear who was calling Shelby at such an early hour.

Muffled sounds of a deep male voice issued forth.

"What? You're kidding me!" Shelby croaked.

More male sounds.

"I can't believe it. How are we going to teach?"

The guy talked forever while Shelby muttered "uh-huhs" and "oh nos."

Monica flipped back the covers and used the bathroom, picking up her own phone on her way back to bed. She navigated to the news feed, and a quick review of the headlines explained Shelby's surprise. Governor Eberhardt's stay-at-home order was official, meaning schools were closed. Teachers were encouraged to teach online as soon as the schools could figure out how to connect with students on devices in their homes. Shelby was freaking out over how she would teach art online.

They had awakened to the reality that they were sentenced to home, both teleworking during a pandemic. Monica had hoped to catch up on sleep from travel, but there would be no spooning and dozing now. They had to acclimate to a new world order, a grim reality from what they were living only a few days prior, and Shelby was freaking out.

I better start the coffee.

While the coffee was brewing, and Monica was setting up her computer and printer at the small desk against a wall that served as a visual divider between her kitchen and living room, Shelby emerged from the bedroom in a hoodie and joggers, her usually ravishing corkscrews an eagle's nest. "I can't believe this."

"That schools are closed?" Monica asked while tinkering with cords.

"That the school won't pay for art supplies that I'd like to send home with students."

"Why not? Students probably don't have any supplies at home."

"That's what I said, but Principal Dickwad says he won't authorize the expense."

"I'm sorry," Monica said while adjusting the printer and plugging it into a surge protector.

Muttering expletives, Shelby hooked her hands around the sink and did a few deep squats, stretching out her back and neck, turning her head from side to side, cracking it. As she rose to a standing position, she leaned over the sink, using it like a ballet barre, extending her legs into the air behind her. More expletives were murmured while muscles stretched and joints cracked.

Even though Monica was accustomed to Shelby bending, twisting, and laying her feet on the back of the sofa to stretch her hamstrings, she had not yet witnessed these angry movements while Shelby swore like a sailor. Throughout the angry performance, Monica snuck peeks, admiring Shelby's shapely body.

"My knees are bruised from sex on the kitchen floor last night," Shelby blurted.

Monica couldn't restrain a small smirk. "Savage."

"I think I'm getting too old for antics like that."

"You mean that wasn't your first time on a hardwood floor?"

Shelby gave Monica some side-eye as she stalked to the coffee maker. "Want me to pour you a cup?"

"That would be grand." Monica booted up her computer.

Shelby clanged mugs and heated milk in the microwave, then whipped the milk into a frenzy with the handheld frother. She finally presented a steaming mug to Monica.

"Mm. Thank you, my love," Monica said before losing her upper lip in the duvet of froth. She tipped the mug back, arching her neck and probing her tongue in search of coffee.

Shelby's previously irritated eyes sparkled with amusement over the rim of her own mug.

Monica made a big to-do about enjoying the brew, leaving a froth mustache above her lip, hoping Shelby would wipe if off with her finger.

"Is this going to be your official home office now?" Shelby asked, ignoring Monica's mustache.

Monica wiped it off on the sleeve of her pullover. "Well, I have my laptop, which I can use from anywhere, but I need a desk for all this stuff, so yeah, I guess so." Monica looked around. "I guess it's kind of stupid to make my office between the kitchen and living room, isn't it?"

Shelby shrugged. "It's temporary. Try coming up with an art curriculum over Zoom, which is a technology I've never used."

"You're tech savvy."

Shelby scowled at Monica as if she were a traitor.

Monica adopted her most conciliatory expression. "Not that I think Zoom is a proper substitute for an art class in person."

Shelby tsked as she moved toward the sofa.

Best to tease this out a bit. "What medium are you teaching right now? Pottery? Painting?"

"It's a mixed bag for high school. Upper-level classes are more focused, so yes, I have several pottery classes. All of the students' clay is at school, though, so I'm going to have to make arrangements for them to pick it up and bring it home." She dropped onto the sofa, set her mug on the coffee table, and buried her face in her hands. "I only have a few days to get ready."

"No classes today?"

"No. Everyone has to get their shit together to teach from home and set up Zoom accounts."

Monica joined her on the sofa and turned on the TV to CNN. They watched the footage in astonishment—men and women in biohazard suits loading corpses into the refrigerated semi-truck containers. Numbers flashed on the screen, indicating the number of estimated cases and the mounting death toll, New York leading the world in souls claimed by COVID.

"Holy crap," Monica exclaimed, hypnotized by the grim images. "This is worse than anything I ever imagined."

"No kidding. I'm sort of scared, Mon."

"Me too." Monica muted the TV.

They watched in silence for a few minutes, then Shelby asked, "You're sure you don't mind if I shelter in place with you?"

Monica scooped up Shelby's hand and squeezed it. "I'd be honored."

"I'm going to have to set up a classroom in your house."

"*Mi casa es su casa,*" Monica said, gesturing around her. "Wherever you like."

"I'm thinking the light in the four-season porch would be good for painting."

Monica nodded in agreement, picturing an easel at the opposite end of her loveseat arrangement by the fireplace.

"And I could set up my potter's wheel in your extra bedroom."

Tires screeched to a halt. Monica pictured the cumbersome wheel that she had seen in Shelby's studio, recalling lots of water and soupy clay on top of a large machine that occupied a lot of space. She immediately worried that the clay soup would splatter the walls and soak into the throw rug on the hardwood floor. "That's pretty big and messy, isn't it? How about we put it in the basement?"

Shelby stiffened. "The basement? It's dark and unfinished down there. Spider webs all over the place." She flitted her fingers theatrically.

"But…but…doesn't it splatter clay far and wide? Isn't there lots of water involved?"

Shelby shrugged off the technical details. "We can put some plastic down."

Pandemic or not, Monica didn't want a potter's wheel in her extra bedroom.

Shelby searched Monica's face, evidently picking up on Monica's trepidation. "I can leave my wheel in my studio at my house. It's super heavy to carry anyhow, and who knows how long I'll be teaching from home. It might be for only a few weeks, which wouldn't warrant transferring it over here."

"Right…"

"Come to think of it, I miss my studio. I haven't spent much time in it since we started dating, what with working all day, cooking dinner for you, and then shagging you on the weekends."

"I've cooked dinner a few times too." A tingle ran down Monica's spine, signaling that she might have pushed Shelby back to her own house.

Shelby shoved off from the sofa and returned to the kitchen, leaving Monica to wonder where they stood. "Um... I'll clear out some space in the four-season porch for your easel and stuff."

Shelby's back was to Monica as she stirred some blueberries into her bowl of yogurt. "No need. I decided I want to use my studio because I have all my supplies there, and the lighting is perfect. That's why I bought that house in the first place. Beautiful studio space."

"Oh." Monica's mind scrambled to comprehend her lover's mood, the pandemic, and their new work situation. *Should I ask her if she's going to spend the nights with me here?*

Before Monica could misspeak again, possibly making things worse, Shelby dove into her yogurt, hips resting against the kitchen island, and scrolled through social media on her phone.

Subject closed.

Monica shifted her gaze from Shelby to the sliding glass door where a drift of dirty snow had melted considerably yesterday but had frozen again overnight. Winter dragged on. The washing machine beeped, reminding her that she needed to transfer the load to the dryer. She set her coffee aside and jumped up from the sofa, grateful for a diversion. When she returned to the kitchen, it was vacant, so she peeked into the four-season porch, where she saw Shelby texting on her phone.

"Um. I'm going to shower and go to my meeting at the physician's house," Monica said.

Shelby didn't look up. "Okay. I'm trying to figure out my day and plan my week. See you later."

Monica wanted to ask if Shelby would be here when she returned but didn't want to sound pathetic, or worse, come off like she was annoyed with Shelby's presence. She hesitated, briefly considering saying *I love you,* but thought that might sound forced, so she elected not to say anything at all. She ducked out and went about her morning routine, all the while processing whether they were sheltering together or not.

9

Monica used the twenty-minute drive to Aqua Vulva to transition from fear about the pandemic to focusing on the questions Matt Breuer and the Minneapolis detective might ask Nicole about the murders of her two patients.

Monica wasn't a big believer in coincidence, flirting with the notion that Ms. Adler's and Ms. Remington's deaths were somehow related to Nicole performing their surgeries. Maybe there was a thread that strung the victims and Nicole together. Maybe not. Mere proximity to Nicole's practice could be a viable explanation. Two trans women murdered in the Midwest were likely to have had their surgeries done by Nicole.

At the Aqua Vulva sign, she turned into the long driveway. After meeting Nicole, the playful sign didn't quite fit with her personality. Of course, the purpose of their meeting and topic of conversation hadn't exactly lent itself to joviality, so maybe there was another side of Nicole that Monica had yet to discover. Or maybe Geoffrey had created the sign without Nicole's input. That seemed a more likely explanation—that he brought the humor and mischief to the relationship.

While driving, she actively looked for critter cams and spotted a few more on her right, the opposite side she had studied on her way out yesterday. *That crafty Geoffrey.*

As she got out of her truck, she patted herself on the back for wearing suede gloves and a brown car coat to ward off the morning cold. The sky was an ugly pewter, the March weather mimicking her mood, seesawing between the promise of spring and the last vestiges of winter.

Neither the Easter-egger chickens nor the Labrador met her this time around, and the driveway was bare of vehicles, indicating she was the first to arrive.

She retraced her steps down the tangled path, tossed the critter cam a smile over her shoulder, and walked up to the icy deck. As she knocked hard on the front door, curled flakes of dried stain shook off and swirled into the breeze.

Nicole opened the door wide. "Good morning, Monica. Please come in."

"Thank you. Chilly out here."

The yellow Labrador circled Monica, nudging her hand like Beach Boy had in Belize, which seemed like a lifetime ago now. "I didn't catch your dog's name when I was here yesterday."

Nicole cast an endearing look at the drooling 80-pounder. "Marvin."

Hearing his name, Marvin immediately nudged Nicole's leg, so she scratched the top of his head. "He's my geriatric pup. Twelve years old, but you wouldn't know it by the spring in his step. He's been through thick and thin with me. I've had him since residency training."

"Wow. A best friend. I'd love a dog like Marvin."

"I'm sure you could find one at the shelter. They're overflowing and need people like you to adopt."

"Uh-huh." Monica briefly considered the idea. *I'm going to be at home teleworking so...but for how long?*

They proceeded to the kitchen table, apparently Nicole's favorite working space.

Across the hall from where they stood, a formal dining room overlooked the deck through a sliding glass door, a slice of lake beyond. In contrast to the bare table from yesterday, the oval dining table was now covered with a floor-length tablecloth with crimson flowers and mossy green leaves. Creases still evident, it looked fresh out of an Amazon box.

The tablescape didn't stop there. Pale green placemats with dark green piping held leaf-shaped dinner plates with salad plates layered on top. Loosely knotted napkins echoed the floral print of the tablecloth, resting in the center of the salad plates. A full set of silverware and stemware were placed in strict adherence to etiquette, probably by a surgeon obsessed with detail. Champagne flutes conjured an excuse for a celebration. A dried floral centerpiece with tapered candles completed the Pinterest-inspired tableau.

Monica pictured Nicole scurrying around the table in the middle of the night, resting her hand on her hip and admiring her work, a homespun treatment for insomnia. "Are you preparing for a dinner party?" Monica asked politely.

Nicole blushed, wringing her pink hands. "No. When I can't sleep, I like to tinker with my china and set a beautiful table. It relaxes me. Reminds me of the holidays when I was a child, and Easter is around the corner."

"Nicely done. It's beautiful." Monica shifted, returning her attention to Nicole.

"Thank you." For the first time, Nicole looked pleased with herself, letting some of her previous guard drop.

Monica draped her coat over an extra chair and sat at the scratched oak table. Nicole's laptop and a growing stack of medical records occupied a pie wedge across from her.

"Coffee?" Nicole asked.

"If you have some made, sure."

Monica watched Nicole—clad in jeans and a cable-knit sweater, familiar rainbow crocs on her feet—tinker at the coffee pot. "Cream and sugar, right?"

"Black is fine today." Monica decided the solemn occasion begged for a bitter taste in her mouth, so she wouldn't drink too much, get amped up, and shoot off her mouth in some direction.

Nicole joined Monica at the table with two mugs of black coffee.

"I like your hairstyle," Monica said, eyeing the Farah Fawcett locks.

Nicole shook her head like she was in a shampoo commercial. "Geoffrey blew it out and curled it before he left."

"He's got skills like a professional."

Nicole smiled, the stress lines around her mouth smoothing. "I'll tell him."

"Did he work in a salon before becoming a device rep?" Monica couldn't help but dig. It was her nature.

Nicole laughed. "Heavens no. His first career was working in a club, becoming a manager, then a co-owner. He tired of the nightlife business, and worked at Injectafyl, but I don't think his heart was in selling breast implants."

"He was both a club owner and medical device rep?"

"Yes. He did the Injectafyl gig only part-time for a short while. He ultimately sold his ownership interest in a Miami club called The Flaming Flamingo."

Instead of retrieving her legal pad and pen from her attaché case, Monica made a mental note. She cradled her coffee, attempting to look conversational while interrogating. "Fun name."

"The name was the only fun part."

"Really?"

Apparently not her favorite topic, Nicole said in a rushed monotone "Geoffrey said the bartenders would rob them blind if they weren't behind the bar every night. He and his partner divided the schedule, but it was grueling work, six nights per week, including booking live musicians on the weekends. They were wedded to the place. Combine that with driving all over town during the day to meet with plastic surgeons to peddle breast implants, and he was exhausted."

"Just hearing about it sounds exhausting."

"By the way, this conversation is privileged, isn't it? Like, you're not going to share it with the detectives or IRS, are you?

"What we discuss is attorney-client privileged. I won't share it."

Nicole registered that and cautiously continued. "The Flamingo made a pile of cash, so it was a lucrative gig for him. They always paid everyone in cash but had stacks left over. Geoffrey was having difficulty squirreling away that much cash after he met his living expenses." Nicole lowered her voice to a conspiratorial level. "Storing and laundering is harder than you think."

Monica raised her dark eyebrows, hoping Nicole wouldn't blurt that out to the detectives.

"Very different world than your legal world or my clinical world," Nicole was saying. "No one at the club got a legit paycheck with taxes withheld, which means there was ample room for skimming. He was relieved to get out because he wasn't sure his business partner was being honest about cash management."

Monica tilted her head in question.

"Drug money is pretty common in Miami. Geoffrey suspected his partner was laundering money for a Cuban gang that spent a lot of time at the club."

Monica nodded even though she had zero experience in such matters. Her curiosity naturally pulled her gaze to the sofa in the living room where Geoffrey had watched TV the day prior. All was quiet. "I don't know anything about gangs."

"You don't want to."

"Is Geoffrey out back tending to the chickens?"

A low, raspy chuckle and shake of the blonde waves. "When he heard the police were coming, he found an excuse to leave. Doesn't much care for the heat, so he's running errands in Apple Grove."

"He's had some bad experiences with law enforcement?"

"Let's just say that he views the police through his Miami club lens, which is different than my Midwest doctor lens, but not a whole lot different from my trans lens. Let's just say that I have a love-hate relationship with the police."

Their conversation was interrupted by a low rumble from Marvin, followed by a series of deep barks. He scrambled out from under the table and trotted toward the front door as Monica heard two car doors slam.

"Speaking of the heat," Nicole said, springing to her feet. "I believe they're here." She nervously smoothed the front of her celery-colored sweater.

"You'll be fine," Monica said. "No need to be nervous."

"Easy for you to say," Nicole said under her breath as she walked down the long hallway.

A few seconds later, Nicole returned with the handsome Matt Breuer and another gentleman.

"Hi, Monica," Matt said. "Thought I recognized your truck outside. Do you represent Nicole?"

"Yes. The hospital retained me."

"Awesome. You always make things run smoother." He smiled and turned to a middle-aged man wearing jeans and a navy windbreaker with the Minneapolis Police Department logo on the breast.

"This is Detective Heinz."

Monica extended her hand despite the pandemic warnings. The guidance on what they should be doing, or not doing, was so contradictory and confusing. "Monica Spade."

"Paul Heinz, Minneapolis Homicide."

He had a firm, warm grip and compassionate, sharp eyes. His black face was a bit weathered and wrinkled, but Monica assumed that came with the territory of being a big city detective.

"Please, sit and use some hand sanitizer to ward off the coronavirus," Nicole said, again demonstrating with a few foam pumps. "I insist."

"Oh, is that all we need?" Matt asked, pumping the foam and smearing it between his fingers.

Nicole harrumphed. "Hardly. I'm guessing it's an airborne pathogen like the flu. We should all probably be wearing surgical masks."

Monica chuckled nervously. "I ordered some on Amazon last night, but it indicated they wouldn't be shipped for three weeks."

"I think the Department will be issuing them to us in a few days," Detective Heinz said.

"We aren't violating the governor's order by meeting, are we?" Nicole asked.

"Homicide investigations are an exception, and they need to be conducted in person," Matt said.

"Law enforcement is an essential function to society," Monica added.

"Well, I'm not symptomatic, and I haven't been to New York in years," Nicole said.

"Me either," everyone chimed.

"Would you gentlemen like a cup of coffee?" Nicole asked.

"Sure," the men said in unison.

Once they were all seated with sanitized hands and steaming mugs in front of them, Matt cleared his throat. "As I indicated in our call, Dr. Kershaw, Detective Heinz has some questions for you about Michelle Adler and Veronica Remington, your former patients."

"I'm happy to help," Nicole said. "I feel so awful, like I'm somehow to blame. Those poor women and their families. How devastating."

Not missing a beat, Detective Heinz asked, "Why would you feel like you're to blame?"

Here we go, Monica thought. *When will my clients ever learn to wait for a question instead of blurting out their emotions?*

Nicole's gray eyes filmed over as she said in a dramatic voice, "I transformed them into targets for hate and ugly prejudice. I can't help but wonder if their tracheal shave scars were too obvious, so they were clocked. Or worse, if someone is targeting my patients to attack me for doing sex reassignment surgeries." She buried her face in her hands and gasped, then heaved with exaggerated gulps, which Monica came to recognize as real sobs.

Monica patted the doctor's shoulder patiently.

Paul and Matt exchanged curious glances, and Monica read their suspicious minds. *They think that Nicole is acting. Trying to hide something behind a smoke screen. Not making a good first impression. Must right the ship.*

"I know this is emotional for you, doctor, so take your time," Monica said. "When you're ready, let's listen to Detective Heinz's questions and answer them one at a time."

As wily as a gumshoe and twice as smart, Detective Heinz didn't rush in with another question. Instead, he sipped his coffee while the doctor dabbed her face with a tissue, blew her nose, shook off emotional tremors, then focused on him through glossy eyes.

Monica was thankful she didn't volunteer more.

"We'll get to the specifics of the surgery in a minute," he said. "I want to start with your background and why you think someone might be targeting your surgical practice as opposed to another plastic surgeon's practice."

Nicole walked him through the same minefield of hatred and bias that she had explained earlier to Monica, except in a more emotional and strident voice, wrapping with, "My practice is worse than an abortion clinic. What the fuck was I thinking? Why do I put myself through this?" More face-burying in chafed hands.

Heinz again glanced questioningly at Matt, then said, "That doesn't give anyone the right to murder your patients. Have you personally received any death threats?"

Nicole said through splayed fingers, "Hundreds over the past four years."

His expression revealed that he didn't hear that answer very often. "We'll need those. Are they by email, letter, voicemail, in person, or all of the above?"

Nicole's hands fell to the table. "My staff delete the emails, and I personally burn the letters in the burning barrel out back." Nicole didn't even flinch while telling the detectives a slightly different version than what she had told Monica—that Geoffrey burned them.

Monica made a mental note, acknowledging to herself that the inaccuracy might be imprecision rather than deceit. In the relentless pursuit of truth and justice, she always caught her clients' discrepant versions of events, sometimes snowballing into complex false narratives. A revised version might be the result of a faulty memory or more intentional, such as a witness protecting a lover, a cop protecting a partner, a lawyer protecting her retainer, or a judge protecting his record for the next election. Monica had no idea how the system stood up to scrutiny over time. Making sausage was a cleaner business.

Heinz studied the doctor. "Do you remember any names of people who threatened you? Anyone specific stand out in your mind?"

The blonde waves swooshed from side to side, and Nicole said through a steadying breath, "No. They all run together over the years. I'm sorry. Maybe I should have kept a list."

"Doesn't give me much to go on. Two women in different cities murdered the same way, both patients of yours. I think it's the same killer, so anything you could tell me about death threats might help me to catch him."

"Would you mind telling me the details of the murders?" Nicole asked.

Heinz set down his pen and sipped some coffee. A man comfortable with long silences, he moved slowly and methodically. "Can you stomach looking at the crime scene photos?" Heinz asked in his calm, low voice.

"I'm a surgeon."

He moved his large hand inside the breast of his windbreaker, fished around, then removed a dozen 4x6-inch photos. He spread them on the table.

Before them lay photos of two different women at two different locations, but they both had one garish and horrific characteristic in common—both were stark naked and defiled with red spray paint. The outline of an erect penis was sprayed from pubis to breast on each woman. The base of the penis was flanked with scrotal sacs, just two blasts of graffiti red paint without any detail. The depiction was crude, at best.

"Oh. My. God." Nicole breathed. "Sick."

The coffee in Monica's stomach burned. "The killer couldn't have made a clearer statement."

Detective Heinz remained silent, studying Nicole.

"A sinful disgrace," she hissed, her eyes spitting fire.

Heinz nodded, then gestured to the six photos on his left. "These are of Michelle Adler, the Minneapolis victim." He waved over the others on his right. "These are of Veronica Remington in her Chicago apartment."

Michelle had a bullet hole to her forehead while Veronica suffered a gaping neck wound from either a blade or a garrote, Monica couldn't tell which. Michelle was lying on a scuffed hardwood floor, blood spattered on the yellow wall behind her. Veronica lay spread-eagle in a dark pool of blood on a rust-colored rug with an Arabic design.

Nicole picked up a photo of each woman, nodded in recognition, fresh tears streaming down her face. "I knew these women. I was honored to be a part of their lives and help them live their true identity. Gender-affirming surgery was just one step in each of their journeys. All for naught. Now tragically dead." She cocked her head to the side, glancing at Heinz and Matt. "Whenever you operate on someone, no matter the reason, you share a bond with that person as a result of the experience. I feel their pain as both their surgeon and a trans woman myself." She growled like an angry dog, "You have to catch this monster and lock him up forever." She returned the photos to the table and wrapped her hands around the hot mug before her, her eyes pinging among her three guests.

"That's why I'm here," Heinz said.

Monica studied the graffiti, so crude and garish against their cyanic skin. "Unbelievable."

"What can you tell me about each woman?" Heinz asked.

"Both Michelle and Veronica were so happy when I last saw them. Pleased with their aesthetic results, and everything was working beautifully."

Heinz nodded. "Tell me more."

"Their visits were ordinary. Unmemorable. They were pleased. If my patient is happy with her results, then my life's work is meaningful." She paused, a grimace and a shake of the head. "That fucker extinguished their beautiful souls." Nicole studied Heinz's face. "If he's sentenced to death, I'd give the lethal injection myself."

Here we go again, Monica thought, *emotional outbursts leading to dangerous declarations.* Monica placed her hand on Nicole's forearm. "Let's not express private thoughts."

Nicole blinked her steely eyes, gathering herself. "I'm sorry. I'm just so fucking angry."

Heinz checked some sort of box in his mind while studying Nicole. "We don't have the death penalty in Minnesota."

"For crimes like these, maybe you should," Nicole said, her chin jutting out.

"How about we return to the medical facts?" Monica prompted.

Nicole shook out her hair, hopefully discarding further impulses to blurt her homicidal intent to the detectives.

They all returned to studying the photos. Both surgical results were aesthetically pleasing, despite the red spray paint defiling them. The breast implants were modest, but well-shaped. Their bottoms looked more attractive than Monica had imagined. Trimmed pubic hair. Proper labia majora. Smooth skin running down to the neovagina. The surgical wounds were well-healed and attractive, if not for the crude, red scrotal blotches obscuring the finer details of Dr. Kershaw's work.

"I just can't believe it," Nicole said.

I feel like I'm going to vomit, Monica thought.

10

After a few more beats, Heinz said, "Michelle Adler was shot in the back of the head with a 9-millimeter bullet."

"That would explain the starred exit wound in her forehead," Monica said through her nausea. "Did you recover the bullet?"

"As a matter of fact, we did," Heinz said. "Dug it out of piece of trim work in her entryway. She was shot at point blank range. My guess is that she turned to lead the killer into her apartment, so I think she knew him. A person usually doesn't turn her back on a stranger in her doorway."

Reasonable deduction. Monica tried to ignore the carnival crawling up the back of her throat.

"Isn't every bullet unique to the barrel of the gun it travels through?" Nicole asked.

"That's right," Heinz said. "The rifling of each barrel leaves a distinctive striation on the bullet."

"Find the gun and match the striation," Nicole said.

"Unfortunately, the likelihood of finding the gun is low. We need a suspect with motive, means, and opportunity. Then we'll look for the gun. Anyway, we don't need a murder weapon to charge and convict."

Nicole picked up a few photos and studied them. "Is it just me, or is the red paint used on Michelle Adler a different shade than that used on Veronica Remington?"

Heinz's eyes narrowed in admiration. "Good eye, doctor. At first, we thought it was due to their different skin tones. Michelle is pale as pale can be, but Veronica has darker skin reflective of mixed ethnicity."

Nicole turned and tilted a few photos, playing the overhead light against them. "I think they're different shades of red. Isn't that something a crime lab could discern?"

"Yes. The Minnesota State Crime Lab confirmed that the red paint used on each woman is a slightly different shade. Probably different brands—Krylon, or Rust-Oleum, or some off-brand. Each manufacturer has its own shade of red. I doubt it's a major clue, but we've made a note."

"Depends on what's available at the local hardware store," Nicole said. "Did you check stores near the victims' apartments for red spray paint, hopefully recovering some security cam coverage of who bought it?"

Heinz blinked patiently. "We're talking about Minneapolis and Chicago. Big cities. Lots of spray paint moves off the shelves for graffiti and legitimate projects alike. The security cams are full of people. Besides, I don't think we're dealing with an impetuous killer who shops for his materials down the block from the victim's apartment building. That would be sloppy and unprofessional."

"Are you looking for someone more diabolical? Someone who buys the materials days in advance?" Nicole asked.

Heinz nodded. "Yes. These are preplanned and organized. He brought the materials with him. The crime scenes are very orderly. Clean with the exception of blood spatter from the wounds. No chaos. No sign of a struggle. Greet the victim. Kill her from behind. Strip her. Paint her. Leave quietly. Fifteen minutes, tops. Blend in with other people on the street when fleeing the scene. No evidence left behind, certainly not the paint cans. No fingerprints on doorknobs. No sexual assault. No hairs on bedsheets or in drains. Put it this way, we got lucky with the bullet, but it still isn't much help. We have to pursue other angles, like talking to you."

Monica rubbed her chin in thought. "How would the killer know they both had vaginoplasties?"

Detective Heinz tapped his temple with his index finger and pointed at her. "Go on."

"Even if they were clocked by a tracheal shave scar—which you hid very well, doctor—the killer wouldn't know they had vaginoplasties unless he had inside knowledge. That makes me wonder if he infiltrated the trans community."

"As in, knew them personally, stalked them on social media, or had access to their medical records," Detective Heinz said. "That's why we're here. We've already spent hours interviewing people who knew the victims personally as well as scouring the victims' social media. We hit dead ends within online comments and communities. Since we didn't flush out any viable suspects, we're pursuing the surgical connection, which leaves the medical record and Dr. Kershaw's practice."

"I'll work with the hospital to check for external hacking into their medical records," Monica said, "even though I think that's a long shot."

"Will you let me know what you find out?" Heinz asked.

"Of course." Monica scribbled a note on her to-do list.

"I also suspect the killer photographed his work," Heinz added.

"Is that common for serial killers?" Nicole asked.

"Sometimes. He might be using it as proof to show someone else. He might be collecting the photos like trophies, reliving the experience by looking at them later. These two murders have a flair for the dramatic with a very clear message —the killer hates trans women."

Bile ran up the back of Monica's throat, reminding her of the first time she viewed the gruesome crime scene photos of the young man stabbed multiple times by Stela-the-Slayer. *Please stop me from tossing my cookies again,* she pleaded silently to a higher power. "Is Ms. Remington's cut to her throat from a knife or garrote?" Monica asked.

"Garrote. That's why it isn't the clean slice that a blade would make," Heinz said.

"Although I've seen neck flaps fall open after a blade slice, making the wound look sloppy," Monica said.

Nicole's eyes blinked at Monica in surprise.

Matt nodded at Heinz. "Monica and I were involved in a multiple stab wound murder trial a few months ago. If it weren't for Monica's fast thinking, we wouldn't have reached a just outcome."

Detective Heinz regarded Monica, respect flashing in his eyes. "I'm glad you have some experience in these matters, Ms. Spade."

She nodded, a little self-conscious that her experience was so limited.

Heinz continued, "In Veronica Remington's case, the Chicago coroner wrote in his report that the wound's edges represented wire rather than a blade."

"Wire, huh?"

"That's right. Could be anything from guitar strings to utility wire, of a finer gauge, of course."

Monica pondered that. "Guitar wire presents an added flair."

"I wouldn't overanalyze it," Heinz said. "In my experience, the specific material is usually what's readily available without leaving a trail of evidence, deadly, and cost-effective."

"Okay," Monica said. "Any DNA on the women's bodies other than their own?"

"No. Neither appears to have been sexually assaulted. While there is semen, or ahh...clitoral secretions on Ms. Remington, whatever you want to call it—"

"She had a penectomy," Nicole said. "It's a clitoris now. However, she still has semen because she still has a prostate. No sperm production because the scrotum produces that, and it was removed." She waved her hand casually. "'Clitoral secretions is fine."

"Okay," Heinz said respectfully, clearing his throat. "Ms. Remington had clitoral secretions on her...labe...ah—"

"Vulva," Nicole supplied.

"Yeah. Vulva, and in her underwear, possibly indicating sexual stimulation before being murdered, but there's no sign she had male sexual relations in the vagina...you know—"

"Penetrative sex in the neovagina," Nicole supplied.

"Right," Heinz looked grateful. "The coroner didn't find any evidence of penetrative sex in the neovagina, just Ms. Remington's own DNA on her bottom and in her underwear. No one else's."

"Again, narrowing the field of possibilities for suspects," Monica said. "A serial killer who isn't into torture or sex. He's a bigot and sending that message only."

"Precisely," Detective Heinz said. "Or, as Dr. Kershaw said, perhaps a message for her, since both victims were her patients."

"I knew it," Nicole groaned. "Someone trying desperately to stop us from doing these procedures."

"I'm struggling with that a bit, though," Monica said. "Wouldn't he just kill you, Nicole, if he wanted to stop your practice?"

Nicole turned on Monica. "Do you think the fact that they're my patients is mere coincidence?"

"I just don't want to assume anything yet," Monica said in a gentle tone.

Detective Heinz cut in. "This definitely isn't the work of a random killer. Those scenes are messy with signs of a struggle, littered with broken furniture, and other signs of violence. Random killings usually involve beating and sexual assault—either before or after the victim is unconscious."

Monica winced, pushing her cup of coffee aside, and considered leaving for the bathroom to splash cool water on her face. "As gory as these photos are, they don't depict a fight, that's for sure."

"These are preplanned by an intelligent person who knew the victims were transgendered on the bottom, I mean … had…ah—"

"Vaginoplasties," Nicole supplied.

"Right," Heinz said. "Someone who knew they had vaginoplasties, and probably someone experienced at murder."

"You think he's killed before?" Monica asked.

"Most likely."

"Trans women?"

"I don't know," Heinz said. "Nationwide, police databases are full of violence against trans women. My team is scouring the databases for the graffitied messages we see in these two cases."

"I'm impressed that you're being so thorough," Nicole said.

"Murder is murder, and I take my work seriously. I also have an interest in serial killers."

"I just want you to know that I'm grateful for your dedication," Nicole said to Heinz.

"Catching a serial killer can take years, can't it?" Monica asked.

Heinz nodded and turned to Nicole. "If you don't mind, doctor, I'd like to get some background information about your practice."

"Whatever you need."

"When did you start doing sex reassignment surgeries?"

"About four years ago, give or take a few months."

"How many have you performed?"

"More than a hundred."

"All male-to-female?"

"No. A few were female-to-male."

"Let's turn to Michelle Adler."

Nicole pulled the stack of medical records closer, resting her elbow on it. Her laptop was within reach but closed.

"Do you remember her?" Heinz asked.

"Yes. I didn't at first, but once I reviewed my medical record and looked at her photos—the ones we took in the office as well as what you have here—some familiarity returned."

"Anything stand out about her?"

"A nice young person. Gender dysphoria and depression, of course. Most struggle with that, but she was living as a woman, had completed a year of hormone therapy, and was ready to take the final surgical steps. She was cautiously optimistic."

"Did anyone accompany her?"

"Yes. Her boyfriend."

"Name?"

"I don't know. I didn't write it down. I should have, and I do now when I meet with patients, but that wasn't my habit a few years ago."

"Does the name Mario Rodriguez ring a bell with you?"

"No," Nicole said. "Do you have a photo of him?"

Heinz removed his phone from his pocket and thumbed through his photos until he found what he was looking for, then held it up to Nicole.

Monica caught a glimpse of curly, long hair framing a Latino face.

Nicole studied the young man's photo and, after some hemming and hawing, said, "Maybe. I think so, but I can't be 100% sure."

"That's fine," Heinz said. "When did you perform Ms. Adler's surgery?"

Nicole promptly leafed through the medical record. "Here's my operative note. February 3, 2018."

"Two years ago," Heinz said, jotting the date in his small notebook.

Monica flipped over one of the photos of Michelle Adler, and, written on the back in black ink was her name, address, and *"DOD February 3, 2020."* Her eyes popped, and she blurted, "Oh my God, she was killed on the second anniversary of her surgery."

Heinz looked like he had been dope slapped. "What? Let me see."

She showed him the back of the photo.

"You said you did the surgery on February 3, 2018, right, Doc?" Heinz asked.

"Yes."

Monica looked at the back of one of Veronica Remington's photos. Again, her name and address were written on the back with "*DOD December 11, 2019.*" Her voice diving into ominous territory, Monica asked, "Doctor, can you look up the date you did Veronica Remington's surgery?"

Nicole licked the tip of her index finger and rifled through a second stack of papers, her fingers scrambling over the pages in search of her operative note. Once she found it, she held it at arm's-length, reading aloud, "December 11, 2017."

"Two years," they all said in unison.

"See?" Matt said, "I told you Monica was helpful. Not like the defense *law-yers* we usually deal with." He pronounced *lawyers* like *liars*.

"Thanks for…whatever that was," Monica said, her mind racing. "I'm no longer struggling with a direct connection to Nicole's practice." *Who would have access to those dates? Did someone hack into the medical record? I need to alert Al Bowman. What about patients whose second anniversaries are approaching?*

She snapped out of her own analysis to Heinz asking, "Doctor, can you provide us with a list of the names and dates of all your sex reassignment surgeries?"

Nicole looked at Monica, who looked at Heinz. Monica knew exactly why he was asking.

"Why don't we start with a list of dates only," Monica said. "If you get any hits of murders two years from the surgical anniversary, then you can give us the name, and we can confirm whether she was a patient."

98

Heinz rolled his eyes, his jaw falling in exasperation. "It would make it a lot easier if we had the names and addresses. Then we'd know where to look and who to look for."

"I'm sure it would," Monica said, "Unfortunately, Dr. Kershaw's living patients haven't authorized her or Community Memorial Hospital to tell the police that they've had sex reassignment surgery. Their information is private and confidential. Now, if you come back with a name of a deceased patient to confirm she had surgery by my client, that's different. However, at this time, we'd be happy to share only the dates of the surgeries with you."

Heinz pointed to the medical records under Nicole's elbow. "What's the difference between those patients and Adler and Remington, who we've been openly discussing?"

"You're investigating Adler's and Remington's deaths as homicides. That outweighs their right to privacy under the law, hence the exception under HIPAA."

"The law never makes sense to me," Heinz said. "So, you're telling me, if I get any matches for homicide dates, then I can come back for names?"

"Either that or get a court order signed by a judge. If you come back with a court order, then we could release the entire list of names, dates, and addresses."

Heinz scratched his head. "I'll talk to the County Attorney and get back to you. In the meantime, can you email me the list of all dates of sex reassignment surgeries?"

Monica nodded at Nicole, who said, "I'll call one of my staff and have them run it right away."

"Thanks." Deep in thought, Heinz's gaze traveled over the living room and its view of the watery ice reflecting the sky like a slab of granite. "Is there anything special about the date of two years from a surgery from your perspective?"

"No. It doesn't mark any day of significance. It's well past the period when we would see patients back in clinic for follow-up, that's for sure."

Heinz scribbled in his notepad, then looked at Monica. "I'm worried about the patients whose two-year anniversaries are approaching."

"Me too," she said in a dead serious tone.

"Is the hospital going to warn them?" he asked.

"I'll be discussing that with the president of the hospital," Monica said.

"If you give me the list of names and contact info, we could warn them," he said.

"Thanks for the offer. I'll pass it along."

He narrowed his eyes. "I'm not sure you're taking the circumstance as seriously as we are."

"I can assure you I am. Just because I have a duty to protect patient confidentiality doesn't mean I don't share your concern. Our interests are aligned, Detective, but I also have to protect patient confidentiality under the law."

"I think you're just trying to protect the hospital's reputation, but you're putting the lives of patients at risk by not warning them. I could charge you with obstruction of justice."

"First, patient safety is paramount, and I think we can protect the privacy of trans patients while maintaining the hospital's reputation. What if the next second-year anniversary is a month away? We have time to catch the killer before he strikes again. Secondly, obstruction of justice is a stretch, and you're waaay out of your jurisdiction."

Heinz bristled, glancing at Matt's reaction.

"Let's not get ahead of ourselves," Matt said in an equable tone. "Monica said she'll provide us with dates. If we need to get a court order for names, we will. In the meantime, I trust Monica will discuss warning future patients with the hospital."

"Okay, but only for now," Heinz said. "The clock is ticking. If there's another murder, the blood is on your hands, Ms. Spade—"

Monica's green eyes lit up. "Stop right there, Detective Heinz. The clock has been ticking since last December. If you'd caught the killer after the Chicago murder, Ms. Adler wouldn't have been murdered in February. The only person at this table with bloody hands is you."

Like a referee in a boxing match, Matt patted the air between Heinz and Monica. "Hold on, hold on. Back to your corners. We're all on the same team. We have a plan. Let's cool the rhetoric and keep working together."

Heinz reluctantly swiveled his alarmed eyes from Monica to Matt, then reset his features and turned to Nicole. "What about Veronica Remington, the Chicago patient. Do you remember her?"

If Nicole was upset by the fireworks, she didn't show it. "I've been trying to distinguish her from a few other patients, but I don't have anything specific I can tell you."

"Was she accompanied to her visit?"

"I honestly can't remember, and I know I didn't document that anyone was with her. That was over two years ago and, as I said, I've changed my practice since then. Now, I always write the names of friends in the record."

"How about the fact that she was from Chicago. Was that unique?"

"No. My patients come from all over the country."

Heinz scratched the salt and pepper stubble covering his jaw. "And you can't think of anyone specifically who might want to harm you by murdering your patients?"

Nicole shook her head slowly, her gaze never wavering from Detective Heinz's probing eyes.

"Well, if you do think of someone or something, here's my card." He fished a few business cards out from the back of his notebook and handed one to Nicole and one to Monica.

Monica reciprocated with her own. "Any other questions or requests?"

"Not that I can think of," Heinz said, then turned to Matt. "Do you have anything?"

"Just a few questions," Matt said. "Dr. Kershaw, do you have a clinical team that does these surgeries with you?"

"Yes," Nicole said.

"Do the same people assist you in clinic as well as the operating room?" Matt asked.

"There's a clinic team and an OR team, with a few people who occasionally overlap. Aside from FMLA leaves, my team has been the same for four years."

"Can we get their names?" Matt asked. "We might want to interview them."

Not before I do, Monica thought, and jumped in before Nicole could answer. "I'll talk to Nicole and make a full list for you, Matt. Should I email it to both you and Detective Heinz?"

"Please," Matt said. "I don't have any other questions."

"Nicole and I will work on gathering more information," Monica said, more politely this time.

Detective Heinz gathered up his grisly photos and stuffed them back in his coat pocket. "Thank you for your time."

The men rose and Monica showed them to the door, leaving Nicole alone with her thoughts.

When Monica returned, Nicole was pacing, her fingers speared into her hair, a tormented look on her face. "What are we going to do?"

"We're going to methodically approach this in cooperation with the police while trying not to breach the privacy and confidentiality of any of your other patients," Monica said.

"What if others have been killed, and Detective Heinz just doesn't know about them yet?"

"We'll cross that bridge when we come to it."

"What if the killer strikes again before they can catch him?"

"I'll discuss that with Al Bowman. I'm worried about patients who had their surgeries two years ago from today. And tomorrow. And the next day. We need a complete list with names and dates of surgeries to see if we need to warn someone."

"I'll ask my assistant to run two lists—one with names and contact info, and one with just dates of surgeries."

"Thanks. Let's not get ahead of ourselves until we see those lists. If we start warning patients, we might unnecessarily freak them out."

"Is that possible at this point? Two women have been brutally murdered."

"That's my point," Monica said.

"I suppose you're right."

"And the media would most likely get wind of it."

"I'm sure Al would be thrilled about that," Nicole said sarcastically. "Our surgical program would be ruined. On the other hand, would Al really put our reputations ahead of warning patients?"

"Of course not. I'm just saying that we might have several days, or even weeks, before the next surgical date, so we might catch the killer before then."

"Are we willing to gamble?"

"Until we know more," Monica said, "what would the warning be, anyway? 'Hi, this is Community Memorial Hospital. The second anniversary of your surgery is approaching, and we're concerned you might be murdered that day. You won't see it coming because you'll know the killer. He'll shoot you or slit your throat. Best not to trust anyone that day. Any questions?'"

Nicole suddenly swung her arm out wide and slammed her open hand into a cupboard, rattling the dishes inside. "Dammit. Who cares what the message would be as long as we can save a life? I'll sit with my patient that entire day if I have to."

Monica felt like an airborne cat after a good scare, her feet returning to the floor after a pathetic vertical jump.

Marvin barked and came to Nicole's side, sniffing her. She crumpled over, resting one hand on her knee and soothing the dog's head with the other. "I'm sorry, Marvin. Mommy lost it for a second. It's all good. You're good."

"Rest assured, Nicole, I'm having the same reaction as you on the inside. I'll discuss the entire situation with Al today."

Nicole straightened, color flooding her face and neck. "Thank you. This is all just so overwhelming, compounded by a fucking pandemic. I feel like I'm losing my mind."

"I can only imagine the frustration and sadness you're experiencing. Maybe playing piano or exercising would be better for you than whacking cupboards."

Nicole smiled, but it was bittersweet. "That would be more productive, no doubt."

"We don't want you to injure those talented hands, do we?"

Nicole examined the palm of her hand, now bright red. "That hurt."

"Looked like it." Monica moved to the table and sat. "When you're ready, I'll take the names of the people on your surgical team. I need to talk to them before the detectives do."

11

Once in possession of the list of employees on Nicole's clinical and surgical teams, Monica shrugged on her brown coat and silently cursed her stomach to stop growling at such an embarrassing decibel level. She stuffed her notepad in her attaché and followed Nicole and Marvin to the front door. Howling through the cracks of the battered door, the wind seemed to sense the ominous set of circumstances in which they found themselves.

They exchanged talk-to-you-laters, and Monica stepped out onto the slippery deck.

"Drive safely." Nicole's friendly warning was lost on a gust.

Monica leaned into the spring gale and hopscotched across the deck to the cobblestone path, also riddled with patches of ice. As she emerged from the shrubs surrounding the curved walkway, the treetops swaying and moaning above her, she spotted Geoffrey at the back of his pickup truck in the detached garage.

No time like the present to get a better read on him, she thought, slanting toward him instead of her own truck.

His back to her, he was clad in jeans, a forest green barn coat with the lapel turned up at the neck, and a matching green fedora. As she drew near, he registered her boots crunching on the gravel and turned. "Hello, Ms. Spade."

"Please, call me Monica. How are you today?" She tucked into the oversized garage to escape the wind chill.

"Cold but stocked up on supplies." His gloved hand gestured to the bed of his massive Ram pickup truck, which she guessed cost roughly the same as her house. Brown paper bags of groceries filled the black bed liner.

"Did you leave anything behind at the store?" She marveled at the amount of toilet paper he had purchased, outstripping Shelby by several rolls.

"Nicole told me to stock up with a month's supply of everything, so I did," he said. "How did the meeting with the detectives go?"

Monica shrugged, not giving anything away. She was fishing, so she tossed in some chum. "You know cops."

He snorted sarcastically. "All too well. Usually shaking me down for bribes in my former life. I wanted to stay and support Nicole, but she practically threw me out. How is she?"

Monica catalogued Geoffrey's response. First, Nicole had lied to Heinz about who had burned the letters. Had she lied about throwing Geoffrey out too? No client was perfect, but she had hoped for an honest one for this file in contrast to the pathological liar in her last case. She returned to the conversation with deceptive instincts. "She seems to be doing okay."

"These murders have shaken her to her core," Geoffrey said. "I think this pandemic is going to put her over the edge because she can't operate, which is like oxygen to her, you know?"

"I think suspending all of our life activities is going to be hard on everyone. Nicole is lucky to have your support."

"If only she'd take my advice."

Monica raised her eyebrows.

"I'm trying to convince her to take a few days off, go to Miami with me to escape this cold, colorless landscape, but she won't budge."

"Probably isn't wise to leave in the middle of an investigation—"

He waved his hand dismissively, cutting her off. "Not that. She doesn't want to risk getting the coronavirus by traveling or mingling with our friends down there. She's worried that Florida will be the next Wuhan."

"She isn't the only one. Given what's happening in Italy and New York, the experts on CNN are predicting—"

"*Pfft.* Those cities are totally different, the way they live on top of each other in apartment buildings. It isn't like that at my place in Miami."

"You have a place?"

"I kept my house in South Beach. It's fully paid for, so why not?"

All that cash from the club. "Great vacation spot. I'm jealous." It was her first official lie of the day, which she considered impressive given they had just met with police.

"You should visit us there sometime. I'll show you around." He scanned her, this time lingering over her face. "You look suspiciously tan for this time of year. Sets your green eyes on fire."

On fire? Seriously? "We just returned from a week in Belize."

"Nice. Where?"

"Placencia."

He ran the back of his gloved hand over his unshaven face, thick with whiskers that would chafe Nicole's inner thighs. "Haven't been there. Been to Ambergris Caye, though."

"Placencia is south of Ambergris. Not sure Belize is allowing any U.S. citizens in now."

"Fortunately, Florida has no such limitations." He smiled, the veneers on his large teeth strikingly white against his beard. "I know all the best restaurants and clubs. I'd be happy to show you around. You like to dance?"

"Not as much as my fiancée."

He cocked his head. "Your fiancé likes to dance?"

Monica clarified, "She does."

His smile broadened, and Monica immediately saw the club owner's side of him. "Maybe mention it to Nicole next time you see her. She needs to get out of here and shake loose a little, but she needs some encouragement from someone other than me."

"I'll think about it after the investigation."

The smile slid off his face. "Fucking investigation. Could take forever. Can't they do their jobs without her?"

"Probably not."

"What a clusterfuck," he said.

"Uh-huh. Well, I should be going." A cock-a-doodle-doo from behind the garage signaled the end of their tête-à-tête. "Does that rooster have a name?"

"Sounds like Blizzard, an ornery white silkie," he said. "Time for me to check their food and water."

"Fun hobby."

He grunted. "If they don't watch it, we'll be having chicken dinner soon."

She couldn't tell if he was joking or in a slaughtering mood, which sent a chill down her spine. "I'll leave you to it, then."

He flicked his gloved finger on the brim of his hat and turned toward the inside.

She watched him walk through the garage to a service door on the opposite end. When he opened it, Monica spotted a small barnyard with coops and chicken wire strung from here to eternity. He stepped through the door and swiftly closed it behind him.

She stayed present in the moment, allowing her eyes to roam over the back of the garage, a plywood workbench and light brown pegboard on the wall above it. A vast array of tools hung there—wrenches, hammers, screwdrivers, pliers, a roll of blue painters tape, several rolls of duct tape, some spools of wire. *Wire?*

Her feet started walking before her brain could analyze her paranoia. Her subconscious told her she was investigating, but maybe her imagination was simply overactive. Either way, she found herself standing at the workbench, studying three different spools of wire. There was a medium gauge that was coated in green plastic. Not good for slicing skin. A large gauge of silver wire that looked thick and difficult to bend. Not practical for a garrote. And a spool of thin, copper wire that looked sharp and pliable. Perfect for killing someone from behind.

Her eyes swept the bench for cans of spray paint, but she didn't see any.

She quickly retraced her steps between the two vehicles, a silver Range Rover with tinted windows—which she assumed was Nicole's—on her right, and Geoffrey's Ram pickup on her left. Both seemed ostentatious for Apple Grove, where the median income was less than the price of either vehicle. She wondered if the handgun that Nicole had mentioned was resting under the driver's seat of the Range Rover. Expensive cars, handguns and a club owner. Hm. Didn't fit the profile of the humble surgeon, that was for sure.

She sliced through the wind to her beater pickup truck. As she drove out, she waved at the critter cams then serpentined her way to Highway 53 south. The clouds skittered across the clearing sky, as she drove past farm fields on one side of the highway and boat dealerships, car dealerships, landscaping businesses and nurseries—all closed per Governor Eberhardt's Order—on the other side.

Once she was cruising along at a steady speed, she called Al Bowman to give him a status update. Jim had lectured Monica and Nathan on his rules for corporate clients to keep their law firm running. Number one: provide regular reports to the person paying your bills. Rule number two: bill every second of your time working on a matter, including driving to and from meetings. Rule number three: send out monthly bills to keep the cash flowing as steady and strong as the Chippewa River. Rule number four: act like you're an expert at everything when your client calls. Rule number five: never turn down a project.

Her phone number must have popped up on Al's screen because he greeted her with, "Hi, Monica. Bet you're calling to update me on the police investigation." He actually sounded in a good mood despite the halt on elective surgeries and the overhaul of his hospital system to meet the potential demands of COVID patients.

"I am," she said. "I'm sorry to tell you this, and forgive me if I'm telling you some things you already know, but someone intentionally targeted and murdered two of Nicole's patients, spray painting a penis and scrotum on their naked torsos. There's no question that it's a hate crime. The crime scene photos are unspeakable. There are no words..."

He groaned. "What a fucked-up world we live in. Any leads?"

She noted his rare vulgarity, and attributed it to unprecedented stress. "The detective from Minneapolis is coordinating with the Chicago police department. Nicole didn't have much to add other than she, herself, has been the subject of violent threats in the past."

"The hospital has received hate mail too," he said. "Our security department has thwarted some threats against her as well as removed protestors from the top floor of the parking ramp."

"Did security save any of the hate letters?" she asked. "Do they have any suspects that we should be turning over to the police?"

"You'd have to ask the head of Security." He sighed. "Makes me wonder why we offer sex reassignment surgeries. It's one thing to offer plastic surgery, quite another to open the hospital to such vehement controversy, making us a target. I just don't know anymore..."

"No need to decide anything today. Give it a few weeks." In reality, Monica didn't like crossing the line by offering her opinion on business decisions, but she also didn't want Al to act rashly. She allowed a small silence before saying, "Well, I hate to pile it on, but the detectives are concerned that other transgendered patients might have been harmed too. They want a list of all of Dr. Kershaw's surgery dates, so they can—"

"Wait a minute," Al said. "How would a deranged killer discover who Nicole's patients were in the first place?"

"That's why the police want to interview Nicole's clinical and surgical team members as well as have me check to see if the medical records of Michelle Adler and Veronica Remington were hacked."

Al snorted like a pug, sputtering, "Our reputation will never survive if someone is hacking into our medical record and tracking down our patients to murder them."

"I wouldn't jump to that conclusion quite yet—"

"Would you come to the hospital for plastic surgery if you knew a killer was going to hack your info and track you down?"

"Well...no, but we aren't going to release that information to the public, mostly because we don't even know if that's what happened. We're just investigating the possibility right now."

"This is a nightmare for our plastic surgery brand."

"Let me look into things." She took a breath and added, "There's something else—"

"What else could there possibly be?"

"We need a list of all of Nicole's gender-affirming surgeries to see what the dates are because—"

"How many has she done?"

"She estimates about 100 cases."

"Jesus. It seems like she just got here."

"She's been operating for four-and-a-half years, so they've added up. Al, more importantly, we discovered that the two murdered patients were killed on the second anniversaries of their surgeries."

"Come again?"

"I'm concerned about patients whose second-year anniversaries are approaching. I need the surgical list to see how many there are. Then we need to decide if we should contact them and warn them."

"You can't be serious!"

"I'm not joking around. If another patient is murdered, everyone will demand to know why the hospital didn't warn her, given the information now in our possession."

"Start warning 100 patients?" He asked in disbelief. "They might go to the press or post on social media. We'll lose control of the narrative and irreparably damage our reputation. This could make the national news!"

"Don't go there just yet, Al. We need to see the next surgical anniversary date. We might have to warn only one or two patients. Better yet, if we can catch the killer before the next date, there won't be a need to warn anyone."

"Do whatever you need to do, Monica. I'm all out of ideas and resources."

"I'll do what I can to run a parallel investigation to the police."

"You have my full support."

"Thanks," she said, getting the green light to sink several hours into the file. "Right now, I need to interview the members of Nicole's clinical and surgical teams before the police do."

"They're all on furlough since we can't do elective surgeries right now."

"Maybe I can visit the employees at their homes or interview them by Zoom."

"Just get to the bottom of this shitshow before another patient is killed."

"Rest assured, Al, I'll try. If the next second-year anniversary is tomorrow, we'll have to warn her. Hopefully, it will be several weeks from now, so we can catch the killer before we're forced to make this public."

"A murder investigation during a pandemic sounds like a perfect storm to shut down our hospital forever." She could hear the defeat as his voice trailed off.

"Don't give up yet, Al. We'll make it through this nightmare, and I'll do my best to solve these murders before they hit the media. Soon, we'll be on the other side of these problems."

"I hope you're better at solving serial murders than the police are, but the odds are against you."

"I'm aware."

He told her he'd email her the contact information for his head of Information Security, and they hung up.

The severity of what she now faced dropped like an anvil on Monica's shoulders. A serial killer was specifically targeting trans women in a cold blooded, pathological plot to send a message. The police didn't have any meaningful evidence or leads, even though they had been working on the cases for a few months already. What made her think she could do a better, quicker job than the police? If another patient were killed, the hospital would be blamed for not warning her. *Well, we can't let that happen.* She gripped the wheel tighter. *I won't let that happen.*

12

As Monica turned onto her tree-lined street, she was welcomed by toppled garbage cans rolling to and fro in the wind gusts reminiscent of *The Wizard of Oz,* a movie she had never liked. She had no idea why it was an American favorite. Scraps of recycled papers swirled into the air, and she couldn't stop from looking up at the tree branches, half-expecting to see the evil monkeys.

She turned into her driveway, surprised that Shelby's Jeep wasn't there. Feeling lonely and burdened, she trudged down to the curb and wrestled her garbage and recycling cans back up the driveway, tucking them into a corner of the garage. Sometimes being an adult sucked. At work. At home. At life.

When she entered her kitchen foyer, the house was quiet but for the wind whistling around the eaves. No Shelby. No food cooking on the stove. Despite the fact that they had spent the last week together in paradise, or perhaps because of it, Monica missed Shelby. She felt isolated. Out of sorts. Restless. Upset. And hungry. Bordering on hangry.

Since she was usually at the office during daylight hours, being home at midday was like playing hooky from school, something she had done only once on senior skip day in high school. Even then, she hadn't much enjoyed it. Her parents both had worked full-time and had shared their philosophy that *everyone worked all the time. Anything less was unproductive, bordering on irresponsible.* Anxiety suddenly surged inside of her that she wasn't at the office, her full phalanx of assistants on standby to help her with a to-do list the size of Texas. To ward off feelings of helplessness and loneliness, she decided that food was in order.

She shed her coat and went to the fridge. Shelby had crammed it with groceries, enough food to feed her high school art class for a month. Monica counted 5 half-gallons of milk. *Last week tequila shots, this week milk shots.* In true Shelby fashion, the drawers were brimming with healthy choices—fruits, yogurt and veggies—all as appetizing to Monica as dog food.

She grabbed an onion roll, slathered mustard and mayo on it, layered cheese and chipped beef, lay a thin pickle slice on top, then reluctantly added a piece of red lettuce. Ignoring the apples and oranges, she opened the cupboard for chips and was elated to see a bag in every flavor. With a *pop* and a *whoosh*, she opened a bag of Sun Chips and poured a generous amount onto her plate.

Balancing her plate and a pint glass of milk, she plopped herself down on the cerulean sofa in front of the TV and clicked on CNN. A male anchor with a black pompadour watched her take a large bite as he droned on.

Soon, the footage changed to grotesque images of the COVID crawling over New York City. The death toll hit her like a tsunami. More jarring images showed hospitals overflowing: patients on gurneys in the hallways, patients lying motionless in ICU beds, patients hooked up to ventilators. Healthcare providers were covered from head to toe in gowns, gloves, and shields. When interviewed individually, the bags under their eyes were dark, accentuating the raw fear radiating from their eyes. All looked haggard, deep lines in their cheeks from masks.

The mayor of New York had officially closed the city—no school, no dining in restaurants, no bar hopping. The place was a ghost town, yet hundreds of patients still died every day from respiratory complications. With no treatment, the doctors were baffled as to how to combat the savage virus.

Monica swallowed hard, dumbstruck by the stealth of COVID, like a snake slithering through the grass, its tongue licking the air, zeroing in on vulnerable prey.

She turned off the TV in the interest of preserving her psychological well-being. COVID on top of Dr. Kershaw's patients being murdered. Her reality was worse than a creative novel. She looked down and was surprised to see that her palms were sweaty and she was wringing the paper napkin on her lap.

No longer in the mood for food, she wrapped her uneaten sandwich and set it in the fridge with the glass of milk. She grabbed her laptop and a glass of ice water, then proceeded to her four-season porch. Now bathed in sun, the view from the porch raised her spirits. Even though the wind was battering the neighborhood, the temps were edging above freezing, so the mega drift of snow in her front yard had melted from four feet in height to less than a foot, signaling that spring was still scheduled to appear.

She called Shelby.

"Have you seen the news?" Monica asked.

"A nightmare. I turned it off." There was a pause during which Monica heard Shelby arranging objects. "Mon, you aren't watching the news, are you? It will throw you into a depression."

"No. I left the TV for the front porch. What are you doing?"

"Setting up my studio for teaching online. I like this space. Looks good and feels good to be back in it."

"I'm happy for you." Monica didn't say that she was relieved the potter's wheel wouldn't be splattering clay soup all over her extra bedroom.

"What's new?" Shelby asked.

"Do you have any groceries over there?" Monica asked. "I feel guilty that you shopped for us, and all the food is over here."

"My cupboards are bare, but I'm guessing you'll return the favor someday." Hint. Hint.

"Consider it done." *I'll find the time somewhere.* "Want to get together for dinner tonight?"

"Of course. I'll come over in a few hours, okay?"

"Sounds great."

"What are you making?" Shelby asked.

No clue. "A surprise just for you."

"That sounds mysterious."

"You'll love it." *As soon as I figure out what it is.*

"Aw, thanks, hon." Shelby grunted, giving the impression she was lifting a boulder.

Monica heard scraping on the floor.

"Love you," Shelby said on a puff of air.

"See you later."

They rang off.

Monica stared out the window, not focusing on anything in particular, the chaotic wind mimicking her scattered thoughts, her brain analyzing how to protect everyone's interests in a serial killer's plot to annihilate trans women. *We're in a pandemic. We closed our law firm. A serial killer is on the loose. I have to save patients and the hospital's reputation.* She called Kathy.

"Hi, Mon. Miss me already?"

"Terribly, and not just your cooking."

The familiar hearty laugh bubbled. "I brought homemade caramel rolls to the office while you were on vacation last week. To die for."

"And I missed them? That sucks," Monica said.

"Who knows when we'll be back together."

"Hopefully in a few weeks."

Kathy snorted. "Don't hold your breath. They're saying COVID could be as bad as the 1918 Spanish Flu Pandemic."

"How is that even possible?"

"I have no idea." Kathy clacked away on a keyboard. "I suppose you're calling to see what I found out about this Geoffrey Gold guy."

"Yep."

"Not much. Still digging. He isn't the only Geoffrey Gold on the East Coast. It would help if you could get me a middle initial and a date of birth."

"Not likely to happen soon. What do you have so far?"

"If his middle initial is "S," and he's 38 years old, then he has an average criminal history."

"Of what?"

In a bored tone, Kathy said, "Attempted bribery of a public official."

"When was that?"

"Eight years ago."

"What was the resolution?"

"Guilty plea with a deferred prosecution."

"Hm," Monica said. "He co-owned a club in Miami called The Flaming Flamingo. I bet he's got a colorful past there."

"I'll look up The Flaming Flamingo too."

"Thanks. Anything else on him?"

"Some civil cases. Sexual harassment. That was settled. Another business, a construction firm, sued him for breach of contract. That was settled too."

"I bet those are related to the club as well. Not very salacious or dangerous, that's for sure," Monica said. "I wonder where he's from originally."

"You don't think he's from Florida?"

"I don't know," Monica said, "but I'll make a point to find out."

"Okay. I'll look up The Flaming Flamingo and get back to you."

"You're a gem. Maybe check social media too."

"Will do." Kathy was obviously chewing something. "I wish we were back at the office. I'm gonna get fat eating my own cooking all day."

"Me too," Monica said. "I'll probably add COVID-19 pounds."

Kathy laughed. "I just can't live without dessert each night, but I make an entire pan of it. Maybe I'll start individually wrapping them and dropping them off at everyone's houses."

"Feel free to add me to your delivery route."

"You and Shelby?"

"Yeah, just use my address. She's over here for dinner most of the time, and, come to think of it, she's always in a better mood if she gets dessert."

"What is she doing about art class now that school is closed?"

"Preparing to teach online."

"Oh dear."

"I know, right?"

"Parents are going to turn into homeschool teachers."

"I feel for them," Monica said. "And the teachers too."

They paused a minute, then Monica said, "Well, I should return to work. I have to talk to Information Security at the hospital about the breaches of two medical records."

"Should I open new matters? Are the patients suing the hospital?"

"No. They're murder victims who both had gender-affirming surgeries performed by Dr. Kershaw."

Without hesitation, Kathy asked, "What are their names? I can do a background search on them as well."

Monica supplied Michelle Adler's and Veronica Remington's names and addresses. "Thanks, Kathy. I didn't even think of doing that. Maybe you'll come up with more than the police have."

"That's what I'm here for. So, you think someone peeked into their medical records, located their addresses, stalked them, and killed them?"

"Dr. Kershaw seems to think someone is targeting her patients to send a message to her."

"Huh. It would have to be a pretty strong grudge to kill her patients. Want me to do a background search on her too?"

"You're turning into my own private investigator."

"Can't stop myself."

"We make a good team," Monica said, "even if we don't get to work face-to-face. Nicole's former name was Nicholas Kershaw, and she already told me that she was charged with a few disorderlies in college for lipping off to the police during protests and parades."

"Got it. I haven't showered yet today, so it's a good thing we aren't working sitting next to each other."

"Silver lining to teleworking, right?" Monica said, then added, "I also have to interview Dr. Kershaw's clinical and surgical teams."

"Why?"

"Because Detective Paul Heinz from Minneapolis and Matt said they want to, so I have to talk to my clients first."

"You and Matt are becoming attached at the hip the way you're working on cases together."

"Now that you mention it, we did work together on the Saudi Arabian murder trial, the Stela-the-Slayer murder trial, and now this. So yeah, I guess we've shared some intense experiences together."

"And you're still friends, which usually isn't the case between cops and defense attorneys."

"Ugh. I'm not a criminal defense attorney. I only orbit around the criminal justice system."

"Ha!" Kathy barked. "Keep telling yourself that, boss. You're in it up to your eyeballs."

"I just wanted to be a hospital attorney. What am I doing?"

"A great job, that's what. Keep it up, so you can afford to pay me."

Monica smiled. "In that case, I should get back to my to-do list."

"Ta-ta," Kathy sang and hung up.

Monica made quick work of contacting the head of IS at the hospital, who connected her to his medical record privacy guy, Sam Moua.

"Can you look up the medical records of Michelle Adler and Veronica Remington, and tell me if anyone from outside the hospital hacked into them?" Monica asked.

"Sure. You know there are thousands of hack attempts on our medical record system every day, right?"

"Really? By whom?"

"You name it. Individuals. Governments."

"Which governments?"

"Mostly China and Russia."

"Why?"

"To steal research information—like if we're working on treatments for COVID or something. They also try to steal patient financial information and sell it on the black market."

"And those hacks have been linked to governments?"

"Yeah," he said as his fingers clickity-clacked across the keyboard in the background. "We report them to the FBI, and they've told us that the IP addresses go to government-owned military buildings."

"Get out. Nothing the FBI can do about that. Way above their pay grade," Monica said. "Anybody else hack you?"

"Small jobs, like attempting to hold our medical record ransom for a bitcoin payment."

"Were they successful?"

"No. One froze our system for about an hour until we rebooted and cleaned off everything. We lost about two hours' worth of data, but that was all."

"Did you reply to them?"

"Not in the words I wanted to use, but we politely declined their ransom demand."

"Well, this potential hack involves murder. We need to see if the killer hacked into two medical records, looked up their addresses, stalked them, and killed them."

"Holy shit!" he exclaimed. "Adler and Remington?"

"Yes." She listened while he clicked away, *humming* and *ohing*.

While she waited, Monica again found herself gazing out the window. She began to wonder if she should offer to hang up and let him do his job. "Do you want me to call you back in 30 minutes?"

"Nope. I'm almost done."

She sipped some water and processed what she knew so far.

Finally, he said, "I don't see any hacks into either of these medical records."

She didn't know whether to feel relieved or discouraged. "Oh."

"Do you want me to check for internal breaches on these charts as well?"

"Internal?"

"Yes. I could check if there are employees who have entered these medical records but had no work reason to enter them. In other words, someone who isn't part of the care team."

"I hadn't thought of that. Does that happen? Employees snooping on patients?"

"Yes. Curiosity is a powerful drug, especially on plastic surgery patients, which these two obviously are."

"What happens to employees who snoop?"

"They're fired," he said in a matter-of-fact tone.

"In that case, yes. Please check both of the records for internal breaches as well."

"When do you need this information?"

Thank God he wasn't going to make her wait on the phone for that search. "Can you give it to me later today or tomorrow?"

"Tomorrow."

She supplied her contact info and they rang off. She pondered the medical care of Michelle and Veronica. *What if someone at the hospital killed them? Al would have a coronary. Come to Community Memorial where a member of the staff is lurking in the shadows, waiting to kill you. Maybe the physicians are vampires too...*

13

By late afternoon, Monica had sent emails to each member of Dr. Kershaw's team introducing herself and suggesting she meet and prepare them over Zoom for the police interviews. The reality was that she would be conducting her own investigation as well, which she looked forward to.

While she thought about what she needed to learn, she got cracking on a romantic dinner for Shelby. She already missed their intimate dinners in Belize, the sound of the surf serenading them, the air thick with the scent of exotic flowers, the gold specks in Shelby's eyes glinting in the candlelight, the love simmering between them.

Instead, she was swept up in swirls of cold weather, a raging virus threatening to kill all of humanity, and a murder investigation that required all of her wit and ingenuity to crack before the killer struck again. She hoped Nicole would send her the surgical date list soon.

Lacking in gourmet imagination or skills, she racked her preoccupied brain for something to prepare. She knew her way around grilling meat but didn't want to fight the wind to grill on her deck. *What to make on the stovetop?*

She thawed a pound of ground beef and sautéed it with onion because she could never go wrong with those two ingredients. Since she started cooking in college, those staples had provided a solid foundation for any dinner dish, from tater tot casserole to lasagna. She splashed some red wine over the mixture, then watched it soak in and simmer off. In true *Diners, Drive-Ins and Dives* style, she added pinches of basil, salt, pepper, chipotle pepper, smoked paprika, and garlic powder—never measuring, just sprinkling and pouring. A jar of cabernet marinara sauce dove in, chased by a can of fire roasted tomato slices. She put the glass lid on the pan to let it simmer. Red sauce with meat. Check.

Scanning the pantry, which Shelby had stocked like a ship on excursion to the arctic, Monica eyed a package of penne pasta. She boiled it to *al dente* texture, then mixed it with the sauce. For her final step, she transferred the mixture to a glass baking dish, grated parmesan cheese over it, and placed it in a 300-degree oven. The pasta dish would be ready whenever Shelby walked through the door—a steaming hot meal for her steaming hot fiancée. Check.

She opened a bottle of fine drinking wine, inhaled the fruity aroma, and took a grateful sip. One of life's small pleasures. She eyed her bare tabletop, comparing it to Nicole's elaborate tablescape.

That won't do. She dug around in her drawer of placemats and came up with a matching set of red checkered placemats and napkins. Scarlet red candles completed the romantic setting. Check.

If she were cooking for herself, a salad wouldn't have entered her mind, but since Shelby loved veggies, Monica forced herself to make a tossed salad with dried cranberries, candy-coated walnuts, cherry tomatoes and cucumbers, dressing it with a light vinaigrette. *Yuck.* She searched the pantry and found some croutons, which she would generously sprinkle over her own salad to provide crunching cover. Shelby would assume Monica was eating lettuce while she was secretly enjoying the buttery croutons. Salad for Shelby. Check.

A glass of wine later, the wind blew Shelby through the door, the setting sun at her back. Monica spread her arms wide, welcoming her lover home.

"What smells so delicious?" Shelby asked, tossing her yellow jacket on a chair, the color a vibrant harbinger of spring.

Her eyes caught on the lighted candles and red-checkered table linens. "It's like a cozy Italian restaurant in here."

"Pasta-bake and salad?" Monica offered.

"Sounds delicious." Shelby fell into Monica's arms and hugged her tightly, as if they were swaying in high seas on the deck of a ship.

"How's my sexy fiancée?" Monica whispered, the air whooshing from her lungs under the weight of Shelby's bear hug.

"Nervous as hell about teaching online. My students won't have the right supplies at home, I'll probably screw up the Zoom meeting, and the school has forbidden the students from picking up their clay, or other supplies, at school. What else could go wrong?"

Monica ran her hands over Shelby's soft jersey, pressing her thumbs and palms into the tight cords around Shelby's shoulder blades.

"Oooh," Shelby moaned, her knees buckling and hips falling against Monica's.

A surge of something hot ran from Monica's fingertips to her toes. "Would you like a glass of wine before dinner?"

"I think I want a margarita—Belizean style."

"I'm pretty sure I don't have the ingredients—"

"We do. I bought them."

Monica liked the sound of "we."

Shelby gave Monica a peck on the cheek. "First, a drink, then you can give me a back rub."

Monica pictured Shelby's bare back, her cocoa-butter-soft skin heating up under Monica's touch. Her libido shot off like a cannon. "Anything you want."

"I'll hold you to that." Shelby released Monica and went to the booze cupboard. She removed a bottle each of Silver Patron and Cointreau, the seals unbroken.

"I see you bought top shelf," Monica said, amused.

Shelby raised a warning brow. "I'm not making jungle juice wapatui, you know. This isn't college."

Monica's lips pulled into a smile, her dimples prominent. "I'm down with expensive booze. We're adulting now, and it only makes sense to buy the good stuff. More importantly, I didn't realize you knew how to make a margarita from scratch."

Shelby withdrew her iPhone from her pocket and touched the screen. "I'll google a recipe." She turned to the fridge and removed a lime and a bottle of organic agave nectar, swinging it from side to side in Monica's face. "This is the secret."

Monica angled her head, her emerald eyes dancing with delight. "And all this time, I thought it was the tequila."

Shelby poured equal parts nectar and Cointreau into a shaker, then added a jigger of tequila. She squeezed half a lime and dumped in the juice, not bothering to measure. A shaved clementine peel jumped into the shaker along with a fistful of ice. With her strong, artist hands, she shook the shaker, her hips swiveling, her boobs jiggling a little, her eyes locked on Monica's.

"I think you missed your calling as a club bartender," Monica said. "I can see you in something very skimpy... entertaining customers."

Shelby waggled her chestnut eyebrows, a quirky extension of the corkscrews streaming out from around her temples. She dumped the mixture into an Old-Fashioned glass and sprinkled some margarita salt on top, also a new addition to the stores of their pandemic vessel. *Aye, Aye, Captain. Stocked to the hilt.*

They clinked glasses, and Shelby tossed back a healthy swig of her concoction. "Whoo-hoo, baby!" She smacked her lips. "That's tasty. Want a sip?"

"Too much wine on board." Monica patted her tummy. "Maybe next time."

"I think this will be my go-to pandemic drink to cushion the impending Armageddon."

Monica rolled her eyes. "Not there yet. Time for a back rub." She steered Shelby by the shoulders over to the sofa. "Sit your booty on the ottoman in front of me."

They set down their drinks, and Shelby ripped off her jersey, her sports bra crisscrossing her ripped back.

Even after six months of dating, a half-naked Shelby still took Monica's breath away. Shelby's unique scent—a hint of light floral mixed with a dead-sexy muskiness—filled the air. Monica quickly rubbed her hands together, warming them.

"Do you mind if we watch Norah O'Donnell during cocktail hour?" Shelby asked. "I want to catch up on the news since I forced myself not to watch it all day."

"I thought you just said you needed your reality softened?"

"I do. I think a drink and a back rub will help me absorb the news. Who knows what the crazed president did today?" She turned on the news at a low volume.

"I may not be able to tear my eyes away from your gorgeous body for Norah O'Donnell," Monica said. "She doesn't do it for me."

"Yeah, I'm sexier than Norah," Shelby said in a sultry voice. She unexpectedly lay back in Monica's lap, the top of her head resting on Monica's bellybutton, her eyes not on the news at all.

Tiny freckles covered the milky skin above her pert breasts, currently contained in black cups. Her ribcage caught on an inhale when she glanced up to see the hunger in Monica's stare. "Does this turn you on?"

"Seeing you practically naked, lying in my lap?" Monica asked. "Hell yes."

"Maybe you want to give me a front rub instead of a back rub?"

Blood rushed south so fast that Monica could actually feel herself grow warm with anticipation. She didn't need to be asked twice. She splayed her fingers across Shelby's torso, stroking the defined abs and the delicate corners of her ribs. Her body was perfection, not an ounce of fat in sight.

Shelby moaned. "Mmmm. You have great hands."

Monica leaned over and kissed Shelby's breasts through the fabric.

Surprising Monica, Shelby grabbed Monica under her arms and pulled her breasts into her face, nuzzling them through the fabric of her V-neck, a Brewers' baseball shirt.

"What are you doing?"

"Enjoying your sexy chest." Shelby's melodious purr was like beachy wind chimes, instantly transporting Monica back to their romantic haven in Belize.

Monica delighted in the nuzzling then raised herself up. "Aren't you hot tonight?" She slid her hand down Shelby's tummy, circling her naval, tickling it, then dipping the tip of her index finger in. She quickly withdrew and held her finger to Shelby's nose. "Literally found some sand in your bellybutton."

"My kind of vacation. You should check for more, but lower this time."

"On my way." Monica quickly unbuttoned and unzipped Shelby's jeans, sliding her hand under a lace bikini brief, until she reached the holy land. "Someone is very wet." She kissed the curls on top of Shelby's head while playing with her, careful not to slide too close to the bundle of nerve endings.

"Someone was listening to Cardi B all afternoon while setting up her art studio," Shelby said in a breathy voice.

"Interesting choice." Monica tilted her head to recall some of Cardi B's songs. "Did the erotic lyrics make you hot?"

"Mmhmm."

Cardi B wasn't Monica's cup of tea, but Shelby liked dirty music, so Monica planned to capitalize on it. "Sing something for me."

Shelby squirmed under Monica's touch, moaning self-consciously. "Of Cardi B? You know I can't sing."

In a raspy, director voice, Monica said, "Rap for me, dirty girl. You know you want to."

Shelby squinted, trying to see if Monica was joking or serious. "I can't remember all the words."

Monica's fingers circled Shelby's hot spot. "Sing while I play with you. No freebies. You have to work for your orgasm tonight."

"Oh fuck," Shelby growled, as her hips hitched up. "Here goes." She cleared her throat, and ground out in a naughty voice, "You fucking with some wet ass pussy."

Monica almost laughed at Shelby's attempt to sound badass, but smothered her amusement, instead focusing on swirling her fingers over Shelby's delicate bud. "Keep going, sexy diva."

Shelby's eyes flashed dangerously. "Bring a bucket and a mop for this wet ass pussy." There was a husky confidence to her tone, but her straight-laced, white-girl style verged on *Saturday Night Live* material.

"Keep singing, sexy." A heady spark of desire traveled through Monica, as she lowered Shelby's jeans, allowing her hand more access. She gently inserted two fingers into Shelby's tight, wet heat, then flexed her wrist and moved in and out.

Shelby's neck tensed, her veins straining under her tan. She licked her lips and rasped, "Put this pussy right in your face, swipe your nose like a credit card..." Her voice caught, as her hips gyrated into Monica's hand, the hard planes of her abdomen flexing and releasing.

Those Cardi B lyrics coming out of Shelby's teacher-mouth were positively scandalous, ramping up Monica's desire. She rewarded Shelby with her thumb rubbing over her swollen nub, faster now. "That's it. Keep rapping for me. You know you want to."

Shelby sang between jagged breaths, "This pussy is wet, come take a dive...fuck...Mon...yes."

Monica arched over Shelby's flushed chest, now rising and falling in quick succession, and moved her fingers and thumb in a faster rhythm. It was time to drop the caramel in Shelby's macchiato. "I like the sound of that, babe, diving into your wet ass pussy...I wanna see you come for me. Keep singing, you slutty little rapper."

Like smoke, lust blew into Shelby's eyes as her hips hovered off the ottoman, chasing Monica's hand and fingers.

Monica worked Shelby into a frenzy for a few minutes, then whispered into her ear, her face buried in the mass of corkscrews, "Sing for me, or the fingers will stop."

"Make..." Shelby said on a moan, then, with herculean effort in a tremulous voice, "Make it cream, make me scream."

Monica could feel the tremor building in Shelby's vagina, the walls throbbing around her fingers, Shelby's thighs quivering.

"That's it. Give me your wet ass pussy," Monica said into Shelby's ear, then stuck her tongue in for a swirl.

The combination pushed Shelby over the edge, as her hips thrust wildly toward the ceiling and froze while Monica expertly drew out the orgasm.

Shelby shredded the air with a "Whoa...fuck...yes."

Monica continued her circular motion, as Shelby gasped and tumbled. When Shelby clenched Monica's wrist, she slowed her rhythm so Shelby could ride out the waves.

After coming down and catching her breath, her chest blotchy from ecstasy, Shelby said, "Unfuckingbelievable, Mon."

Monica cupped Shelby's pussy and held her while she nuzzled the side of her head. "You're so sexy when you sing for me. The hottest."

"Oh. My. God. Who knew?" Shelby giggled devilishly. "I'm such a bad singer."

That's true, Monica thought, but said, "You're awesome. When you're ready, my credit card nose will be waiting for you."

Shelby readjusted her limp body and offered her face to Monica, her pupils dilated with pleasure, a satisfied smile on her face. "Kiss me." She grabbed Monica and pulled her down to her face.

Monica's lips met Shelby's in a lip-smacking crash, their tongues diving deeper into the liquid heat, uniting them. Monica was sucked into a whirlpool of hot desire. The room started spinning and Monica's mind left her body, floating above the realities and brutalities of a mounting pandemic and a serial killer on the loose. She no longer cared about the outside world, her law firm, her colleagues, her clients, anyone. All that mattered was exploring the warmth of Shelby.

When Monica opened her eyes, she was surprised to find herself lying lengthwise on the sofa, Shelby snuggled up against her, their legs entwined, their fingers speared into each other's hair.

Shelby smiled against Monica's plump lips, raw from a shameless pummeling.

"You are the absolute best kisser," Monica said.

"Yahtzee!" Shelby whispered in a teasing voice.

Who goes from dirty rap to family dice games in the span of an orgasm? Monica's mind, already reeling from wine, woman and song, wanted more nakedness, more love, more of Shelby's mouth and talented tongue. "Let's roll the dice again, shall we?"

She didn't give Shelby the opportunity to reply, claiming her mouth.

Shelby inched up slightly and snuck her hand into Monica's cheeky bikinis, her fingers going to work.

14

The next morning, Monica received a call from Dr. Kershaw. "I just got my surgical list. Bad news. The next second-year anniversary of a surgery is in four days."

"Four days?" Monica asked in disbelief. "How are we going to catch the killer in four days?" She pictured telling Al Bowman. *Ouch.*

"They haven't been able to catch him for two months, so I'm not optimistic," Nicole said in a defeated tone.

"Shit. We promised to email the list of dates to Matt and Detective Heinz, so they'll see that and want to warn the patient right away."

"I think we should beat them to the punch and warn the patient today," Nicole said. "I have her contact info."

"Who is she?"

"Carissa Beachley, a California surfer."

"With a name like that, I'd hope so. She came all the way from California to see you?"

"Yes. The waiting list for gender-affirming surgeries in California is much longer than mine."

"What city does she live in?"

"She isn't really tied to one city. I remember her telling me about her roaming lifestyle in her van, driving up and down the coast, following the 'dope waves,' as she put it."

"Hm," Monica said. "If we can't find her, then maybe the killer won't be able to either."

"I have her cell phone number...assuming it's still good," Nicole said.

"Okay, but hold off for now. Give me a few days to see what I can do."

Nicole scoffed. "Monica, do you really think you can do in a few days what the police haven't been able to accomplish in two months?"

Thanks for the vote of confidence. "I have to, don't I?"

"Why can't I call Carissa right now?"

"How would you like to be her? Wouldn't it be better if we could spare her that worry altogether?"

"If I were her, I'd want to know right now."

"Nicole, I also represent the hospital and Al would prefer that we not start calling patients because word will get out. What if Carissa posts it on social media? That could destroy your reputation as well."

Nicole sighed heavily. "I'm in a no-win situation. If she gets killed, it's on me. I'd never be able to live with myself. The guilt! What about her family? They'd be devastated, then they'd sue me for failure to warn her. And they'd win. It would be criminal not to warn her. I don't have a good reason not to call her right now."

"I agree with the possibilities as you've described, but I'm begging you for a little time. Two days, max. If I can't solve this in two days, then you'll still be able to give her two days' warning."

Nicole was silent.

"I'll pay for your plane ticket to join her in California for the day of the anniversary if that would make you feel better."

"It isn't about me feeling good, Monica. It's about doing the right thing."

"I agree and I'm completely on board. All I'm asking for is two days. Do we have a deal?"

"Fine. Forty-eight hours, but that's it."

"Deal. Email me the list of only surgical dates so I can pass it along to Matt and Heinz."

Monica heard some typing. "On its way now."

"Thanks." Monica allowed a short pause before saying, "Don't share the master list with anyone, okay?"

"Can I send it to you and Al? That would make me feel better."

"Of course. I'll let him know the two-day plan."

"Forty-eight hours, Mon. Not two days."

"Right. I'll stay in touch."

Later that day, Monica held a Zoom call to speak to the group of nurses and surgical assistants who comprised Dr. Kershaw's clinical and surgical teams. In a pre-pandemic world, she would have met with each of them in person at the hospital. That wasn't in the cards, though, so they trialed the technology that, while not new, hadn't been used in the regular course of legal business.

Monica had begun the Zoom meeting with the entire team in attendance, providing them with the background of the two murders and giving them some general instructions about talking to law enforcement. She stressed that they should answer all questions honestly and be forthcoming with work information while not offering irrelevant details about their personal lives. In other words, she didn't give a hoot about their personal lives but didn't want to expand the police investigation to the hospital itself.

After an hour of going around the boxes of faces on her flat screen, asking each of the six employees about their jobs and how much time they spent with Nicole and the transgender patients, one-by-one, she had said goodbye to all but Jane Krajewski and Derek Russell. Jane was Nicole's dedicated clinic nurse, and Derek was Nicole's right-hand physician assistant in the operating room. Of all the people on the two teams, Jane and Derek worked most closely with Nicole on a daily basis, becoming close acquaintances with her and her patient population.

Jane was Zooming from her house, her backdrop a large Kitchen-Aid mixer on a white countertop. She was a middle-aged woman with brown hair piled on top of her head in a messy bun. A loose blouse with a flower pattern covered her ample curves. Her rosy-cheeked, round face was free of makeup and she looked like she had just come in from the outdoors. She had an easy, broad smile but her eyes blinked incessantly. Monica wondered if the blinking was prompted by having a camera in her face and a lawyer on her screen, or whether she blinked nonstop off-camera as well.

"I'm so nervous about this," Jane said.

"Why?" Monica asked.

"I just…feel like I might say something that hurts the hospital, or worse, Dr. Kershaw."

Monica looked into the camera with her most reassuring lawyer face—as opposed to her menacing one—and said, "Jane, unless you describe watching Dr. Kershaw kill her patients, there's nothing you could say that would reflect negatively on the hospital or Dr. Kershaw."

"Are you sure? I mean, I just don't know…"

Both Derek and Jane stared straight ahead into the camera, Derek as expressionless as a gravestone. In contrast to Jane, Derek was sitting at the hospital, his background a mixture of speckled ceiling tiles and seafoam green walls.

He wore a green surgical hat and a mask loosely draped around his neck. Thick, brown chest hair popped out of his V-necked green surgical garb. He viewed the world through thick, plastic OSHA glasses that Monica assumed were intended for surgeries.

He had mentioned at the beginning of the call that he was scheduled to return to the operating room after they concluded, so Monica wanted to be mindful of his time, not squander it on Jane's irrational fears. Sometimes, one witness's worst fear was also the worst fear of others, so discussing it provided an opportunity for Monica to teach the group. Here, however, judging by Derek's nonparticipation in the conversation, she guessed he wasn't benefiting from Jane's insecure ramblings and Monica's handholding. The two women might as well have been comparing brands of tampons.

"Jane, why don't you think about that for a minute, and I'll come back to you." Monica focused on Derek. "You mentioned you have a surgery to get to, so let's address any questions or concerns you might have, then you can drop off the call."

He unmuted. "Um. Yeah. So, what's my role here?"

"To meet with the detectives and answer their questions. They'll ask you how long you've been working with Dr. Kershaw, what types of surgeries you assist her with, and whether you remember or spoke to the two patients who were murdered."

He nodded dispassionately. "The answer is, ever since she started here, and all of her gender-affirming surgeries. I talk to the patients briefly before the surgeries, then afterward when we round on them in the hospital."

"So, were you working at Community Memorial before Dr. Kershaw arrived four-and-a-half years ago?"

"I've been coming to Apple Grove periodically for five years as a *locum tenens* physician assistant."

Monica was familiar with *locum tenens* physicians and nurses, but hadn't yet worked with a *locums* physician assistant. She had met retired physicians who liked to travel around the U.S. doing *locums* work, and there seemed to be an active community of traveling nurses, which the hospital routinely relied upon to backfill nursing shortages. These were people who stayed at the hospital for about three months, then moved on.

"Where is your home?" Monica asked.

"Northern California," he said.

"Where?

"I live part-time in Sacramento."

"What hospital do you work at?"

"UC Davis Medical Center."

Monica made a note. "Do you split your time between Sacramento and Apple Grove? If so, why did you choose Wisconsin in March? Shouldn't you be back in California?"

Her question drew a small smirk. "Trust me, not by choice. Dr. Kershaw scheduled several surgeries in February and March, so I agreed to help her out."

"I see. Since she can't do any elective surgeries under the governor's order, will you return to Sacramento?"

"It depends. The hospital is still paying me, so I'm helping out with emergency cases like gallbladders and trauma. I'll leave when they want me to."

"Gotcha. Now, with respect to the victims, do you remember either Ms. Adler or Ms. Remington?"

"Not really. The surgeries all blur together after a while."

Monica logged that. "How far in advance do you meet the patients?"

"The morning of surgery."

"Not in the clinic?"

"Sometimes, but not usually. I round with Dr. Kershaw on post-op patients then take calls for her regarding any patient concerns."

"So, you see the patients more post-operatively than pre-operatively?"

"Exactly. They're usually in the hospital for four days or so. Unless there's a specific issue with their care that would stand out, I wouldn't remember them."

"That makes sense," Monica said, jotting down his answer. "Derek, do you have any questions or concerns about speaking to the detectives?"

"Not at all," he said, his inscrutable face the color of bread dough under the fluorescent lights.

"Then feel free to drop off the call and attend to matters in the OR."

"Don't mind if I do," he said.

"I'll be in touch when the detectives want to meet."

"You have my email address." He unceremoniously left the meeting.

And now there were only two. Jane looked calmer. "I was up all night thinking about this."

"What specifically?" Monica asked.

Disbelief colored Jane's eyes and fear played at the creases in her forehead. "Someone has to be targeting Nicole."

"Why do you say that?" Monica was surprised that both Nicole and Jane had automatically jumped to this conclusion.

"I don't think it was a coincidence that the two murdered patients both got their surgeries here. You can get this surgery at other hospitals too, so I think someone is hacking Nicole to get her list of patient names."

This new twist caught Monica by surprise. "Not hacking into the medical records but hacking into Nicole's computer account at the hospital?"

"That's what I think."

"Does she keep a list of names of transgendered patients?"

"Yes," Jane said. "She has a log of all of her surgeries. It's required for her board certifications. I helped her assemble it."

Monica thought that was a major leap from simply infiltrating trans community online activity, but she felt compelled to address it. "So, if a person hacked her account, then he could theoretically find that list?"

"Yes."

"I'll check with Information Security," Monica said. "Have you ever seen any hate mail or emails to Dr. Kershaw?"

"Dozens."

"From whom?"

"You name it. White supremacist groups. Individuals. QAnon. Weirdos. The list goes on and on. Sickos, all of them."

Now that they were alone, the unvarnished Jane was more talkative and surer of herself. She reminded Monica of her aunt with a few glasses of wine on board.

"I didn't realize Dr. Kershaw's work was that controversial." A white lie meant to prompt more.

A guttural hoot escaped Jane. "Are you kidding me? Do you keep up with the news?" She waved her hand. "We live this stuff every day."

"Do you think that's partly because the practice is located in Apple Grove?"

A head shake. "The letters and emails mostly come from people *outside* of Apple Grove."

Monica nodded, again impressed with how progressive Apple Grove was for its size.

"Then there's Dr. Kershaw herself. Since she's trans, and very much out there advocating for trans people at parades and on social media. Like, for example, she's been very vocal that trans females should be able to participate in women's sports. She's drawn a lot of criticism and hatred."

"I'm sorry to hear that, which leads me to question whether you can think of anything specific that would help catch the killer."

Jane wiped her hands over her face, taking a minute. "Frankly, I don't know why I keep working in plastic surgery. My husband wants me to transfer to a less visible role in general surgery, but I really like Dr. Kershaw. She's a kind person, and, as far as surgeons go, she's easy to work with."

Monica was frustrated that Jane didn't answer specific questions, but if Jane needed to get some emotions off her chest before she met with the detectives, then Monica would listen. Better to have Jane blurt this stuff out to Monica than to the detectives. "Are surgeons difficult to work with?

A sarcastic hoot flew from Jane's broad lips. "They can be pretty stressed out, especially if they were on call and up all night doing surgeries."

"Tired and grumpy?"

"That's a start." *Blink, blink, blink* over an apologetic smile. "Controlling. Obsessive. Opinionated. Impatient with staff. Throwing things. Yelling. But Dr. Kershaw takes her time with each patient, and she's really nice to staff. She also lets me do my job. Doesn't micromanage, you know?"

"That's refreshing." Monica made a note and thought about how to get them back on track. "Tell me what you remember about Michelle Adler and Veronica Remington."

"Like Derek said, the patients all blend together after a while. Nothing really sticks out about either one of them, so I guess that's a good thing, right?"

"Dr. Kershaw mentioned that Michelle Adler's boyfriend accompanied her. Do you remember him?"

"That's pretty common, so no. Dr. Kershaw has a better memory about the details because she spends a long time talking to the patient, family members and partners, if they come. She usually puts all that information in her notes."

"Michelle Adler is from Minneapolis. Does that jog your memory?"

Jane smiled patiently. "We get quite a few patients from Minneapolis. There's a pretty big trans community there with a lot of resources, support and connections."

Monica was hitting roadblock after roadblock. "I think the detectives will show you photos from the homicide scenes. Will you be okay with that?"

"I'm a nurse."

"I get that, but homicide scenes can be…what should I say…gruesome?"

"As a nurse, I deal with gross stuff—mostly bodily fluids—all day, every day."

"Have you ever testified in a criminal trial?"

Jane's eyes expanded in surprise, and the blinking momentarily stopped. "No."

"How about a civil trial? Have you given a deposition or testified in any type of case?"

"Never. I haven't even served on a jury. I have no experience with the legal system."

Monica absorbed that piece of info. "Well, I can't predict where this homicide investigation will go, but testifying down the line is certainly a possibility."

"That's what scares me." The blinking resumed.

"Anything specifically?"

"I just don't want to hurt Dr. Kershaw or the hospital?"

"Do you know something that you aren't telling me?"

"Not that I can think of."

"Then let's concentrate on your job and what you remember. Do you recall anything about Veronica Remington from Chicago?"

"Not really," Jane said. "Sadly, we tend to remember only the patients who complained about things...the squeaky wheels."

"I get it. Same in my business."

There was a pause while Monica waited to see if Jane raised anything else.

"Do you think my life is in danger?"

"I don't think so," Monica said. "Trans women are being targeted, not cisgender nurses." She waited to see if Jane had a reaction to that other than blinking.

"So, Dr. Kershaw is a big target, then, right?" Jane asked.

"Potentially," Monica said.

Jane mulled that over, her expression going from troubled to terrified. "So, this meeting with the detective will be in person?" Jane asked.

"Yes. I'll email you as soon as I hear from either Detective Heinz or Breuer."

"Okay."

"You have my email address if you think of anything else," Monica said.

"Can I email you with questions before the meeting?"

"Of course."

They ended the call and Monica pushed back from her desk. CNN was on, but the volume was muted. She stared at the silent screen and thought about how she could move this investigation along at a faster clip. She had a lawyer's intuition that someone on Dr. Kershaw's team knew something valuable but she had to figure out a way to unearth it. There was no substitute for meeting face-to-face.

15

Considering the images on CNN—rising death toll and falling stock market—Monica recalibrated her understanding of how the world used to behave. Everything felt upside down, which wasn't conducive to focusing on murder clues. She made some chai tea and added a smackerel of honey. More accurately, she turned the honey bear upside down and squeezed hard to a count of three. While the honey steeped with the tea bag, she microwaved and frothed half-and-half into a pillow that occupied a third of the mug. *I need a bigger mug for teleworking.*

Returning to her desk, mug of tea in hand, she thought about Derek the PA. Like many healthcare providers she had met, he seemed overworked, over-scheduled and stressed, lines etched deep between his brows. Rare was the rosy-cheeked Jane who had manifested her nervousness by rapid-fire blinking. Of course, Jane wasn't familiar with the legal system, so she was understandably frightened. Monica was used to this reaction from healthcare providers.

In this case, neither Jane nor Derek had a vivid recollection of either Michelle or Veronica, but did they possess something useful about Dr. Kershaw?

She emailed Detectives Heinz and Breuer the names of the six team members, indicating they were available to meet in person and Monica would accompany them. She added that the infectious disease doctors encouraged everyone to meet outdoors if the weather permitted, but if inclement, the conference room at her law firm would work as long as everyone kept a suitable distance between them and remained masked.

Two seconds after she sent the message, her phone rang with Matt Breuer's name on the screen.

"Hey, Matt."

"Thanks for getting back to us so quickly," he said. "Detective Heinz asked me to follow up with the hospital employees and report back to him. He has his hands full in Minneapolis and Chicago, so it will just be you and me."

She heard voices and radios crackling in the background and pictured him at the police station, hunkered down in his cubicle.

"The fewer people we have at the meeting, the better," she said.

"Rest assured, I'll be following the new guidelines. They seem to add a new requirement every 12 hours." He paused a minute then asked, "Is the hospital overflowing with COVID patients?"

"They have a few positives, but Al told me that no one is on a ventilator. Yet. It isn't like New York, that's for sure. The governor's order appears to be keeping the COVID rates at bay."

"Since the clinic is closed and surgeries are scaled back, it's a perfect time for Dr. Kershaw's team members to talk to the police, right?"

"When isn't a perfect time to chat with the friendly Detective Matt?" she asked with perfect sarcasm. "Most of them aren't going to be helpful, but you're free to speak to all."

"Really? Tell me about those who might be helpful."

"Dr. Kershaw's clinic nurse, Jane Krajewski, and Derek Russell, the physician assistant who helps Dr. Kershaw in the hospital with surgeries."

"And the others?"

"They're like the supporting cast of *Gilligan's Island*. They don't know anything or recall the victims. However, I want to make them available to you, so you can chat with them if you like."

"For the sake of completeness, let's schedule them for 30 minutes each, back-to-back. For Nurse Krajewski and PA Russell, let's do an hour each."

"Sounds good," Monica said.

"How about the day after tomorrow?"

"What? I was thinking tomorrow, if not today."

"Today is completely out of the question and I can't tomorrow. We're in mandatory officer training all day."

"Can't you get an exemption for a time-sensitive murder case? We have four days until the next second-year anniversary date."

He blew a raspberry. "I know. I got your email. I hope you plan to warn the patient."

"Al Bowman doesn't want to. I promised Dr. Kershaw and him that I'd try to solve this in the next couple of days so we don't have to."

"Solve this murder case in the next few days?" he asked with incredulity. "You're cracked."

"While y'all are in your officer training seminar, someone has to work on it."

He let her insult slide. "Serial murder investigations can take years, Mon. One day of training is a speck of dust in the universe."

"Maybe for the police, but not for me."

He uttered a couple of *heh hehs.* "With limited resources and the power of one, you go for it."

"Watch me," she said with more bravado than she had intended. "I don't have to wait around for you guys."

"Not even Detective Heinz talks smack like that. I seriously think the hospital should just suck it up and warn the next patient."

"We will when we need to."

"If you don't, then we'll have to. Don't make us get a court order for her name."

"No worries. We'll do the right thing."

"You're the most stubborn lawyer I've ever worked with."

"A lie, I'm sure."

"Different topic," Matt said. "Did you check with the hospital to see if anyone hacked into the medical record of either Ms. Adler or Ms. Remington?"

"Yes. No external hacks, so the Information Security guy, Sam Moua, is going to analyze their medical records to see if anyone internal to the organization improperly accessed them."

"You mean, like some diabolical Dilbert sitting in a cubicle in the basement?"

"Whose only hobby is murder?" she added. "Yes. Only the care team should be accessing the chart, so that's what Sam is tracking down for me."

He pondered that a minute. "Good thinking, Monica."

"That would be Al Bowman's worst nightmare. No. Maybe a pandemic is his worst nightmare. He's living two nightmares."

"Sucks to be him."

"All we need now is for the media to pick up the scent of murder and follow the trail back to the hospital."

"I can picture Tiffany Rose broadcasting live in front of the hospital." He switched to a falsetto. "'Patients who've had gender-affirming surgeries at Community Memorial are being targeted and slain in their homes, male genitalia painted graffiti-style in red on their naked torsos—'"

"Not funny."

"I wasn't trying to be funny. I think there's a solid line connecting the two murders to Dr. Kershaw and her practice. I like Detective Heinz's theory that someone might be targeting her with a personal message. If that isn't newsworthy, I don't know what is."

"I'm pretty sure that theory was the first thing that flew out of Dr. Kershaw's mouth when he asked her about herself, but I'm not necessarily buying it—"

"You're right to be skeptical," he said. "If Dr. Kershaw was the only target, then why hasn't the killer tried to harm her?"

"Million-dollar question." Monica was tempted to say that Nicole is protected by big, bad Geoffrey Gold, who was conspicuously absent when the detectives visited. Even though she and Matt were friends, and she could trust him to investigate fairly, she owed a duty to her client. For reasons Monica had yet to discover, Nicole hadn't wanted the police to know Geoffrey existed. He wasn't Monica's cup of tea, but that didn't make him a killer either.

"Based on what she told us," Matt was saying, "there are too many possibilities to track down in four days, especially since Dr. Kershaw didn't save any of the hate letters and deleted the emails—"

"Which the hospital server wipes off the system in 30 days anyway." She shook her head. "We'll catch a break. Stay positive."

"I'm always positive, but I'm also realistic. It's going to take stellar detective work over the course of weeks, a clue left behind by the killer, and a healthy dose of luck to catch this guy."

She grunted in response.

"Warn the next patient, Mon."

She grunted again. "I'm going to hang up on you."

"On a different note, how are you and Shelby doing with the shelter-in-place order?"

A visual of them making love on the sofa during the evening news flashed through her mind. "Oh, you know. We're scraping by."

He laughed. "Like everyone. What is she doing for art classes now that the schools are closed?"

"Teaching online."

"That sounds like a challenge with teenagers."

"Yeah. She's pretty nervous about it."

"So, she's in one room teaching art, and you're in the other practicing law?"

"No," Monica said. "She has a studio at her house, so she's doing her Zoom classroom from there."

"Just like painting by numbers on YouTube, huh?"

"Don't say that to her," Monica said. "She isn't in a good mood about having to transfer her curriculum to an impromptu online format."

"Isn't art always impromptu?"

"Shush. Don't you dare say that! Shelby labors over each curriculum, whether pottery or water coloring."

"Learn something new every day."

"So, are you and Nathan staying together or apart?"

"He didn't tell you?"

"No. What?"

"We moved in together."

"Congrats. His house or yours?"

"His. He's much pickier about furniture and decor, and I don't really care one way or the other."

"He has good taste," she said, recalling the few times she had been in his house.

"My house is now on the market."

"Hope its sale isn't impacted by the pandemic or the falling stock market." She couldn't help the doubt from seeping into her voice.

"Me too. Unprecedented."

"We'd have to look back at 1918, I suppose."

"If you hear of anyone looking for a house, send them my way."

"Be happy to."

They rang off and Monica emailed Kathy to set up the meetings with Dr. Kershaw's staff.

As she glanced around her quiet living room, the walls felt like they were closing in. There was a reason she went to law school and practiced at a busy firm—she liked being with people. Seeing them. Laughing with them. Arguing with them. Sharing meals with them. Faces. Voices. Wisecracks. Body language. Interaction. Companionship. She had been teleworking for only a few days, but she was lonely. She missed her colleagues and the chatter and clatter of office life.

She wondered if Shelby was just as lonely, toiling away at her home studio, teaching a bunch of apathetic high school students who were highly distractible under the best of circumstances. *I should do something nice for her. Maybe surprise her by buying groceries and delivering them.*

Monica's heart fluttered at the prospect of doing a good deed for her lover, then seeing the delight and appreciation sizzle in her eyes. She justified the diversion to let her mind process clues.

She clicked on the website for the local grocery store, which was now offering curbside pickup, and bought the healthy essentials that Shelby liked to eat during the day— salad makings, apples, bananas, milk. A pack of RX Fitness bars in chocolate and sea salt flavor. Some chips for the hell of it, and a few bottles of wine.

She left for the store and Shelby's house. *I hope she's surprised.* Anticipation built in her chest, as she drove down her charming street in her aging truck. The weather was mild, the sky clear, and the temperature nice enough for a light jacket. Delighting in a much nicer day than yesterday, kids were riding their bicycles despite snow patches here and there.

At the store, the employee set the bags in the passenger seat and Monica was off. The buzz of love and the prospect of giving something nice to Shelby lifted her spirits.

When she arrived, there was a shiny white Mercedes coupe in the driveway, the temporary plates as bright as the showroom sparkle. She could practically smell the new car interior from the street.

Monica didn't want to block the car in on Shelby's narrow driveway, so she parked on the street and carried the groceries to the back door of the one-hundred-year-old house. The drafty walls and ancient electrical system were eclipsed by its charm, the front veranda being one of the features Monica admired most.

The kitchen door was unlocked, so she carried in the groceries and set them on Shelby's cutting block, which served as her center island in the tiny kitchen.

Women's voices, one lower than the other, carried from the general direction of the art studio, so Monica followed the sound. As she drew near, she heard the unmistakable sound of a woman mumbling through tears, her voice cracking. The voice didn't belong to Shelby, and was saying, "I don't know what I'm going to do...closed...no yoga...for who knows how long?"

Suddenly feeling like an intruder barging in on a delicate conversation, Monica paused on the threshold of the studio. *What if Shelby views my arrival as a violation of her privacy? Maybe I should leave...*

Monica weighed her options. Silently retreat to her truck, leaving the groceries behind. Or, clear her throat to announce her presence, assuming she had a right to be there as Shelby's fiancée. Her heart and pride steered her toward the latter. She tiptoed around the corner and peeked her head into the studio.

Before her sat Shelby on a paint-splattered stool, her arm draped around a gorgeous blonde, buttery tendrils framing her face then flowing over her shoulders. Tears fell from her stunning Barbie doll eyes, so sad and broken. Her heart-shaped scarlet lips were puffy and trembling.

If her celebrity good looks weren't enough, she was wearing hot pink tights and a white crop top with cold shoulders that didn't look so cold with Shelby's arm draped across them.

Monica recognized her competition immediately—Coco Rivelli, yogi extraordinaire—owner of The Yoga Studio. Shelby's ex-lover, the woman who had cheated on, then lied to,

Shelby, all but destroying her belief in trust and fidelity. That had happened only one year ago. Monica had warily navigated Shelby's emotions, a turbulent sea of mistrust, ultimately convincing her that true love and commitment were not only possible but also within her reach, if only she turned her heart over to Monica.

Monica took a step into the studio. Coco looked like she weighed the same as Monica's left butt cheek. Every sinewy muscle was visible under blemish-free skin, probably nourished by arugula for lunch and a protein bowl for dinner.

Shelby and Coco were engrossed in an intimate conversation, their personal connection unmistakable and flashing like a neon sign.

"Ahem." Monica cleared her throat self-consciously.

Their heads snapped up and registered her presence.

Shelby blurted a gurgling sound in surprise.

Each of the three women was as startled as the other, their eyes darting and roaming like the gunslingers in *The Good, the Bad, and the Ugly*. Monica silently called dibs on *the Good,* then immediately felt insecure in the presence of two beauties because neither Coco nor Shelby qualified for the role of *the Ugly.*

Her insecurities flaring like Clint Eastwood's temper, she threw her shoulders back and reminded herself that she was Shelby's fiancée and had a right to be there.

Shelby's arm withdrew from Coco's shoulders as fast as a rattlesnake. She hopped off the stool to stand before Monica in her bare feet. "Monica! What are you doing here?"

Monica purposefully allowed her eyes to swivel back and forth between Coco and Shelby. "Obviously, interrupting something."

"No...it isn't what it looks like," Shelby stammered. "Such a cliché." She threw her paint-stained hands in the air, searching for the right words, if there were any. "What I meant to say is that... I was..."

"Consoling me," Coco said, a hint of Italian accent hanging off lips that Monica wanted to punch.

Monica gave Coco her high-voltage, Spadish death stare. *Go ahead, Coco, make my day.*

"Shelby was consoling me because I'm so very sad that I closed my yoga studio business," Coco continued, "and am losing money by the minute."

Monica didn't give two shits about Coco's yoga studio cash flow. "I'd be sad, too, if I had to drive around a white car that had 'Bitch' painted in red on the side."

Both Shelby and Coco gasped in shock, Coco's eyes suddenly going from sad to alarmed. *A study in Acting 101*, Monica was sure.

"What?" Coco exclaimed. "You didn't."

"I will if I catch you with my fiancée again," Monica said between clenched teeth in a low, steady voice, loaded with venom.

Shelby covered her mouth, her eyes filling with panic.

Coco patted the air with her palms. "Fear not, Ms. Spade. I would never attempt to seduce your Shelby. She's spoken in glowing terms about how much she loves you..." Coco seemed at a loss for how to finish her thoughts, so she shrugged a rippled shoulder and inclined her gorgeous head, throwing a thick chunk of hair toward Monica.

Monica's hands twitched at her sides, balling into fists.

Shelby reached for Monica's arm. "Mon, no need to get angry. Coco just wanted to talk because she's devastated over closing her business and doesn't know what to do."

Monica's muscle fibers twitched at Shelby's touch, adrenaline pumping through her. She wanted to drag Coco by the hair through Shelby's house and throw her tight ass in a snowbank. "Maybe Coco could find another ex-lover to console her and caress her shoulders."

Shelby's fingers wrapped around Monica's forearm, but Monica shook her off. "And you." She turned her fiery emerald eyes on Shelby. "We're engaged. Is this your idea of fidelity? Is this your idea of social distancing during a pandemic?"

Shelby's expression turned defiant, telling Monica what she needed to know—that Shelby thought she could do whatever the hell she pleased.

For the first time since arriving, Monica actually focused on Shelby and was astonished to see that she had highlighted ribbons of her hair a shimmering silver to match her new spectacles, also high octane silvery white. They weren't metal frames, but a high-resin plastic, designed to frame her eyes like a modern painting. New look. Very *avant-garde. Did Coco help you pick them out?*

Shelby's mouth was moving, indicating she was speaking, but Monica couldn't hear anything above the jet engines roaring in her head.

Shelby stopped spewing forth schoolgirl platitudes and leaned in face-to-face. "Monica! Snap out of it! Nothing is going on—"

"I'm not a fool," Monica growled. "Don't lie to me. I won't be your doormat. Find yourself another sucker to shelter at home with."

She turned on her heel and stormed out, her heart exploding with rage. As soon as her boots hit the driveway, she jammed her hand in her coat pocket and felt around for a tube of lipstick, as if it were a six-shooter. *Bingo!* On her way down the driveway, she held the lipstick to the side of Coco's car and ran a straight line from headlight to tailpipe. *Consider yourself warned, bitch.*

16

Three hours had passed since Monica had blown up and stomped out of Shelby's house, defiling Coco's status symbol.

Three hours of Monica not returning Shelby's calls or texts.

Three hours of steam still hissing from Monica's ears.

Three hours of Monica's blood still boiling.

Three hours of confusion over Shelby's intentions—innocent or traitorous?

Three hours of confusion over her own behavior—losing her shit and vandalizing property.

Three hours of rebuffing Shelby and doubling down.

Three hours of holding onto resentment.

Not that Monica was counting the hours.

She half-expected Shelby to show up at her kitchen door, which is what she had done the last time they had fought, coincidentally over the same pussy poacher. Putting an end to that fight, Shelby had apologized and promised that she didn't have any lingering feelings for Coco, that Monica was her one and only. Now that Monica thought about it, had Shelby ever promised that? Had she been forthright and clear, or had she used vague, evasive and deceptive language? Monica's emotions were a hopeless jumble.

She second-guessed her decision to propose marriage so soon in their relationship. They had known each other only three months in January when Monica had popped the question on bended knee at the ice sculpture garden. Shelby had said yes, but here they were, only in March, and Monica had walked in on Coco and Shelby. *Bad things happen in threes. A pandemic. A serial killer on the loose. Shelby and Coco reuniting. Could my life get any worse?*

After being on the receiving end of Shelby's adoring glances, Monica was sick to her stomach at recalling the way Shelby had been looking at Coco. Not in an *I-want-to-fuck-you* way, but in a fully connected way. The way two people who really know each other feel. In a we-were-once-intimate kind of way. The way a lover carries the burden of pain for her partner. *Is Coco really an ex?*

Monica had never learned much about Shelby's relationship with Coco, other than Coco had broken Shelby's heart by fooling around on her, all the while denying infidelity. Monica felt like an outsider, not privy to the nuances of Shelby and Coco. The chemistry that made them tick. Their shared jokes. Their favorite sweet nothings. What they liked in bed with each other. Her mind spiraled into vivid images of Shelby and Coco making love. Big mistake. Rage began building inside of her. Again. Her heart raced and adrenaline coursed through her veins. She wanted to hit someone. Something. Anything.

"Arrrrrgh," she growled for the hundredth time, pushing away from her desk. She needed an outlet for her pent-up emotions. Wishing she could go to a CrossFit class and throw around big, heavy barbells, she realized she had nothing for workout equipment at home. The irony struck her that she had met Shelby at a CrossFit class when she had needed to blow off nervous energy during the Saudi student murder trial. Shelby had patiently taught Monica all the moves, both in the CrossFit Box and in the bedroom. Since the Box was now closed, however, Monica had to think of an alternative to release her violent energy.

She instinctively went to her sliding door and cracked it open. A light breeze tickled the sunny afternoon, the snow melting into puddles in her yard and dripping down the rain gutters from her roof, the sound methodical as a metronome.

Plunk, plunk, plunk. She inhaled the fresh air, calculating how many layers she would need for an outdoor run.

Fifteen minutes later, decked out in tights, a base layer with a wool long sleeve, and her CrossFit shoes, she was running down her street, feeling free and alive.

The atmosphere in the neighborhood seemed more like a Saturday than a workday, her neighbors outside, cleaning and organizing their garages. People walking their dogs on the sidewalks. An early spring had sprung in the frozen tundra and, for once, people were at home sheltering in place to witness it. Everyone seemed to be pretending they were on a staycation during spring break.

Monica ran and ran, her body carrying her faster and farther than it had in ages. Her emotions transitioned from feeling unhinged to feeling unchained. Glorious. Free. Settling into a pace that suited her, she gleefully burned off the vicious toxins that had built up in her body.

As the endorphins permeated her brain cells, her anguish dissipated into the clear air. Stride after stride and breath after steady breath, her Shelby troubles faded to the background as her physical prowess rose to the foreground. Finally, somewhere after mile four or five, she felt herself breaking free of the endless loop she had been watching in her mind's eye—replaying the scene at Shelby's art studio and recalling the snippets of conversations she and Shelby had initially had about Coco.

The heavy ache around her heart subsided when she found herself in Nathan's neighborhood. How that had happened, she didn't entirely know, but she was currently running by his modern house. The heat of the day had passed, and the freezing temperatures of a March night drifted along the streets, making her limbs feel heavy and stiff. She eased up and slowed her pace to a walk, circling back to Nathan's. She realized she craved a warm beverage and a ride home, if he was willing and available. If he wasn't, an Uber would do. If they were still operating, that was.

She pulled out her phone and texted him. *Hey Nathan. I was out for a run and ended up in your neighborhood. Can I drop in for a cup of tea and bum a ride home?*

Feeling slightly foolish and a little like a moocher, she paced the sidewalk in front of his house, pulling her knees up to her chest, attempting to stretch out her rapidly cooling muscles.

The red front door swung open, and Nathan came bounding down the steps and sidewalk toward her. "Hey, stranger! I didn't know you were a runner!"

"Neither did I!" Her dimples appeared with her smile.

Despite her sweaty appearance, he gave her a light hug and pulled her by her gloved hand toward the front door. "It's getting cold. You need some dry clothes, girl."

Her spirits lifted. "Now that you mention it..."

"Did you run all the way from your house?" he asked.

"I did. Honestly, I didn't have a plan but was just out enjoying the sights and sounds of spring." Fib. "My legs brought me here." Truth.

"Sights and sounds of spring, huh? That's a long run for someone who doesn't run regularly." He ushered her into his house, closing the door behind him. "I'm impressed."

"Come to think of it, my legs are starting to feel a little crampy." An involuntary shiver overtook her.

Nathan, clad in tight jeans and a sweater, eyeballed her. "Would you like to soak in our hot tub out back while I run your clothes through the wash?"

She pictured Nathan and Matt in the tub and all she could think of was testicle soup. Hard pass. "Um. No thanks. Maybe just a quick shower to warm up...if you wouldn't mind?"

"Hot shower it is. Come along." He turned and motioned for her to follow.

"You're a lifesaver. Muscles I didn't even know I had are starting to cramp up on me."

"If I decide to run a half marathon someday, I'll drop by your house and you can return the favor." He angled through the modern living room, Monica in his wake, and turned down a short hallway into a black and white checkered bathroom. "There are clean towels hanging on the shower door. Set your running clothes outside the door and I'll pick them up. In the meantime, I'll find a pair of joggers and a sweatshirt for you when you get out of the shower."

"How sweet of you," she said, then bravely added, "I'll have to go commando in your joggers."

"No worries. I'm loaning you the ones I always go commando in."

She covered her face at the images populating her mind. "Please, no."

He guffawed. "Just joking. Don't worry about it." He slid the pocket door closed. "Now, hop in the shower, and take your time."

Monica luxuriated in the shower for several minutes, shampooing her hair and applying conditioner, both Aveda products. *Leave it to Nathan to carry only top-shelf hair products.* They had so much in common—at both work and home—and had grown closer after coming out and leaving the DSW law firm. She and Shelby hung out with Nathan and Matt on weekends, and Monica found Nathan to be one of the easiest lawyers to work with. Her name was listed first in the firm, Spade, Daniels & Taylor, but Jim was the real boss, and Monica and Nathan were just students of Jim's wise counsel.

She toweled off and turbaned her hair in a thick, cream-colored towel. He even had lotion and a hairbrush on the counter. *What a guy.* She emerged a warm, but exhausted, woman in baggy black joggers and a designer sweatshirt that was so cuddly and soft on the inside she considered stealing it.

Nathan was at the stove making tea.

"I'm sorry for barging in on you like this." She hopped onto a padded bar stool at his kitchen counter and sank into the leather backrest.

As he poured a mug of tea, he said over his shoulder, "Are you kidding me? I've been climbing the walls teleworking. I need people. I'm no good alone at home. If you think you're leaving anytime soon, you're wrong."

"You too, huh? I thought I was the only one going nuts."

"Cream or sugar?"

"Both."

He added them and set the steaming mug on the counter before her. "Here you go, partner."

She wrapped her hands around the mug and inhaled, the peppermint aroma invigorating. She sipped at the hot liquid and wasn't surprised that it tasted heavenly.

A beeping sound came from a room off the kitchen. "Your clothes are done. I'll throw them in the dryer." Nathan disappeared for a second, and she heard the opening and closing of washer and dryer doors.

"That was fast," she said when he returned.

"I did a speed wash. They'll be dry in 20 minutes. Would you like a piece of toast with some whipped avocado and sliced hardboiled egg?"

She inclined her head and smiled tentatively. "Sounds intriguing."

"It's my new shelter-in-place snack." His usual enthusiasm for legal files seemed to be replaced by food. "Watch and be prepared to be amazed."

He sliced an avocado into a cup and whipped it with avocado oil, salt, and a dash of lemon juice, all the while bemoaning his litigation practice that was on hold or quickly evolving from in-person deposition testimony to Zoom testimony.

"Same for me," she said. "I've already met with hospital employees via Zoom."

He removed a hardboiled egg from the fridge and carefully sliced it into thin disks. Next, he made two pieces of sourdough toast, spread the guacamole, and decorated them with the egg slices. A sprinkle of salt and pepper followed. "Madame, my original concoction just for you." He slid the plate over to her. "Enjoy."

Monica usually dipped chips into guacamole, but the crisp toast and egg on top made a refreshing *après*-run snack. "This is really tasty, Nathan. Just what the doctor ordered."

"I'm here to serve, darling. Now, a beverage for me, and I can assure you it won't be tea."

She smiled. "It's five o'clock, so you're entitled."

With speed and dexterity, he made himself a mojito, a sprig of fragrant mint sprouting from the side. He air-toasted Monica, drank heartily, burped, and declared, "Fucking crazy time we're living in."

"Really fucking crazy," she said while chewing.

Like a smooth bartender, he quickly cleaned up after himself, then placed three square bowls on the counter. Monica watched as he filled one with honey roasted peanuts, the next with meat sticks he was chopping into bite-sized pieces, and the third with thinly sliced rosemary and garlic cheese.

"You're a godsend," she said, sneaking some peanuts.

He smiled broadly. "Are you ready to move onto something stronger than hot tea?"

"How about a glass of water?" she asked.

"Carbonated or flat?"

Did I die and wake up in a fancy restaurant? "Flat please. I'm beginning to think I might not be able to afford this restaurant."

"Wait until you see the wine list," he said with tantalizing bravado.

He served her a glass of ice water then sidled up kitty corner from her across the bar. "So, tell me what's really going on. Why the marathon run today?"

When she tried to speak, her throat constricted. "I... caught..."

In a compassionate gesture, he reached for her hand and covered it with his own. "It's okay, Mon. I'm here for you."

Her body surprised her by releasing a fire hydrant of tears. After a time, she spotted a box of Kleenex on the counter and plucked several tissues, placing them over her eyes like a washcloth. *Get ahold of yourself. How embarrassing. Nathan will assume the worst—that one of my parents died from COVID.*

After a time, she lowered the wet wad of tissues and looked at his narrow face, aquiline nose, and compassionate brown eyes, realizing for the first time that he hadn't shaved, giving him a scrappy look to match his perennially long bangs. Nor had he said a word while she was crying. No *"what's wrong?"* or *"What are you crying about?"*

She eyed him suspiciously. "You haven't asked me why I'm so upset."

"Always too smart for your own good." He tipped his glass and lowered his chin in acknowledgement. "Go ahead, tell me why."

Her bloodshot eyes widened in surprise. "You've already spoken to Shelby."

"No need to be upset," he said. "She called me a few hours ago, spilling her guts and crying on the phone for, like, an hour."

Monica hiccupped in response to that bit of news. She shook her head and chomped into the guacamole toast.

Nathan jangled the ice in the bottom of his drink and pushed off his stool. "Ready for something stronger?"

"You're a fast drinker, and you're stalling." She shook her head at him.

He started making himself a second mojito. "You know I've been friends with Shelby for several years—long before I met you."

"I realize."

"I'm the one who introduced you two at the Rascal's baseball game."

"I remember."

"I knew you'd be a perfect match. You're both so sweet, smart and beautiful. Anyway, I love you both, so why don't you start from the beginning, and tell me all about it?"

"I think you should tell me what Shelby told you."

He made a zipper sign across his lips.

"Are you our marriage counselor now?" she asked sarcastically.

He shook his head, his nutbrown eyes amused. "First, you're not married, and second, I'm not qualified. I'm just a good listener who is friends with both of you, and I want to see your relationship succeed." He rolled his hand in the air for her to start talking. "Go ahead."

17

"It's pretty simple. I walked in on Shelby and Coco Rivelli, the yogi sensation who put the *ass* in *vinyasa*."

He blinked slowly, allowing a slight smile. "I'm pretty sure it isn't pronounced '*vinyassa*.'"

"Work with me here." Her eyes tightened into slits like a dog ready to bite.

"And what were they doing when you walked in on them?"

"Shelby's arm was around Coco's shoulders, like this." She imitated, exaggerating some cozying and shoulder squeezing.

"I can see how that might have upset you."

Her lower lip trembled, so she bit down on it. "I wanted to kick Coco's ass, but I think I did one better by running lipstick down her white Mercedes."

Nathan unsuccessfully suppressed a smile. "I might have heard about that. I also heard the lipstick streak didn't completely wash away at the car wash, so Coco had to bring it back to the dealer for a deeper scrub and buff."

"Ha! Mission accomplished!"

He let her victory hang in the air for a minute. "The dealership charged her a pretty penny because they were technically closed due to the order."

Monica slapped her hands together. "Perfect! I could see the wax in the lipstick sort of glomming onto the shiny new finish."

He nodded and raised his hands, keeping his elbows tight to his ribcage. "Who knows. More importantly, I take it you haven't spoken to Shelby?"

She lowered her hands to her thighs, her shoulders slumping. "No. I have some pride too, you know. She might be better looking than I am, but fuck, she acts like she owns the relationship, you know?"

He nodded and sipped his second concoction.

"She treats me like I'd be marrying up if I were to be so lucky to become her wife. Maybe it's time that she looked at me the same way."

He reached for some cheese, and she followed suit. Nathan wisely let silence surround them, only soft music playing in the background.

Monica settled after a few lingering hiccups, setting the cheese on a napkin in front of her.

"You don't really believe that you'd be marrying up, do you?" he finally asked.

She slowly shook her hair out of the towel, allowing the long strands to hang over the sweatshirt, halfway down her back. "No, not really. I'm more confident now that we have our own law firm, and I'm not in the closet any longer. The last couple of years have shown me what I can accomplish, and that has been a huge self-esteem booster. But let's face it, I know Shelby's prettier than I am, and she knows it. And she's sweet. At least, I always thought she was. Now, I'm not so sure."

He nodded, then disappeared around the corner to the laundry room. He returned with a basket of clean clothes. "Here you go. Do you want to put on any of these before we continue?"

"Maybe my bra and undies." She grabbed the basket and traipsed into the bathroom to add her warm undergarments and tank, then re-dressed in Nathan's comfortable joggers and sweatshirt. She felt better when she returned to the kitchen.

"Thanks for taking care of me, Nathan. I should probably go instead of burdening you with my personal life."

She waved her hand over her front. "I'll wash these sweats and return them—"

"Oh no you don't. We're just getting started with this pity party. You sound depressed, and you're not leaving here until you feel 100 percent better."

"Ugh. There isn't anything to say."

"There's always something to say. Go on. Get it off your chest."

"I'd rather hear what you and Shelby were talking about."

Expecting this question, he sewed his eyebrows together in a genuine look of tenderness. "I want to keep each of your words in confidence, especially since I suspect some words might be coming from a place of anger. However, I can tell you that she loves you and has no intention of rekindling a relationship with Coco."

Monica squinted hard at him. "What makes you so sure?"

"Coco is engaged to someone else."

Monica's eyebrows shot up.

"And, before you think that Coco was visiting to take Shelby for one more spin around the block, she wasn't."

Damn him for knowing me so well! She stared at her tea.

"Aren't you going to ask me to whom Coco is engaged?" he asked.

Monica slowly raised her chin. "I suppose, although her fiancée shouldn't be relevant. Let me guess, she's one of Shelby's exes."

"She is a he."

"What? A he?"

"Yes. Coco is engaged to a man. A doctor in town." He rubbed his hands together, delighting in the juicy tidbit.

"A man? She's bi?"

"Either that, or she's trying it on for a certain lifestyle, no?"

Monica inclined her head. "Is that even a thing?"

He rubbed his thumb against his index finger, the universal sign for *cashola, dinero, moolah.*

"What kind of doctor? What's his name? Does he work at Community Memorial? Did he give her the Mercedes?" Monica asked.

"Family practitioner. Steve Olson. Boring, middle-aged guy. Shelby said he works for a clinic in a small town south of Apple Grove for—wait for it—" He played the drums on the counter.

A short eternity passed.

"Adventist Health System, a highly conservative, religious organization that doesn't tolerate queers."

Her hand flew to her mouth. "Does he know she's a lesbian?"

He shrugged. "How could he not? She cut a pretty wide swath through town, shagging every woman in sight."

Monica scowled because that shag-a-thon had included Shelby.

"Coco obviously has commitment issues," he said.

"Now she's engaged to a sugar daddy. Good luck with that, dude."

"Who knows what their deal is? The point is that it doesn't concern you or Shelby." He popped some peanuts in his mouth, chewing loudly, then washed them down with a swig.

Monica rocked her head in consideration. "Maybe there is justice after all. Coco will be sentenced to the 'happy baby' yoga position in bed for the rest of her life."

Nathan barked at that, spraying some peanut dust across the kitchen. "Never know. They might do it in downward facing dog."

"Too naughty for a religious fanatic," she said, waving him off.

After another swallow, Nathan said, "Shelby insists that Coco wasn't at her house to hit on her."

"And see, I don't believe that. I think she was at Shelby's for one last taste of freedom before prostituting herself for a physician-supported lifestyle."

He raked his hand through his shaggy hair. "Not according to Shelby."

"Can a lesbian really be satisfied in a straight relationship?" Monica asked before absent-mindedly nibbling a slice of cheese.

"Define satisfied."

"Sexually. I think Coco will be fantasizing about Shelby while she's lying in the missionary position with her eyelids taped shut."

"I wouldn't limit her fantasies to Shelby. She might have other women in her spank bank too, but yeah, I agree."

"You can't substitute someone else for what the heart really wants."

He placed his hand over his heart. "Don't I know it."

As if on cue, they heard the garage door open and close, and the handsome Matt Breuer came bustling around the corner, dressed in his detective blue windbreaker and navy slacks. He scanned the kitchen, his face breaking into a relaxed smile when he spotted Monica.

"Hey, Matt," she said. "Welcome home."

"Thank you, Mon. Glad you're here." Despite the greeting, his expression and voice were serious.

Nathan moved in for a hug, but Matt stepped back. "Let me get out of my work clothes first. They say the COVID virus can live on surfaces like jackets. I'm going to hang this up in the laundry room."

"I heard that today too," Nathan said, then turned to Monica, "I've been watching waaaaay too much CNN."

She rolled her eyes. "Me too. Horrible. Makes me want to drink."

"That's why I am. But you're not keeping up." He hiccupped, sounding tipsy.

"Who can keep up with your pace? And who the heck is going to drive me home?"

He smiled. "We might have to ask Matt."

"Sorry for imposing. And sorry for not being a good drinking buddy, but I'm confused about Shelby, and oh by the way, trying to solve a murder case."

"Is there a better reason to drink?" he said through a hiccup.

Matt reappeared in a white ribbed tank and black Lycra boxers, his squat body rippling with muscles. "Sorry for the display, Mon, but my jeans are in the bedroom." He scooted past them, carrying his police-issued handgun wrapped in his shoulder holster.

Nathan whistled a catcall at Matt's thick back.

"This pandemic is leading to the most bizarre experiences," Monica said. "Like me seeing Matt in his undies. He has an impressive physique, though." She raised her water glass. "You're a lucky man."

"I'll drink to that." Nathan toasted Cupid and drank, a mischievous grin plastered on his handsome face.

When Matt rejoined them, he was wearing straight legged jeans and a black V-neck that revealed his chest hair and accentuated his five o'clock shadow. He surveyed the food and beverages. "What are we drinking?"

"Mojito for me and tea and water for the lady."

Matt hesitated a second. "I think I'll have a whiskey." They watched while he poured himself two fingers over the rocks. Nathan and Matt air-clinked and drank, smiling into each other's eyes over the rims of their drinks. Nathan was taller, but Matt's thick hair, mussed just a whisper, made up the difference.

"Good day at work?" Nathan asked.

Matt raised a shoulder and inclined his head. "A few developments that Monica might be interested in."

She gave him her full attention. "Please. I'd love to hear about something other than Shelby and Coco."

Nathan tutted. "Oh shush. There is no Shelby and Coco. Shelby is devastated that you won't talk to her. Heartbroken, really. She's crying nonstop, afraid that she's lost you."

If Cupid had talons, they were digging into Monica's flesh. "Really?"

Matt's blue eyes volleyed back and forth between them. He seemed in no hurry to relay his work news.

Nathan gave her one of his sympathetic looks that he laid on juries when arguing in court. "Really. She's baffled because she loves you so much. She wants to be with you, Mon, and is terrified that you're going to break up with her."

Sensing that their conversation could go on quite a while, Matt turned and washed his hands, then refilled the bowls with peanuts, meat and cheese.

"But I saw—" Monica started.

"Shelby's innocent compassion for Coco," Nathan said. "*Innocent.* There isn't anything between them anymore, and Shelby's okay with that. She's moved on—with you."

Monica twisted in her chair, nervously crossing her legs. "And you're sure of this? I wouldn't look like a doormat for taking her back?"

"Positive. She wasn't taking advantage of you."

Monica tipped up her chin. "Do you think I overreacted?"

He gestured with his thumb and forefinger. "Maybe a little bit, but I can't say as though I wouldn't have done the same thing."

"Thank you," she said, uncrossing and recrossing her legs, unaware of how troubled the gesture made her appear.

"Can you two love birds kiss and make up now?" Nathan asked.

Her eyes flickered with promise. "Am I supposed to make the first move?"

"Yes. You're the one who told her to leave you alone so you could process. You're done processing, so invite her over and clear the air."

Her eyes searched his face. "I wouldn't know what to say."

He squeezed her shoulder. "Start with a text. You'll know what to say when she gets here."

"Here?" Monica said in falsetto. "To your house? Now?"

"No time like the present. She can join us for drinks and dinner."

"Um...that feels a little too...public for me. Plus, what about COVID? Shelby was just canoodling with Coco."

Nathan rolled his eyes. "Canoodling? Is this the 1950s?"

Monica shrugged.

"They weren't canoodling and Shelby is welcome here."

"Let me think about it for a few minutes." She turned to Matt. "What happened today that I might be interested in?"

Matt blinked a few times, his luscious black lashes long enough to brush Nathan's face from a foot away. "Paul Heinz called me. A homicide detective in Iowa City contacted him about the murder of a trans woman."

18

Monica's hand flew to her mouth. "Oh no. A third murder? When?"

"Less than a year ago—in July 2019. On a farm outside of Iowa City," Matt said.

Monica blew out a shaky sigh. "Let me guess. The victim was a patient of Dr. Kershaw's."

"I asked, but they never investigated that angle," Matt said. "At the time, they didn't think it was relevant where she had her gender-affirming surgery. So that's for us to find out."

"Do you know her name or any details?"

"Ingrid Durbin. She was hanged from a rafter in an old red barn."

"Did they rule out suicide?" Monica and Nathan asked in unison.

Matt nodded slowly, his lips turning downward. "A penis and scrotum were spray- painted—"

"Graffiti red on her torso," Monica finished for him.

"From her pelvis to her chest," Matt said.

"Stripped nude?"

"Yes."

"Savage," Nathan snarled. "Just when you think we've come a long way, the haters show us what they're capable of."

"At least, a certain serial killer shows us," Matt said. "Ms. Durbin's murder fits our pattern. If she's one of Dr. Kershaw's patients, I think we need to assume it isn't a coincidence."

"No signs of sexual assault?" Monica asked.

"No," Matt said. "The local detective was surprised because Iowa City is known for being fairly progressive. He told Heinz there's a pretty chill queer scene there, including a pride parade and festival, with vibrant gay bars and minimal violence."

"Iowa," Nathan said in disgust, "Idiots Outside Wandering Around."

"Who hasn't heard that before?" Monica said, poking him in the arm. "You were just waiting to say that."

He smiled, slightly lopsided.

"I've also heard that Iowa City is gay-friendly," Monica turned back to Matt. "Evidence gathered at the scene?"

"No discarded can of spray paint, if that's what you're asking. The barn was messed up under the noose, hay bales and chairs knocked over. Signs of a struggle, basically."

"That's to be expected," Nathan said. "How would you force someone to get up on a chair and stick her own head in a noose?"

"Probably with a gun pointed at her chest," Matt said.

"I'd rather be shot than hanged," Nathan fired back. "I'd tell the motherfucker to suck it."

Matt raised his eyebrows at Nathan's strident, but slightly slurred, retort.

"Ditto," Monica said, "but a messy scene doesn't square up with the prior two murders. Those scenes were neat and orderly, according to Detective Heinz."

"That's why he believed the victims knew their killer," Matt said.

"That isn't to say Ingrid Durbin didn't know her killer," Monica said. "She just didn't agree to being hanged."

"Touché," Matt said.

"What about the rope?" she asked. "Did the killer use an old rope he found in the barn?"

"No," Matt said. "Brand new white, nylon rope. Very pliant and smooth, easy to tie a noose with. The murder was obviously premeditated rather than opportunistic."

"As if the killer had scoped out the place and knew where he was going to hang her from."

"You mean, like he'd been there before?" Matt asked.

"Precisely," Monica said. "Makes me wonder if the killer bought the paint and rope at a local hardware store or brought them with him."

"Only a fool would buy it locally," Nathan said.

"Heinz told me the Iowa City detective checked nearby stores but didn't get any hits."

Monica sat up straighter in her chair. "We have a killer who's traveled to Minneapolis, Chicago and Iowa City, basically hitting the Midwest, bringing his own supplies along with him—spray paint, gun, garrote and rope—and has planned the method of murder well in advance. A gun can be used anywhere, and is a quick kill. A garrote can be used anywhere, but he would have to be quick and stealthy—good with his hands and strong. A rope for a noose, on the other hand, requires a rafter or the like. He would have to be familiar with the building. And if he was forcing her to get up on a chair, he would anticipate she might resist or scream, so he obviously had a gun with him. I think he knew her and had visited the farm previously."

"I think you're onto something," Matt said.

Monica frowned and propped her elbows on the counter, resting her chin in her hands. A vision of Geoffrey Gold and his tools flitted through her mind. "Any other evidence?"

"They picked up a decent set of shoe prints in the layer of dust covering the concrete floor of the barn."

"Oh really?" Monica asked. "Did they save the tread print?"

"Of course," Matt said, "but the chances of matching an old print to a suspect's shoes almost a year later is quite low."

"What was the shoe size?"

"Average for an adult male— about 10, give or take a half size," Matt said.

"At least that gives us something to go on," Monica said. "Did the victim live nearby, like in a farmhouse?"

"Yes. On the same property and alone," Matt said. "No sign of a fight in the house."

"If the killer met the victim in the house and forced her to go to the barn, then we're back to someone the victim knew and trusted."

"That's what they thought too." Matt sipped his whiskey.

"And you said she was murdered last July? In 2019?"

"Yes."

"Which makes me wonder if Ms. Ingrid Durbin had gender-affirming surgery by Dr. Kershaw in—"

"July 2017," Matt said.

Nathan looked at them in surprise. "Were the other two victims killed two years after their surgeries?"

"To the day," Matt said.

"Oh," Nathan said, dropping a fistful of peanuts in his mouth. "Didn't know that." He chewed on that information.

"We have a serial killer who's targeting Dr. Kershaw's patients, tracking them down at their home addresses in other states, and killing them on the second anniversary of their surgeries," Monica said.

"That's the pattern," Matt said, pouring himself more whiskey over the rocks, "and the next victim could be in four days."

"I need a whiteboard to create a map and timeline of the murders," Monica said to no one in particular.

"How do you know the killer could strike again in four days?" Nathan asked.

"That's the next second-year anniversary of a surgery," Monica said.

"You need to call her and warn her," Nathan said.

Matt raised his eyebrows at Monica in an *I-told-you-so* look.

"Give us a chance to catch the killer before we unduly alarm the patient," Monica said in a matter-of-fact tone.

"In four days?" Nathan scoffed. "What planet are you living on? Earth to Monica, cops spend years looking for serial killers. If I were you, I'd warn the patient now."

Matt's eyes bored holes into Monica.

She patted the air at both of them. "I get it. We have the same concern, but I really feel like the pieces are coming together in my mind. I'm seeing a pattern, and I feel like we're closer than we realize."

Nathan narrowed his eyes and shook his head imperceptibly. "The hospital is worried about this going public, isn't it?"

"Wouldn't you be?"

"They can't put their reputation ahead of patient safety," he said.

Monica rolled her eyes. "Oh, for God's sake. You know Al Bowman. He isn't heartless. We have plenty of time. Simmer down." She quickly changed the subject. "What did Ms. Durbin do for work?"

Matt shrugged. "Don't know. That will probably be in the file that Heinz is sending me."

"I just wonder if there's any connection among the victims with respect to their work lives," she said. "We have to analyze every angle."

"If memory serves," Matt said, "Heinz told us that Michelle Adler worked at a large company in Minneapolis—"

"Because she had good insurance," Monica finished.

"Maybe there's a common thread there," Matt said.

"Do you have any photos of the scene?" Monica asked.

"Can't wait to see those," Nathan blurted, then covered his mouth.

Matt gave him some disappointed side-eye. "Heinz told me he's sending everything as a packet. I'd like to talk to Dr. Kershaw again and show her the photos."

"We need to jump on this. Can you get out of officer training tomorrow—at least to talk to Nicole about this latest murder?"

"Yeah. I already cleared it with the chief. What does your schedule look like?" he asked.

She consulted her iPhone. "Let's do it first thing in the morning."

"If it works for Dr. Kershaw, I'm game," Matt said.

Monica typed a quick email to Nicole, requesting the meeting, then looked up at Matt. "If you get the chance to email me anything beforehand, I'd appreciate it."

"I'll ask Heinz." Matt knocked back the remainder of his whiskey. "We need to catch this bastard before he strikes again."

They looked at each other, thinking grave thoughts.

Once again, Geoffrey Gold's face popped into Monica's mind. She didn't like him, but all she had was her own mistrust, topped off by suspicion. Nothing more than conjecture. She had to dig for more information that would actually place Gold at the murder scenes. Cold, hard facts.

"So, if we're done discussing murders that we can't solve tonight," Nathan was saying, interrupting her thoughts, "may I text Shelby to join us?"

Monica winced. She didn't feel like jumping into relationship drama after learning about another murder. Her mind was busy at work, not at romance, and she wanted to review Heinz' file on the Iowa murder. "I don't think—"

"I'll take that as a yes," Nathan interrupted. "Let's see if she's available. If you don't want to stay, then at least allow her to drive you home where you two can talk in private."

"The way you've been pounding mojitos, I'm going to need a new ride anyway," she said in a teasing tone.

"True that, Ghost Rider," Nathan said, "I'm texting her."

Monica realized the alcohol was going straight to his head. "Fine. You win."

He picked up his phone from the counter, his fingers poised to type.

She watched him for a second then grabbed his forearm. "Wait. Maybe I should be the one to text her. I feel like we're triangulating the relationship, putting you in the middle."

He set his phone down. "You're right."

She texted Shelby, *Hey. Want to talk?*

"Should we make dinner plans?" Nathan asked.

Monica's ears perked up. She was much more interested in food than drinking.

Matt opened the fridge, scanning its contents. "We have leftovers from last night—"

"We aren't feeding our friends leftovers," Nathan said on a slur.

"Why not?" Matt said. "That shrimp scampi in tomato sauce over pasta was good."

"Yum. That does sound good," Monica said, following Matt's gaze to the plastic container in the fridge.

Nathan rolled his eyes. "I was thinking of ordering personal pizzas from Za 51."

"I'd definitely go in on pizza," Monica said. "About the time they deliver, I'll be starved."

Nathan quirked an eyebrow at her. "Didn't my guacamole on sourdough toast take the edge off?"

"I didn't eat lunch, and I ran more than six miles! I need more than guacamole-egg-toast."

For some reason, that struck him as funny. He smiled broadly and threw his arm around her shoulders, squeezing her tightly. "My partner, the runner."

Her phone vibrated loudly on the counter, so she picked it up and read Shelby's text. *Of course. When?*

Monica replied, *Now? I'm at Nathan and Matt's house.*

Bubbles appeared, dissipated, then reappeared. *You want to talk there? Is Nathan our counselor now* 😊

Monica permitted a small smile at Shelby's attempt at humor, although she wasn't ready to crack jokes. She texted, *No, but I don't have a car bc I stopped in while I was out for a run. If you want, the guys could drive me to my house, and we could meet there. I was going to ask Nathan but he's drinking mojitos like they're water.*

Shelby's reply was instantaneous. *No need. I'll drive over.*

Following her heart and not overanalyzing, Monica typed, *See you soon. We're ordering pizza.*

Shelby replied, *Oh good. Couples counseling over pizza. I'm in...*

Monica smiled again but didn't reply.

"Judging by the smile on your face," Nathan said, "Shelby is on her way."

"Indeed." Monica's palms suddenly felt sweaty. "I'm not sure it's such a good idea for us to meet here, though, with an audience and all."

"How about if we give you some privacy, then you and Shelby can join us for pizza?" Nathan asked. "You can have the lower level. There's a fireplace and sofa down there."

Monica shrugged. "I'd be willing to check it out."

"Come along," he said, practically skipping to the stairwell. "I'll turn on some mood lighting and start the gas fireplace to give it a cozy ambiance."

Matt watched them walk away. "I'm ordering four personal pizzas. I'll get a variety of toppings." He proceeded to punch in a phone number on his cell.

Monica gave him the thumbs up sign as she followed Nathan. "I don't think I've been down here before."

"I designed and decorated it," Nathan said, flicking on lights as she trailed behind him. "This will be the perfect romantic setting for your reconciliation. Neutral ground, so neither of you has the home field advantage."

"We're not playing the Super Bowl."

"Read Sun Tzu, young padawan. The location of the battleground is just as important as the battle."

"This isn't a battle, you moron."

As soon as they entered the lower level, Nathan threw open his arms in a welcoming gesture. The space was decorated in masculine hues with coffee-colored walls accented by white trim. Too finished to be a man cave, the essential elements were still there—a wet bar, a pool table, and a giant flat screen in front of a U-shaped sectional. She guessed that Matt happily watched football while Nathan perused home décor magazines.

She took the center of the room while Nathan pointed a remote at the gas fireplace in a corner. Blue and yellow flames instantaneously sprang to life. "I really feel like I nailed it with this room."

"It's well done, that's for sure." Monica's phone buzzed, interrupting her intent to compliment Nathan on his decorating acumen. An email from Al Bowman popped up that she quickly scanned. "Oh shit."

"What?" Nathan spun around. "Do not tell me that Shelby backed out."

"No. Nothing to do with Shelby."

"Whew," he sighed.

"Worse."

"Do tell."

"Al Bowman just asked for clemency on his monthly bill for legal services. He said they aren't making any money at the hospital, and he has to cover some other debt first."

Nathan's eyes grew wide. "What are you going to tell him?"

"What choice do I have?" she asked. "It wouldn't make any difference if I said 'no.' If he's out of money, he's out of money. Insisting he pay us, on the other hand, would tarnish our relationship. I have no choice but to give him a pass."

"How much does he owe the firm?"

"Last time I checked, about $25,000, and increasing at a meteoric rate with this murder file."

Nathan whistled long and slow, steadying himself by resting a hand on a barstool.

"I know. We won't be able to make payroll if our clients stop paying us," she said.

"I hope my insurance clients stay current with their bills." He suddenly looked pale.

"I have to tell Jim right away." She forwarded Al's email to Jim.

"Thank God Jim has run a firm before," Nathan said in a slurred voice. "I hate to go all apocalyptic on you," which he pronounced as *acopalyptic*, "but it feels like this pandemic is going to wreak havoc with our lives in more ways than one."

"That's an understatement."

"I need another mojito."

19

"I'd like to believe that COVID will sweep through the country in a few weeks, then disappear into thin air," Monica said, twirling her fingers, "but I don't think that's realistic."

"Only our whackadoo president believes that might happen." Nathan made a scoffing sound. "And we'll all be riding unicorns with butterflies on our shoulders, sliding down rainbows." Nathan's mojito slur deepened as he flapped his arms and slid along the sofa, ultimately landing on its arm.

She smirked, buoyed by his silliness. "I know, I know. It's so overwhelming that I just have to remain optimistic."

"If my first week of teleworking is any indication, I'll be staring into the deep abyss by the end of next week."

She covered her face with her hands and mumbled, "I need Shelby more than ever right now. Why did she have to hook up with Coco?"

"Darling, Shelby didn't hook up with Coco. She told me that Coco unexpectedly dropped by and started crying about closing her yoga studio. Total drama queen. Coco doesn't have any friends outside the studio, you know, so she imposed herself on Shelby." He scrunched his face. "Is 'imposed' the right word? I'm having trouble with word finding tonight. Imposition is what she was." He stared at Monica, not really seeing her, and muttered, "insinuate, impose, innuendo, imposter syndrome, inundate, inanimate, inarticulate," massacring every one of them. "All my favorite 'I' words."

Monica giggled as she lowered her hands from her face. "Shelby would tell you that version because she knows we're friends. She wouldn't confess infidelity to you—also an 'I' word, by the way."

He shook his head slowly, purposefully. "I can see why you'd think that, but I believe her, and I know her. She considers me a confidante too, you know."

"Fine," Monica said with pursed lips. "I'll give her the benefit of the doubt."

"Good girl. Come along." He shoved off from the sofa toward the staircase with a topsy-turvy gait, motioning for her to follow. "We can leave the fire on to warm the room. Let's go back upstairs to see what kind of pizzas Matt ordered."

She moped up the stairway a few steps behind him, half concerned he might stumble and fall. Despite the pitter-patter of her heart beating faster in anticipation of Shelby's arrival, Monica felt like a boulder was dangling from a crane above her head. The killer could strike in only four days, yet here she was, ironing out relationship issues and trying to make sense of a pandemic.

When they returned to the kitchen, Nathan returned to inhaling the remainder of his mojito while Matt described the flavors of the pizzas he ordered. The doorbell rang.

"Must be Shelby," Monica said, rubbing her hands down her thighs. "I'll go."

"Good luck," Nathan muttered into the tall glass, still at his lips.

Monica skipped to the door and opened it wide to a tousled Shelby, the new streaks of silver in her hair shimmering under the outdoor lamps. Her artsy spectacles framed her hazel eyes, now tinged with uncertain specks of gold.

Monica was again startled by the frames. Shelby looked *so different* in silver accents rather than lavender. Unfortunately, Monica had first seen the new frames when barging in on Shelby *consoling* Coco at her art studio, so she was afraid she would forever associate the silver accents with Coco-the-yogi-twat.

"Are you going to let me in?" Shelby asked in a soft voice.

"I'm sorry," Monica said, sweeping her arm to the side. "I was just studying your new silver strands and forgot my manners."

Shelby stepped inside, removing her paint-splattered hands from the pockets of her pewter-colored puffer jacket. Here they were, standing on the threshold of reconciliation, a stilted silence between them.

Monica wanted to smile, say something lovely and warm, then wrap her arms around Shelby, but something held her back. Her heart was still recovering from the art studio scene, and her ego was too bruised for her to make the first move. Or was she embarrassed at her own behavior? She couldn't pinpoint the exact barrier but it was palpable. She widened her stance and lowered her chin.

Shelby, probably possessing a higher EQ than Monica, immediately picked up on Monica's frosty features. Like a shelter dog cautiously approaching a new owner, she tentatively tugged on the hem of Monica's sweatshirt. "You look good in Nathan's sweatshirt. Better than he does."

"Thanks. I showered here after my run and Nathan loaned it to me. Don't tell him, but I might keep it. So soft on the inside." Monica wrapped her arms around herself.

Shelby angled her head, her expression softening. "Uh-huh. I love a rough exterior with a gooey inside."

Monica bristled at being accused of having a gooey inside, but Shelby's voice lacked any guile, so she let it slide. If Shelby wanted Monica back, she was going to have to come up with something more than comfy platitudes. Monica wanted a full-blown apology with an explanation that covered everything from Coco's intentions to Shelby's feelings, past and present. Nothing short of Shelby laying her soul bare was going to patch her gaping wound.

Shelby gazed past Monica to the lower level, where the lights were on, then to the upstairs, where Nathan's and Matt's voices carried.

Monica followed her eyes. "Umm. Nathan and Matt are in the kitchen. We just ordered pizzas. Do you want to say hi to them before we talk?"

"Probably, but I'll do whatever makes you comfortable. Just tell me what you want me to do."

Monica stiffened. "Are you patronizing me?"

Shelby rocked back on her heels like Monica had thrown cold water in her face. "No...ah...I'm...sorry. So sorry. I want everything to get back to normal. You're torturing me." She held up a hand, reaching for Monica's arm, but thought better of touching her. "Not you, personally. What I really meant to say is that being apart is killing me...I'd do anything to fix this. I love you, Mon. Only you."

The vibe was all wrong. Monica was pissed, unable to move from her spot. Reunions shouldn't be this easy. Shelby shouldn't be able to say a few words to smooth over her version, which apparently involved some misunderstanding on Monica's part. Monica, for one, was not mistaken. She had seen them together. Shelby's arm across Coco's shoulders. Shelby's compassionate eyes, supposedly meant for only Monica, washing over Coco. The vision made her chest heave with anger. She felt as hot as she had when she had confronted them. Raw jealousy. Betrayal. Revenge.

No. Their breakup was on Shelby. Shelby was required to lay it all out there, but now she was shifting the focus to Monica, as if Monica held the cards, and Shelby were some innocent bystander to Monica's ill-conceived perceptions. A crazy misunderstanding, that's all. Bullshit. *This is bullshit!*

"Listen, Shelby, this isn't about me. It's about you and your bombshell ex. I walked in on you and Coco, you with your arm across her shoulders, hugging her. The way you were looking at her...like you've looked at me when we're in sync.

Understanding and connection. I know that look." Monica couldn't even describe how brokenhearted she was.

Shelby shook her head in disbelief, but before she could speak, Monica broke in.

"Don't try to deny it, damn it!" Monica exclaimed, her voice rising. "Don't try to twist this into some little misunderstanding, a *not-what-it-looks-like* situation. I know you well enough to know that you were into her. Into the moment. Into her emotions. You were a fucking couple." Her voice hitched, and she unexpectedly started to cry in sputtering little bursts that couldn't be disguised as hiccups.

Shelby took a step closer and lay her hand on Monica's arm, but Monica jerked her arm up, throwing Shelby's hand off.

Shelby's quirky eyebrows shot up, and her eyes widened. She opened her mouth to say something, closed it, then opened it again. "I'm so sorry. There's no connection between Coco and me. There's nothing. She wasn't there for that. She was just scared and wanted to talk to someone. That's all."

Monica looked at Shelby through a thick film of tears, her vision blurry and her ego too attached to her perception to recant. "Don't try to smooth it over. She was there to see if there was a spark before she committed to her doctor. One last chance with Shelby. And, if you ask me, you looked ready and willing to leap."

Shelby's square jaw hit the floor. "Not the case, Mon. Not even close. Coco knows we're engaged. What was I supposed to do? Slam the door in her face?"

"Yes!" Monica blurted without thinking, her voice rising to a new level of volume and pitch. "If what you're saying is true, then yes. For starters, we're in a pandemic. You could've told her it wasn't safe to meet. In addition...even if you wouldn't say that...you told me that she broke your heart. You couldn't even talk about it without becoming unglued, for God's sake. Now you expect me to believe you were this rational counselor to her about her fucking yoga studio closing? Please. How naïve do you think I am? You were comforting her the way lovers do. It was more than a mere discussion and you know it. I saw it with my own eyes."

Shelby stared, dumbstruck.

"Fuck it!" Monica yelled. "This isn't going to work. I don't have anything more to say to you. I thought I was ready to talk, but talking about it is making me angrier because I know what the problem is." Her lower lip trembled.

"What's that?" Shelby yelled back, her own voice almost matching Monica's volume now.

"The real problem," Monica said, going in for the kill now, her voice thick with guttural rage, "is that you take me for granted. You have since the beginning. I pursued you, so you think you're the big fish in our relationship." Drifting toward mockery, she said, "'Shelby, what a catch for Monica. Monica, marrying up.' Well, not anymore. If you think you're some fucking hot diva, then go out there and sleep with all your gushing fans because I'm not one of them!"

There. She had gone and done it now—laid her insecurities bare and bludgeoned Shelby with them. Monica wanted Shelby to feel as hurt as she had felt when she had busted Shelby with her arm around Coco. And, by the look on Shelby's face, Monica had succeeded.

A speechless and pale Shelby stood before her, shellacked by Monica's tirade. When she spoke, her voice was small and frail. "If that's the way you feel..." She turned to the door, her hand on the knob, coughed a sob, hunched her shoulders, then opened the door and slipped out, haphazardly pulling the door shut behind her.

Monica heard Shelby break down on the other side of the door, her sweet, feminine voice producing tortured sounds of wailing that faded as she made her way down the sidewalk to her Jeep. Monica watched through the sidelights as Shelby got in her Jeep and sat staring at the steering wheel for a long moment, crying. After a time, she wiped her face with her hands, turned on the engine, and drove off.

Monica felt empty inside. Ruthless and cruel, none the better for having verbalized her worst fears. Shame crept in where the anger had resided. *I was right, wasn't I? She's always viewed herself as better than me, right? Her ego is the problem, right?*

Monica slowly made her way back to the kitchen, embarrassed beyond belief that Nathan and Matt had no doubt heard every single word. Heat flushed her neck and face. Even the tips of her ears burned in shame.

When she looked at their faces, they reflected what she felt. Surprise. Shock that the *clearing-the-air* talk had taken a turn to the dark side. Darth Monica had fought, and destroyed, Shelby. She wanted to curl up in the Sith Lord's black robe and die. "I'm sorry you had to hear that. I lost control and said a bunch of stuff I shouldn't have said."

"Been there," Matt said before sipping his whiskey.

Nathan cleared his throat. "You don't really believe that you're second fiddle in that relationship, do you? Because I don't think anyone looks at you that way."

Monica shrugged; all of her fight gone. She had unloaded her vile baggage and now had an emotional hangover.

"Monica, you're a catch too." Nathan advanced on her and pulled her into a hug. "Don't let a lack of self-confidence from your youth color what you witnessed at Shelby's house."

She cried onto his tightly woven cotton sweater.

"There, there," he said, smoothing the back of her head. "Let it all out. Maybe some food will help."

She shook her head. "No food. Can you guys just drive me home?"

20

Monica awoke the next morning to sore hamstrings and a chainsaw buzzing through her head. *Maybe going for a spontaneous six-mile run wasn't such a good idea.* Her mood soured as she recalled the spiteful conversation with Shelby. *Maybe telling off the only woman I've ever loved was a worse idea.*

At the kitchen sink, she downed two glasses of water before making a small pot of coffee. While it brewed, she imitated Shelby's stretching moves, resting her hand on the counter and stretching one leg behind her, then the other.

All the while, her mind replayed the scene at Nathan's house where she had showered Shelby with vitriol that she didn't even know she harbored, much less was capable of spewing forth to her lover. Jealousy had brought out a nasty side of her that she didn't know existed. She squeezed her temples as she realized she had actually baited Shelby into a verbal trap, putting words in her mouth, then accusing her of acting on them. *Maybe I overreacted. Maybe I'm insecure and too possessive of her. Maybe I should apologize.*

The shocked hurt in Shelby's eyes had chased Monica through her dreams all night. She had barely slept a wink and now was paying the price for stupidity and cruelty. She was reminded of Eric Clapton singing, *They call it stormy Monday, but Tuesday's just as bad. Lord, and Wednesday's worse, and Thursday's awful sad.* Clapton's 12-minute lament of the classic song was shaping up as Monica's anthem for the week.

Pandemic. Murder. Girlfriend problems. *What day is it, anyway?*

The bottom line was that she faced a full day of work, so she needed coffee and a clear mind to catch a killer. Only three days until the next potential strike. She and Matt had a morning field trip to the blue-bottomed chicken ranch, oddly dubbed Aqua Vulva, owned by Nicole and Geoffrey, unlikely characters living lakeside in the deep woods.

Monica flipped open her laptop when she was settled on the sofa in front of a muted CNN, glancing between the unfolding disaster on the TV and emails from Al Bowman about adding out-of-state physicians to the medical staff, so he could staff an ICU of expected COVID patients. The mass of patients hadn't arrived yet, but he was preparing as if all the citizens of Apple Grove would come gasping into the ER at any second.

The death toll in New York rose as people fled the city for relatives' homes in other states, thereby further spreading the virus. Meanwhile, Trump had convened a task force that he didn't listen to while he threatened to withhold aid from New York and other blue states if they didn't support his crazed political agenda. *Our president is a totalitarian ass.*

She turned off CNN and glanced at her phone. No texts or calls from Shelby. *Should I go over to her house? No. I'm not going to grovel. If she wants me, she has to make the first move. Yes, I went too far...that's true. But, dammit, I was enraged and rightly so.*

Shoving aside regret, she pumped herself full of caffeine and set off for Aqua Vulva.

An overcast day met her while she drove north, the leaden color of the low cloud cover complementing the same hues of the remaining snow piled along the road. A monochromatic landscape void of any green. The perfect backdrop for a discussion about serial murders.

She waved to the critter cams as she wound her pickup truck through the twisting driveway. *Take that, Geoffrey. I'm onto you.*

She opened her car door to hens clucking and the rooster cock-a-doodle-dooing. The flock hopped in an amoeboid shape across the driveway and within a few feet of her, but always out of reach. They struck a balance between looking for a handout versus scattering in fear. She easily counted nine colorful and fluffy chickens as she made her way down the shabby walkway.

A few *rat-a-tat-tats* on the fried front door, and it swung open to Geoffrey. Greasy Geoffrey. Those dark eyes assessed Monica, and the edge of his lip curled up. While performing a creepy half-bow, he said, "Counselor."

God, I hate this place. "Geoffrey."

"Another dance with law enforcement this morning?"

Only a sociopath would consider this a dance. "Will you be joining us? I'd like to introduce you to my friend, Detective Matt Breuer."

Her invitation wiped the cocksure smile off his face. "No. I'll be in the barn."

"I just saw your flock, and they look fine. I think it would be helpful if you joined our discussion."

"Nicole insists she can't concentrate when I'm around."

Yeah right. Monica toed off her boots and followed Geoffrey down the hall. Piano music issued forth from the study on their left, interrupting their progress. Monica lingered in the doorway, listening to the twangy tones produced by the old upright. Geoffrey proceeded toward the kitchen.

As soon as Nicole picked up Monica in her peripheral vision, she said, "Monica, please come in." She continued playing lightly, her fingers effortlessly floating over the keyboard. "I can't believe this. Three. I'm a wreck. Playing helps calm my tattered nerves."

Monica recognized a jazzy version of the Beatles' *Blackbird.* "You have a nice touch."

Nicole smiled through a pained expression, and her fingers abruptly stopped gliding, instead landing on one key, which she jabbed with her index finger while staring at Monica. The key was silent.

Monica raised an eyebrow.

"Dead fucking key," Nicole snarled. "It has to be the D above middle C, a white key that I need for every song." Her right hand floated up the keyboard to the higher-pitched keys. "It couldn't be one of these that I hardly ever use." She struck them for emphasis. "It has to be this one." She moved her index finger back to the D and pounded, producing only a dull thud from the hammer mechanism somewhere in the belly of the wooden box.

"I'm sorry," Monica said.

Nicole waved her hand and turned to face Monica. "Not your fault. I'm waiting for Geoffrey to fix it. He said he ordered the piano wire from Amazon, but it's been several days. So much for Amazon Prime delivery."

"I think everyone is experiencing delays due to COVID," Monica said. "Sounds like Geoffrey can do everything. I've heard that fixing a piano can be tricky."

"Jack of all trades," Nicole said in a honeyed contralto.

Monica nodded politely. *Or Jack the Ripper? Piano wire is sharp...could be used as a garrote...*

Nicole stood and moved toward the arched doorway, pulling Monica back to her. "Please excuse my appearance."

Indeed, Nicole looked as bad as Monica felt. Her eyes had a crazed sheen, no doubt from lack of sleep, and she hadn't bothered to put any concealer over the dark circles under them. Nicole's hair looked like a dry-shampooed egret's nest. She wore the same jeans as Monica had seen her in a few days ago, but she had on a snappy zip-up long sleeve top that accentuated her firm arms and trim waist.

They entered the kitchen, the familiar oak table holding Nicole's open laptop and growing stacks of papers. As Monica moved to the table to set her coat on a chair, she was surprised to see Geoffrey's lower half lying on the floor, waist deep in the cupboard under the kitchen sink. Unfortunately, his hairy, muffin-topped belly was on full display.

"Geoffrey!" Nicole barked. "What the fuck?"

"I'm tightening the faucet handles," his muffled voice said from under the counter.

"Now?" Nicole asked. "The detective is coming any minute!"

"Do you want it fixed or not?"

Her rainbow Crocs started kicking at his legs. "Not now, you dunce. Get. Out. Of. Here."

Monica thought Nicole was being a bit harsh, but maybe that was the warp and woof of their attraction—Geoffrey being annoying and Nicole getting physical.

"Ouch!" he yelled from under the sink. "That hurts!"

"It's supposed to," Nicole hollered back, "Come... out...of...there." She spoke between toe kicks, landing a few more for good measure. Shaking her head vigorously, she mouthed at Monica, "I'm sorry."

"As far as I'm concerned," Monica said, "Geoffrey is welcome to stay." She desperately wanted Matt to meet Geoffrey to confirm her impressions, meaning 10 out of 10 on the suspect scale. Speaking of 10, Monica studied Geoffrey's feet, clad in Smartwool socks, and thought they could pass for size 10, which Matt had said was the size of the tread print at Ingrid Durbin's murder scene in Iowa. A jolt ran up her spine, setting tiny hairs on fire.

Geoffrey slithered his love handles out of the cupboard and sat up in the center of the kitchen, a wrench in his hairy paw. "Jesus fuck, Nicole. You hurt me." He theatrically rubbed his shins, but Monica wasn't buying his act.

Neither was Nicole. "Don't be such a wimp." Nicole moved to his backside and placed her hands under his armpits. "Up and out to the barn. You don't get on well with police, and we both know it. There's no need to add gasoline to this fire."

Nicole was stronger than she looked, hoisting up Geoffrey in one lithe movement. He was just as surprised as Monica, his bedhead standing on end, his lumpy body finding itself in an upright position. He winked at Monica, a gesture she found profoundly troubling.

"Guess it's out to the barn for me," he said. "Can I at least get a cup of coffee before I go?"

"Fine," Nicole said through clenched teeth. She busied herself pouring Geoffrey a coffee while he adjusted his pants and replaced the cleaning supplies in the cupboard.

Monica lowered her head to her iPhone and noticed she had only one bar of reception. "What's your Wi-Fi password? I have only one bar."

"Flamingo2018," Nicole said from the coffee pot.

"Thanks." Monica navigated to her settings and thumbed in the password. She immediately gained a strong Wi-Fi signal. Now that she had their password for Wi-Fi, she wondered if they used it for other apps.

Her mind switched gears to the critter cams in the yard. From her parents' lake place, Monica knew there was a Moultrie critter camera mobile app that would send photos to the user's phone. She decided to strike while the iron was hot, so, lacking any guilt whatsoever, she found and clicked on the Moultrie app to download it. While the app was installing, she set her phone face-first on the table.

A loud thumping at the front door shook her from her clandestine activity. "I'll get it." Monica trotted down the long hallway and threw open the door. Barely allowing Matt time to enter, she grabbed his gloved hand and tugged on him to follow her.

"My shoes—"

"Kick 'em off on your way," she whispered, hustling him along.

He hippity-hopped, untying shoelaces, as they moved down the hallway. "What the—"

"Shush," she whispered, then swiftly transitioned to a casual stride as they entered the kitchen.

As she had hoped, Geoffrey was poised by the sink, shifting his weight from one foot to the other, as he watched Nicole pour cream into his Thermos of coffee.

"Hey guys, Detective Breuer is here," Monica said.

"Greaaaat," Nicole muttered under her breath while replacing the carafe.

Geoffrey spun around to face Matt and Monica. Monica knew him well enough to recognize his immediate discomfort. He looked like a teenager hiding booze and weed in his pockets.

"Detective," Geoffrey said, extending his hairy paw for a shake.

Matt, still unsure what all the fuss was about, gave Geoffrey a healthy shake. "Nice to meet you."

"Geoffrey was on his way out to the barn with his coffee," Nicole said, bumping him with her body to move him along. Nicole turned to Matt. "Can I pour you a cup?"

"Um. Sure. Thanks. Black is fine."

As Geoffrey tried to scoot by Monica, she said, "Feel free to join if you like."

Confused, Matt watched Monica and Geoffrey.

"Too cold for the silkies today," Geoffrey mumbled as he awkwardly stepped around Monica. "Have to get them into the coop and feed them. Maybe when I'm done with chores."

Monica's eyes pierced Matt's double row of long lashes to signal him. True fact. He had two rows of lashes. What Monica wouldn't give for that. *Why do men get all the aesthetic miracles?*

21

"Please, have a seat," Nicole said, as she motioned to the empty chairs at the old table.

Matt turned to Nicole and addressed the topic *du jour*. "I assume that Monica informed you why we're meeting today."

"She said you discovered another murder." Nicole's eyes pinged between Matt and Monica.

"Well, I didn't discover it, but an Iowa City detective contacted Detective Heinz, who you met—"

"The other day," Nicole finished for him. "Do you have photos and details?"

And the impatient side of the surgeon swiftly emerges, Monica thought. She wished Matt had asked some questions about Geoffrey first, but she couldn't prompt that line of questioning without coming across as a traitor to Nicole. So she sat on her hands, literally, waiting to see if Matt would spike the ball she had served to him.

He opened a plastic folder and spread out four photos of Ingrid Durbin. Two photos depicted Ms. Durbin hanging from the white noose, and two had been taken after she had been lowered to a black body bag on the dusty concrete floor.

Monica sucked in a breath at the grotesque photos. *Don't puke. Don't puke. Don't puke.* Matt hadn't emailed anything to her beforehand, so she was seeing them for the first time and was again startled and appalled by the evil depredations of this series of murders. A live, vibrant human being was now reduced to pale blue skin covering a sack of cold muscle, a sagging skeleton, and a sunken face with hollow eyes that remained open but vacuous. To top it off, the disfiguring red graffiti was front and center.

The killer had spray-painted the signature penis and scrotum across Ingrid's torso, but his depiction appeared more detailed than it had been on Adler and Remington. Instead of a crude rendering, the penis was erect and had the tell-tale ring of a circumcision. It was grotesquely large, going all the way to her left nipple. In place of the red blasts of testes on Adler and Remington, the scrotal sacs on Ingrid appeared to be ribbed by several horizontal lines, some of which had dripped. Resembling blood, the rivulets of paint ran down to Ingrid's clean-shaven bottom. If there were an award for ghoulish genitalia, the killer had won the gold medal.

Durbin's diaphanous, hairless skin along her narrow hips and skinny legs accentuated the crimson, almost purplish shade of spray paint. Maybe the blue undertone of death nudged an otherwise lipstick red to a darker hue, but Monica thought this red was a different shade than what the killer had used on either Adler or Remington. Not fire engine red, but deeper and more layered, like an alizarin crimson. Signature red. Serial killer red. Graffiti red.

"That's a statement if I've ever seen one," Matt said into the sad silence. "It's almost as if the killer used a stencil on this victim, unlike the crude spray jobs on the other two."

Monica looked at the photos with a keener eye. "I think you're right. The outer edges of the penis and scrotum are too well-defined to be done freehand."

"To say nothing of the attempted likeness to a scrotal sac," Nicole hissed, as she picked up each photo, studying it closely. Tears immediately formed in her eyes, quickly spilling down her face, free of any makeup. "I recognize her. A gentle spirit and a kind young woman."

"She was your patient then?" Matt asked.

"Yes," Nicole said on a throaty gulp.

"I'm so sorry," Monica said, then waited a respectful silence before asking, "Do you remember Ms. Durbin, specifically?"

"Oh yes. Ingrid. She stands out for me because, like myself, she had an old soul. Soft spoken, she came across as wise beyond her years. We were kindred spirits." Her lips curled down, and she continued in a raspy tenor, "I can tell by my surgical technique, and the design of her introitus and labia, that she was one of my earlier cases." Unchecked tears running down her face, Nicole turned to her laptop. "Let me look her up. Do you have a date of birth, Detective Breuer?"

"Yes." He removed a sheet from his folder. "February 6, 1994."

They watched as Nicole pecked at her laptop keyboard. "Hmm. Yes. Here she is. She was 23 years old when she had her surgery on July 23, 2017."

Matt wrote down the date, then flipped over one of the photos, and read out loud, "Date of death was estimated to be July 23, 2019."

"Why the estimate?" Monica asked.

"She was found by a friend in the late afternoon on July 24th, so the coroner estimated that she had been dead between 12 and 24 hours."

Nicole glanced from the screen to the photos on the table, studying them. "Looks like it from these photos. Nevertheless, two years from the date of surgery. Just like the other two victims."

"Three makes a pattern," Monica said.

"A pattern that smacks of insider knowledge," Matt said, steadying his gaze on Nicole.

Monica visualized Geoffrey sitting at this very table after Nicole had left for work, accessing her laptop and trolling through her list of surgeries, or worse, through the medical records of trans gender patients. Monica wanted to plunge into an interrogation of Nicole about Geoffrey, but she couldn't, at least not in front of Matt. Obeying her ethical duty to her client,

Monica instead chewed the inside of her cheek, waiting. That seemed to be all she was doing during this investigation—waiting. She needed something to go on and she needed it now!

Matt seemed to intuit Monica's discontent, glancing in a triangular fashion from her troubled eyes to her hands, again tucked under her thighs, then back to the photos. He turned to Nicole, waited a few minutes while she reviewed the electronic medical record, then asked, "What can you tell me about Ingrid Durbin?"

Nicole's eyes swiveled from the screen to give him her full attention. "From what I recall, she came with her twin sister to the appointments. Both were very pleasant and soft-spoken. Ingrid had attended a few years of community college, but was struggling with her identity—gender dysphoria—and wanted to explore surgical options. She had already been in therapy for a year and living true to her identity. She and her sister listened attentively and participated in the discussion about the irreversible nature of the surgery and the importance of aftercare, including a commitment to dilation."

"Dilation?" Matt asked.

"Of the neovaginal canal," Nicole said, "so it remains open, and retains its depth and pliancy."

Matt digested that information, then said, "Please, go on."

"She was an easy surgery. I was only a year or so into my practice, so I was still mastering my design and technique, but I think we got a good result for her." She clicked on the photos in the medical record—displayed on her laptop—and turned the screen to Matt and Monica. Before them lay a living Ingrid on an exam table, her knees pushed wide for a spread-eagle shot of her bottom, only a few weeks post-surgery.

Nicole pointed to Ingrid's vulva, the harsh, freshly transplanted labial folds with stitches in curved lines. She spoke in clinical terms about the result. "Here, the introitus is a bit too anterior to the clitoris, making for a little bit of an angle to access the neovagina, but she later reported that it was very functional, and she enjoyed penetrative sex with her lover."

Matt briefly looked at the surgical photos. "Did you ever meet her lover?"

Nicole turned the laptop back to herself, and, attempting to access her memory, stared at the screen while she clicked through more photos, studying her work. "No. I don't believe he ever made the trip to Apple Grove for an appointment."

"Did you document his name?" Matt asked.

"I'm afraid not."

"Is there anything you recall about Ms. Durbin, or her sister, that would provide a clue as to who murdered her?"

Nicole knit her blonde eyebrows together, a single line between them deepening into a worry chasm. "I've been obsessing over that with respect to all the victims since I learned about them. The answer is 'no.' If I had thought of something, I would have called you right away. Have you spoken to Ingrid's sister yet?"

"I just received the Iowa City file this morning," Matt said. "I don't plan to duplicate all of their field work. Detective Heinz, who is the lead investigator, simply asked me to interview you and your staff. You've been helpful, as per usual."

"Well, I hope someone plans to duplicate the initial detective's work in Iowa City, because he obviously failed to catch the killer." Nicole raised her chin in challenge. "In medicine, we value redundancy, because it helps us pick up signs and symptoms that someone else may have overlooked."

Matt straightened as he slid the photos back into the folder. "I'm sure Detective Heinz will take the appropriate steps in his new investigation."

Nicole hummed in consideration. "You seem capable. Why don't you make a few phone calls and ask the questions that apparently weren't asked by Sheriff Rosco from the *Dukes of Hazzard* in Iowa?"

Matt remained impassively professional, apparently not willing to comment on the Iowa detective's performance in front of Nicole. "I'll think about it. By the way, who is the gentleman I met when I entered your kitchen today?"

Daily jackpot! Monica thought, finally removing her hands from under her thighs. While keeping one ear open for Nicole's answer, Monica made a note to herself to call Ingrid Durbin's twin sister, regardless of whether Matt planned to. She planned to get the name from Nicole after Matt left.

Nicole narrowed her eyes. "That was Geoffrey, my partner."

"Physician partner?" Matt asked.

"Romantic partner. He lives here with me."

"Last name?"

"Gold."

"Date of birth?"

"Why?"

"Just doing my job."

"I think not, Detective Breuer. Viewing him as a potential suspect is…not only low…but also lazy. I'm not surprised you guys haven't caught the killer if you're planning to investigate a guy like Geoffrey." Nicole shot out of her chair to her feet. "I think it's time for us to conclude our meeting."

Monica was shocked by the change in temperature. If Nicole was trying to deflect attention away from Geoffrey, she had just accomplished the exact opposite by her indignant behavior. Matt would latch onto Geoffrey like a terrier onto a squirrel.

"Suits me," Matt said. "I'm missing some mandatory training right now, so if we're done here, I'll be on my way." He gathered up his belongings, and with deliberate patience and disappointment, pushed back his chair and stood, now nose-to-nose with Nicole. "I'll note in my report to Detective Heinz that you stopped cooperating at the exact point when I asked for Geoffrey Gold's date of birth."

Monica rose too. "Just a minute, Matt. The doctor has answered every single question about the victims, expressing grief and remorse. The fact that you started quizzing her about her boyfriend is a little offensive, to say the least, and irrelevant to the investigation."

He turned to Monica, as she expected he would. "Everything, and everyone, is relevant until we say they aren't."

Having fulfilled her duty to Nicole, Monica shrugged off the fight since she was 100% in support of Matt investigating Geoffrey. "Suit yourself. I'll walk you to the door."

Matt nodded curtly at Nicole. "Thanks for your time."

Nicole didn't respond or extend her hand.

Monica and Matt quickly retraced their steps down the hallway toward the front door, Matt collecting his shoes on the way. He handed her his plastic folder while he pulled on his shoes and tied his shoelaces. Neither spoke, but when he straightened up, he winked.

She made the phone motion with her thumb and pinky, then said, "Good day, Detective."

He said, "Goodbye" loud enough for Nicole to hear from the kitchen. Monica opened the door for him and patted him on the shoulder as he left.

She returned to the kitchen, where Nicole was slamming dishes into the top rack of the dishwasher. Rather than interrupt, Monica picked up her phone from the table and saw that the Moultrie critter cam app was now fully downloaded. She opened it and, when prompted, entered Nicole's email address, then the same password she had used for their Wi-Fi—Flamingo2018. The app opened. She was now a happy recipient of photos from Geoffrey's critter cams. *We'll see who comes and goes from Aqua Vulva.* She quickly closed the app so Nicole wouldn't notice.

"Why the fuck did Breuer ask about Geoffrey?" Nicole asked.

"Why do we care?" Monica said.

Nicole spun around and rested a hand on her hip. "As I told you, Geoffrey has a checkered past, and I don't want them going off on a wild goose chase investigating him. It might embarrass my standing at the hospital and in the community." She sighed. "We already get enough grief. I don't need more rumor and innuendo."

Monica regarded Nicole, wondering if there was more to it than a colorful background. "This is the last time I'm going to tell you this, but I need you to be straight with me or I can't represent you. If you know something about Geoffrey, you need to tell me."

Nicole flopped into the chair across from Monica, her right knee bouncing up and down, her elbows on the table. "I decided against being straight two decades ago, dear." She smiled at her own joke, then said, "Geoffrey told me he has a criminal record in Florida and New Jersey."

"For what?"

"Petty stuff. Nothing like assault or harm against anyone, but he's afraid the detectives will go apeshit over his criminal records and," she pointed her thumb toward the departed Matt, "you know, consider him a suspect and investigate, then maybe stumble onto his hidden cash. Report him to the IRS. Who knows?"

"Okay. I get that, but the best way to deal with Geoffrey's criminal record is to put it out there, not hide it. You just piqued Matt's interest by getting defensive and clamming up." Monica placed her hand on Nicole's forearm. "Here's my advice. Geoffrey needs his own lawyer. I can't be his lawyer because I work for the hospital, which pays me to represent you. Geoffrey isn't my client. You are, but he needs legal advice."

Nicole rubbed her hands over her face. "I'll talk to him but I seriously doubt he needs a lawyer unless Detective Matt decides to question him."

Monica removed her hand. "Is there anything else I should know?"

"I love him," Nicole said.

When Monica didn't respond, Nicole continued. "He's a good person, he really is. I was going through some insecurities when we met back in 2018." She gestured to herself. "I'm not the youngest woman in a bar, and I just wasn't meeting anyone who I could consider a long-term partner, especially men who would be good with my transition."

Monica nodded.

Nicole raised her hand and made a sweeping gesture. "The men who live and work around here are pretty old-fashioned about how they like their women. When Geoffrey met me and told me I was beautiful—both inside and out—for the first time, I wanted to melt into a puddle of tears. He really cares about me and loves me, you know? I just don't want any hassle for him as the police investigate this."

Monica wasn't convinced that Geoffrey was totally innocent, but she also trusted Nicole's judge of character. "Okay."

"That's the only reason I'm protecting him."

The dining room clock ticked for a few seconds before Monica asked, "I do have an unrelated follow-up question for you. Did you document the name of Ms. Durbin's sister?"

Nicole's facial expression relaxed when the topic switched to patient care. "I think so." She turned to her laptop and typed a few keystrokes.

Monica watched and waited while Nicole read some notes.

"Yes. Here it is. Isobel. Isobel Durbin. I thought it was cute that Ingrid chose a female name like her sister's. Ingrid's previous name had been Luke."

Monica jotted that down. "Very good. That's all I need, so I'm going to be on my way." She rose and gathered her attaché case, stuffing her pen and notepad inside.

Nicole walked Monica to the door. "If I haven't said so yet, I really appreciate everything you're doing for me. I get that I can be a difficult client, but I'm really grateful for your advice."

Monica warmed to the expression of gratitude. "My pleasure. And trust me, you're not a difficult client. Not even close. Let's keep our eye on the ball—cracking this case. I'll find this killer if it's the last thing I do."

Nicole cocked her head. "It just might be. There are only three days until the next anniversary, you know, so I plan to warn Carissa tomorrow, okay?"

"I'm sure we'll be talking between now and then."

When Monica left, she looked directly at the critter cam along the walking path, hoping it would capture her photo so she could see it populate later on her own phone. As she slid into her pickup truck, a *cock-a-doodle-doo* from a rooster wished her farewell.

22

The overcast sky was quickly breaking up, giving way to patches of blue as Monica drove south on Highway 53.

Her mind raced about her current state of affairs. *Will Detective Heinz solve these serial murders on his own? Will this pandemic end before summer arrives? Did I break up with Shelby?*

She pictured the next season of their lives—after this case was over—living outdoors in the summer. This time of year, she usually hauled her outdoor furniture from the garage to the deck, hosed it down and added the chair pads and umbrella. She longed for the easy summer living of reading, grilling burgers, and eating outside under the canopy of trees in her back yard. She had taken Shelby's company for granted, but now, as she envisioned herself doing those activities alone, her heart toppled over a cliff. *Are we really over?*

Her phone rang, jolting her from her lovesick thoughts and a churning stomach. She hit the speaker button. "Hello?"

"Hey, Mon. It's Matt. I only have a few minutes before I join the training session."

"Oh. Hi."

"You sound disappointed. I thought you wanted me to call you?"

"I just thought you were someone else."

"You and Shelby still scrapping?"

"More than scrapping. I have a feeling I pushed her away for good by shooting off my mouth last night."

He whistled softly. "I admit that your bad self probably offended her, but I know she loves you, so, never fear, she'll come around."

"I hope you're right."

"If you want her back, just apologize."

"It's not that easy."

"I do it all the time. Just say, 'I'm sorry,' then hug her. I mean, *really* hug her." He paused a second, then added in a gravelly tone, "Makeup sex is the best."

"Jeez, Matt. I don't want to picture you and Nathan having sex."

He chortled devilishly.

"What are you calling about, anyway?" she asked.

"You gave me the eye and made the phone sign as I was leaving Dr. Snotty's house. I got the impression you wanted to talk about her partner, Geoffrey Gold."

"I did, didn't I?" She retooled her anxious mind to refocus on the puzzling Geoffrey. "He gives me the creeps."

"You say that about everyone. I didn't get a bad vibe when I shook his hand."

"I've spent more time with him, and I can tell you that I don't like him. He's sleazy. He used to be a club owner in Miami, and it shows."

"Strip club?"

"Dance club. The Flaming Flamingo."

"Monumental leap to a serial killer."

"Think about it. Geoffrey would have access to the medical records through Nicole's home laptop."

"Opportunity doesn't mean he actually snooped."

"He has a criminal record in Florida and New Jersey."

"Getting warmer," he said. "I'll look him up when we're done with training today. Anything else?"

"Can't you get someone else to look him up while you're doing karate on mannequins?"

He sighed, so Monica continued, "Geoffrey is handy with wire."

Matt choked on a drink of something, then coughed. "What are you talking about?"

"The garrote that was used to kill Veronica Remington in Chicago. Geoffrey obviously uses wire for chicken coop repairs and this morning, Nicole told me that he knows how to fix a piano. He just ordered some piano wire, which is very sharp, you know."

Matt laughed mockingly. "Those are all circumstantial bits of information that don't add up to a motive, means or opportunity. We have to place him at the scenes of the murders, preferably with a motive."

"Admittedly, I don't see a motive either, but Geoffrey and the victims are all connected to Nicole, and the scenes are all a one-day drive from Apple Grove."

"But these are hate crimes. Why would he hate trans women when he's living with one?"

"I don't know," she said. "A serial killer's mind works in mysterious ways."

"Well, yours certainly does. I'll check him out, but I'm not too excited about Geoffrey as a suspect."

"Okay. You're the detective," she said a little too sarcastically. Since he had so readily shot down her suspicions, she was hesitant to tell him that she was considering calling Isobel Durbin.

"I'll do the detecting and you do the lawyering, okay?" he said.

Game on. "Sometimes they're intertwined, and need I remind you that the clock is ticking."

"Only your clock is ticking," he said. "You should warn the next patient to get this stupid deadline off your shoulders. Proper police work takes time, Mon."

"Would you at least email me the Iowa file so I can work on this while you're in training?"

"I can't. The deputy chief says it's an on-going investigation, so I can't share anything until it's concluded."

"That's bullshit and you know it."

"Rules are rules, Monica. You aren't the District Attorney. Dominique is."

"No. I'm just the person who can help you solve these murders."

"You don't have the right to bust my balls," he said, a hint of irritation surfacing. "You want info so you can protect your clients—the hospital and Nicole. The government is not your client."

"Representing my clients isn't mutually exclusive to finding the killer. I think our goals are aligned."

"Sorry. Still can't release the file."

She grumbled unintelligible expletives.

He ignored her. "Are we still scheduled to interview Dr. Kershaw's nurses and physician assistant at your office tomorrow morning?"

"Yes. Hopefully, the weather will be nice, so we can sit outside."

"Sounds fine to me. I spend a lot of time outdoors on the job. Just tell your clients to dress warm, or they'll get cold and want to leave."

"I'll have Kathy send them a reminder email. Even though we just met indoors with Dr. Kershaw, I don't want to hold these meetings inside. I'm especially concerned about the PA since he travels for work, and he's working on traumas. I consider him a high-risk individual for getting, then transmitting, COVID."

"The advice from the experts seems to change daily, but I think we're taking every precaution short of biohazard suits. See you then."

"Right."

"In the meantime, will you please talk to Shelby?"

She groaned. "I'll think about it."

After they rang off, Monica called Kathy.

"Hi, Monica. You sound like you're in the car again. Do you think about me only when driving?"

"Guilty as charged because I'm driving from Dr. Kershaw's house to my home office, and I wondered—"

"If I had turned up any more dirt on Geoffrey Gold?" Kathy asked.

"Yes. Or Dr. Kershaw. Or The Flaming Flamingo. Or the victims." Monica snapped her fingers. "And, I have a new assignment."

"Why don't you give me the new assignment before you forget."

"We have a third murder victim, Ingrid Durbin. She was murdered on her farm outside of Iowa City on July 23, 2019."

"Let me write that down." Kathy tapped her pen on the desk. "Hm…"

"What?"

"I was just wondering if there was a pattern to when the killer strikes, but so far, we have one in July 2019, one in December 2019, then one in February 2020, so there isn't a recognizable pattern there."

"Maybe the murders have more to do with the killer's schedule and opportunity instead of a pattern of every six months or something."

"That could be," she said, "but serial killer stories always highlight the similarities of each murder—little peculiarities—that mesh with the killer's psychopathy. Like, if he's obsessed with a specific age, ethnicity, day of the month, or something."

"Well, he's clearly obsessed with trans women who had gender-affirming surgery by Dr. Kershaw. And it's obvious that he thinks they should have kept their penis and scrotum, judging by his spray paint jobs. He's a showoff—daring the police to catch him. He's given us the biggest clue yet, which is killing the victims on the second anniversary of their surgeries."

"That's my point. Maybe he has other idiosyncrasies that we haven't identified yet."

"I think we have a lot, considering the next victim could be three days away."

"Whoa, shit. Seriously?"

"Yes. Guess I forgot to tell you that. I promised Al Bowman and Dr. Kershaw that I'd catch the killer before we have to warn the patient."

"Um. I hate to rain on your parade, but—"

"I know," Monica interrupted. "It's a long shot. I get that but I have to try."

Kathy cleared her throat. "I'd get the contact info lined up for the patient if I were you. Now, you have a new assignment for me?"

"Yes. The Iowa City victim, Ingrid Durbin, has a twin sister named Isobel. She attended some appointments with Ingrid. I'd like you to track her down so I can call her."

"Didn't the Iowa police talk to her and file a report?"

"Yes, but Matt won't share the file. He says he can't because it's an on-going investigation."

"Sounds familiar. So, we don't know what Isobel Durbin told the police about Ingrid's murder?"

"I'm more concerned with what she didn't tell them because they probably didn't know what to ask. We know they didn't pursue the angle of Dr. Kershaw because they didn't realize at the time that Nicole's patients were being targeted. That's why I want to call Isobel. I have more context now, so I think I can ask better questions than the local police did."

"I'll track her down for you," Kathy said. "Switching gears to an update on my latest efforts, here's what I have so far. As you might expect, The Flaming Flamingo itself has had a lot of interactions with the City of Miami as well as lots of criminal drama going on outside on the street."

"Oh really? Like what?"

"Don't get too excited. It's stuff you'd expect for a Miami club. The police are called almost every weekend to break up fights outside the club. Lots of disorderly conduct arrests. The Flamingo itself has been cited a few times by the

City Health Department for food storage issues and cockroaches in the kitchen, but nothing that would shut them down. The fire department also cited The Flamingo for exceeding capacity regularly, as well as blocked exits—nothing nefarious—just tables in the way or carts stacked in the wrong place. If the Miami city government system works like I think it does, however, I'd bet that money exchanged hands so the citations were dropped."

"Of course," Monica said. "Nicole told me that the club made piles of cash. Also, Geoffrey suspected his partner was laundering drug money for a Cuban gang."

"That might explain the violence along that entire street. I did some digging into the bars, restaurants, and clubs in a three-block vicinity, and it's a hotbed of criminal activity. In December 2018, there was even a murder in an alleyway behind The Thirsty Pelican, which is located on the same street as The Flamingo."

That news hit Monica like a tsunami. Her head was swimming with questions. "What are the details?"

"I don't have any yet. While widening my research, I stumbled across it in the *Miami Herald*. Suffice it to say that The Flamingo's criminal record is tame compared to what's happening elsewhere in the neighborhood."

"It's probably nothing but that's Geoffrey Gold's neighborhood," Monica said, her voice eerily calm. "I want you to follow up on that murder. Get as many details as you can, okay?"

"Will do. I'll read the articles in the Miami fish wrap a little closer."

"What about the background checks on Dr. Kershaw and the other two victims, Ms. Adler and Ms. Remington?"

"I wish I had something titillating to report, but I don't. I can see why the Minneapolis and Chicago police hit dead ends. Neither victim has a criminal record, and their social media accounts—Instagram and Facebook—have been taken down."

"I see," Monica said, elongating the *eee,* as she allowed her mind to consider more possibilities.

"Are you and Matt still having all of those meetings tomorrow morning at the office with Dr. Kershaw's staff?"

"Well, not in the office. We're planning to sit outside in the parking lot. Maybe I'll lower the gate on my pickup truck and set a blanket on it or something."

"Tailgate meetings," Kathy said. "You're going to need a fire because the temp is supposed to dip into the 30's tonight."

"I'll bring my Hibachi grill and start a little fire to keep us warm."

"Are you kidding me? That won't do a thing. I'll bring my stainless-steel bonfire pit."

"Your what?"

"It's a cylindrical kettle that kicks out the heat. Don and I bring it to Packers games for tailgating. It only needs a few logs to produce a lot of heat."

"That sounds really nice."

"I'll get there early and set up everything, so when your meetings start at nine, we'll have hot coffee, homemade goodies, and a big fire. I'll bring a portable table and chairs too."

"Wow, Kathy. That's going above and beyond, but don't ignore your assignments in the interest of baking."

"Duh. Have I ever?"

Monica didn't know how to respond to that because the answer was probably, maybe, yes.

"I can walk and chew gum at the same time. To tell you the truth, I'm going crazy inside these four walls. Even worse, Don told me he can't eat any more desserts, so I had to stop baking."

"I'm sure we can take some dessert off your hands tomorrow."

"I'll make a spread that our clients will never forget." Her throaty laugh bubbled like a babbling brook.

"No Bloody Mary's, though, right?"

"Wouldn't dream of it."

"Somehow, I don't believe you."

"I do admit to a little RumChata in my coffee now and again. Keeps the toes warm when you're working outside."

"If you say so," Monica said. "That reminds me. Maybe you should email the nurses and PA to tell them to dress warm."

"Will do."

"Yeah. Let me know what you can find out about the Miami murder in The Flamingo neighborhood, and if you can get the contact info for Isobel Durbin sooner rather than later, I'd appreciate it."

"I'm on it. We have a deadly deadline, so we're going to do all we can."

"Never thought of the word 'deadline,' like that, but you're right. We basically have 24 hours before Dr. Kershaw warns the next patient."

"It's a longshot, Mon."

23

Monica clicked off the phone and glanced at her gas gauge, which indicated she had less than a quarter tank. She quickly calculated her best options and decided to hit up her favorite Kwik Trip. A few miles later, she turned onto London Road and pulled into the station next to a gas pump.

Under the service station awning, she pumped gas and gazed at the mix of humanity around her. A construction worker in brown bibs absent-mindedly filled his mud-splattered pickup truck. An optimistic young woman, flip flops on her feet in 40-degree weather, pumped hand sanitizer on her hands. A man in a black suit, trying to keep the nozzle away from his dress shoes, jammed it into the pump and quickly tore off and pocketed the receipt. People going about their business. No one seemed panicked over an impending pandemic.

Still processing the meaning of a pandemic, Monica hadn't wrapped her head around the historic nature of their new reality. *Is this what the bubonic plague was like? People going on with their lives in a calm, normal fashion while entire city populations fell sick and died?*

She removed her phone from her pocket and googled "pandemics." Several sites populated, so she clicked on an article entitled, *"20 of the Worst Epidemics and Pandemics in History."* The first was a prehistoric epidemic, circa 3000 B.C. in China.

The next was a plague in Athens in 430 B.C.

She scrolled lower. The Black Death in 1346 A.D. traveled from Asia to Europe, wiping out half of Europe's population. It was spread by a bacteria carried by fleas on infected rodents. Monica reminded herself that COVID-19 was a virus from bats rather than a bacteria from rodents. She further reminded herself that antibiotics treated one but not the other.

Her scrolling fingers stopped dead in their tracks at the next line: *Cocoliztli Epidemic of 1545-1548.* The sheer naming coincidence intrigued her, so she read on. The viral hemorrhagic fever killed over 15 million inhabitants of Mexico and Central America, and was named "Cocoliztli," the Aztec word for "pest."

Well, I'll be goddamned. A smug smile spread across her lips as she turned off her phone and dropped it back in her pocket. *How apropos. Coco the pest. Named after a deadly virus that killed 15 million people. It could only be better if it meant bitch too, but I can't have everything.*

The nozzle clicked, so she replaced it on the pump, declined a receipt, and screwed the cap back on her tank. A dispenser for hand sanitizer was next to the pump, so she squirted and rubbed her hands a few times, using a paper towel to wipe off the excess.

She couldn't help but feel buoyed by her new discovery. *If we weren't at the beginning of a pandemic, I never would've discovered that Coco meant pest.* She wanted to shout it from the mountain tops but she would settle for telling Shelby. Shelby? *Shit. I can't even tell my best friend because she's enamored with the pest.* Her elation quickly vanished with the realization that she and Shelby were still on the outs. No amount of mental Coco-bashing compensated for the fact that Monica's one-and-only was currently at risk of becoming a one-and-done.

Adding to her woes, she recalled that Shelby hadn't stocked up on Chai tea, and Monica was down to her last few bags. She desperately needed afternoon caffeine if she was going to push herself to work overtime on this case through isolation. She had no choice. Her need for tea required a targeted mission into the potentially infected bowels of Kwik Trip. She opened the driver's door and removed a bandana that she had hanging from her radio dial. She carefully spread it over her nose and stretched the fabric down to her chin, then tied a knot in the back.

Mindful not to touch the door handles when she approached the store, she scooted in behind another customer. She located the limited selection of teas in the back corner and grabbed a box of Lipton orange pekoe. As she walked by the beverage coolers toward the counter, she also remembered that Shelby had purchased only wine and margarita ingredients on her pre-pandemic shopping spree, which meant that Monica's home beer stash consisted of a few Oktoberfest varietals that she had bought several months ago. She opened a glass door and removed a 12-pack of a local lager, and, as she turned for the checkout counter, ran smack dab into the hot Sicilian yogi otherwise known as Coco Rivelli, wearing a fashionable white mask with disgusting glitter specks on it.

The pest!

Coco's Barbie Doll eyes flashed at Monica then settled into undiluted hatred. "Your little trick cost me a lot of money," she sneered through her mask.

"You caused me a lot of grief by trying to steal my girlfriend. Let's call it even." There was no way Monica was going to admit that she and Shelby were on the rocks.

Adopting a cocky stance, Coco hissed, "I could have Shelby back in a New York second if I wanted her. I'm her soulmate, you know. She'd do anything for me."

"Get lost, pest," Monica said, attempting to sidestep her.

Coco moved in front of Monica, blocking her. "Pest? That's the best you can do?"

"I'll bet you didn't know that Coco means 'pest' in Aztec, and you, my dear, were the first pandemic in Mexico in the 1500s. You killed millions."

"What the fuck are you talking about, nerd? I'm second-generation Sicilian." Coco arched her back and thrust out her chest.

"Yeah, but your parents named you after a virus that killed millions, so that's all you'll ever mean to me. A pestilence. Now, get out of my way, flea bag."

Coco's sharp laugh rang out like Cruella de Vil. "I heard you were a geek, but now you've confirmed it with your lame insults. There's no way you'll satisfy Shelby. Did she ever tell you about our threesomes?"

Monica's eyes flashed with anger as her entire body tensed from head to toe.

"Judging by the surprise in your eyes, I'm guessing she hasn't shared her sexual preferences." Coco's voice dove to a conspiratorial whisper. "You see, I like it spicy, so I brought out Shelby's creative side. She was my personal sex slave, but I needed more salsa in bed, so with three, the sex was tangy and hot." She twisted her yogi hand triumphantly in the air with a jangle of bracelets and rings that accentuated her long, red nails. "Shelby grew to appreciate my more sophisticated tastes over time."

A jackhammer roared to life behind Monica's eyes, the *rat-a-tat-tat* pushing out all rational thought. She transferred the 12-pack from her right arm to her left, shaking out her dominant hand.

Coco's devious eyes bored holes into Monica as she continued her vicious diatribe. "Shelby will never be satisfied with a homely, dull, butchy lawyer like you. She needs my charisma, my body, and my imagination." She ran her bejeweled hand down her white jacket and slim hips. "I do things with her that you'd never dream of—"

"Fuck off, pest." Monica's heart thudded in her chest as she flexed her hand, rocking forward on her toes.

"I might just fuck Shelby on the side after I'm married." Coco's rogue eyes danced. "You wouldn't mind, would you?"

Smack! Monica's fist landed in the center of Coco's mask, the source of the vile garbage spewing forth.

Coco staggered back against the refrigerator glass door, her hands moving to her face. Spots of blood stained her glittery mask, which she clawed off with her long fingernails. "You bith! My lip ith bleeding." She gingerly padded her lips with the mask and examined the bright red blood.

Emboldened, Monica advanced on Coco, pinning her against the glass door with the hard 12-pack until she heard the air whoosh from Coco's lungs. "Stay away from Shelby, or I'll break your nose and mess up your pretty little face, you slut."

Coco's eyes grew wide with fear.

Monica gave her one last shove with the 12-pack, hoping to bruise her breasts. "Got it, pest?"

"Yeth. I gob it," Coco mumbled through the blood and her rapidly-swelling lips.

"Looks who's homely now? I hope I knocked out your teeth." Monica turned and walked to the checkout counter, where she quickly paid and fled the store.

When she exited into the cool air, she saw Coco's white Mercedes and was tempted to pour a beer onto the windshield but moved toward her truck. *Someone might call the police,* she reminded herself. *Think calming thoughts and get the hell out of here.*

She tossed the 12-pack on the floor of the passenger side and slid behind the wheel. When she tried to buckle her seat belt, her hands were shaking so badly that she couldn't click it. She let the strap bounce back into the panel and rested her hands on the wheel to settle her rage. The knuckles on her right hand were as red as raw hamburger, so she massaged the tender bumps as she contemplated her current state of affairs. At least one of the in-store security cameras captured her hitting Coco, of that she was sure. That video would be incriminating evidence in the eyes of the police. *I should call Matt.*

She pictured the video being played on social media, possibly in an attempt to discredit her legal practice. *I should probably warn Jim too.*

She pounded the wheel, shooting more pain through her knuckles. Her thoughts seethed with jealousy about Shelby and Coco. *Did they really do threesomes?*

This time, her hands managed to click the seat belt into place, and as soon as she pulled out of the parking lot, she called Matt. She was surprised he picked up since he was in that stupid training.

"You what?" he hollered in disbelief. "I thought I told you to go home and apologize to Shelby."

"I was on my way, but I needed gas and tea, and once I was in there, I decided to buy some beer too. Anyway, Coco started it. She sought me out and got up in my grill, bragging about how she was the only woman Shelby ever loved. Blah, blah, blah. And how they used to have threesomes." Her emotions and pitch soared as she relived the smackdown. "Worst of all, she threatened to fuck Shelby for sport after she married, so I lost it and hit her in the face."

"Aw shit, Mon," he said. "You know that was probably caught on a security camera, right? They hang like cobwebs in the corners of Kwik Trips."

"I know. I know. That's why I'm calling you."

"I won't be able to deep-six it if she files a complaint."

"I wouldn't expect you to." *Okay, I sort of would, but I can't ask outright.* "Besides, I used a 12-pack of beer to slam her chest into the cooler door, too, so it's beyond deep-sixing. You'd have to 'deep-twelve it.'" She chirped with nervous laughter.

"You sound hysterical," he said. "Are you okay to drive?"

"I'm fine." She looked at her hand, now clenching the steering wheel. "My knuckles hurt like hell, though."

"You didn't break them, did you?"

"They look straight to me, so I'll ice them when I get home."

He sighed long and hard. "Did you break her nose?"

"I didn't hit her nose. I just split her lip."

"Most people won't press charges over a bloody lip unless they're trying to prove something, or they plan to seek a restraining order."

"She confronted me, then goaded me into it!"

"Settle down and get ahold of yourself. I know that, and I'm sure your lawyer would argue that, but assault is assault. Couldn't you have saved the punch until she came outside where there aren't as many cameras?"

"I momentarily lost my mind," Monica said in a defeated voice. "By the way, did you know that 'Coco' means 'pest' in Aztec, and that the Cocoliztli was an epidemic that killed 15 million people in Mexico in the 1500s?"

"What the fuck are you rambling about? Are you drunk?"

"No. I'm just saying Coco is a pest, is all." Monica realized that her google discovery might not be that clever after all.

"Are you on mind-altering medication?"

"This is me, sober. Anyway, Coco probably doesn't want to make our fight public because she's engaged to that Adventist doctor. She wouldn't want him to know about her lesbian relationship with Shelby or their kink."

"Whatever. I'm a little worried about you, Mon. You need to check your fury and clear your mind. Don't do anything stupid. In fact, don't do anything at all. Just go straight home and chill. Don't call Coco, or email her, or text her. Understand?"

"Got it. Now that I think about it, I'm sure Coco won't file a complaint." She relaxed her grip on the wheel, glanced at the speedometer, and eased up on the gas. "Okay. I'm driving home now."

"Good. Go for a run when you get there. Just calm the fuck down. And don't believe a word Coco said. Nathan and I have known Shelby longer than you have, and we never heard anything about threesomes."

Monica groaned. "Stop it. I can't even bear to think about it."

"Take it easy. Shelby loves you."

"Right," she whispered sarcastically.

"Work on your relationship for a few days and dial back the amateur PI gig on this murder investigation, okay?"

She blinked at his insult, rage building again. "Did you just call me an amateur PI?"

"I'm sorry," he mumbled. "I meant a detective, not a PI. You aren't a police detective, Mon. I'll tell you as soon as I learn something."

She clenched her jaw and ground out, "I have a client to represent and you're in training all day!"

"I know, and you're doing a good job. Just stay in your lane and do legal work, not police work, okay?"

"If *you* did the police work, I wouldn't have to!" She hung up on him, and a few blocks later, she called Jim Daniels. She could hear something sizzling in a pan and kitchen noises in the background as she downloaded the confrontation.

"You what?" he asked.

"I punched her in the face and bloodied her big fat lip."

"Way to take care of business, 007 Spade. I'm proud of you." He let loose a few "*heh, hehs*," in his deep baritone, as if he were slapping her back in the locker room. "By the way, you're on speakerphone, and Dominique is with me. We're in my kitchen, prepping meals since both of our offices are closed."

"Oh fuck," Monica said too loudly. "Hi, Dominique. I hope you don't think less of me."

"Not at all, Monica. You earned my respect during our last murder trial."

"Thanks, but I feel like I didn't do anything."

"You were the hero, and you know it," Dominique said. "Nevertheless, I wouldn't advise punching out women who've slept with your fiancée."

"At least not under security cams," Jim added. "Rookie move. You have to find a place where there aren't any witnesses."

"Jim!" Dominique snapped. "Don't listen to him, Monica. If Shelby presses charges, a judge might order you to take some anger management classes, and you might be reprimanded by the State Bar Association."

"Ohhh shit," Monica moaned. "I hadn't thought of that."

"We'll beat all that," Jim said. "I'll represent you."

"I doubt she'll file a complaint," Monica said. "She can't risk her sugar daddy fiancé learning about her sexual preferences. He's a religious fanatic who doesn't tolerate homosexuality."

"Maybe you've got nothing to worry about," Jim said. "I'm glad you called to warn me, though. I'd invite you to join us for dinner this evening, but we're supposed to be sheltering at home."

"Thanks, but I have to work this case and attend to my relationship issues."

"Maybe burn off some excess energy before you do legal work," Jim said. "Go for a run or something, okay?"

She didn't bother telling him that she'd already done that this week and didn't plan on a repeat. When she turned into her driveway, Shelby's Jeep was there but Shelby wasn't in it. *What is she doing here?* A new surge of anxiety shot through her.

24

Monica pulled in behind Shelby's Jeep, blocking her in. She grabbed her tea and beer, got out, and entered her house. The lights were on, but Shelby was nowhere in sight. Monica removed a few cans from the boob-bashing box and placed them in the fridge, cracking one open for herself in the process. Yeah, it was only noon, but her boxing nerves needed alcohol and she was confused. A pandemic. A murder investigation that was kicking her ass. A fiancée crisis. Suddenly, day drinking sounded acceptable since social customs were falling like flies and she didn't know what she was doing professionally, talking smack that she could catch a serial killer in a few days. *I'm an idiot. I don't even know what I'm doing.*

She hoped the buzz would dull the pain in her knuckles and slow the Indy 500 turbo-charged cars racing through her mind. The first sip of cool liquid soothed her, so she tossed back a few long swallows. *I can do this.*

The sounds of slamming drawers sprang from the bedroom, which she interpreted as Shelby packing. *Not a good sign.* Tapping her foot nervously on the kitchen floor, she allowed her breaking heart to battle against her bruised ego. Pride would watch Shelby walk out the door. *Serves her right for cozying up to Coco. I'm an accomplished lawyer, not a doormat.* That would surely result in a failed relationship with the only woman she had ever loved. That would also be so dumb on so many levels.

She drummed her fingers on the counter, allowing the battle to rage on. *What do I really want? What would make me feel the best when waking up tomorrow morning? Alone or with Shelby?* The sound of a closet door sliding open echoed from the bedroom, indicating her lover was one step closer to departure.

Another drink for courage and she found herself rapidly swallowing her pride with the beer. She left her can on the counter and followed the rummaging sounds to her bedroom, where Shelby had her suitcase open on the bed, tossing clothes in helter-skelter.

"Hi, Shelby," Monica rasped, unexpectedly on the verge of tears.

Shelby whipped around, her chestnut corkscrews fanning out like swings suspended from the top of a carousel. "God. You scared me. I didn't hear you come in." She placed her hand over her heart, dried streaks of clay clinging to her fingers and sleeves.

"I'm sorry for everything I said at Nathan's house," Monica said, tears spilling over her long lashes. "That stuff about you being a diva isn't true. You've never acted like a diva...never acted like you're the big fish in our relationship... and...I...just..." Her voice unpredictably broke into a higher octave like a teenage boy going through puberty. "I was just hurling insults because I felt hurt and insecure about seeing you with Coco, knowing that you loved her once, and she broke your heart." She paused briefly, then finished in a choppy mix of raspy-cry, "I'm so sorry. Please forgive me."

Shelby's expression changed from guarded to compassionate, her eyes assessing and reassessing Monica's contorted face and wringing hands. "I didn't expect you to... um...I don't know what to say to that." Shelby threw her hands in the air, an artsy gesture. "Please believe me that I don't have any feelings for Coco. It's over. It's been over for a long time. I love you, but if you can't trust me, or think that I'm using you, or not committed, or whatever, then we should just break up now."

Fortunately, Shelby's voice hitched on the last suggestion, so Monica knew that breaking up was just as unpalatable to Shelby as it was to her.

"That isn't what I want," Monica said at the same time Shelby asked, "Do you want your ring back?"

"No," Monica said while Shelby muttered, "Me either."

A glimmer of hope sprang to life in Shelby's questioning eyes. "I love you..."

Niagara Falls burst over Monica's lashes. Between the thunderstorm in her head and the rapids obscuring her vision, she wasn't sure if she had heard Shelby correctly. "I love you too, if that's what you just said. My head is pounding and my ears are ringing so loud that—"

"You too, huh? I've had a headache all day. Nothing is going right...the kids don't have Zoom hooked up at home yet...so I ruined a few clay pots by myself..." Shelby shook her silver-streaked curls to clear her thoughts, then said again, more deliberately this time, "I love you with all my heart, Mon. I don't want to break up."

Monica felt her shaking lips smile of their own accord, as she wiped away tears with the backs of her hands. "Me either."

"Because I really like this ring." Shelby extended her left hand, the overhead light bouncing off the brilliant sapphires. The braided gold band shimmered against her contrasting clay-stained fingers.

Surprised, Monica looked at Shelby for confirmation and instantly realized that she was messing with her. When Monica saw the loving smile, she knew she had her old Shelby back. "And see, I'm just in it for the sex."

Shelby growl-laughed but remained a step away, now anxiously rolling the engagement ring between her thumb and forefinger. "Can you promise me that you won't be suspicious if you see me talking to a friend, or even ex-lover, in town?"

Monica angled her head and attempted to blink away the drops on her lashes. "I can't promise I won't be a little jealous, but I can promise not to…um…be suspicious or get out of control." She paused, blinked away more tears, then asked, "Are there a lot? Of these ex-lovers, I mean?"

Shelby shrugged and shook her head. "Maybe a few, but I never felt the same way about them as I do about you. I was single for a long time, so yes, I dated. Not a huge amount, but enough. I occasionally run into exes around town, usually when I least expect it. Like, when I'm out of art supplies, and I have to make an emergency trip to Michaels. My hair is usually tucked up into a ball cap, I'm not wearing any makeup, and I haven't showered, then *whammo*, I run into an ex." She laughed at herself, but the smile slid off her face when she saw the hurt look in Monica's eyes.

"Well, your shabby look is my best," Monica said.

"Stop it," Shelby said. "I don't know why you keep putting yourself down. You're the most beautiful woman I know."

Monica rolled her eyes. "Now I know you're lying. I'm average. An average lawyer. An average cook. An average runner. An average fiancée. An average-a-lot-of-things, but a below-average detective, that's for sure."

"See?" Shelby exclaimed. "That's what I'm talking about. You're the hottest and smartest woman I know! You even have your own law firm now. I mean, seriously, you've been in the news umpteen times for your last couple of murder trials. What are you talking about? You're the star of Apple Grove!"

Monica snorted. "That's only because Tiffany Rose can't find anything better to report about."

"She probably has the hots for you to boot." Shelby waved off that conversational thread and turned to her bag, resting next to her suitcase. She searched inside it, finally coming up with a ring box. "And don't ever call yourself an average fiancée, because you're my hot, successful lover, and it's high time that I put a ring on your finger."

Monica was gobsmacked. Of all the scenarios she had imagined for this showdown, having Shelby pull out a ring wasn't one of them. Shelby taking a knee in front of her was even more mind-blowing. *Am I dreaming?* She slapped herself lightly on the cheek.

From her kneeling position, Shelby leaned her head back and regarded Monica with sheer adoration. "What are you doing, Monica Spade?"

"I'm slapping myself to make sure this isn't a dream."

"Rest assured, it isn't." Shelby cleared her throat. "I've been waiting a few days to do this, and I wasn't sure I'd get the chance, so I'm not blowing this one. I know you asked me to marry you, and I said 'yes,' but now I'm asking you to be my wife, too. Attorney-extraordinaire Monica Spade, will you marry me?"

Shelby popped open the lid on the black ring box, the internal light illuminating the braided gold band, which looked even shinier and newer than Shelby's.

"It's beautiful. Everything I'd ever want in a ring." Monica gently removed the gold band from the box and slid it onto her finger. "Best of all, it matches yours."

"Denise had actually set it aside months ago, guessing that I would want to buy it for you."

"Smart woman," Monica said under her breath. "But she's closed now. How did you get it?"

"I called her and she met me in the parking lot."

"Aren't you two something!" Monica held it up to the light, admiring it.

Shelby placed her hands on Monica's hips and pulled herself up, now toe-to-toe and curve-to-curve. She ran the back of her fingers along Monica's jawline and pulled her in for a gentle kiss.

The thunderstorm in Monica's head gave way to sunshine, floating butterflies, flowers blossoming, and fragrant lilacs filling her senses. Suddenly, all was right with the universe, and her body was overcome with the promise of spring as she turned Shelby's exploratory kiss into a real one.

When their lips unlocked a few moments later, and they rested their foreheads against each other, Monica said, "I missed you."

"Me, too. Kind of surprised that your mouth tastes like beer in the middle of the day."

"Oh. Yeah. That. I needed to dial down my amped up self before talking to you."

"Hm. I'm glad you did. So, now that I've given you a ring, will you introduce me to your parents?"

Monica's head started spinning again. "What? My parents?"

"You know. Roger and Colleen. I've stayed at their lake house but never met them. Are you ashamed of me?"

"I'm already confused from kissing you, but now you're confusing me even more. Of course, I'll introduce you as soon as they return from Arizona. I'd never be ashamed of you in any way, shape or form. Duh. I love you." Monica could feel Shelby smiling. "You're teasing me, aren't you?"

"Yup."

"Whew. I thought you were angry or something." They separated, and Monica toppled into those hazel eyes again. She ran her thumb and forefinger down one of the new strands of silver in Shelby's hair. "I like what you've done with your hair and new glasses."

Shelby's grin widened. "I thought you'd never notice."

"The first time I noticed, you were with Coco, so I was startled. Then I thought maybe she had helped you dye the streaks, and I couldn't...think straight. Well, you know what happened."

"I changed up my look for you, Mon." Shelby slipped her arms around Monica's waist. "Coco wasn't around when I colored these streaks or bought these cheapy specs at CVS."

"Oh."

"I'm an artist. I like to switch up my look." Shelby smiled reassuringly. "To keep things exciting and mysterious."

Heat crept up Monica's neck. "Trust me, you're all the excitement and mystery I can take."

"Can we finally close the Coco subject?"

"Done." Monica debated internally whether to confess to bloodying Coco's lip. "I'd rather talk about setting a date for our wedding."

"This summer?" Shelby asked, completely ignoring the burgeoning pandemic.

"June?" Monica suggested. "If we aren't still in a pandemic, that is."

"So depressing. I can see why you're drinking." Shelby's hands moved to Monica's arms. "I'd love to get married this summer. Are you serious?"

Seeing the joy light up the gold flecks in Shelby's eyes sent Monica over the moon. "Yes. Outdoors, right?"

"Absolutely," Shelby said. "I'll decorate the back yard like you've never seen. You won't even recognize it when I'm done. Oversized lights will be strung from tree to tree..." Her gaze drifted past Monica as she continued verbalizing the details, which Monica realized had probably been rolling around in Shelby's head since she was a teenager.

"Let's have a drink and talk about it," Monica said, longing for the remainder of her beer while she listened to decorating ideas.

"Good idea. I have some color palettes to run by you." Shelby squeezed Monica's sore hand in delight, skipping down the hallway toward the kitchen, pulling a wincing Monica with her. Monica swallowed the groans of pain from the fire-tipped arrows running from her knuckles to her brain.

An image of Matt Breuer materialized in Monica's head. *Apologize and get it over with. Makeup sex is the best.*

As they entered the kitchen, Shelby was prattling on about how Joanna Gaines' palette of grays was so limited. She proceeded directly to the wine rack and selected a bottle. While sinking the corkscrew, she said, "A subtle light, slate gray for background colors, accented by a mauvy pale purple—but without looking purple—that sits between violet and pink in the color wheel." Shelby popped the cork. "Mon, are you listening to me?"

Monica blinked several times after draining her beer and suppressing a belch. The knuckles on her right hand were throbbing, so she secretly massaged them. "Yes. Absolutely. Pewter tablecloths with pale pink flowers."

Shelby cocked her head and hip at the same time. "No. That's not even close. Pink is not a part of our world, certainly not on our wedding day."

"Okay." Turning away to hide a burp, Monica opened the fridge and grabbed another beer. "Maybe it would be easier for me to imagine if you showed me some pics on Pinterest or something."

"Good idea," Shelby said while pouring herself a healthy glass of wine. "I'll share my Magnolia wedding board with you."

"Can't wait." Despite all the uncertainty swirling around in her, Monica managed to pin a seriously enthusiastic expression on her face.

"Do you have any wedding ideas?" Shelby asked.

"Um...not right now." Monica lowered her head, holding the full can of beer against her throbbing knuckles. "I do have something I need to confess to you, though."

Shelby's body stilled, and her voice became cautiously low. "What's that?"

"I hit Coco Rivelli in the face today."

"What?" Shelby asked, confusion crinkling her forehead.

"About an hour ago. At the Kwik Trip," Monica mumbled, her chin lowered toward the floor.

Shelby flew to Monica, put her hand under Monica's chin, and raised her head to look at her troubled emerald eyes. "You hit her? In the face? At a gas station? Why?"

Monica looked at the ceiling for redemption, finding none, she groaned as she met Shelby's gaze. "We ran into each other by the beer cooler. I had just removed a 12-pack. Anyway, she blocked my path, telling me that you two were soulmates...and...that you liked threesomes...and you were essentially her sex slave...and that she planned to fuck you on the side after she married the rich doctor." Monica put her hands up. "Her words, not mine."

"That bitch!" Shelby spat. "Soooo not true." Shelby turned to the counter and rested her palms on its cool surface. "Not even close. Never been there. Never done that." Hands still placed in front of her, Shelby snapped her head around to look at Monica. "You know I'm telling the truth, right?"

Monica saw the vulnerability in the flinty gold flecks, Shelby's worried brows the shape of tildes, her lips parted in question.

"Yes. I believe you. She had me going for a second, though, so I punched her in the mouth and bloodied her lip."

Shelby sucked in a breath and slapped her palms on the hard granite. "Oh my God, Mon. I wish I could've seen that!"

No expression of sympathy for Coco. So far, so good. Monica thrust out her right hand for Shelby to examine. "My knuckles are a little sore."

Shelby grasped Monica's hand, gingerly examining it, then softly caressing it.

Monica longed for Shelby's caresses, her hands running over her body, squeezing her in all the right places, her fingers tickling and delighting. How many hours had it been now? Too many for Monica's fragile heart to endure. Warmth spread up her arm and charged into her heart.

Shelby intensified her knuckle rubs, causing Monica to flinch momentarily, but the warm finesse was worth every second of pain. *Oooohs* and *ahhs* escaped Monica's mouth.

After a few hot minutes, Shelby released Monica's hand and sipped some wine. "Did you chip any of her teeth?"

"I doubt it. Just bloodied her lip."

Shelby giggled devilishly. "I'm sure you shocked the shit out of her."

"Looked like it."

"She deserved it. She's such a fucking manipulator."

"I just hope she doesn't file a police report against me."

Shelby thought about that for a moment. "I doubt she'll go to the trouble."

Monica air toasted.

After staring at each other for a few minutes, Monica asked, "Want to order takeout from The Broken Spoke for dinner?"

"What a great idea." Shelby glanced at the microwave clock. "But we still have several hours before dinner."

"I know. I was just predicting that we won't have much time to prep a homemade dinner tonight."

Shelby arched a brow. "Why is that?"

"I want to see if I can find all the splotches of dried clay on your body."

Shelby quirked a smile.

"And I want to give the Spoke our business during the pandemic so they don't go belly up."

"Speaking of belly up, let's move this party to the bedroom."

25

The next morning, Monica rolled into the empty parking lot of Spade, Daniels & Taylor, where Kathy's dark SUV was parked cattywampus across the neatly painted white lines. This was her last day to crack the case before Nicole called Carissa to warn her. She felt like a fool for boasting that she could catch a killer quicker than the police. What had she been thinking?

She sighed as she emerged from her truck. The blue sky promised full sunshine, so, by noon, maybe they could shed their jackets.

"Hiya, boss," Kathy said through a Green Bay Packers face mask while adding a log to a fire licking the crisp morning air from a stainless-steel drum.

Monica gave Kathy a faux disapproving look before pulling up her bandana over her nose and mouth. "We all know who's the real boss around here. Good morning to you too. What a fantastic fire." She thrust her hands out to the yellow flames, the sparkling gold band on her left finger glinting in the morning sunlight.

"Thanks. Don and I love it. Lots of heat without a mess."

"You've created the quite the cozy atmosphere," Monica said, taking it all in. A table and four chairs sat a few feet from the fire, and the back of Kathy's SUV served as a kitchen counter where there was an industrial-sized coffee pot brewing at full steam.

"Only the best for our clients."

"The aroma of coffee outdoors warms my heart."

"Wait till you see what else I brought." Kathy removed the lids of several plastic containers holding caramel rolls, cookies, muffins and bars.

"Holy sugar high," Monica said. "We won't get cold meeting outside with the amount of calories and caffeine in this buffet."

"Help yourself before the others get here," Kathy said. "Paper plates and napkins are on your left."

"Don't mind if I do." Monica grabbed a plate and pried a caramel roll away from the teeming pan of a dozen. She poured herself a cup of coffee, adding a healthy amount of cream.

Kathy joined Monica at the table, her own mug of coffee between her hands. As Monica lowered her bandana, Kathy's clever dark eyes followed Monica's fork from roll to mouth.

The first bite of caramel roll didn't disappoint, the soft, gooey dough practically melting in Monica's mouth, giving her a blissed-out look that told Kathy she had hit the jackpot.

"These are heavenly," Monica mumbled while chewing. "Yummmm."

Kathy beamed as she dug into the pocket of her large down jacket and came up with a miniature bottle of RumChata. She cracked open the top and poured some in her coffee, then held it out to Monica. "Care for a little nip?"

"What the hell," Monica said. "It's a pandemic, we're holding meetings in the parking lot, and there's no way I'm going to catch the killer before we have to warn Carissa. If we're going to fail, let's get a buzz on while we do."

The crows cawed approval from the treetops surrounding the lot.

Monica drank her spiked coffee and had to admit it was the ying to the caramel roll's yang. RumChata, a portmanteau of rum and horchata, added a creamy flavor to the coffee. There was something horribly incongruent about sitting next to a roaring fire, drinking booze, and eating tasty treats in preparation for witness interviews in a rapidly failing murder investigation.

"Before we turn to business, what's new with you?" Kathy asked, her eyes tracking to Monica's left ring finger.

Unable to suppress a smile, Monica extended her left arm and flexed her hand in a gaudy display of her new engagement band.

Kathy's *whoop* sent a few crows fleeing from the trees as she took Monica's hand in her own. "What a beautiful ring. Simple, yet sophisticated. Shelby has fantastic taste. Did you two set a date yet?"

Monica smiled through caramel. "This summer. Shelby is working out the details."

"We'd better be invited. Indoor or outdoor?"

"You will be. Probably outdoor."

"You should send out *save the date* cards."

"I'm sure Shelby will do that." Monica took another bite.

"I'm so happy for both of you. Congratulations."

"Thank you." Monica chewed for a few seconds, then asked, "In other news, did your searches turn up anything?"

"Nothing at the moment," Kathy said. "I thought I'd work while we interview witnesses out here."

"Did you bring your laptop?"

"All charged and ready to go. I even get the firm Wi-Fi out here."

"Awesome. Maybe you can get me Isobel Durbin's phone number this morning," Monica said. "I want to call her today, my last day to solve this before we warn Carissa."

"That's a lot of pressure to put on yourself. We've got very little to go on."

"*Et tu, Brute*? No one has any faith in my ability to..."

Their conversation was interrupted by Matt driving into the parking lot in an unmarked, four-door sedan that was obviously a police car.

Dressed in a police-issued bomber jacket, jeans, and scuffed brown boots, he approached them, holding his hands out over the fire. He spied the treats in the back of Kathy's SUV. "Nice party. You two go all out for your hospital clients, don't you?"

"This is for you, Detective Breuer," Kathy said flirtatiously.

"I don't believe we've met," he said, extending a hand. "Matt Breuer."

"Kathy Holt." She reached up and shook his meaty hand. "I brought hot coffee, caramel rolls, muffins, and bacon for breakfast. Help yourself. My husband told me I can't bring any of it home because we're getting fat." She rose and pumped hand sanitizer into her hands then opened the lids on the containers.

"Bacon?" Monica asked, craning her neck. "I didn't see the bacon."

"I'll get you some." Kathy snagged several slices with a silver tong and dropped them onto Monica's plate.

"This smells and looks delicious," Matt said. "Thank you for going to all the trouble. I feel like I walked into a family brunch."

Kathy's melodious laugh picked up Monica's spirits. "Tailgating is more like it."

"I can get behind that." As Matt was pouring himself a cup of coffee and taking one of everything, a hot-rod motorcycle's thunderous crack shattered the peaceful morning air.

They turned to the deafening sound, as a man on a black and chrome chopper turned into the lot and made a wide circle while downshifting, the engine shooting off a few more cannon blasts. The slicked-up rider rolled in next to Matt's car, killed the engine, popped the kickstand with his heel, and rested his large boots on the pavement. "I'm looking for Monica Spade."

Quite the entrance. "I'm Monica. You must be Derek from our Zoom call."

"Guilty as charged." He slowly unwound his body from the massive bike and sauntered over, his thick boots, black leather chaps, and riding jacket squeaking with his tough-guy swagger.

As Monica made the introductions, Derek shook their hands, still wearing his tight, black half-gloves. Kathy described the buffet, and Derek removed a small bottle of hand sanitizer from his jacket pocket, squirting some on the tips of his fingers.

"Thanks for the spread," he said, his voice low and gravelly.

"Please, help yourself," Kathy replied.

He pushed his reflective riding glasses onto his head, which was covered in a black knit cap with the *Harley Davidson* logo printed on it. "Not only do I get the pleasure of a beautiful woman's company, but also her cooking. My lucky day." He grinned teasingly at Kathy, his smile a hodgepodge of overlapping teeth.

"Flattery will get you everywhere," Kathy said. "Can I fix you a plate?"

"I'd love that." While he watched her, he poured himself a grandé cup of black coffee. "Mind if I sit?"

"Please do," Matt said.

The three sat while Kathy fussed over Derek's plate.

"Do you still have an hour for an interview this morning?" Monica asked.

Derek slowly moved his leather-clad hand to his side and pawed a silver-linked chain that could anchor a battleship in a storm, tugging until a pocket watch emerged. He clicked open the silver lid and read the time. "I'm meeting some friends for a rally in Tomah in a few hours."

"What type of rally?" Matt asked.

"Motorcycle."

"You sure don't fit the stereotype of a healthcare provider," Matt said.

Derek's iceberg blue eyes pierced the morning air. "You mean the bike?"

"Yeah."

Derek chuckled. "It's my day off, so I'm doing my thing."

Monica studied Derek's profile, his eyes bulging a bit like a guppy, his pasty white face covered in sandy stubble, his thin eyebrows almost invisible.

Kathy set a full plate before him and he dug into the caramel roll, taking a large bite.

"Watch out for patches of black ice on the roads," Matt said. "Got down to freezing last night."

Derek moaned an indifferent *uh-huh* while chewing.

Kathy returned to her SUV kitchen, tidying up, then resting her hip against the car, looking at her phone, fading into the background.

"There's still sand on the road from winter," Matt said. "We see a lot of spring motorcycle accidents around curves on the county highways." He gestured with his hand. "The bikes skid right off the road."

Derek washed down a bite with coffee. "I'll be on the lookout." He lifted his gaze to Kathy. "Kathy, these rolls are dynamite."

She glanced up from her phone, a broad smile accentuating her dimples. "Thank you."

Derek returned his attention to Matt and waited.

Monica recalled Derek's quiet demeanor from their Zoom call. He had spoken only when asked a question and had answered concisely and efficiently. Some people were reserved on Zoom and chattier in person, but Derek appeared equally reticent live.

"Do you know why we're meeting today?" Matt asked.

"Monica mentioned that two of Dr. Kershaw's trans female patients were murdered." He turned to Monica. "Sorry. I forgot their names."

"Actually, since I spoke to you, a third was discovered," Monica said.

Derek's freakishly oyster-blue eyes flashed at her. "Really?"

"Yes. The victims are Michelle Adler, Veronica Remington and Ingrid Durbin," Matt said. "Do you recognize any of those names?"

Derek paused from eating, his hands resting on each side of his plate. He angled his head and stared at the large building that housed Monica's law firm, then said in a monotone, "Maybe. Over the years, all the patients' names blend together, but they sound familiar."

"Would it jog your memory if I showed you photos?"

Derek's leather-clad shoulders shrugged. "Maybe."

Matt removed a plastic folder from his backpack and spread the now-familiar photos of the gruesome crime scenes on the table. "These are the three victims at the scenes where they were killed."

All eyes were on Derek and his reaction. His gaze roamed over the photos, but he didn't pick any up to study them like Dr. Kershaw had. "Sick paint job."

Kathy peered over Matt's shoulder; her studious eyes startled but not panicked. Her Packers mask prevented Monica from reading her entire expression.

"More than a paint job," Matt said. "The killer appears to be sending a message."

Derek nodded.

"Care to comment?"

"He obviously hates trans women." Notwithstanding the gore, Derek resumed eating a piece of bacon and looked at Matt, holding his stare.

"Most people would find it difficult to eat while looking at these."

"I scrub into surgeries that make these photos look like a walk in the park," Derek said around a bite. "And we learn to eat when we get the chance because it might be several hours before we get out of the OR again."

Matt's eyes roamed Derek's face. Sometimes, people just talked and talked without him having to prompt them. Not Derek. After a strained silence that could have been interpreted as respect for the victims, Matt asked, "How long have you been a PA?"

"Seven years."

"Where did you go to school for that?"

"UC Davis."

"Where's that?"

"Sacramento."

"How many years is that program?"

"Three."

"Did you grow up in Sacramento?"

"Yep."

"Still have family there?"

"My mom was my only family, and she died when I was in the PA program."

"I'm sorry," Matt said.

"Thanks." Derek shrugged off the sympathy.

"What brought you to Apple Grove to work with Dr. Kershaw?"

"I was on the surgical team at UC Davis Medical Center for sex reassignment surgeries, and I was interested in seeing other parts of the country, so I signed a contract with a *locums tenens* company to do some travel work, and that's about the time Dr. Kershaw joined Community Memorial to start her program."

"So, you started the program with her?"

"Yes."

"Have you received any hate mail?"

Derek paused a minute at the non sequitur question, squinting through short, sandy lashes. "Not that I can remember."

"Been targeted by any hate groups or protestors?"

"No. I'm not the face of the program, and when I leave the hospital, I'm riding my Harley, so people generally don't make the connection."

"Travel to any other parts of the country for work?" Matt asked in a friendly, conversational tone.

"I'd like to, but between Sacramento and Apple Grove, my hands are full right now. I've been encouraging Dr. Kershaw to hire a full-time PA, but she says she likes me too much, and I don't want to move here full-time." If Derek took any pride in Nicole's loyalty or flattery, he didn't show it by smiling, shoveling another bite into his mouth.

Matt nodded, watching Derek calmly finish the food on his plate.

"Can I get you something else?" Kathy asked.

"No, thank you." Derek neatly folded his napkin over the plate and sipped his coffee.

"Do you recognize these victims?" Matt said, gesturing to the photos once again.

"Yes and no," Derek said. "Their faces look familiar, but I couldn't tell you who is who or remember any details about them."

"Anything at all that might help us find the killer?"

"In general, I'd say this group of patients is scared before the surgery but very grateful afterward."

"How so?"

"It's a big, transformative surgery. Very painful, but when we round on them post-operatively, even though they're in a lot of pain, they seem immediately pleased with the results. Dr. Kershaw is very good at what she does."

"Do you socialize much with her?"

"On occasion. We aren't riding buddies, but we have dinner together once in a while."

"Have you met her partner, Geoffrey?"

There was a pause in the cadence of question and answer, Derek's guppy eyes traveling over Matt's face. He appeared to be choosing his words wisely. "Yes."

Monica was growing bored of Derek's abbreviated answers.

"Where?" Matt asked.

"I was in Miami with Dr. Kershaw when they first met," Derek said with a flat affect, then added "and I've been out to their poultry farm on Lake Wissota."

"You were in Miami with Dr. Kershaw?" Matt asked. "When was that?"

"Oh, I don't know. A year or two ago, Dr. Kershaw and I attended a plastic surgery conference focusing on gender-affirming surgeries. The whole gamut—eyebrow reshaping, tracheal shaves, breast implants and vaginoplasties."

Monica perked up. Derek hadn't mentioned this trip on their Zoom call.

"Tell me about Geoffrey," Matt said.

Derek suddenly seemed eager to talk. "He was a breast implant device rep, hawking his wares out of a booth at the vendor hall of the conference. Dr. Kershaw struck up a conversation with him, and they hit it off right away. First, his medical device company hosted us on a little boat cruise with other physicians, then he invited her to a club he co-owned, and she dragged me along as her wingman." He stopped, stared toward the building again, and clicked his fingers. "What was the name of that club?"

"The Flaming Flamingo," Monica supplied.

He flinched like she had stabbed him in the ribs, quickly turning toward her. "Right." He performed some type of assessment of her eyes, then reached into his pocket and removed his mask, also black with a *Harley* logo. "Almost forgot to put my mask back on after eating." He crinkled his eyes at her, but they lacked any warmth.

"What was the club like?" Matt asked.

"Not my scene. Slick Miami guys out on the prowl. Women too fast for my taste. I'm more of a pool hall kind of guy."

"No DJs in pool halls," Matt said.

"Or freaks," Derek muttered through the mask.

Monica recoiled but maintained an inscrutable expression. *Freaks?*

Matt didn't let that one slide. "What do you mean by freaks?"

Recovering quickly, Derek said, "Let's just say I was uncomfortable with the eclectic mix of gangsters, Russian hookers, doped-up rich kids, and people pretending to be someone they weren't."

Matt considered Derek's list. "By 'people pretending to be someone they weren't,' are you referring to trans women?"

Derek shrugged. "Nah. That's people being real. Remember, I do sex reassignment surgeries for a living. I just don't care for disingenuous people who are masquerading for the night at a club. That's all."

"Uh-huh," Matt said.

"Anyway," Derek said, refocusing on Geoffrey, "those two have been inseparable since."

"What do you know about Geoffrey?" Matt asked.

Derek jammed a thick finger into his right ear and twisted a bit. "Not much. I think he sold his club when he moved up here. I don't know if he's still a sales rep for the breast implant company." He again looked over Matt's shoulder. "What was it called?"

"Injectafyl," Monica said.

He turned to her again, slower this time. "Yeah. Injectafyl. You know more about Geoffrey than I do. Matt should be interviewing you."

She smiled. "Part of my job."

"Anything else about Geoffrey?" Matt asked.

"He and I didn't really hit it off. Still don't. Just not my type of guy. That doesn't mean he isn't good to Dr. Kershaw.

They have a chemistry, but there's just something about him…" The leather-clad shoulders shrugged again, slower than molasses. The gesture came off as very deliberate, as if he were trying to signal Matt.

"Okay," Matt said. "Well, we don't want to keep you from your rally, and our time is about up. Here's my card if you think of anything else I should know."

Derek accepted Matt's card and slipped it into the deep pocket next to the pocket watch, and who knew what else. "Thanks for your hospitality this morning. I assume this will turn into a court case, and you'll want me to *testilie* at some point?"

Monica chewed her lower lip, wondering if she'd heard him correctly. "I'm sorry. What?"

He chuckled. "A term we use in the OR—*testilie*—instead of testify."

Monica and Matt exchanged looks. "If there's a criminal trial, we will want you to testify truthfully," Monica said.

"And I would plan to do that," Derek said formally. He stood abruptly so they did too. After shaking hands with a mystified Monica, then Matt, Derek lingered over Kathy. "Best caramel rolls I've ever had."

She blushed above her mask. "Thank you."

"And bonus, the cook has beautiful eyes."

Instead of replying, she turned to organize her already-organized buffet.

Derek strolled back to his motorcycle like a man who had the day at his leisure. He swung his leg over the seat and balanced the huge bike between his legs. With the turn of a key, the low engine coughed to life, and he gave it some gas with a twist of his right hand. The loud cracks smacked the morning air while the engine warmed. He lowered his sunglasses, casually surveyed the parking lot, and nodded at the group. Up went the kickstand, in went the clutch, and down went the gear shift with his toe.

His right hand twisted the throttle, and the bike rolled forward with the roar of a lion. As he was making the turn out of the parking lot, he accelerated again, a thunderclap of horsepower echoing off the building windows.

"Expensive bike," Monica said. "Wonder if he rode it all the way from Sacramento."

"Quite the charmer," Kathy added. "Overdid it, if you ask me."

"Real badass," Matt said after the roar faded in the distance. "I didn't like his remark about disingenuous people masquerading for the night."

"Or *testilying*," Monica said.

"I've heard a few old-timers use that word, but it's generally ill-advised when meeting with law enforcement," Matt said.

"I wonder what Nicole and Geoffrey would think about his views of club goers," Monica said. "The only thing that resonated with me was his dim view of Geoffrey."

Matt rolled his eyes.

26

They had a few minutes before the first nurse was scheduled to arrive, so Kathy and Monica ran into the office building together to use the restroom. On their way out, Monica checked her emails. "Shit."

"What gives?" Kathy asked.

"Sam Moua, my Information Security contact at the hospital, reviewed all three victims' electronic medical records to see if there were any internal breaches."

"You mean, like a hospital employee looking at them?" Kathy asked.

"Yes."

"Did Sam find anything?"

"No," Monica said. "He reviewed the electronic footprint for access to their charts and confirmed that only the employees who provided direct care entered their charts."

"That's good news, right?" Kathy asked, as they descended the steps to the parking lot.

"From the hospital's perspective, absolutely," Monica said with a wholehearted lack of enthusiasm.

"But," Kathy said, "I hear a *but* coming."

"I'm concerned that the hospital looks too squeaky clean on this. It's no coincidence that Nicole's patients are being murdered. There's a murder pattern that links the killer to her, so she's obviously implicated. As a bystander, a victim, a target, a witness, a suspect, I don't know." Monica considered the information in the patient charts. "The fact that only the care team looked at the charts means that I'm much more suspicious of the care team itself. That includes Nicole and her boyfriend, the greasy Geoffrey, because he lives with her and has access to her laptop."

"All roads leading back to Geoffrey?" Kathy asked with a healthy amount of skepticism. "Sounds too easy to me."

As they joined Matt at the table, Monica said loud enough for him to hear, "I still have this premonition that Geoffrey, former club owner and purveyor of breast implants, inappropriately accessed Dr. Kershaw's laptop to look at patient charts. For the protection of the next patient, I think you should haul Geoffrey in for questioning."

Matt guffawed. "Yeah, right. Based on your dislike and Derek's shrugs?"

"What if Geoffrey *is* the killer?" Monica said. "You could keep him in jail over the next anniversary, thwarting his efforts."

"The best way to protect the next patient is for the hospital or Dr. Kershaw to warn her," Matt said.

"We've already been over this," Monica said.

"If Geoffrey is the killer," Kathy said, "why hasn't he killed Nicole? Wouldn't he hate her too?"

"Not if he wanted to use her for information to find his victims," Monica said. "Moreover, if she turned up dead, he'd be an obvious suspect." Monica looked at Matt, her mind working.

"That's a good theory, Mon, but it's a stretch to use and live with someone you supposedly hate just for information," Matt said. "Besides, Dr. Kershaw is a smart woman, and I would bet money that she'd notice if her lover was killing her patients. She knows the dates the victims were killed, so she can recall if Geoffrey was at home or away during those times."

"Love can be blind."

"Either way," Kathy said, "I'm betting that Dr. Kershaw's career will dry up soon because the hospital can't keep a lid on this investigation forever."

"There's a good chance," Monica said, "especially if Geoffrey is the killer."

"Let's not get ahead of ourselves." Matt closed the lid on his laptop. "I don't know if I share Derek's opinions of people. He seemed arrogant to me."

Monica refreshed her coffee and sat down across from Matt, unpacking her own laptop and setting it on the table. "Mm."

"Just so cocksure of himself. I've never liked guys like that."

"He definitely wasn't intimidated by you, the investigation, or the interview," she said.

"Like it was an ordinary, everyday occurrence. You'd think the guy would express some surprise or shock at seeing three of his patients brutally murdered, but no. Nothing. Eating his caramel roll. Checking his fancy pocket watch. Looking forward to his bike rally in Tomah. Not taking any interest in the investigation. Something didn't fit with that guy."

"Could just be his personality," she said. "He does surgeries and handles traumas. Are you doing any background checks on him?"

"Just sent the email to an officer to do that very thing." Matt gestured to his laptop.

A car pulled into the parking lot, and Monica immediately recognized Nurse Jane Krajewski. Even through the windshield, fear colored Jane's expression. She got out, quickly adjusted a pink surgical mask over her face, and bustled over to their conference area. "Am I in the right place? Are you Monica Spade?"

Matt and Monica rose. "You are, and I am. Sorry, I have a mask on while we're meeting outside."

After introductions and a trip through Kathy's buffet line, a shaky Jane sat down at the table with Matt and Monica.

Kathy pulled up a chair next to the fire and opened her laptop, close enough to eavesdrop but not be part of the conversation. Tweeting birds and the faint hum of traffic provided springlike ambient noise.

Matt went through his standard introductions and got down to brass tacks quickly, running Jane through the names of the three victims. As she had during their Zoom meeting, Jane's eyes started blinking nonstop. Her surgical mask hung loosely from her left ear as she nibbled her way through the plate of Kathy's treats, her lips bouncing back and forth between a shaky smile and closure.

"Do you remember Ms. Adler, Remington or Durbin?" Matt asked.

"Monica asked me the same question, but we didn't discuss Ingrid Durbin." Jane glanced nervously at Monica, then returned her attention to Matt.

"Ingrid didn't surface until recently," Matt said.

"I don't remember Michelle or Veronica, but I remember Ingrid because she was our first patient from Iowa."

"That's a positive development," Matt said. "If I showed you a photo, would it help you remember all of them?"

"It might."

"My photos are from the crime scenes. Most people find them upsetting."

"I can handle it," she said, setting down her plastic fork.

Matt removed the stack of photos and solemnly placed them on the table in front of her, as he had for Derek. He silently assessed her while her eyes consumed them.

As Monica had expected, Jane's face quickly contorted into anguish and rivers spilled from her eyes. Monica pushed the box of Kleenex toward her.

"I'm so sorry," Jane said. "I thought I could handle this, but...looking at their dead bodies...so brutally murdered." She began sobbing, mumbling through gasps, "The fear...the terror that must have gripped Ingrid. No one should have to die like that."

Jane dropped her head into her hands, her brown, messy bun spilling chunks around her face like a curtain. "I feel so sad for her."

After a solid two minutes of watching her cry, Matt asked, "Do these photos jog your memory as to any details about the victims that might help us?"

Elbows resting on the table, her face still in her hands, Jane said in a muffled tone, "Only Ingrid. I remember that her sister accompanied her to the first visit. They were so young, so cute, so innocent looking. Naïve farm girls. Well, a girl and a boy, but then Ingrid had her gender-affirming surgery." She flicked a hand. "You know what I mean."

"Of course," Monica said, patting Jane's shoulder. "Do you remember anything specific about Ingrid?"

"No," Jane groaned. "I wish I did."

"Was Ingrid satisfied with her surgery?" Matt asked.

Jane raised her head, wiping away tears and resituating her mask over her nose and mouth. She seemed to gain some control by performing that familiar task. "I think so. She came to all of her post-operative visits and was compliant with the dilation therapy."

"Did her sister still accompany her?" Matt asked.

"No. Maybe a boyfriend, but I'm not sure of that."

"Do you remember his name?"

"No. You could look at Dr. Kershaw's notes."

"We did, but it isn't there," Matt said.

"I'm sorry. I don't remember."

"Do you remember the sister's name?" Matt asked.

Jane stared at Matt for a second, then clicked her fingers. "Isobel. Ingrid and Isobel. Twins. I thought their names were so Midwestern and charming."

"Did Ingrid or Isobel ever mention anyone threatening them?" Matt asked.

Jane slowly shook her head, indicating no.

"Did you ever see or hear threats to Dr. Kershaw or yourself?" Matt asked.

"As I told Monica, yes. Many times. Dr. Kershaw is considered a pariah by people who think gender is defined by your sex organs. We get hate letters and emails from sickos all the time."

"What do you do with them?" he asked.

"At first, we forwarded them to the hospital Security department, but then they became so commonplace that we just deleted them."

"If you still have some, it might help," he said.

"I'll see what I can do."

"Do any stand out in your mind? Any names? Gangs? Groups?" Matt asked.

"No. I'm sorry that I'm not more help, but I just tried to forget them. Push them out of my mind. I never imagined I'd be sitting here talking to you about murder."

Matt glanced at Monica with the frustration borne of dead ends. "I understand. I encounter this type of situation a lot. People don't save evidence because they hope that the threat, or situation, or whatever, will pass. Sometimes it doesn't. It only gets worse, and we find ourselves here."

"I realize that now," Jane said. "I'm sorry."

Matt adopted a softer tone as he explored a new topic. "Do you work much with Derek Russell?"

"He comes to the clinic to confer with Dr. Kershaw, and sometimes they see a patient together in clinic, but that would be rare."

"For him to join you in clinic?"

"Yes. All of his work is in the hospital."

"Tell me what you know about him," Matt said.

"He lives in Sacramento. He's been coming here for at least three years, maybe longer. We discuss patients on the phone quite a bit. Their appointments. Their follow-up visits. Any complications. Their meds. He can be a bit rough around the edges, but he's always patient-centered. Nicole speaks highly of him—says he's the best assistant she's ever had in the OR. Apparently, he's very dexterous with the instruments."

"Ever do anything socially with him?" Matt asked.

"Derek?" she asked in surprise.

Matt nodded.

"Only work functions. A birthday party here, a department party there."

"Is it true that if he isn't at work, he's riding his bike?"

"I guess so. I don't know him well enough to say what he does in his free time."

"Ever see him get angry or rough up anyone?"

Her eyes widened. "Oh heavens, no."

"Has Derek told you about his life in Sacramento?"

"Now that you mention it, not really. We've only discussed work matters."

"How about Dr. Kershaw's partner, Geoffrey Gold," Matt asked. "Have you met him?"

"On a few occasions, he's joined us when we've been out with Nicole. I've met him maybe twice."

"Did you talk to him?"

"Personally? Just the two of us?"

"Yes," Matt said.

"I'm sure it was only a few words," Jane said. "So, I don't remember what we talked about."

"What, if anything, can you tell me about him?"

"Um..." She ran her fingers through her hair and reworked her bun. "He's from Miami. Used to own a club. Said something about buying a bar in Apple Grove and turning it into a tropical club with live music." Her eyes narrowed as she looked at Matt, then Monica. "He's not a suspect, is he?"

"Everyone is a suspect until I rule them out," Matt said.

"Oh dear."

"Please don't be alarmed, and don't share what we've discussed with anyone else. This conversation is confidential," Matt said.

"I won't," she said. "I just wish I could be more helpful. I feel so useless."

"You've been plenty helpful," Matt said. "I don't have anything further for you, but if you think of something, please call me." He fished out a business card and gave it to her.

After Jane departed, Matt went into the office building to use the restroom. Monica stretched her legs, pacing around the fire.

Matt rejoined them, and the glint of Monica's engagement ring pinged him in the eye. "Wow! Is that new?"

"Yeah. Shelby gave it to me last night."

"I see you took my advice," he said in a smug tone.

"I did." She lowered her hand.

"What did you think of Jane's interview?" Matt asked.

"She confirmed some impressions I had."

"You mean that you don't like Geoffrey?"

"I just get bad vibes. Could be anything. Could be something. I need more data points."

Just then, a car pulled into the lot.

"Looks like our next nurse witness is here," Monica said.

"Let's get these over with," Matt said.

Monica was convinced the next few nurses wouldn't be able to top Derek and Jane, but she would watch patiently while Matt interviewed them.

27

After the last nurse left, Matt turned to Monica. "You were right. They didn't have anything earth-shattering to say."

"That's what I gleaned from my Zoom interviews."

"Well, I still have to write up a report on each one, then share my findings with Detective Heinz."

Monica registered that chain of information sharing. "I hope you and Heinz decide to interview Geoffrey after you talk."

He quirked an eyebrow at her but didn't say anything as he pushed away from the table and stood. "Thanks for your hospitality, ladies. I better get going."

"Please call me immediately if you learn something new," Monica said.

"I expect you to call me if you learn something new." He leaned in closer. "Warn the next patient, Mon."

"I'll call her myself if you bring Geoffrey in for questioning."

"This isn't a negotiation." He turned to Kathy. "Your cooking is fantastic. Thank you for bringing the delicious treats."

After Matt left, Monica and Kathy remained at the table.

"Sitting out here next to the fire was a great way to hold meetings," Monica said. "Thanks for making it happen."

"You're welcome. Now that spring is here, the weather will only get nicer, so meeting outside is an excellent option."

"Did you discover any helpful info this morning?"

"As a matter of fact, I did." Kathy slid a slip of paper across the table toward Monica. "Here's Isobel Durbin's phone number. From what I can tell on Facebook, she recently married a guy named Jake Martin. If that phone number doesn't work, let me know and I'll message her on Facebook."

"Thanks." Monica tapped the edge of the paper with her finger. "I feel horrible about calling her to dredge up the details about Ingrid's murder from last summer. The pain must be horrendous. I couldn't imagine losing my sister like this."

"I didn't know you had a sister," Kathy said, tilting her head.

"Elizabeth. She's five years older. I don't mention her much because we aren't super close."

"Where does she live?"

"Minneapolis."

Kathy raised her eyebrows. "That's only 90 minutes away. Do you see her often?"

Monica shrugged. "Only on holidays. She's a busy pediatrician, and her husband is a neurosurgeon. They don't have the time for the likes of little old me."

"I doubt that. I'm sure Lizzy—"

"No."

"Beth—"

"Never."

"Lizbeth."

Monica snorted. "She goes by 'Elizabeth' only. There are no nicknames."

Kathy's eyes twinkled above her mask. "I can see why you might not be close."

"Yep."

"Well, back to Isobel Durbin Martin," Kathy said. "As far as you calling her, and peeling the scab off the wound, if I were her, I'd want the killer found, convicted, and sentenced to death, so I'd be willing to relive some of the pain to achieve that goal."

"Minnesota, Iowa and Illinois don't have the death penalty."

"Just the same," Kathy said, "I think Isobel would want to talk to you if it would help solve the case."

"I'll call her today," Monica said. "Did you find out anything more about that murder in the Miami night club district?"

"I did, and you're not going to believe it. I didn't know whether to say all of this in front of Matt or not, so I was waiting for him to leave."

"You have my attention."

Kathy jammed her leopard print cheaters onto her face and read from some scribbles on a legal pad, her eyes also bouncing up to the screen on her laptop. "In the alley behind The Thirsty Pelican, which is a few doors down from The Flaming Flamingo, a cross-dresser who went by the name of Destiny Diamond was found beaten to death with a metal pipe."

Monica covered her mouth and whispered, "Did Destiny work at The Flamingo?"

"No. She was just a frequent flyer there. Her real name was Norman Gutierrez, a third generation Cuban American."

"Was she naked? Was there a penis and scrotum painted on her pelvis?"

"No paint. She was found fully clothed. And she wasn't a trans woman, just a cross-dresser. Here's a *Miami Herald* photo of her with some friends at the bar." Kathy turned her laptop for Monica to see.

The wind was knocked from Monica's lungs as she looked at the grainy photo. "Holy shit! That's Geoffrey next to her." Monica pointed at the screen for Kathy to see Geoffrey standing with his arm around Destiny Diamond's waist, a few other people flanking them.

"I had no idea. The caption doesn't mention anyone else by name and I've never met Geoffrey," Kathy said. "What do you suppose that means? Were they dating? Were they just friends? Or was she just a regular at the club?"

"I don't like the connection," Monica said. "Can you email that article to Matt? Maybe that's enough for him to bring Geoffrey in for questioning."

"Will do."

Monica pondered the new information while squinting at some robins flying in and out of the trees, making their nests. After a long minute, she asked, "What was the date of the murder?"

"December 14, 2018."

"Let me look at my notes from my last meeting with Nicole." Monica rummaged through her attaché and came up with the yellow legal pad she had been using for this case. She curled the first few pages over the top and scanned her handwritten notes. "Here it is."

"What are you looking for?" Kathy asked.

"Nicole and Derek went to a conference in Miami in December 2018, but I don't know the exact days. I wonder if they were there when Destiny Diamond was murdered."

"Good catch," Kathy said. "At this point, nothing is coincidental."

Monica turned to her laptop and googled "2018 plastic surgery conference in Miami." Her mind clicked when she read the first search result. "Holy boob job."

"What?" Kathy asked.

Monica read aloud, "The 2018 International Society of Aesthetic Plastic Surgery Conference will be held December 10-14 in Miami. ISAPS is the world's leading international body of board-certified plastic surgeons, and this year's meeting is expected to draw more than 1,500 participants."

"So the conference and the date of the murder overlap."

"Even if they didn't, it isn't uncommon to spend a few days on either side of a conference for a little R&R. That's probably when Nicole dragged Derek along to Geoffrey's club as her wingman," Monica said.

"Maybe Ms. Destiny Diamond hit on Derek, offending him," Kathy said. "What did he say about the club? The women were too fast for his taste?"

"He called them 'freaks,'" Monica said, "and when Matt asked him to elaborate, he said, 'people pretending to be someone they weren't.' Sounded like he was referring to Destiny Diamond if you ask me."

"So, he beat her to death in the alley?" Kathy asked in disbelief. "That's a major overreaction to being turned off, or even disgusted, by someone. I mean, really."

"We don't know if something happened between Derek and Destiny. Maybe Destiny came onto him. Maybe they had sex in the alley, and he hated himself for it. I don't know. I'm not an expert in the psychology of a killer's mind. Who knows what damage lurks behind his guppy eyes and snaggled teeth?"

Kathy squinted. "Maybe Destiny was Geoffrey's girlfriend, and he discovered her having sex with Derek in the alley. Maybe Geoffrey killed her in a jealous rage."

"Wouldn't Derek have reported that?" Monica asked.

"Maybe Geoffrey killed her after Derek and Dr. Kershaw left that evening."

"That could be," Monica said, "but it wouldn't explain an on-going rampage against trans women."

Kathy followed Monica's gaze at the birds. "Maybe it sparked a deep-seated hatred that he could no longer control, unleashing a fury against trans women. As you said, he later had access to the medical records for Michelle, Veronica and Ingrid on Nicole's laptop at home. He could've gotten their names and addresses."

"That's true," Monica said. "Both Geoffrey and Derek are suspects in my mind, and I don't like either one of them. Let me talk to Isobel Durbin. Maybe she has info that could tip the scale toward one or the other. In the meantime, could you dig into Derek Russell's past in Sacramento?"

"I'll get right on it," Kathy said. "Wow. The morning just flew by."

The women folded and packed up the portable table and food, leaving the steel drum to burn out. They agreed to talk by phone later. Monica drove straight to her house, which was empty.

She situated herself comfortably in the mid-afternoon light, the sun dodging a bank of building clouds, and dialed the number for Isobel Durbin. Her call went to voicemail, but the greeting indicated it was Isobel, so Monica knew she had the right number. She left her name and number and hoped Isobel would return her call.

She decided to do some googling herself and typed in "Derek Russell, Sacramento." Only his position as a PA at UC Davis Medical Center populated, confirming what he had told them in the parking lot. She pondered his situation and why he chose to become a *locums*. A light bulb turned on in her mind, and she thought that the Community Memorial HR Department should have a complete file on him. She called Becky Smith, the HR person who regularly assigned Monica employment contracts to review.

After they exchanged greetings, and Monica explained her role in the investigation, Becky asked, "What can I do for you?"

"I'm interested in the file on a *locum tenens* physician assistant by the name of Derek Russell. He's from California —"

"UC Davis Medical Center in Sacramento," Becky finished. "I'm familiar with him. He's been coming here for several years."

"I'm always amazed that you know everyone," Monica said.

"Well, we're not as big as you might think, and Nicole's subspecialty program for gender-affirming surgeries is relatively new," Becky said. "Let me pull up PA Russell's electronic file."

Monica heard keyboard taps on the other end of the line. "Yep. I have it here. What would you like to know?"

"What were his physician references from UC Davis like?"

A few key strokes and Becky said, "The usual letters indicating the dates of employment. He's in good standing on the medical staff. No issues."

"Did you call anyone there or just rely on written references?"

"For a *locums* staff member, we would rely on the *locum* agency to do the primary verification of credentials and employment. The agency would then send the info to us electronically. If anyone was going to talk to surgeons at UC Davis to get a handle on Derek's skills, it would've been Dr. Kershaw. I guess you'd have to ask her."

Monica made a mental note to follow up with Nicole. "Would you mind asking the *locums* company to confirm that Derek still works at UC Davis and is in good standing? And that he doesn't have a criminal history? Maybe they could do another background check."

"They're supposed to run one every two years," Becky said. "Let me just get to that part of the file." More keyboard strokes, then, "Hmm."

"What?" Monica asked.

"I don't see one in here. I'm sure the *locums* did one but just forgot to send it to us. They're very thorough."

"Let's hope they simply forgot to send it to you. You never know what will show up on those."

"I'll call them right away and let you know what I learn."

Monica's phone screen lit up with an incoming call. "Hey, Becky. I have to run. I have another call coming in."

"Sounds good. I'll catch up with you later."

28

Monica recognized the number on her screen as Isobel Durbin's.

"Hello. This is Monica Spade."

"This is Isobel Durbin. You left a message about Ingrid, my sister?"

"Yes." Monica took a deep breath. "I'm so sorry to bother you by raising the topic of Ingrid's death again, but I'm assisting the police in Minnesota and Wisconsin in the investigation of three murders of trans women, your sister being one of them."

There was a sigh, followed by Isobel saying in an anguished voice, "I already gave a lengthy interview to the Iowa City police last July."

"I realize that," Monica said, "but since that time, more information has come to light, so we have a few more questions for you that the Iowa City detective probably didn't ask."

"Who are you with again?"

"I'm an attorney in private practice. I represent Community Memorial Hospital in Apple Grove, Wisconsin, where Ingrid had her gender-affirming surgery."

"Oh," Isobel said with surprise. "What does the hospital have to do with the investigation?"

Monica chose not to answer that and instead asked, "Do you remember Ingrid's surgeon, Dr. Kershaw?"

"Of course," Isobel said. "She was awesome."

"As it turns out, three of her patients, including Ingrid, have been murdered."

"What?!" Isobel exclaimed.

"Yes. In addition," Monica said, "they all had the same defiling symbols spray-painted on them, in graffiti red."

"You mean, male genitalia?"

"Yes. The killer's signature."

"Were they hanged too?"

"No. One was shot and the other's throat was cut."

Isobel sobbed for a minute then asked in a jagged whisper, "So, the hospital thinks the killer is targeting Dr. Kershaw's patients?"

Smart girl. "As do the police. When the Iowa City detective spoke to you last year, he didn't make the connection because the other two murders hadn't happened yet—"

"Why aren't the police calling me?" Isobel snapped, her tone becoming defensive. "How do I know you're who you say you are?"

Monica wasn't surprised that Isobel was skeptical. She had a right to be. "As I said, I'm working closely with Detective Matt Breuer in Apple Grove and Detective Paul Heinz in Minneapolis. I'll share what you tell me with them. In the meantime, feel free to google me. I'm Monica Spade of Spade, Daniels & Taylor in Apple Grove. I represent the hospital and Dr. Kershaw. I can wait while you google me."

There was silence for a few seconds, but Monica didn't hear any keyboard strokes.

"Fine. I believe you," Isobel said, "but I don't want the detectives calling me too. I want to get this conversation over with in one call. Ingrid's murder is just too hard to relive, and discussing the details brings back so much pain. You don't understand. Dredging it all back up again will destroy me for the rest of my day. I'll be emotionally shot and won't be able to focus when I return to work."

"I can only imagine," Monica said in a tender tone. "I hope you can take some comfort in knowing that there are people like me who want to catch Ingrid's killer. To do right by her and bring the killer to justice. If that helps make some of the pain worthwhile—to know that we want to catch the killer as much as you do—then maybe we can talk for five minutes."

Monica heard a sharp intake of breath and a door open to the sounds of the outdoors—car traffic, the wind hitting the phone, birds chirping.

"I'm at work but just left on break," Isobel said. "We can talk while I walk around the block. The truth is that I'd do anything to help find her killer."

"I'll try to be brief and to the point," Monica said. "Thank you for your time."

"What do you want to know?"

"Do you remember meeting other members of Dr. Kershaw's care team?"

"Yes."

Finally, someone who remembers something. "Can you tell me about them?"

"Well, there was Jane, Dr. Kershaw's nurse. She seemed nice. I think I met her a few times—at clinic visits."

"Okay. Anyone else?"

"After the surgery, in the hospital, the nurses who cared for Ingrid were all really nice and understanding. I'm sorry I don't remember their names. There was one guy, though, Dr. Kershaw's physician assistant..." Isobel's voice trailed off.

"Uh-huh," Monica prompted.

"I think his name was Derek."

"Yes. What do you remember about him?"

"He was very professional and a good listener. Caring and gentle. Ingrid said he had the softest touch among the providers when he examined her. He visited her every day in the hospital, then actually did an annual follow-up visit in Iowa to make sure she was happy with the results, to see if she had any lingering complications, and to make sure everything was working okay. I think he brought a questionnaire with him that Ingrid filled out."

"Oh really?" Monica's blood ran cold, the hairs on her arms standing on end. Neither Nicole nor Derek had mentioned annual follow-up visits, making Monica wonder if Derek had scanned the questionnaire into the medical record.

"Yes," Isobel was saying, "We were really impressed by that type of long-term attention. I met Derek leaving Ingrid's house on the first anniversary of her surgery, but I didn't get to say hi to him on the second anniversary because I was at work."

A river of dread flooded Monica's mind as she pictured Derek at Ingrid's farmhouse, rope and spray paint in hand.

Isobel continued, "He said it was his favorite part of the job—visiting the patients for the first two years after their surgeries."

"Did anyone come with him?"

"No. As I recall, he rode his motorcycle, which we thought was sort of cool. He said he loved seeing the countryside, and the air in Iowa smelled so fresh."

"That's interesting." Monica had driven through Iowa on numerous occasions and never thought the air was any fresher than in Wisconsin. "You're sure Derek visited Ingrid the second year, right before she was killed?"

"She said he was planning to, but I didn't hear how it went. She died right after—" Isobel's breath caught, and she blurted, "Oh my God! You aren't saying that *he* killed her, are you?"

"No," Monica said very slowly and carefully, "but this is important information that I'm going to share with the police today." Even though her own voice sounded calm, her worst fears soared on a gust of adrenaline. She could barely formulate a coherent thought to ask another question.

"You would think Dr. Kershaw would have told the police about the annual visits," Isobel said.

"As I said, the Iowa police never spoke to Dr. Kershaw." *And I'm not convinced that Nicole knew about the annual visits*, Monica thought but didn't say. "Did Ingrid mention the precise date Derek planned to visit? Was it a few days before she was killed?"

"Maybe a week or so, but I can't remember. At the time, I didn't consider it very eventful. Just another appointment. You know, unmemorable. It fit together in my mind because it was the second anniversary of her surgery. We didn't talk for a week or so, then, when she was found dead, well, I had just forgotten about everything leading up to her death because my mind was shattered into a thousand pieces. In fact, I hadn't thought about Derek, or his visits, until you called today."

"Visits? As in multiple?" Monica asked.

"No. Just the two, I mean."

"Got it. And you didn't get the chance to ask Ingrid how her second visit with Derek went because she was found dead on July 24th. Is that correct?"

"Exactly. It wasn't uncommon for us to go a week or so without talking, since we both worked and had busy social lives."

Monica let a brief silence settle over the phone, hoping Isobel might volunteer more useful information. When she didn't, Monica asked, "After Ingrid died, did you have the opportunity to enter her house? Was there any evidence of Derek's visit? The questionnaire? His business card? Anything?"

Isobel was breathing harder now, and Monica pictured her striding with purpose down a sidewalk, an anguished look on her face. "Let me think. I remember going through her things, sorting them. It was so painful. So sad. So hard on my parents. But no, I don't remember seeing any evidence that Derek had visited."

"So, you aren't sure whether he visited or not?"

"No. For all I know, he never arrived."

"Okay. But when you last spoke to Ingrid, she mentioned he was planning to visit, right?"

"That's right. She was looking forward to it."

"Did she keep a calendar? Did you, or the Iowa City police, look at it?"

"Not that I know of. She had a cell phone, of course, and my fingerprint unlocked it. I opened if for the detective and he took it. They never told me if they found anything on it, and I didn't get it back, not that I wanted it back."

"I wonder if the Iowa detective still has it," Monica said.

Isobel said, "Excuse me," to someone, which reminded Monica that Isobel's break time was probably coming to an end.

"I'll make sure Detective Breuer follows up on Ingrid's cell phone. Maybe she had the appointment in her phone calendar," Monica said.

"Thank you, Ms. Spade. You were right. I am relieved to know that there are people who still want to catch Ingrid's killer."

"Rest assured, we'll try our hardest," Monica said. "Listen, I want to be respectful of your time while you're at work. You've shared very important information with me, and I'm going to discuss it with Detective Breuer right away. If you think of anything else, please feel free to call me at this cell phone number."

"Do you think Derek is the killer?" Isobel asked.

"We have to analyze everything. I don't want to jump to conclusions."

"Okay," Isobel said. "Will you let me know either way?"

"Of course," Monica said. "Thank you for taking the time to talk to me today."

As soon as they hung up, Monica called Sam Moua in Information Security at the hospital.

"Sam, I'm so glad I caught you on the first try."

"What's up?"

"Can you look in Michelle Adler's, Veronica Remington's and Ingrid Durbin's charts, and tell me if there's a questionnaire in them that would've been completed one year after their surgical dates, and then again one year after that."

"What are the dates of their surgeries?"

She supplied them to him. "Can you look soon? Like in the next 30 minutes?"

"Sure. I'll get right on it."

As soon as she hung up, she equivocated on whether to call Matt or Al Bowman next. She gazed out the long bank of windows, the building clouds presaging rain. *If I tell Al that Derek is the number one suspect for serial murders, will Al remove him from the staff, thereby tipping him off?*

She called Matt.

"Hey, what's up?" he asked. "Kind of busy at work."

She heard radios crackling and people talking in the background.

"I wouldn't be calling if it wasn't important. I spoke to Isobel Durbin, Ingrid Durbin's sister."

"I was thinking about calling her myself, but hadn't looked in the Iowa City file for the number yet. What did she have to say?"

"That Derek Russell visited Ingrid at her house on the first anniversary of her surgery, then planned to visit her on the second anniversary as well."

"What?" he asked.

She heard a door open and close, blocking out the background noise.

Monica repeated what she had just said.

"Did Dr. Kershaw tell us that was part of the surgical follow-up plan?" he asked. "Do surgical teams do house calls? I think I'd remember that."

"She said she usually saw her patients for a few months, then got occasional cards from them, like over the holidays."

"That rings true," he said. "Do you think she knows that Derek visited Ingrid?"

"I intend to ask her," Monica said. "Want to meet me at her house?"

"Sure. What time?"

"Hopefully soon, but I haven't arranged anything yet. I'll text you as soon as I know. Did you find out anything about Derek's background in California? Does he have a criminal record?"

"The officer I assigned to run the search hasn't reported back."

"I can do stuff in half the time it takes you people," she muttered.

"Come again?" he said.

"Nothing. Just tell your lackey to hustle up. In the meantime, I'll call Nicole then let you know what time we plan to meet."

"Simmer down, Mon. I know you don't want to warn the next patient, but don't overstep."

She swallowed a nasty retort and asked, "Did you get an email from Kathy with a *Miami Herald* article attached showing Geoffrey with his arm around Destiny Diamond's waist?"

"Huh? What are you talking about?"

She explained that Destiny was killed at the same time Nicole and Derek were visiting Miami, and that Destiny could've been Geoffrey's girlfriend.

"Really? That is interesting. More than a coincidence."

"That's what I'm telling you!"

"Don't do anything rash," he said. "This is still a police investigation so I don't want you going rogue."

She rolled her eyes, hung up on him, and dialed Nicole.

"Hello, Monica. What's up?"

"Hi. I'm wondering if we can meet today."

"About what? Do you have a crack in the case?"

"Sort of. I need to talk to you."

"Geoffrey and I are making a surgical strike at the grocery store right now, but we should be home in thirty minutes or so. Do you want to come over?"

"If you wouldn't mind," Monica said.

"What is it about?"

Monica hesitated because she wanted to see Nicole's reaction in person. On the other hand, she wanted Nicole to look up the medical records and get her head in order. She decided to spill the beans. "Derek Russell making house calls to surgical patients on the first and second anniversaries of their surgeries."

"What?"

"Yes. Is that part of your post-operative protocol?"

"Noooo," Nicole growled in an astonished whisper.

"Well, we need to look at the medical records together. He made a follow-up visit to Ingrid Durbin one year after her surgery, then planned to make a second one shortly before she was killed."

"That doesn't make any sense to me," Nicole said.

"That's why we need to meet in person. I'll download everything to you, and we can look for his note in the medical record."

"He never mentioned those visits to me, and I'd remember something like that."

Monica decided not to mention Geoffrey's relationship with Destiny. "Okay. I'll see you in an hour to talk about the implications of this. Matt Breuer will join us."

"Right. See you then."

No sooner did Monica end that call than Sam Moua called her back.

"Did you find any post-surgical questionnaires in the medical records?"

"None," he said.

"Did you find a note by Derek Russell indicating he visited the patients on the first or second-year anniversaries of their surgeries?"

"Hang on," he said. "I can look for that."

She waited patiently while he opened each of the three women's medical records and looked for the dates in the progress notes. "I don't see any entries by PA Russell after the patients were discharged from the hospital."

"Thanks," she said. "That's what I needed to know."

Monica went to the kitchen and made herself a cup of tea to go, as the day had gotten away from her. The drive to Nicole's house would take about 20 minutes, and she needed the energy boost. She texted Shelby. *I might be home late. Don't wait for me for dinner.*

Shelby replied, *Work again?*

Monica typed, *Yes. Things are heating...*

Before she could complete her thought, the Moultrie critter cam app on her phone alerted her that she had new photo from Nicole and Geoffrey's house. She opened the app and clicked through the photos. The implications of what she saw added a dangerous twist to her existing suspicions. The photos were of Derek riding to Nicole's house and parking his bike next to the garage. Derek had told them that morning that he was attending a bike rally in Tomah, which was at least 90 minutes south of Nicole's house. Had he gone to the rally at all or had he lied to them?

She tried calling Nicole but it went straight to voicemail. She had only a few seconds to decide how to leave a message without disclosing that she had downloaded their critter cam photos. After the beep, she said, "Heads up, Nicole. I have it on good authority that Derek is headed to your house."

Feeling confident that she provided a sufficient warning to Nicole and Geoffrey, Monica gathered her attaché case and shrugged on a coat. The thought also occurred to her that they should be getting the same critter cam photos as she did, since it was their app in the first place. *Duh.*

Her phone rang. "This is Monica."

"Tiffany Rose here," she said flirtatiously. "Long time, no see. How are you?"

Tiffany was the Bambi darling of the Apple Grove TV news reporters. She had covered the last two murder trials Monica had been involved in and had hit on Monica while interviewing her. Monica didn't have anything against Tiffany. She just didn't care for her thick makeup, bleach-blonde hair, skinny body and short, short dresses. Nothing personal. In all fairness, however, Tiffany had made Monica a local celebrity by interviewing her so often.

"I'm doing fine," Monica said in as formal of a voice as she could muster. "Kind of busy at work right now. What can I do for you?"

In her inquisitive, honeyed tone, Tiffany said, "I heard there's an issue at the hospital."

"Tiff, I don't have time for rumors about monkeys running loose—"

"Do you have time to confirm that three of Dr. Nicole Kershaw's trans female patients have been murdered?"

Oh fuck! Who is her source? Monica attempted nonchalance. "You can't believe everything you hear."

"That isn't what my source tells me," Tiffany said. "This is serious, Monica. I think you better check it out."

"Give me 24 hours?" Monica asked.

"I'll give you until tomorrow morning at 10, but I'm not letting go of this. I called you as a courtesy because I know you sometimes speak for the hospital, but my station manager is breathing down my neck to prepare a segment for tomorrow."

Monica swallowed hard and said in her most reassuring tone, the one she used to bamboozle judges and sway juries, "You have my full attention, Tiff. I'll be sure to get back to you before 10 a.m. tomorrow."

"Great. Maybe we can meet over breakfast and discuss it."

"Restaurants are closed, remember?"

"Right. Stupid pandemic. You could come over to my apartment—"

"I don't think so, Tiff." *I do not have time for your nonsense right now.*

Tiffany removed the coating of amour from her voice. "I'll wait to hear from you."

"Thanks for the courtesy call."

Monica hung up and decided she had better update Al Bowman on her way to Aqua Vulva.

29

Once she was in her pickup and cruising along on Highway 53, she called Al.

"It's been a while since I've heard from you." He sounded like he needed a friend.

"I've missed you too, but I've been working on the investigation into Dr. Kershaw's patients. I wish I had better news for you, Al, but there are two suspects related to Dr. Kershaw and the hospital."

"Oh shit," he said in a mix of angst and exhaustion. "How many patients were murdered?"

"The present count is three." She decided not to include Destiny.

"Could my life get any worse? Patients with COVID are starting to come into the emergency room, I'm losing money ass-over-tea kettle, and now patients are being murdered."

"I'm sorry to tell you this, but one of the suspects is a member of Dr. Kershaw's surgical team, a PA named Derek Russell."

"Never heard of him."

"No reason you should have. The other suspect is her live-in lover, Geoffrey Gold."

"One suspect is my employee and the other is my plastic surgeon's lover? I don't know whether it sucks worse to be her or us. The hospital is going to take a beating in the press. I'd better bring Public Affairs up to speed."

"Good idea. I need to talk to them as well. Tiffany Rose called me 10 minutes ago. She's already heard about the connection of murder to Dr. Kershaw. I have no idea who her source is, but I promised to reply to her by 10 a.m. tomorrow."

"Can you be our spokesperson for the news?"

"Be happy to. Just so you know, if the killer is Dr. Kershaw's boyfriend, he probably got the victims' names and addresses by looking at her laptop, which she regularly brings home with her."

"Again, pointing all the arrows right back to the hospital. That would be an indictment of our medical record security."

"I agree. There's an equal chance that Dr. Kershaw's PA is the killer though."

"Why?"

"He's kind of a jaded, biker dude from Sacramento, but we don't know much about him. Detective Breuer is investigating his past. He's a *locum tenens* who helped Dr. Kershaw start the program, and he visited—"

"For Christ's sake, don't we do background checks on *locum* staff?"

"Funny you should ask. I already spoke to Becky Smith in HR. She said the *locums* agency is supposed to run the criminal background check, but she didn't see one in Russell's employment file. She was going to call them and track it down."

"Seriously. What type of a criminal background would indicate a serial killer?"

"Hard to tell. Serial killers are sociopaths. Surprisingly, a history of arson is a common theme among serial killers."

"Arson? That doesn't make any sense to me whatsoever."

"Some signs make sense, others don't. Early childhood trauma or abuse makes sense. A history of cruelty to animals makes sense. Neither arson nor wetting the bed makes sense to me."

"I'm pretty sure none of those is asked on our employment application, but a conviction for cruelty to animals or arson would show up on a background check. Last I checked, it wasn't a crime to wet the bed." Al fake-laughed at his own joke.

He sounded a little crazed to Monica. "Even so, if Derek was convicted as a juvenile, then his criminal record might be sealed, and later expunged for good behavior—"

"So, it would appear clean on a search nowadays," he finished.

"Precisely."

"You're telling me we could've hired a serial killer without any clue?"

"Yes."

"How is he connected to the victims?"

"He visited one of the victims on the first anniversary of her surgery and was scheduled to visit her on the second anniversary. She was killed on the second anniversary, to the day, like the other two victims."

"Which places him at the scene of the murder."

"Maybe. If he followed through."

"I've never heard of a second anniversary house call. Is that part of Dr. Kershaw's protocol?"

"I don't think so, but I'm driving to her house right now to talk about it."

He groaned. "I'm really glad you're working this case, Monica. I need to check if this PA is scheduled to work, and we need to cut off his access to the building and computer system."

Finally, someone who appreciates me. "Give us two hours, Al. If he is the killer, we don't want to tip him off."

"Oh right. I'll just alert security to call me if he shows up on campus. I'm currently living my worst nightmare as president of a hospital. I should've listened to my mother and gone into banking."

"I'm so sorry. I'll do what I can—"

"To transport me to a new reality?" he scoffed.

She remained silent.

"I'm sorry, Monica. This news is pretty mind-blowing. I'm really grateful for what you're doing, but I'm just so overwhelmed right now."

"I understand."

"Update me as soon as you and the police decide what to do."

"I will. Take care."

She finished her tea and tried to remain optimistic but was reminded that she couldn't polish a turd. The facts were the facts. Three of Nicole's patients had been targeted, murdered and defiled. A fourth victim was brutally murdered in an alley behind Geoffrey's club on a night when Nicole and Derek could have been visiting the club. *Mere coincidence? I don't think so.*

As Monica drew closer to Lake Wissota, a wall of stirring black clouds hovered above her like the Death Star. A few miles down the road, icy raindrops thrashed her windshield, testing her old wipers. She suddenly remembered that she hadn't texted Matt with a time to meet. She called him.

"Hey," he said.

"I'm almost to Dr. Kershaw's house. Sorry I didn't text you sooner, but I got distracted. My mind is racing a million miles per second. If you can break away right now, Nicole said she could meet with us."

"It will take me thirty minutes to get there," he said.

"I'm still 10 minutes away," she said. "I'll chat with her for 20 minutes while we wait for you."

"I'll leave right away."

"By the way, you should know that Derek will be there too."

"What? Why? I thought he was headed to a biker rally in Tomah."

"That's what he told us, but...well...I don't know if you noticed, but Dr. Kershaw has several critter cams strapped to trees in the woods surrounding her house—"

"I saw them," he interjected.

"Of course, you did," she said. "You're a detective."

"What of it?"

"Through a series of events, I now receive the photos from Nicole's cameras on my phone through my Moultrie critter cam app."

"Clever girl. I'd need a search warrant to do that."

"And see, I'm a private citizen, so I'm licensed to snoop."

"And, that's how you saw that Derek is at her house?"

"Yes. Nicole and Geoffrey are grocery shopping, so I left her a voicemail about Derek coming to her house."

"Okay," he said in a calm voice that she found condescending. "Let's not assume that fireworks are going off just yet."

"Whatever. I'm concerned, Matt."

"I'm leaving the station right now."

She turned her wiper blades to high. "The sky is spitting a mix of rain and snow up here."

"Drive safely. The forecast is for thunder snow this evening."

"I'm slowing down as we speak. Just get here as soon as you can, okay?"

"Keep things low key until I do," he said.

"No worries. I'm good at low key. I won't play my hand until you arrive."

"Good girl."

She chafed at "good girl" as she took the next exist for Lake Wissota. By the time the Aqua Vulva sign came into view, a bolt of lightning streaked across the sky, followed five beats later by a thunderclap. Her wipers were working overtime, creating a bank of sleet at the edges of her windshield.

When she emerged from the winding driveway to the garage, she saw Derek's Harley Davidson chopper still parked by the garage, the sleet pinging off the chrome and accumulating on the seat. The garage door was closed and no one was in sight.

She turned off her lights and sat for a minute, the wind intensifying and the sleet hammering the roof of her truck like a million BBs being dropped from a box of ammo. Her pulse heightened with the anticipation of a confrontation, her breathing coming in shallow bursts. She suddenly realized that she was entering the lion's den, and if either Derek or Geoffrey was the killer, she would be in grave danger. *I'm not the police. I don't know how to defend myself. Maybe I should wait for Matt.*

30

She pondered her options, then decided she was being a wimp. Nicole was her client, dammit, and Monica owed her a duty to help her in all things legal. She also owed the hospital a duty to figure out what the hell was going on. *I can probably get more info than Matt. Once he arrives, they'll all clam up.* She took three deep breaths, envisioning herself on a yoga mat, the floor heated and the yoga studio cast in the orange glow of battery-powered candles. *Time to put on my big girl undies and be brave.*

She opened her door, the sleet greeting her like a swarm of bees stinging her face. She ice-skated down the cobblestone path, waved to the critter cam, and was stepping onto the wooden deck when she heard a loud bang. *Was that thunder or a gunshot?*

Convincing herself the crack came from inside the house, she crouched down and darted off the cobblestone path, tracking to the left side of the house, the opposite direction of the deck and front door. If someone was about to flee the house, she didn't want to meet him on the sidewalk. Unarmed, and her pickup truck sitting in the driveway, she already felt like a sitting duck.

She was plunged into dark gray on the back side of the house, her suede boots no match for the slippery leaves and puddles of wet snow. Energized by fear, her lashes fighting a battle against the sleet while her eyes scanned the deck area behind her, she focused on calming herself as her vision adjusted to the stormy evening.

I wasn't imagining a gunshot, was I? She forced herself to listen through the sleet slamming the house, her ears ringing from the thunderclaps. She inched along the edge of the house, bumping into shrubbery and struggling for balance on the wood chips. At one point, she stepped into a hole, the icy water spilling over the top of her boot and soaking her foot.

She reached a large window overlooking the lake, soft light casting a glow into the wall of rain. She didn't have the benefit of shadows playing on the ground due to the heavy rain, so she couldn't tell if anyone was in the room or not by looking at the snow-splotched lawn. She had to risk a peek into the window. She held her breath, moved her face to the bottom right corner of the large picture window, and looked inside.

Oh fuck, I'm too late.

Before her in the center of their informal living room, was a standoff between Geoffrey and Derek, with Nicole caught in the middle. Derek, who was a few inches taller than Nicole, had his left arm crooked around her neck in a headlock, a gun in his right hand and pointed at her head.

Geoffrey stood six feet away, facing them, also wielding a handgun. He was pointing his gun directly at Derek, his arm steady and finger on the trigger. Geoffrey had no shot, however, because if he pulled the trigger, Derek could shoot Nicole. Even worse, if Geoffrey missed Derek, his bullet would hit Nicole.

Their lips were moving, all talking at once, but Monica couldn't hear a damn thing through the window and weather. Geoffrey looked straight-up pissed, Nicole horrified, and Derek a psychopathic calm.

Monica had to save Nicole. Of that, she was certain.

Scenarios ran through her mind as the lightning flashed, and another thunderclap shook the house, causing the lights to flicker. Monica heard Marvin, who was at Nicole's side, howl. The lights came back on for Monica to see Marvin bare his teeth at Derek, advancing on him. Risking his tactical advantage, Derek quickly lowered his gun and shot Marvin in the head, reminding everyone that they were one second away from the same fate. Marvin crumpled at Nicole's feet, blood and brain splattered on the rug next to him.

Nicole's mouth opened wide and words that Monica couldn't hear flew out. Her expression changed from abject horror to fury, her body thrashing against Derek.

Their struggle didn't last long when Derek tightened his arm around her neck and pistol-whipped her against the side of the head. Dazed, Nicole slumped against Derek, and the standoff resumed.

Monica used the thunderclaps and streaks of lightning to her advantage, raising her cell phone to the window and taking a photo of the threesome. Her fingers turning to icicles, she leaned against the house and texted the photo to Matt with the message, *Hurry!*

She stuffed her phone in her pocket and wondered how she could save Nicole in the next few minutes before Matt arrived. *I need a diversion, but I can't end up in the same room with them, or Derek will shoot all of us.*

Monica recalled what Nicole had told her during one of their meetings. *We're armed to the gills. I have a conceal and carry permit and a gun in my car at all times.*

Monica memorized where everyone was standing in the room then ducked back down to a crouch and ran pell-mell through the sloppy terrain, slipping and sliding, even falling to her hands and knees at one point. She scrambled back up and finally made it to the garage. She entered through a service door and went to Nicole's Range Rover, which thankfully was unlocked.

Her hands cold, wet, and smeared with mud, Monica rubbed them on her jeans, then opened the driver's side door. With her numb fingers, she searched under the driver's seat. *Success!* Her fingers clasped around a smooth, leather carrying case. She set the case on the seat, hands shaking, and unzipped it. What appeared to be a .45 automatic lay next to a full clip of bullets. She examined the gun and clip in the glow of the interior car lights, jammed the clip into the grip, and racked and chambered a round.

Carrying the gun at her side, careful to point it down and away, she picked her way across the wet gravel, shielding her eyes from the downpour with her other hand. She avoided the squeaky front door that would give her away. Besides, she would be visible if she walked down that hallway to the living room.

Instead, she quietly and carefully snaked up the slippery deck, now cast in shades of silver with each lightning burst. She crept to the sliding door off the dining room, which was out of view from where the three were in a standoff.

She unzipped and removed her wet boots, and using the pounding rain and steady drumbeats of thunder as cover, she opened the sliding door, stepped inside, and slowly closed it behind her. In a crouching position, she scurried along the wall dividing the dining room from the living area.

"Don't do it, Derek," Geoffrey was saying. "We can all get out of this together."

"Slide your gun over here, prick. I'm gonna make it look like *you* killed her."

"Then you're going to have to kill me too. And how will that look to the police?"

Derek was silent, so Geoffrey pressed on. "If you kill us both, you'll have a sloppy mess on your hands. Too many clues, Derek. The police will figure out it's you."

Once Monica was at the edge of the wall, she expected she would have a clear view of the group. She dropped to her tummy and army-crawled the last few feet to the archway. Once there, she removed her phone. She clicked on the camera and extended her arm, holding the phone just around the corner. By looking at the screen, but not sticking her face out, she could see the threesome—still glued to the same spots—in the living room.

Derek's and Nicole's backs were to Monica, Marvin at their feet, blood pooling around his body. Geoffrey was facing them from about six feet away, off to the right of Monica's shooting lane if Derek was her target. Thankfully, Geoffrey's position would allow Monica a clean shot at Derek.

Nicole was a different story because she was glued to Derek. If Monica missed Derek, she would most likely hit Nicole. On the other hand, Nicole's life looked like it was about to meet a swift end in Derek's hands, so what did Monica have to lose?

Am I really capable of shooting someone? What if I'm wrong? What if Geoffrey is the killer? Her mind racing, she considered that possibility. *He doesn't have a gun to Nicole's head. Derek does. Analysis over.*

She stopped second-guessing herself and took a photo of the threesome. Then she turned on her phone's video camera and placed it face down on the floor, since she couldn't video and shoot at the same time. At least it would capture the audio recording. Her photos and video might be the best evidence of the dilemma she faced, because she had no idea if Geoffrey would support her later. She was experienced enough to know that people's perceptions and agendas weren't always the same when they later gave statements to the police.

Gun cradled in both hands, she inch-wormed around the corner, her hands and face now in full view if anyone glanced her way. Geoffrey was facing her, but his chin was tipped up, and he was looking at Derek. As she steadied the gun and took aim, if Geoffrey noticed, he didn't flash his eyes or flinch. He easily could have, dashing her plans and throwing them into a new standoff that would be as pointless as the one they were in now, but Geoffrey remained focused on Nicole and Derek.

A loud thunderclap rattled the house, the lights flickering again.

"Why, Derek, why?" Nicole asked in a strangled voice.

"They're freaks. You're a freak. After Destiny used me in Miami—"

"Destiny Diamond?" Geoffrey asked with genuine surprise. "How did she use you?"

"She seduced me," Derek spat. "Lured me to the alley. Gave me a blowjob, then when I undressed her, I saw..." He coughed in disgust, unable to finish.

"That she was a man?" Geoffrey finished for him.

"A freak. All freaks," Derek yelled. "I beat him. And you know what? It felt good...*right*. He deserved to die for deceiving me. For deceiving everyone."

Geoffrey blanched in surprise and Nicole gasped.

"She was my friend, you bastard," Geoffrey growled.

"Serves you right, you sick bastard," Derek said. "That kill was sloppy and unprofessional. A nightmare, really." He laughed maniacally. "No style or signature, and I was covered in blood. Unacceptable. Disgraceful. No. I realized I had to up my game to be a contender among the best. For the professionalism of it, you know? There's more competition for creative kills than you might think, so I did my homework, studying the craft of those who came before me. I had to up my game." His voice rose in pitch, deranged and sarcastic. "You know us psychopaths. We love the thrill of the kill."

"They were our patients!" Nicole screamed.

"Quiet, you bitch!" Derek yelled, tightening his arm around her. He turned to Geoffrey and said with a snarl, "Put the gun down or it's over for you too."

Geoffrey must have noticed Monica at some point because he suddenly provided the opportunity Monica needed. He raised both hands to the ceiling, the gun still in his right hand. "Then why don't you take your best shot and kill me before you kill Nicole."

Thunder pounded the house and a bolt of lightning crackled close by, sending them all into darkness.

"Geoffrey, no!" Nicole exclaimed.

Oh shit. I lost my chance. Monica's eyes plunged into darkness, her head throbbing and ears ringing. She listened for commotion or gunshots in the living room but all she could hear was the sleet pelting the house.

After a few seconds, the lights flickered back on, illuminating the same standoff. Geoffrey's hands were still in the air, his gun pointed at the ceiling. Taking the bait like a hungry shark, Derek moved his gun from Nicole's head and aimed it at Geoffrey.

Take the shot! a voice in Monica's head screamed. *You've got him dead to rights.*

Monica aimed her gun at Derek's leg. If she missed, the worst she could do was to maim Nicole. If she hit Derek, she had no doubt that Geoffrey would finish him off, that is if Derek's trigger finger didn't shoot Geoffrey on his way down. *Shoot before the lights go out again!*

Rapidly blinking her wet eyelashes, she squinted to place the bead in the sight, wavering between Derek's ass and thigh. She exhaled and eased the trigger back with her frozen index finger.

BAM! The deafening crack of a gunshot stunned everyone, as the gun recoiled in Monica's hand. She quickly leveled it, again aiming at Derek just in case he turned on her.

Derek fell to the floor instantly, his handgun skidding across the hardwood and under a coffee table. He groaned in pain, his hands clenching around his thigh. "Motherfucker! I'm gonna kill you," he screamed at Geoffrey. His homicidal eyes swept the floor, but Marvin's dead body obscured the location of his gun. He didn't realize it was Monica who had shot him.

As Monica had anticipated, Geoffrey didn't waste a second. He fired two more shots into Derek, slamming his chest and rolling him back onto the floor.

Nicole shrieked, then bolted sideways onto the sofa.

Gurgling sounds came from Derek's throat as he lay face up.

Geoffrey advanced on Derek, towering over him. Monica couldn't see Derek's face from her low angle, but she heard Geoffrey say, "This one is for Destiny, you fucker." She heard another shot.

Monica slammed her eyes shut and retreated around the corner into the dining room, raising herself into a sitting position, her back against the wall. A drum corps banged in her head, adrenaline and fear leading the cadence. *Please, God, forgive me.*

31

Monica's brain and body dissolved into a puddle. She was overcome with remorse but still as high-strung as a horse on race day. She pulled her knees to her chest and rested her chin on them, clutching the gun in a vice grip. *I shot Derek,* her mind involuntarily told her over and over. Wet to the core from sloshing around outside, she was shaking from head to toe, the adrenaline of battle kicking her paranoia into overdrive. *I heard him say he killed those women... I did the right thing...*

"What the fuck happened?" Nicole asked Geoffrey in the living room. "I thought I heard a gunshot when you raised your hands over your head."

"Over there," Geoffrey said. "Your lawyer shot Derek in the ass."

"Where? Where is Monica?" Nicole's voice sounded strained and thick.

"In the dining room," Geoffrey said.

Thunder hit, lightning flashed, and the lights went out again.

"Monica?" Nicole asked, her footsteps drawing near. "Monica, are you here?"

Monica opened her mouth to respond but no words came out. Suddenly, they heard another crash, and the front door slammed against the wall, hinges creaking and the old, dry wood shattering.

The thud of heavy boots filled the hallway along with the beam from a powerful flashlight, sweeping left to right and back again.

Monica was facing the door, so she automatically pointed the gun at the commotion.

"Apple Grove police! Drop your weapons!" Matt yelled from the dark hallway.

She had completely forgotten about Matt, but recognized his voice, his arrival snapping her back to reality. She released her grip on the gun, leaving it on the floor next to her, and raised her hands above her head. "Matt! It's me! Monica!"

His flashlight blinded her. "Are you all right?"

"Yes. I shot Derek."

"I heard the gunshots." The beam left her and illuminated Nicole's ashen face. She thrust her hands into the air. "I'm unarmed. Geoffrey is behind me in the living room. Derek and my dog, Marvin, are on the floor. Dead. Derek was the killer." She jerked her head around, pointing with her thumb.

The electricity was still off and Matt was still too far down the hallway to see Geoffrey or the dead bodies of Derek and Marvin sprawled on the bloody rug.

He treaded carefully in his wet boots, squishing and squeaking, gun still in hand, but lowered. As he passed Monica on the floor, he patted her shoulder, then cautiously entered the living room, the smell of death and gunpowder hanging in the air. After his eyes swept over everyone and everything, he pointed his flashlight at Geoffrey. "Set your weapon on the floor, Geoffrey."

"Sorry, man. I forgot. I'm in shock." Geoffrey knelt and carefully lay his gun on the rug, outside the expanding ring of dark blood.

"Anyone else here?" Matt asked.

As if responding to his question, the lights flicked on again, casting the living room in a yellow glow.

"No," Nicole said. "Just us. Derek was going to kill us, but Monica saved my life." She gestured to Geoffrey. "Both our lives."

Matt regarded the cut on Nicole's cheekbone, blood trailing down her cheek, then swung around and looked at Monica, comparing her angle to the hole in Derek's head, and his bloodied chest and pelvis. "From that angle?"

Monica didn't move from her spot, wrapping her arms around herself, rocking back and forth. "No. I shot him in the leg or butt. I don't know which. Geoffrey shot Derek after he fell to the floor."

Matt turned to Geoffrey. "Is that right, Geoffrey?"

"Yes. Monica shot him in the ass, and I shot him in the chest and head."

His eyes still on Geoffrey, Matt asked, "Why did you shoot Derek?"

"He was holding Nicole hostage, a gun to her head. He said he was going to shoot her, then shoot me. He didn't know that Monica had sneaked into the dining room and was behind him."

"Why was Derek going to kill you?" Matt asked both Nicole and Geoffrey.

"Because I asked him why the hell he was visiting our patients two years after their surgeries," Nicole said. "I sure as fuck hadn't approved it."

"How did you find out about the visits?" Matt asked.

"Monica called and told me she wanted to talk about them, so we arranged to meet here. I assume that's why you're here too. She said you were coming."

"That's true, but why did Derek show up?"

"I don't know," Nicole said. "He was here when Geoffrey and I got home from shopping. When we pulled in, he was leaning against the garage door, smoking a cigarette. We saw on our trail cams that he had arrived about 20 minutes earlier. He said he wanted to catch up on the police investigation before he left for Sacramento. Since the hospital stopped doing all elective surgeries, he was ending his *locums* coverage a few days early."

"Did he come inside with you?"

"I invited him in," Nicole said. "He helped us bring in the groceries, then sat at the kitchen table, making small talk. I brewed a pot of coffee, and Geoffrey went into the living room to turn on the TV. Thinking back on it now, Derek was obviously here to find out what we knew about the police investigation. When I asked him about the post-operative anniversary visits, he pulled a gun on me. He put me in a headlock and walked me out to the living room, his gun at my head. That's when Geoffrey quickly removed a gun from the holster above his butt crack, and pointed it at Derek, throwing us into a standoff."

"Is that how it happened, Geoffrey?" Matt asked.

"Yes. I actually had my back to Derek and Nicole while standing in front of the TV. Derek didn't realize I could see their reflection in the picture window, though, so when I saw he had a gun to Nicole's head, I unholstered mine as I turned to face them."

"Nice move," Matt said. "Did Derek confess to the murders?"

"We stood there forever, yelling at each other, then Marvin growled at him, so Derek shot him." Nicole's speech was choppy. "Poor Marvin." She covered her face with her trembling hands. "He was such a good dog."

"I actually witnessed Derek shooting Marvin when I was outside, looking through the picture window," Monica added in a hushed tone from the dining room.

"Did Derek confess?" Matt repeated, now staring Geoffrey in the eye.

Geoffrey nodded. "He confessed to killing Destiny Diamond, a good friend of mine, when he and Nicole attended the plastic surgery conference in Miami. Her body was found by the dumpster behind The Thirsty Pelican, brutally beaten. She didn't deserve to die like that. No one does. Derek said they went outside together and he discovered she was a guy. He went on about how messy that murder was, and how he needed to up his game to compete. With other serial killers, I guess.

But yes, he admitted that, after he killed Destiny, he started targeting and killing their patients. He didn't list off their names or go into more detail."

"Okay," Matt said. "Then Monica arrived and shot him from behind?"

"Yes," Geoffrey said. "While Derek was talking crazy, I happened to glance toward the dining room, and I saw Monica lying on the floor, her gun pointed at Derek. I was shocked as fuck, but I kept a poker face and raised my hands, taunting Derek to shoot me. The dumbass took the bait and pointed his gun at me. I saw his index finger curl around the trigger, but before he could get a shot off, Monica shot him, dropping him to the floor."

Matt spun around and looked toward Monica. All he could see was her wet socks. "Good job, Monica. Didn't know you were carrying now."

"Totally fucking agree," Geoffrey said. "Thanks for saving my life, Monica. One second later, and I'd have been a goner."

Monica gave them a thumbs up from around the door jamb. "Not my gun. Got it from Nicole's car."

Matt holstered his gun and put on a pair of blue latex gloves. He removed a baggie from his jacket, stepped around the pool of blood, and swiftly unloaded Geoffrey's gun, dumping it into the bag. "Do you have any other weapons on you?" he asked Geoffrey.

"No," Geoffrey said.

Matt's boots squeaked as he approached Monica in the dining room. He knelt beside her and patted her on the knee, then quickly unloaded her gun and dropped it into a second baggie. He sat back on his haunches and regarded her. "Mon, you're white as a ghost and sopping wet. We need to get you dried off and warmed up. More police will be here in a second. They'll want a statement from you."

"Okay," she said, a shiver racking her body. "I…just…"

"I understand. You're in shock. How did you know that Dr. Kershaw had a gun in her car?"

"She told me. Under the driver's seat. I left the case on her seat. You can go check it out."

"Remember to tell the officers that when they take your statement. You saw Derek about to kill her so you ran and got a gun to shoot him, right?"

"Yes."

"You'll be fine." He stood and held out a hand. "Can you get up?"

She grasped his hand and allowed him to pull her up to her feet.

"I'll get a dry towel for you," Nicole said, disappearing into the bedroom wing.

She returned with a towel and a clean sweatshirt. "Take off your wet top, dry yourself, and put on this sweatshirt. Quick, before the other officers get here."

Matt returned to Geoffrey in the living room, and they spoke in hushed tones. Monica did as instructed, peeling off her sopping jacket and collared shirt. Nicole gave the towel to Monica and waited while she dried herself.

Still feeling like she was in a horror movie, Monica was surprised at how much better she felt after removing the cold, wet clothes, like the first layer of the nightmare falling away.

"Put the sweatshirt on," Nicole said.

Monica quickly pulled the sweatshirt over her head, then dried her hair with the towel while Nicole hovered like a mother.

"Better?" Nicole asked.

"Yeah." Monica focused on Nicole. "You have a nasty cut on your cheekbone. We should wash that out and apply a bandage."

Nicole gingerly palpated around her cut. "I suppose. Let's go to the kitchen sink."

The ringing in Monica's ears, as loud as a swarm of cicada bugs, was interrupted by police sirens increasing in intensity. Through the open front door, they heard car tires grinding to a stop on the gravel driveway, then several car doors opening and closing. Matt trotted down the hallway and went out the front door, now slouching off its hinges against the wall.

"Come along," Nicole said, guiding Monica by the arm. Geoffrey trailed behind them. "Sit down at the table, Monica. Geoffrey, turn on the gas fireplace in the corner. The front door is wide open." Ever the commanding surgeon, Nicole quickly filled a tea kettle and turned on the stove.

Monica inched closer to the blue flame of the gas fireplace as she watched Geoffrey disappear down the hallway toward the front door.

Soon, a parade of officers and crime scene investigators stomped down the hallway to the living room, passing a traumatized Monica and attentive Nicole. They watched through the opening in the shared wall as photos were taken, samples collected, and body bags used for both Derek and Marvin. Nicole asked them to leave Marvin so she and Geoffrey could bury him properly in the yard, but an officer explained that they needed to remove the bullet from his skull as evidence.

"Fine," Nicole said, "but can you cremate him then?"

"You can make arrangements with the coroner," the stern-faced officer said, as he and a second officer carried the body bag out.

Monica drank two cups of hot tea as she helped Nicole wash and bandage her cut, then suffered through a police interview. An officer simultaneously interviewed Nicole in the dining room. Only after the police moved outside and Geoffrey had hammered the front door closed, did Monica think she was capable of driving.

"How are you doing?" Nicole asked when she returned to the kitchen. "You're still white as a ghost."

"Better. I've calmed down and warmed up, thanks to you." She raised her hands over the table. "Look. My hands aren't even shaking anymore."

Nicole reached out and clutched Monica's hands, holding them in her own, which were warm, sturdy and strong. "Monica, you saved my life. I can't thank you enough."

Monica blinked back tears. "You're welcome. I hope you can put this dreadful experience behind you."

Nicole released Monica's hands and shook her chunks of hair, some blood staining the large bandage over her right cheekbone. "There's no way I can continue practicing medicine in Apple Grove. My reputation is ruined. A serial killer for a physician assistant." She snorted in disbelief. "I'll have to start over someplace else."

Monica nodded in agreement.

"Maybe I'll go to Miami with Geoffrey and start a practice there." Nicole sipped her tea. "He'd love that, and, of course, there's a strong demand for plastic surgery in the land of beaches and bikinis."

"I suppose so," Monica said.

Nicole regarded Monica, her eyes softening in genuine appreciation. "I wish you well, Monica. You're a smart lawyer, and, as it turns out, a good shot with a .45."

"Is that the caliber of your gun? I wasn't entirely sure when I removed it from your car, but I'm familiar with automatics, so I just did what my daddy taught me."

"He did well, and so did you," Nicole said.

"I wish you and Geoffrey the best." Monica stood, gesturing to her front. "Mind if I—"

"Keep the sweatshirt," Nicole said, reading Monica's mind. "I won't have much occasion to wear a Packers' sweatshirt in Miami anyway."

"I suppose not." Monica wondered if she would ever wear it again herself. She glanced around for her wet jacket and shirt, which Nicole had folded and placed on a chair. Monica picked them up and walked toward the dining room.

Nicole followed, and they shook hands at the sliding door. A deep sense of sadness filled Monica, all the way down to her sopping socks. She didn't know if it stemmed from the shared experience with Nicole and their bond over battle, or if it was her part in shooting Derek. Either way, profound loss swamped her heart.

After mumbling more goodbyes, she stepped outside and pulled on her wet boots, intending to remove them as soon as she got in her truck. Getting across the icy deck was an adventure in itself, the cobblestone path even worse. When Monica emerged from the wooded area onto the gravel driveway, the blue and red flashing lights on the emergency vehicles blinded her. Cutting the glare with a hand to her eyes, she picked her way around the vehicles to her truck.

As soon as she started the engine, the passenger door opened and Matt climbed in. "Hey, Mon, are you okay to drive?"

"Yeah. I warmed up by the fire and had two cups of tea." She cranked the heat to high and removed her boots, setting them on the floor on Matt's side.

"The bravery you showed tonight was amazing. Not many cops would have had the guts or skills to do what you did."

"Thanks."

"I looked at the photos and audio recording you texted me. Good move to verify everyone's story."

"I thought the evidence might come in handy. You never know what people will say."

"Isn't that the case?" he said. "I also wanted you to be the first to know that my officer got back to me on Derek's criminal background in California. The court records indicate he changed his name from Donald to Derek when he was 18 years old. The officer searched the records of Donald Russell and found a juvenile record of arson, shoplifting, and disorderly conduct citations."

"Did you say arson?"

"Yes."

"I wonder if he was cruel to animals and wet the bed."

"Trademarks of the serial killer," Matt said.

"We'll never know, will we?" She cocked her head and looked at the windshield, now covered in sleet. "I'm sure that Detective Heinz will be grateful for the info we gathered and for..." She couldn't verbalize the grisly details yet again. "I just remembered that I promised Isobel Durbin I'd call her."

Matt patted her hand. "You're a first-rate detective, Mon."

"Not an overzealous amateur PI anymore, huh?"

"Sorry I said that. I was wrong."

She patted his leg. "I was the one who was wrong about Geoffrey. I obviously still have a lot to learn."

He smiled affectionately at her. "Listen, when I'm done here, would you and Shelby like to come over for pizza and beer? Just to process all of this?"

Monica considered his invite. "Why don't you two come over to my house? Once I get home and shower, I won't want to leave, but I'd like to talk it all out with you."

"Nathan and I will come over." He rested his hand on the door handle, ready to get out.

Interrupting their moment of silence, a red gloved hand banged hard on Monica's window.

"Fuck!" she shrieked in surprise.

Tiffany Rose stuck her face close to the window, a yellow rain slicker hood pulled over her blonde hair. "Monica, do you have time for a comment?"

Monica's heart was tachycardic, her nerve endings on alert. "Jesus." She turned to Matt.

"Oh. Sorry I forgot to warn you. Tiffany just arrived in the WQOD van."

"How did she get here so fast?"

"I'm sure they picked it up on the police scanner."

Monica turned back to Tiffany and cracked her window. "Sure. Matt is getting out, so you can get in his side."

"See you later." Matt jumped out and Tiffany slid in and closed the door.

"Hey, Monica. Are you okay?" Tiffany asked. "You look horrible."

"Thanks. I'm fine. Didn't you already get statements from the police?"

"Yes, but I want to confirm their story with you and get the hospital's perspective. We'll run this story on the 10 p.m. news, so I need something quick."

"Fire away," Monica said.

"Is it true that you shot a serial killer?"

"Yes."

"Wow. You're our local hero."

"I don't know about that. I just happened to be in the right place at the right time, and I did what I considered was necessary to save lives."

Tiffany nodded in amazement. "Is it true that Dr. Kershaw's plastic surgery patients were being targeted for murder?"

Deep down inside, Monica groaned. She had to be honest but still preserve the hospital's reputation, seemingly mutually exclusive goals. She would describe Derek's name change and deception to become employed at Community Memorial.

32

A lifetime later, Monica's heart rate returned to normal when she turned into her driveway. The lights were aglow in her house, and she had learned through texting that Shelby was making dinner. She parked next to the kitchen door, so she wouldn't have far to walk in her wet socks.

When she opened her door and turned to get out, her back tightened and her legs screamed in agony. Her muscles were protesting against the abuse from sloshing around outside, sprinting across Nicole's property, army-crawling on the hardwood floor, and being juiced on adrenaline. *I need a hot shower.*

She chicken-hopped up the stoop and sloshed to a stop in the kitchen entryway.

Shelby turned from the stove. "Hey! You're…Oh my God, Mon. You look horrible." She dropped a ladle into a bubbling pot and rushed to Monica, grabbing her arms. "Are you okay?"

"Not even close," Monica said. "I need a hot shower, then I can tell you all about it."

Shelby's gaze traveled the length of Monica, lingering on her wet socks. "Where are your boots? Why are you running around in a storm in wool socks?"

Monica gazed into the alarmed eyes of her lover. "My boots are in my truck. Stepped in a hole…totally wet… probably ruined—"

"And this Packers sweatshirt," Shelby interrupted. "I've never seen it before. Whose is it?"

Despite the trauma she had just experienced, a smirk pulled up the right corner of Monica's lip. She had only texted Shelby that she would be late because "some stuff" had happened at Nicole's house, but now she could see Shelby's imagination at work.

Through a massive shiver that racked her entire body, Monica said, "Listen, I just need a long, hot shower, then I can explain everything. Nicole gave me this sweatshirt because my clothes were wet. Do you want to follow me into the bathroom?"

"Nicole?"

"Dr. Kershaw."

"Oh. Let me help you." Shelby dropped to her knees and grabbed one of Monica's wet socks. "Put your hand on my shoulder and lift your foot." She peeled off Monica's socks, tossed them in the kitchen garbage, and followed her down the hall to the bathroom. Surprisingly, Shelby didn't interrogate Monica until later, after the shower and several layers of warm clothes.

They sat on the sofa with bowls of homemade ham and bean soup while Monica downloaded the entire ordeal between slurps. The parking lot conversation with Derek in his biker leathers. Her phone call with Isobel Durbin. Window-peeking in the storm. The hostage standoff. Finding Nicole's handgun in the car. Crawling across the dining room floor. Shooting Derek in the ass. Geoffrey's cold-blooded kill shot to Derek's forehead after he had already shot him twice in the chest.

"I just can't believe it!" Shelby exclaimed. "And you figured it all out on your own, then saved Nicole and Geoffrey?"

"After talking to Isobel Durbin, I was 99 percent sure that Derek was the killer. I knew he was in Miami when Destiny Diamond was killed in the alley behind The Thirsty Pelican. Nicole had explained that Derek was her wingman when she went to visit Geoffrey's club, which is a few doors down. During our parking lot interview, Derek had told us he didn't much care for the atmosphere at the club. He referred to trans women as 'freaks,' but when Matt called him out on it, he muttered something about people pretending to be someone they weren't. He spoke with such disdain and disgust."

"That's fucking twisted," Shelby said.

"When Isobel told me about the house-call anniversary visits, my antennae shot up. I'd never heard of any legit provider doing that. Later, when I spoke to the head of HR at the hospital, and she told me she didn't have a criminal background check on Derek, I was scared. Scared for Nicole's life."

"You're so smart," Shelby said. "And brave." She nudged Monica with her shoulder. "You're like a detective starring in your own Netflix series."

Monica rolled her eyes. "Mind you, Geoffrey was still pretty high on my list of suspects, but while I was lying on the floor in the dining room, my gun pointed at Derek's ass, Derek confessed. The timing couldn't have been better. I recorded it on my iPhone."

"Did you play it for the police?"

"Yeah," Monica said, slurping more soup. "Even though Geoffrey corroborated my story, it was still nice to have it on my phone."

"So, Geoffrey was innocent after all."

Monica hummed. "He certainly didn't have any problem shooting Derek twice in the chest and once in the forehead. Can't blame him though. Destiny Diamond was his friend."

"Well, Derek deserved it," Shelby said.

"While true, I sort of got the distinct impression that it wasn't the first time Geoffrey had shot someone."

"The important thing is that you're home safe with me now." Shelby took Monica's empty bowl and set both of their bowls on the coffee table. She held Monica's face between her hands and looked at her. "You're my hero. I love you."

A circus of emotions erupted in Monica, and she was sure her eyes looked wild. "I love you too. Coming home to you means everything to me."

Shelby leaned in and kissed Monica's forehead, then her eyelids, then her nose, then her cheeks, and finally her lips. Not in an *I-want-to-jump-your-bones* way, but in a loving, caring, gentle way.

Unfortunately, their tender moment was interrupted by knocking on the kitchen door.

Shelby flew back.

"That will be Matt and Nathan," Monica said, sliding a soothing hand over Shelby's leg. "I forgot to tell you that Matt said he wanted to come over and talk, and I said it was okay."

"Good. I'd like to see them."

Monica went to the door and let the guys in.

"Oh, you poor dear," Nathan said, pulling her into a hug.

"I'm fine," Monica said with more gusto than she actually felt.

"Hey, Shelby," Matt said, holding up a 12-pack of beer. "Have room in your fridge for this?"

"Sure," she said. "Can I interest you in some homemade ham and bean soup?"

"I'd love some if you have enough." He glanced around. "I thought we were going to order pizza."

"No need," Shelby said. "I've got dinner ready."

He moved to the stove and breathed in the aroma, sliding his arm around Shelby's waist and hugging her. "This looks delicious. Thank you for making it, and thank you for being here for Monica."

She leaned her cheek on his shoulder. "My crime fighting girlfriend definitely needs a beer and some healing conversation."

"She's like a Marvel superhero, isn't she? After the Stela Reiter trial and the Derek Russell shooting, I might have to issue her a license to kill."

"Matt, that's horrible," Shelby said.

"I'm just a small-town lawyer," Monica said. "Seriously, I didn't sign up for this."

"They definitely didn't have a class in law school on knife fights and sharpshooting," Nathan said.

Monica punched him in the shoulder. "I feel like I'm the only lawyer who gets herself into these messes."

"These situations do seem to find you, don't they?" Matt said. "You've exercised true valor, Mon. More so than many cops I've seen."

"I'll drink to that," Shelby said.

"None of us is holding a drink," Nathan said, thrusting out his hand and swishing it in the air.

"Let's remedy that right now," Monica said, moving to the fridge. "Who would like a COVID cocktail?"

Nathan said, "I would," at the same time that Shelby said, "Count me in."

She removed the tequila and Agave syrup.

"Who'd like a bowl of soup?" Shelby asked.

"Yum," Nathan said. "What kind?" He glided over to the stove and hugged Shelby.

Monica was overcome with affection as she rounded up the margarita ingredients, and gathered in the small space with her friends. Her frayed nerves settled and her confidence reappeared. She was proud of herself. Despite being faced with the seemingly impossible task of catching a killer in a few days during a pandemic, she had done it. She had prevailed against the odds and maintained her sanity in the process, if only by a thread. Through it all, she felt like she had grown as both a lawyer and a person.

Shelby removed some cheesy, garlic bread from the oven and peeled away the aluminum foil. The steamy aroma floated around them, mixing with the savory smell of the soup.

Matt and Nathan *ooohed* and *ahhhed* at the same time, rubbing their tummies like little boys.

"I love cooking for y'all," Shelby said in a comfy southern drawl, her characteristic broad smile returning.

Monica twined her fingers through Shelby's then returned to making drinks. "And I love your cooking."

"I think we should live here after we get married," Shelby said.

Monica stopped pouring tequila midair. "It's up to you, but I was thinking that we could build an addition onto the house for a new art studio for you."

Shelby hopped up and down. "Seriously?"

"Yes. And we're getting a dog," Monica said. "Let's go to the shelter this weekend to adopt a pup that looks like Beach Boy."

"That sounds perfect," Shelby said.

From a few feet away, Matt said, "Look, a special news alert is on TV. There's Tiffany."

"Let's turn it up," Nathan said, running to the TV remote.

Images from Dr. Kershaw's driveway flashed before them, police cars and an ambulance in the background.

Her yellow hood pulled low and tight around her face in the rain, Tiffany said, "Local Attorney Monica Spade was a hero tonight, saving Dr. Nicole Kershaw from being shot by a serial killer named Derek Russell. We learned that Russell, who worked at Community Memorial Hospital as a physician assistant, was responsible for at least four brutal murders. Three of the murders were of trans women who were patients of Dr. Kershaw's. Earlier tonight, Spade entered Kershaw's home to find Russell holding Kershaw hostage and in a standoff with Kershaw's boyfriend, Geoffrey Gold, a former Miami club owner. Both Spade and Gold shot Russell to save Kershaw's and Gold's lives. The police told me there is no longer a threat to Dr. Kershaw's patients. Monica Spade protected the public from a violent serial killer, this latest act of heroism on the heels of the Stela Reiter stabbing trial. Spade appears to be turning into Apple Grove's local superwoman.

Tiffany Rose reporting from Aqua Vulva on Lake Wissota. Back to you, Keith."

*** THE END ***

Message from the Author

If you enjoyed *Graffiti Red Murder*, I would be grateful for your review on Amazon or Goodreads. I'd also love to hear from you about whether you would like more Monica Spade. Hop over to my website at www.alexivenice.com and use the contact form. Or, email me directly at: alexivenice [at] gmail.com

If you haven't already, it isn't too late to read the first two Monica Spade novels, *Conscious Bias* and *Standby Counsel*. Available on Kindle Unlimited.

"An impeccably well-written legal drama with a slow burn romance front and center. Look for a surprise twist at the end of this book, too!" Goodreads Reviewer - 5 Stars

A standalone legal drama, laced with a woman's personal growth, that explores visceral bias, cultural alliances, and the power of love in Apple Grove, Wisconsin.

Trevor McKnight, a young, white male, is charged with the murder of Abdul Seif, a Saudi Arabian foreign exchange student.

Newbie Attorney Monica Spade's physician clients plan to testify at trial that Trevor's punch to Abdul's head killed him. Monica is shocked when her bosses at her all-male law firm warn her not to cross the powerful McKnight family. Facing death threats and career-ending consequences, Monica must decide whether to expose the truth in a bigoted environment.

In her personal life, Monica joins a CrossFit box to blow off stress. During class, she meets Shelby St. Claire, a high school art teacher. For the first time in her career, Monica considers coming out of the closet for Shelby.

"Conscious Bias has mystery, law, a slow burn of a romance, and intrigue all rolled into one...The humor, deceit and bias in this story really help to move things along in a great way, and I appreciate the fact that Monica and Shelby take things slow instead of diving right into a relationship headfirst." Goodreads Reviewer - 5 stars

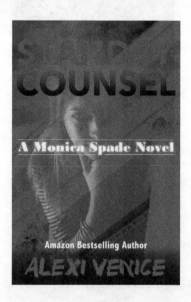

***** Recipient of a 2020 Lesfic Bard Award *****

"A sexy legal thriller that deftly blends an international terror plot with romantic obsession. Highly recommended." - *BestThrillers.com*

A full-length standalone legal thriller.

Monica Spade insists she isn't a trial lawyer, much less one who represents dangerous criminals. Despite her protests, Judge O'Brien orders Monica to serve as standby counsel for a young woman accused of repeatedly stabbing her boyfriend.

Setting aside her abject fear, Monica drags herself to the jail to meet her new client, Stela Reiter. A demure Romanian, Stela looks more like a meek librarian than a person capable of overpowering and stabbing a young man to death. Unlike Monica's other clients, Stela is coy and secretive during their interview.

Meanwhile, Monica's girlfriend, Shelby St. Claire, is keeping secrets of her own, forcing Monica to question the foundation of their relationship. Curiosity being Monica's trademark, she digs into the backgrounds of both women.

Monica uncovers sexual innuendo and layers of international intrigue, then deadly forces come after her, including a Ukrainian thug who will stop at nothing to get what he wants and two suspicious federal agents. Stuck between an unrelenting judge and a killer in a pink cardigan, Monica pursues the truth in court while fighting to keep Shelby and herself out of harm's way.

Set in the dead of winter in surprisingly progressive Apple Grove, Wisconsin, Standby Counsel will keep readers' hearts racing.

"Among legal thrillers, STANDBY COUNSEL excels in its depth of characterization. The chapters devoted to Monica's romantic life are no less gripping than those devoted to the primary plot. While *Standby Counsel* is the second book in the Monica Spade Series, it's a perfect entry point for new fans. Highly recommended." *Best Thrillers.com*

***

If you're looking for a gritty crime drama series with more explicit romance, check out my *San Francisco Mystery Series*. A six-book series that explores the heartbreak and struggles of Dr. Jen Dawson, Detective Tommy Vietti and District Attorney Amanda Hawthorne. Will their unique love triangle survive solving crimes and life together?

★★★★★ *"Couldn't love this series more if I tried...Most amazing mix [of] love, action, thriller, and...comedy!"* Amazon Reviewer

BINGE READ NOW

Story Description for *Bourbon Chase, The San Francisco Mystery Series, Book 1:*

"Venice is a fabulous crime/mystery and suspense writer. She knows and understands the legal system and that is conveyed in her storytelling. The action and drama feel very authentic. The interplay between the police and the DA's office is written with a keen eye, keeping it quite realistic. Additionally, the story is nicely paced; readers are engaged from the first page and yearn for more. Even though Bourbon Chase is titled a mystery, it contains a lovely undercurrent of romance. The romance is beautifully threaded throughout the story and contributes wonderfully to the overall story arc." *5 Stars The Lesbian Book Blog*

In *Bourbon Chase*, Jen Dawson is an emergency room physician training for a triathlon in San Francisco. Her boyfriend, Tommy Vietti, is an experienced detective loyal to the police force, his Italian family, and Jen.

Amanda Hawthorne is a charismatic District Attorney who prosecutes criminals while fending off attacks from mobsters. As San Francisco's most eligible lesbian, Amanda has her choice of female companions, so why is she attracted to Jen, who is supposedly straight?

When one of Jen's colleagues becomes a suspect in a murder investigation, Tommy and Amanda invade Jen's professional life. Jen sticks up for her physician colleague but discovers she has more in common with Amanda than just butting heads. Will Jen stay with Tommy or choose Amanda?

Enjoy the entire six-book series: Bourbon Chase, Amanda's Dragonfly, Stabscotch, Tinted Chapstick, Sativa Strain and #SandyBottom.

"This book (heck, the whole series) is FANTASTIC! Rarely do books get into my thoughts like these did - I would think about them during the day at work. The two main characters, Amanda & Jen, are people I wish were my real friends (maybe I need to get out more?) Anyhow, the books are so good & I cannot recommend them highly enough... The story line is great, the writing is great, my only complaint is that there aren't more books to the series! More! More! More Venice! :)" *5 Stars - Goodreads Reviewer*

Both *The San Francisco Mystery Series* and the *Monica Spade Series* are available on Amazon and in Kindle Unlimited.

Acknowledgements

I am deeply grateful for the love and support of so many people through the numerous steps from story creation to publication, in this instance—10 months.

My friend and colleague, JC, brought substantial prosecutorial and writing expertise to the table while juggling a busy litigation practice and family. I appreciate the subject matter expertise and suggestions during the design phase.

Annie Cregan, a retired New York City police officer, reviewed the second draft and provided awesome commentary regarding police procedure.

Rob Bignell edited the third draft, and I'm grateful for his on-going tutelage and edits.

Megan McKeever brought her considerable professional skills to the party and edited the dickens out of the manuscript at a point when I really needed some critical feedback and style pointers to bring my writing to the next level. I'm fortunate that Megan took me on as a client and didn't hold back, knowing I wouldn't shrink from constructive critique.

Elizabeth J. Wilson was kind enough to lend me some of her otherwise adventurous time for proofreading. Not only is Elizabeth a speed reader, but she's also incredibly sharp about crime scenes, legal jargon and life experience. I'm blessed to have made her acquaintance and am thankful for her keen eye.

My friend and colleague, Erin, came in clutch as the final, final proofer, then *poof!* it was gone. Okay, she did more than proof, requiring me to work hard…again. It's always worth it in the end.

Finally, I thank Bo Bennett and the entire team at eBookIt.com for doing the heavy lifting of publication.

About the Author

Amazon bestselling author Alexi Venice writes legal thrillers and crime drama with LGBTQ leads and wlw romance. Her bestselling legal thriller, *Standby Counsel, A Monica Spade Novel*, received a 2020 Lesfic Bard Award. Venice is a member of International Thriller Writers and a patron member of The Lesbian Review.

Venice's 32-year legal career informs her legal, medical and crime fiction. She is legal counsel under a different name at an international healthcare system, specializing in preparing nurses and physicians to testify in court in both civil and criminal trials. Venice's heart, imagination and life experience inform her romantic drama.

When she isn't writing, Venice can be found on the lake boating with her family. Venice is married and lives in Wisconsin.

Connect with Venice on her website: www.alexivenice.com or by sending her an email: alexivenice [at] gmail.com